DISSECTION

A MEDICAL & POLITICAL THRILLER

bancroft
press

Cristina LePort, MD

Cover Design: Alex Kirby (www.misterkirby.co.uk)
Interior Design: TracyCopesCreative.com
Author photo: Brystan Studios (Aliso Viejo, CA)

978-1-61088-557-7 (HC)
978-1-61088-558-4 (PB)
978-1-61088-559-1 (Ebook)
978-1-61088-560-7 (PDF)
978-1-61088-561-4 (Audiobook)

**bancroft
press**

Published by Bancroft Press
"Books that Enlighten"
(818) 275-3061
4527 Glenwood Avenue
La Crescenta, CA 91214
www.bancroftpress.com

Printed in the United States of America

To my husband Peter, the best thing that ever happened to me.

CHAPTER 1

THE WARNING

D r. Rajesh Nirula stopped chewing on his hamburger. All his attention zeroed in on a sheet of tan paper. Folded in two, it had the thickness and size of a birthday card. Nirula had seen and held such cards many times in his forty-three years of life. His first thought: My birthday came and went three months ago. His second thought: Why would the card show up in my hospital mail-slot without a return address or even my name on the envelope?

But it was the card's message that turned his face muscles limp: "YOUR HEART ATTACK WILL ARRIVE WITHIN 1 HOUR."

A heart attack? The leading cause of death in the world? A chill went through the doctor's spine. Just last week, to satisfy his curiosity, he had run his heart attack risk profile through an algorithm. *The results:* His chances of having a myocardial infarction any time soon were less than 1%. How could this stupid card be right? Then he remembered: Up to 25% of people who suffer heart attacks have no known risks beforehand. His heart paused and pounded as this possibility invaded his consciousness.

His entire life flashed through his mind: India's misery, America's richness, the pizzas he had twirled in college, medical school, emergency medicine at the Washington D.C. Capitol Hospital, and the most beautiful American girl he had ever seen who was now his wife.

The doctor's eyes hadn't blinked once since reading the card for the first time. The black spread of words on the tan paper had seemed to acquire a life of its own, shouting a scornful threat to everything he had accomplished so far.

Nirula reflected briefly on his two children. Despite his job as an emergency room physician facing deadly traumas and illnesses every day, he had never given much thought to leaving the kids behind at an early age. In fact, he had never felt mortal up until now. What would his family do without him?

Something on the paper suddenly drew his attention. Just below the word "will" was a small gray disk. With one finger, he briefly touched it. Burning hot.

"Shit," he said as his fingertip turned red. He clenched the card and quickly surveyed the busy cafeteria crowd. Nobody seemed to have heard him. He ran his hand through his hair. Still thick. He took a deep breath, then began massaging his closed eyelids. Good genes, exercise, and avoidance of unhealthy substances had kept his body in shape. He was still in his prime. Or so he had assumed before today.

After a moment, Nirula opened his eyes and stared at the burger. The yellow cheese had solidified, droplets of fat spotting the dish below. His heart protested in his throat. Not the best cardiac-prudent food. The smell of fried grease drifted from the grill and hung in the air. A fleeting sense of nausea bloomed from his stomach. Was the card a joke? Who would send him something like this? Fear receded like a wave from the shore and crashed into anger.

Suddenly, he had an idea. Those Congressional idiots had gone too far. First the ban on large sodas, then the trans-fats prohibition. Washington DC was becoming worse than New York City. Congressmen often asked the Capitol Hospital's doctors for advice. Just because Nirula had expressed his support of legislation against fast foods didn't mean they had to use him as a guinea pig for such scary advertisements. Who were those morons trying to convince with this crap? A message like the one on the card would only piss people off, push the public to hurriedly eat more junk food before the government made it disappear. Nirula sighed and glanced at his watch. His lunch break had taken longer than planned. January was a busy month in the ER. After the holidays' intoxications, arrhythmias, heart attacks, and suicides came the flu season, which was now in full swing.

He flung the card onto the table with a two-fingered gesture underscoring relief and vindication, reassembled his hamburger, and finished it off in four giant bites. The Coke, in several long slurps, was next to disappear. Soon the remnants of his lunch hit the trash can, right along with the tan card.

CHAPTER 2

TOMBSTONES

Nirula rushed out of the cafeteria and zoomed through the hospital corridors. He bumped into familiar personnel without acknowledging them, his mind deciding whether to give any more attention to the ominous tan message. By the time the emergency room door closed behind him, the nausea was back. The ER's familiar turmoil and cacophony usually energized him in his role as master of life-or-death situations. Now noise and confusion overwhelmed him, made him feel weak.

A heavy sickening pressure rose from the center of his chest and spread like an oil spill to reach his jaw. He placed his palms on an empty gurney and bent over. What was happening to him? Was this indigestion? Should he grab a couple of Tums? A red flag, waving in his head, demanded immediate attention. To students and patients, he often told stories about people stricken dead of myocardial infarction thinking that burping was all they needed to do to save their life. Was he in the fits of denial—on the verge of becoming one of those casualties? Doctors were, after all, the worst patients.

Perhaps "seeking medical attention," as doctors put it, was in order. But what was Nirula going to tell the ER doc—that he had read a card about having a heart attack and was afraid he was having one? That sounded just like one of his crazy ER patients. Oh, wait. He was the ER doctor in charge today.

He tried to move, but his muscles didn't respond, as if rebelling against an action that could endanger his life. Only his arm went up, and only to wave at the female intern on the other side of the room.

An incremental mixture of bewilderment and dread surfaced on her face the closer she got to him. Nirula touched his forehead; it was cold and clammy. He guessed his color closely matched the green of his scrubs.

"Who's in charge?" he said, his voice quivering.

The young woman in the white coat stopped. Her mouth hinted at a smile, but dismay chased it away as her eyes widened.

"You are," she said. "What's the matter, Dr. Nirula. Are you feeling sick?"

"I mean," he said, then placed his right fist on his chest to counteract the vice-like pain behind his breastbone. "Who's the senior resident? I'm afraid the cafeteria food is finally killing me."

"Doctor." She pointed at his clenched hand. "You're giving me what you taught us to be the universal sign for chest pain. Are you having chest pain?"

He nodded. The woman's fair-skinned cheeks got paler. Her eyes roamed around, searching for something or someone.

"It's probably nothing," Nirula reassured her, as sweat poured from all his pores and tight pain slithered along his left arm down to his pinky. "But let's grab an EKG, just in case."

She fetched the machine herself, eyes darting back at him, full of concern. Good for her. She didn't wait for the tech. Great intern. He was in good hands.

In his new role as patient, Nirula crawled up on the gurney. Being "on the other side" was a new experience, and not one he relished. Screw the idiot who said that suffering one's own illnesses made them a better doctor.

Curtains were pulled. His scrub shirt went up to expose the part of the chest where the worst symptom seemed to be originating. He noticed a moment of hesitation in the young woman's fingertips when she started applying electrodes to his skin. A mentee wasn't supposed to see her mentor's naked body parts. Her doctor-patient relationship was clashing with the student-mentor one.

The sticky leads tickled his skin, but Nirula didn't laugh. He held his breath to make sure no chest motion would interfere with the instrument's work. The machine spat out his fate with a buzzing noise that seemed to last forever. He read his diagnosis in the blue eyes of his intern. The woman swallowed hard and sighed. She looked around again, this time with the jerkiness that comes from panic. There's no good way to give bad news.

"What is it?" Nirula asked without reaching for the tracing. "The real thing?"

She nodded. "Tombstones," she said.

She was still treating him as a colleague and a teacher, not just a patient, and her gravity conveyed flawless professionalism. It was as if she was saying, "Okay, the bad news is that you have the worst possible EKG tracing, showing a massive heart attack involving the entire left ventricle, colloquially called 'tombstones' by doctors because the electric waves look like tombstones, and because of the high risk of sudden death. The good news is you're one of us, and we'll take care of you." For using medical slang describing the worst news of his life, Nirula felt grateful. He clung to the good news to avoid plunging into the black hole of despair expanding inside him.

"Call Bob Green, the cardiologist," he said, glancing at the pink EKG sheath fluttering in his doctor's hand. "Tell him I need to go to the Cath lab STAT. Call code STEMI—you know, S-T- Elevation-Myocardial-Infarction. Give me the whole shebang—aspirin, statins, beta blockers. You know. You've been here long enough, and you're a good doctor."

She nodded. Her tight mouth trembled slightly and her head inclined at the compliment. Then she snapped to attention like a soldier ready to fight. Nirula needed someone like her—someone willing to fight to save his life. She yelled for assistance, gave orders to the nurse in charge and, as ER personnel swarmed the space within the curtains, took his pulse. She was in charge. Everything he had taught her now swirled in her head, ready to set the right things in motion.

Nirula was just a patient. Nothing for him to do now but wait. He welcomed the numbing effect of morphine. The pain remained, but Nirula didn't care as much. A beeping started at his side. Someone had connected him to a monitor. He pitied his heart, struggling to beat despite the blood supply being chocked off. Plastic prongs entered his nostrils and the cold, dry hissing of oxygen penetrated his nose. He took deep breaths. His lungs gulped in the magic gas in an attempt to rescue the heart muscle.

A booming voice announced "Code STEMI" as if from a distant tunnel. Despite the mind-numbing drugs, automatized action jerked Nirula's muscles and kicked in adrenaline like a conditioned reflex. The beeping accelerated. No need to rush to any patient. He was the one needing rushing to. Nirula admonished his own body to stand down at once, but his heart didn't get the message. The monitor announced a few extra beats, followed by pauses that felt like skips and thumps in his chest.

Rapid drumming translated into a hammer-like pounding. Was this what ventricular tachycardia felt like? His thirsty heart tried to push blood against closed valves, but could only manage to make his neck pulsate. A relentless vice kept on squeezing the life out of his chest, protesting the sudden whipping of adrenaline. An ominous feeling of emptiness and impending doom washed over him. He couldn't die. What would his wife and his children do? He had to take control of his destiny.

"Listen," Nirula groaned, shaking his intern's wrist. "If I need a zipper—I mean a coronary bypass—the only one I want touching me is Steven Leeds."

Then the room started to spin. The gurney sucked him in. As he felt the cold defibrillator paddles on his chest, his eyes rolled back into a sheet of blackness.

CHAPTER 3

DISSECTION

D r. Steven Leeds slid a cap over his thinning black hair, reached for a sponge, and stepped on the pedal to switch on the water. Behind the shiny surgical shield, dark, deeply-set eyes still showed a hint of smart irony, ready to detect any bit of life's fun. Then seriousness took over in preparation for the task ahead, and a light fog coated the shield as he took a cleansing breath. He glanced through the open door of the operating room to see his last patient for the day, already under anesthesia, unaware of the surrounding flurry of activity leading to the forthcoming surgery.

The male patient, naked and overweight, looked vulnerable spread on the operating table, his skin pierced by tubes and catheters, waiting for Steve's hands. Leeds inhaled the smell of betadine. He cherished the fact that he stood at the pinnacle of his career, having mastered the art of life and death at the tender age of thirty-nine. Only a few more grueling hours left before his reward at the end of the day. The smiling face of a dark-haired woman flashed into his mind and sent a fleeting shudder of pleasure through his body. Soon he'll be in Silvana Moretti's arms for the entire night.

"Dr. Leeds." The charge nurse's voice made him turn. "Dr. Green, from Cath lab. He said it's very urgent."

She waved his cell phone. Damn. Emergency case. Leeds's eyes glided to the clock. Did Bob Green mess up a procedure? Not likely. Not Green. If Steve were to have a myocardial infarction, he would want Green to open his artery. For Steve to get a case from him, the patient must've been a disaster.

Steve dropped the sponge, dried his hands on a paper towel, and reached for the phone. The frantic exposition erupting from the speaker caught him by surprise. What was Green talking about?

"Are you sure?" Steve interrupted his colleague. "Nirula wants me? He hates my guts."

"Why?" Green asked.

"Why?" Steve stared at his sponge, which was leaking red betadine at the bottom of the sink. "I thought everybody knew. Weeks ago, we had a big fight over Silvana Moretti's brother."

"I heard about it," Green said. "I didn't know you were involved."

"Silvana and I are dating," Leeds said. "Her brother dropped dead of myocardial infarction after Nirula discharged him from the ER, instead of listening to her and admitting him to the hospital."

"Look," Green said, "no time to discuss that now. This guy is dying and he asked for you by name. Obviously, he doesn't hate you that much—not when he's having a massive heart attack. Take it as a compliment that he wants you despite everything. After all, you're the best."

Leeds had to take the case. Not because he needed to keep up his reputation, and not because that loser deserved it, but because fixing hearts was his job. He had worked very hard at it for most of his adult years, and was proud of how good he had gotten. More proud than of anything else on Earth. And this probably was going to be one hell of a case, one that only he could successfully handle.

"No worry," Leeds said. "I can be professional. Did something go wrong with stenting? What artery is the culprit?"

"That's just it," Green said. "All the arteries are culprits. I've never seen anything like it. The guy has no risks for heart disease, no calcium in his coronaries, no plaque. The wall of both coronary arteries just dissected, splitting apart into dead-ended channels. Every time I deployed a stent, the wall dissected more, like pulled-apart Velcro. Better stop short of a full metal jacket where you couldn't plug in any grafts."

"Okay," Steve said. "Send him over. I'll do him now."

The thin and wrinkled charge nurse nodded at his side. Steve watched her solving the problem Green had created by dumping his case on the busy

OR schedule, setting in motion a disruptive domino game. She knew what to do. Steve could count on her. He had just enough time for a phone call before Nirula hit the operating room.

"Have the Resident talk to the patient and family," he told her. "Explain that we got bumped by an emergency."

Adrenaline rush time. Steve loved the feeling, despite the stress. His eyes went from the clock to the scrub sponge. Should he have the nurse make his call? No. This was a call Steve had to do himself. He dialed. The phone rang and rang. The door at the end of the corridor thumped open and gave way to an entity announced by beeping and hissing sounds. Bags of fluids dangled from metal supports, as Nirula's gurney rolled in and shuffled toward the operating room. Steve had to scrub immediately. Better just have the good nurse cancel his date and leave all explanations for later. He had to focus on the task ahead.

"Hello," Silvana Moretti's voice answered in his ear.

Her voice never failed to lift something inside him. She had that effect, despite everything that had happened to her in her life. Widowed at the age of thirty-one, single mom. And then, five years later, her brother had to die. Well, he didn't have to, but he did. Thanks to Dr. Nirula. There should be a cap on bad luck. What was Silvana going to say when she found out that Steve was going to save the life of the doctor who had basically killed her brother? Steve could just imagine. How could he blame her? Now Steve had to find the courage to tell her.

"It's me," Steve said. "I have an emergency surgery. No idea how long it's going to take. I'll call you when I'm done, but I'll probably need a rain check. Sorry."

"I understand," she said.

But she didn't understand. Not yet. Steve was going to make it very complicated. He had to.

"Listen." His voice got softer as he spoke. "Better you find out from me. The patient is that ER doctor Nirula. I hope it's okay."

Silence followed. The beeping of monitors and hissing of pumped air reached him from a distance. Nirula was in the OR getting prepped for surgery. Steve had to go.

"Nirula?" she said. "He had a heart attack?"

"Weird," Steve said, trying to steer conversation away from the conflict. "Had no underlying risks. All arteries are clean. He suddenly dissected everything."

"How does that happen?"

Steve started to answer, relieved by the topic at hand. He glanced at the OR door and focused on slowing down his explanation. "In a dissection, the layers separate. It's rare. And I've never seen all coronaries at once."

"How's he doing?"

How's he doing? She cared? That was news. No problem with doing surgery on her enemy? Good for him. For both doctor and patient.

"Not good," Steve said. "I got to go now. Or he'll do even worse. Rain check."

"Listen," she said, a strange break in her voice. "I hate to tell you now, but no rain check. Nothing to do with the case. Was going to tell you tonight. We should stop seeing each other. It's me. I'm not ready. Too many deaths in my family. I need to focus on my daughter."

Lightness faded from inside, as Leeds' brain isolated the essential message from the mumbo-jumbo he had just heard. Had she just said, "We should stop seeing each other"? The air became too dense to breathe. In English, that meant she was breaking up with him. Steve felt as if a brick had hit his chest and lodged inside his ribcage. And now Nirula was waiting. Steve had taken the case and had to walk into the OR, even if all he wanted to do was to get out of the hospital, drive to Silvana's home, and find out what the heck was going on.

"I thought we were good," he mumbled.

"You're good," she said. "You're the best thing that's ever happened to me. But not now. You should move on. Don't wait for me."

Then she was gone. Steve looked at the phone's blank screen, sighed, placed the phone in his scrub pocket, reached for a new sponge, and started scrubbing. Everything had seemed fine. Better than fine, great. Silvana's dark lustrous hair draping over her naked breasts came to mind as a painful reminder of how big a loss he had just incurred. He scrubbed harder, until his hands burned from the betadine, but his mind kept on going.

He had known Silvana for—it seemed a lifetime, but Steve had met her only five months ago, because of her invention. She was a biophysicist, and super-smart. At first, Steve wasn't sure what a biophysicist did for a living. He had fallen in love during her presentation of a new device predicting impending heart attacks and strokes. Her abstruse algorithms intimidated and alienated most of the MDs present, but Steve had felt a growing desire to possess the beautiful body of the woman who could come up with such mathematical descriptions of sound waves.

"Doctor," the charge nurse announced, "you're needed in the OR immediately. The patient had to be shocked out of ventricular fibrillation several times."

Steve threw the sponge and walked to the designated room, hands up in the air, but the thought of Silvana wouldn't stay behind. Thanks to her, for the first time in his life, his personal happiness had matched the wonderful sense of satisfaction of fixing hearts and saving lives, at least until five minutes ago, when his world collapsed. The relationship he had waited and worked for during most of his adult years was gone, but why? Steve continued to ask himself that question as he pressed his shoulder against the OR door.

CHAPTER 4

LEFT MAIN

Steve grabbed the steaming latte from the hospital's café counter and checked his texts. Nothing from Silvana. Unable to see her last night, and too early to call her this morning, Steve was in limbo, like those souls marked by original sin—not good enough for Heaven or for Hell—punished for a sin he had no idea he had committed.

"Hey." Green joined the coffee waiting line next to him. "Thanks for taking the case yesterday. How is he?"

Green lifted his tired eyes and ran his hand up to his receding hairline. Despite the fresh shave and crisp shirt, Green looked the way Steve felt; like shit. After the arduous surgery, Steve and Green had spent the night battling Nirula's shock, recurrent arrhythmias, and bleeding from chest tubes. But Steve had to deal also with the Silvana factor, an all-encompassing depressive state of misery that hiked up the impact of all other problems by several notches.

"Finally stable," Steve said. "The surgery was a nightmare."

"I can't believe it." Green said. "You couldn't even use the mammary arteries for bypass."

"Dissected as well," Steve said. "In my entire career, I've never seen anything like it. Luckily, the radial arteries were okay. I can't wait for him to wake up to ask him if he has any clue what messed him up like that."

"He doesn't seem the type who does hard drugs," Green said, his brow rising. "Let's go see him."

The Capitol Hospital's CEO thought he'd bundled up enough against the piercing January air. But after just a few minutes of waiting, his hands, though gloved and tucked in his coat pockets, felt numb. He stomped his feet on the crunchy frozen ground and looked at the snow coating the school's playground. Before the doors opened at day's end, kids of different ages were tossing snowballs. Yells of fun filled the air.

The CEO smiled as he recognized the puff of red hair sticking out of a purple snow hat. He waved and called his daughter's name several times. At last, the seven-year-old lifted her large green eyes and ran into his arms. He swept up her light frame and held her tight. The girl's legs wrapped around him, wet shoes dripping mud on his cashmere coat. It was worth it. Whenever Daddy picked his sweetie up from school was a big deal. Not often could the CEO leave work at such an early time. Today, he had made it happen, thanks to the postponement of a finance committee meeting.

"Daddy," she said in his ear, "are you home today?"

"Yes," he said, giving the girl a tight squeeze. "Let's go before I freeze."

He reached home fully briefed on all kinds of school adventures. Once inside the dark and silent house, his coat went immediately into the dry cleaner's bag.

"Mommy's still at work." He unloaded the large backpack from his daughter's thin shoulders. "Just you and me."

What he had in mind was a good fire and some hot chocolate followed by quiet daddy-daughter time. Reading a book could also be fun. He had a lot of catching up to do. He walked to the fireplace and lit the gas. The fire appeared with a thump and the heat brought him a sense of peaceful well-being. He turned and on the entry's floor, noticed his daughter's purple snow jacket and matching hat and gloves.

"Look, Daddy," she said, picking up a bundle of papers from under the mail slot. "The mail."

"Later," he said. "Put your stuff away first. Then you can help me make some hot chocolate."

In the kitchen, he reached up to the cupboard for a pot and two mugs. Muffled steps followed him. He glanced back at his daughter dumping the bundle of mail on the table. Envelopes, papers, and magazines fanned out. His daughter would do anything not to put her clothes away, but an argument didn't seem like a good way to start their afternoon together.

"Oh, a birthday card," she said, picking up a tan envelope. "Looks like one of those with the music inside. Whose birthday is it?"

"You can open it," he said. "Probably an invitation from one of your school friends. But first hang up your jacket and put your hat and gloves away, so tomorrow morning you don't waste time."

Slow, reluctant-sounding steps receded to the entry room. He took milk from the refrigerator, measured two cups, poured the liquid into the pot, and placed it on the lighted burner. The crackling of logs consumed by fire broke the silence as the Chief Executive Officer waited for the milk to heat up.

When the shuffling of papers started again behind him, he verified that his daughter's short purple coat now hung at the front door's side. His wife would be proud. Rules were to be obeyed and chores were to get done, all without fights or complaints. Even if he rarely exercised his fatherly authority, the CEO hadn't lost his touch, though he knew he'd have to learn to do better in the future. The years ahead were bound to get trickier.

He glanced back and what he saw filled him with pride—a little girl excited about reading the mail. Better than playing those stupid videogames. The CEO added chocolate powder to the warm milk. Was he going to get clumps? Last time he did. He grabbed a wooden spoon from the drawer and stirred, pressing against the small powder clusters. Today everything had to be perfect.

His daughter kept reading out loud, stopping at every word. "Your.

Heart. Attach."

"That's great," he commented without turning, holding the dripping spoon over the pot. "You can read so well."

"Attach," the girl went on. "No. Attack. Will. Arrive. With. No, within. One hour. What does this mean, Daddy? And it doesn't work. The music doesn't work. Ouch."

"What's the matter?" The CEO stopped stirring and turned.

The girl was sucking her index finger. Distress carved the suggestion of a frown on her young forehead. Had he failed to protect her from harm? But what in a card could hurt her?

"It's hot," she whined, waving the tan paper. "And it's broken. There is no music."

He took the card from the small hand and lifted the flap. Black printed words appeared: "YOUR HEART ATTACK WILL ARRIVE WITHIN 1 HOUR."

"What the—?" he started. Then he stopped, remembering his daughter.

His hand glided over the dark letters, exploring the surface, looking for the entity responsible for causing his little girl such pain. His index fingertip landed on a strange small disk. His hand jerked away from burning pain.

"Sh—" he whispered. He looked at the young, puzzled face. "The music has burned out."

"You said a bad word," she mumbled while still sucking her finger.

"Sorry. The card is just a silly trick," he said, but the thumping of his heart didn't agree with that assessment. "Someone will pay for these stupid jokes. Come here."

He squatted down to her level, his arms open in invitation, the card still in hand. She took a step toward him, but the injured finger stayed between her lips. As he closed his arms around his wounded little girl, the card, just dangling there, seemed to mock him. His eyes paused on his watch: 5:18.

What had made him do it? Did he believe that within one hour hell would break loose? Was his chocolate going to get clumps on account of the freaking card? He shrugged and patted the girl's back until the damaged finger came out for inspection. The sight of the red fingertip caused his fatherly heart to pound with anger at the irresponsible sender of the tainted missive. He stood up, stomped his foot on the trash container, and threw the card and envelope away. Hearing the lid's soft thud gave him satisfaction.

"Look." He pointed at the pot. "See how smooth the chocolate is today."

The girl stepped closer. The CEO picked up the wooden spoon and got ready to stir again, when his phone played the hospital's ringtone. No peace for him. Work followed him no matter where he hid. As he stirred the thick brown liquid, his other hand reached for the phone from his shirt pocket.

"Yep," he answered. "Who is this?"

"Dr. Leeds," said the voice at the other end.

"I'm home with my daughter," the CEO cut in. "Can we talk tomorrow?"

"Sorry," Steve insisted. "I think you need to hear this today, in case there's something to it. You may want to make an announcement."

"Okay." Professional diplomacy suppressed annoyance. "But give me the quick version."

"It's about Dr. Nirula," Steve said. "You know, he had a coronary artery bypass last night."

"Wow. Sorry to hear. How is he doing?"

"He's doing fine," Leeds said. "Just woke up."

"That's great." The CEO squashed a powdery lump against the pot's side. "But why are you calling me now?"

"It's going to sound crazy," Steve went on. "But Nirula said that just before he experienced his symptoms yesterday, he received a strange card. Like an announcement. That he was going to have a heart attack within one hour."

The wooden spoon clattered to the floor, splattering chocolate droplets all over the tiles. The CEO turned to his daughter. She stood at his side, a white ceramic cup with a red heart between her hands—it was her favorite cup. The girl's eyes were on the fallen spoon. His hand shook as he shut the burner off.

"Where is it?" he whispered, but his words sounded like a scream. "What did the card look like?"

"We don't know for sure," Steve said. "We looked for it in the cafeteria trash, but it was too late. I know, it's probably the morphine that has Nirula acting crazy. And the pump-run does strange things to the brain too."

"No. I believe you." The CEO's mouth felt too dry to shape words. "Did Dr. Nirula say it was a tan card, like a birthday thing?"

"Yes," Steve said, after a short pause. His voice sounded as if modulated by puzzlement. "How did you know?"

"I, I just got the same thing in the mail," the CEO moaned. "A little while ago. My daughter opened it."

"You better come into the ER." Steve's voice sounded too calm to be natural. "Both of you. Just in case. We should warn the hospital staff and employees about this."

"Yes," the man gasped. "We're on our way."

His fingers rubbed against his thumping heart. He had to remain calm, do what needed to be done, and think and feel later, for her sake. He squatted down again, peeled the small hand off the heart cup, and kissed the red fingertip.

"We are going to the hospital," he told his daughter.

"But, Daddy." She smiled. "My finger is all better."

"I know, sweetie." He tried not to moan. "I'm afraid we may have picked up some bad stuff from the card you opened."

He watched happiness turn first into disappointment, then fear. But she didn't protest. Smart girl. Must've seen the panic in her daddy's eyes. This was insane. A few frantic minutes later, after getting back into the car again, he drove as fast as he safely could. Soon, the freeway rush-hour traffic made him slump in his seat. Had he been stupid? Calling an ambulance would have been the right thing to do. But for what? He looked at the rear-view mirror for the round rosy face he loved more than his own life. Only seven years old. Where was she?

"Are you okay?" he asked her for the third time in ten minutes.

No immediate answer came from the back seat. A fistful of panic hit him in the pit of his stomach as the image of a lifeless daughter flashed into his mind. He turned, thankful for the traffic jam. The girl smiled.

"Yes," she answered. "How many times are you going to ask?"

A half-hour later, father and daughter sat in the Capitol Hospital ER, she on a gurney, he on a metal chair, both hooked up to cardiac monitors. The concert of beeps drove the CEO crazy. His body jumped at any change in the girl's heart rate. The substitute for Dr. Nirula, a short, thick-set doctor in his thirties, stood in front of him. The doctor had failed to react to the man's title. He had listened to the CEO's story with a fixed "I know it all" stare. So far, the only thing the CEO had heard from this doctor was what his hospital couldn't do for him.

"What do you mean?" the Chief Executive Officer asked. "You won't admit us for observation? Do you know who I am?"

"Yes, sir," the doctor said. "You already made that very clear. And I understand your concern after what happened to Dr. Nirula, but we aren't allowed to admit people without symptoms. Besides, your daughter is only seven. The chance that she's coming down with a heart attack is as close to zero as you can get."

The CEO stared straight into the doctor's unfeeling eye. Didn't the moron understand that, at the very least, the girl needed to stay to be observed? Human beings can't fit into algorithms. Common sense wasn't taught in medical school.

"No admission," the CEO asked, "for the high risk of something fatal? Says who?"

"You, sir." The doctor pointed his finger at the CEO's chest. His mouth twisted in the imitation of a smile. "You insisted on no exceptions. Is this a test?"

The doctor acted as if something secretive had been going on between the two of them, and somehow the doctor had outsmarted his boss-patient. The CEO shook his head and lifted his hands in an "I give up" gesture. Peeling off the monitor leads, the doctor gave him a wider smile, waved goodbye, and left.

The CEO handed his daughter her sweatshirt. The girl's puzzled look made his stomach sink. Must be confusing for a seven-year-old to get schizophrenic messages from her dad. Was he acting crazy? Almost an hour had passed and nothing had happened yet. Could it be a hoax? But what about Dr. Nirula? A hell of a coincidence for his heart attack to arrive within one hour, just like the fucking card said it would. And now the CEO had to call his wife, to fill her in on the seemingly senseless events.

He donned his shirt and buttoned up outside the hospital curtain while his daughter got dressed. Her shadow from the halogen light quivered on the white screen. The oversized hospital gown came off and the sweatshirt slid down. The CEO pulled the curtain back. The head that appeared through the shirt collar didn't have her usual rosy cheeks. The girl's irises rolled back into the eye sockets, her lips darkened to a purple color, and the small body crashed onto the gurney.

"Help!" the CEO screamed, his hands shaking her limp shoulders. "My daughter is dying! I need a doctor!"

Long moments later, the "Code Blue" team rushed into the narrow space, headed by the very same ER doctor the CEO had recently come to despise. The CEO suppressed a strong desire to strangle him, but stepped back and stood helpless outside the pulled curtain to allow the team to work on his little girl. His paternal heart stopped at each "No pulse" call. His body shuddered with every announcement of defibrillator shock.

A few interminable minutes later, pain struck him for real. The CEO clenched his chest, unsure what to do. How could he interfere with his daughter's chance of survival? His eyes searched the ER for someone else who could help him. His heart thumped faster and faster. He felt dizzy and dropped onto his chair, head buried in his palms. He needed his wife, now, to tell her how much he loved her and ask her for forgiveness for not having saved their daughter. He deserved to die, not his little girl. Then the green scrubs appeared between two of his fingers. He forced his head to lift, his eyes to look. It was Dr. Leeds approaching.

"Dr. Leeds." The CEO reached for the doctor's hand.

The doctor stopped. He stared at the CEO. A flicker of recognition appeared on his face, then turned into relief.

"I heard the code," he said, looking at the CEO. "I knew you were coming. I'm between cases now. Are you okay?"

"No," the CEO said. "I'm in trouble too. But please help my daughter first."

The doctor grabbed his arm. One professional look apparently was all Leeds needed. Thank God for someone who knew his stuff. Dr. Leeds would take charge. The CEO knew his reputation. His daughter was in good hands. He could pass out now. A merciful dark blanket of oblivion overtook his consciousness.

At 9:45 PM, Steve pulled up his bloody gown, peeled off his gloves, and walked out of the operating room to find the CEO's wife. The waiting room was deserted, but Steve knew where to find her. He walked to the intensive care unit.

The middle-aged woman sat wrapped in a hospital blanket on a chair next to a bed occupied by a sleeping young girl. Despite her short brown hair, which was ruffled, and her dazed appearance, Steve judged the woman attractive. As he approached, she lifted her make-up-smeared eyes.

"He's stable." He saw her forehead relax. His favorite reward. Tension receded from his back muscles. "I had to bypass all his major coronary arteries."

She nodded. Her chest moved with a deep sigh, and her eyes came to life.

"How?" She hesitated, as if the question was too big to put forward. "What happened? How can they both get a heart attack at the same time? The police went to our house to search for clues."

Steve wished he had an answer, so the same questions could stop swirling in his own head. Did the woman know about the card? He took a breath. But she didn't wait for his answer, turning back to the girl's heart monitor, her eyes glued to the wiggly EKG lines, as if only she, the mother, could drive and maintain the daughter's heart function during her sleep. Explanations could wait for later.

"I heard." He touched the woman's shoulder and pointed his chin at the hospital bed. "She's okay also."

"Yes." The mother's mouth stretched into a ghost of a smile. "Dr. Green placed a stent into the opening of the main artery, the one in charge of sending blood to most of the heart. God bless him. And you. She was already dead."

"I know." Steve watched tears well up in the woman's tired eyes. "But she's still with us now. That's what counts."

Her face turned to the nurse's station with an expression of awe. Green sat busy at a computer. Leeds squeezed the woman's shoulder in salute and went to join his colleague.

"Shit." Green looked up from his notes. "What's going on? Three cases in two days with the same freaking dissections? I told my partner to call you right after shooting the guy's coronaries and not to waste any time stenting. Just call you, let you do the job. Meantime, by sheer luck, I could stent the left main on the girl. Can you imagine a bypass at age seven?"

"Great job." Steve shrugged. "But how's this even possible? What's this, an epidemic?"

"I'm afraid not." Green turned back to the computer. "The FBI may be asking you a few questions."

What was Green saying? FBI, as in Federal Bureau of Investigation? A door to a scary, unknown world flung open in Steve's mind.

"The FBI?" he asked. "What does the FBI care about heart attacks and coronary dissections?"

"While you were in surgery," Green explained, "the police retrieved the card announcing the heart attack from the CEO's trash. Apparently, the daughter opened it first. That's what he told the ER doc, then he looked at it for some time. Three cases, counting Nirula. Not a coincidence."

"Do you mean," said Steve, his breathing accelerated, "that these may not be natural events? What do they think they are? The FBI usually comes in for cases dealing with serial killers."

"That's right." Green nodded. "They're going to investigate to determine if that's what we're dealing with."

Steve glanced at the child's room. Who would want to kill a seven-year-old girl? Perhaps, he thought, she was collateral damage.

CHAPTER 5

FEDERAL BUREAU OF INVESTIGATION

Steve sat in his seventh-floor office at Capitol Hospital. He hadn't heard from Silvana since the day of Nirula's surgery. It was like having a loved one physically missing for three days. One would fear the person dead, but without any evidence to confirm or disprove the worst, he would have to go on, with the uncertainty poisoning every event of his life. No matter what, Steve had to find out the reason Silvana had ended their relationship. He touched the name "Moretti," held his phone to his ear, as he had done without success many times in the past few days, and swiveled his chair around to the window.

The Capitol's white dome, stacked against the silver wintry sky, uplifted him a bit. To the left had stood the traditional Christmas tree only weeks ago. Now it was gone, just like the first Christmas Steve had spent with Silvana and her delightful daughter Patrizia. For the first time since he could remember, he had forgone attending his own family's annual Christmas reunion, placing his old, easily distressed mother at risk of stroke, all to remain with Silvana, who was busy with an urgent project: a governmental secret, no less. Had there been tension then? Now that Steve thought of it, she had acted worried, nervous. He had attributed this to deadline pressure. Had he ignored some signals?

The phone rang and rang. Was Silvana not hearing her phone? But the call went to voice mail again. Had she seen the caller ID, then touched the rejection key in response? With nothing to lose, he would have to pay her a surprise visit. Perhaps after his next meeting. He might as well, since the rest of his afternoon schedule had been ditched to make room for the FBI.

At 3:00, a knock at his door announced the entrance of two men. The first one led the way into the room without waiting for Steve's invitation. His light brown hair was worn in a crew-cut, and his slit-like eyes were the color of water. As Steve sprang up and came around to greet him, he estimated the man to be in his mid-thirties. A neck too thick for his starched white shirt, biceps-filled sleeves, and a black suit with the jacket bulging at his side gave away the man's profession even before introducing himself.

"Jack Mulville," the man said as if imparting an order. "FBI. Criminal Investigation Division."

His left hand shoved forward a gold and blue badge with an eagle insignia. His right hand held a business card between two thick fingers. Steve took the card, placed it on his desk, and shook the man's hand. He might as well have shaken a brick. The FBI man must've cracked a few during martial arts training. Good thing the agent was on Steve's side.

"That's Kirk Miner." "Karate Man" thumbed the man behind him. "Private investigator from New York. He consults for the N.Y.P.D. on medical crimes. My boss, for whatever reason or favor, political or otherwise, thought Miner could help. He's tailing me the next couple of weeks."

"Kirk." The second man showed Steve a plastic wrapped FBI ID card bearing his name above an expiration date two weeks in the future. "No politics involved here. I have some medical background. The New York Police Chief heard of this unusual situation and recommended my services to the FBI director, who officially hired me as a consultant."

Intense dark eyes, a fit body without superfluous thickness, a sport jacket, pressed tan pants, and black sneakers. No gun bulges. Steve shook Miner's hand and decided he would deal with him any time over "Karate Man," even if the FBI guy didn't vouch for the PI's usefulness.

Mulville parked himself on the edge of one of the two available chairs. Kirk waited for Steve's hand signal to loosen up his jacket and sit on the other one. He placed one of his business cards on the desk. Steve went around, sat on the other side, and placed the card in a desk drawer.

"How can I help you gentlemen?"

Mulville pulled out a small electronic device, touched a key, placed the gadget in front of Steve's fingers, and then leaned back against his chair. As he crossed his legs, his buttoned jacket tightened up around his weapon.

"Please state your full name and credentials," he ordered. "Speak clearly."

Steve stared at the device. It reminded him of a past malpractice deposition. What was going on? "Do I need a lawyer?"

"Of course not." Mulville's quick smile involved only the sides of his mouth. "We're only gathering info."

"Well." Steve fingered the recorder. "You know how it is. Doctors are uncomfortable around recording stuff. Lawsuits and all that."

"I have a good memory." Kirk waved at the gadget. "We can kill the recorder, if it's okay with FBI policy."

Kirk side-glanced Mulville. Mulville shrugged. His hand snapped the recorder off while retrieving a phone from his breast pocket. Kirk winked at Steve.

"Let's cut to the chase," Mulville said, "before our asses grow roots. Dr. Leeds, what's the incidence, in general, of coronary dissections?"

Steve looked at the wall behind the men. Should he have prepared for this? Good thing the recorder was off.

"Off the top of my head," he said, "dissections are found in less than one in one thousand procedures done for chest pain. If you want a more precise answer, I would have to look it up."

Mulville showed no reaction. His thumbs went to work on his phone. Kirk nodded.

"You said in your report…" Mulville scrolled through documents on his phone. "…that all the major coronary arteries were dissected. What's the chance of that?"

A faint spray of saliva erupted from Mulville's mouth. His eyes locked on to Steve and didn't move as the back of his hand came up to wipe his lips.

Steve blinked a few times.

"Very rare." Steve cleared his voice. "I remember one report about a few patients having more than one artery involved. They all had a genetic condition that weakened the arterial wall. But the chances of two patients coming down with the same lesions in one week? Plus a seven-year-old kid? Almost nil."

"What can cause coronary arteries' dissection?" Mulville's thumbs kept typing. "Besides the condition you mentioned."

"Several things," Steve said, "most of which don't apply to our subjects."

"Indulge us." Mulville waved his hand in encouragement.

"Pregnancy." Steve's tone sounded condescending. "High blood pressure. Okay, the CEO is fifty-one and has hypertension, but his BP was controlled. Other causes can be drugs. Cocaine or methamphetamines. All patients had a negative drug screen. Even excessive exercise has been associated with dissection. Dr. Nirula exercises quite a bit, marathons and all, but at the time of his event, he was sitting in the cafeteria eating lunch."

"Wow," Kirk said. "I better cut down on my running."

"I get the picture," Mulville said with a tone of impatience and a snappy glance at the PI. "So there are some possible predisposing factors. Two of the people are related, one has high blood pressure, and the third one is an exercise freak. Could someone have had access to medical records with this information?"

Where was this guy going? Did the FBI know something about the tan cards?

"But why would one send an announcement," Steve asked, "a warning, if the purpose is hurting or killing somebody? Why send a card and give someone a chance to get to the hospital?"

"Perhaps they want to cause panic," Mulville said.

"Not just panic." Kirk glanced at Mulville. "In this case, people got real heart attacks. They easily could've died."

"It doesn't make any sense," Steve said. "Let's assume that these people were predisposed to coronary dissections, which I don't believe, and who-ever sent the card knew their medical history, for which there is no evi-dence. How would they predict that the dissections would happen within one hour?"

"Unless they caused the dissection." Kirk stressed the word "caused."

"Caused?" Mulville's eyebrows tented into an inverted V and his mouth morphed into a sarcastic grin. "How can you cause a dissection with a card? Miner, are you an expert in voodoo medicine as well?"

"Doctor," Kirk said, ignoring the question, "how can someone from the outside cause dissections?"

"I suppose you could cause trauma to the chest." Steve upturned his mouth in sign of guessing. "We sometimes see it after car accidents."

"But nobody was beaten up," Mulville said, "or was in an accident. We've got to find out what these three people have in common, where they went, what they did."

"Okay," Kirk said. "So we all agree this is highly unusual, and unlikely to be a coincidence. So far, the only things the three have in common are the cards."

"Card." Mulville stressed the letter D. "One card. And the description of another."

This investigative stuff was exciting, Steve decided. The FBI in his office was a first for him. Steve was there as an expert witness; part of the team. His stress level dissipated.

"Any prints?" Steve asked. "Besides the patients'?"

"Doctor." Mulville put out his palm like a stop sign. "If you don't mind, we're asking the questions here. This is now an official, ongoing criminal investigation. We're here to gather information, not to supply any."

"Not just a plain card." Kirk ignored the signal and looked at the doctor as if calling on his expertise. "A card with a sound box."

"Yes," Steve said, "both patients mentioned that it looked like a musical card, but it didn't work and the music box was very hot. Did your tech have a chance to check it out?"

"Our tech analyzed it this morning." Kirk said. "It looks like a regular sound box for greeting cards. But it's difficult to tell for sure because it was all melted down…"

"Miner." Mulville's palm stuck out again. "As I said, we're not here to discuss findings from an ongoing investigation. Doctor, we need your permission to talk to your patients about what, if anything, happened when they opened the card."

"Three days out of surgery," Steve said, "Nirula should be able to answer questions. The hospital CEO was operated on the day before yesterday, but he was awake this morning. And the girl didn't require surgery. She might have gone home already."

"Fine." Mulville stood. "Let's go see them. We need to find out who would want them dead. Doctor, please remain available for questions, as they may come up in the future. Kirk here will stick around for a few days to investigate."

"Before you go," Steve said, "shouldn't we make this public? Warn people?"

"And spread raw panic?" Mulville said. His look portrayed a deep contempt for stupidity. "Absolutely not. Just warn the hospital people. Urge them not to open any cards. And to keep their traps shut. Gotta go now."

Mulville's chin signaled the door. Kirk remained seated. The FBI guy looked puzzled, but the PI didn't budge.

"Jack," Kirk said, "let me chat a bit more with the doctor. I'll join you in the ICU in a few moments. Only one person at a time is allowed in anyway."

"Fine." Mulville's tone made the word sound like "fuck." "But you and I need to talk. Soon. And remember what I said."

He shrugged himself out of the office without saying any good-byes. Kirk looked back at the door as if to make sure he was gone, then smiled at Steve—a real smile, with all his facial muscles.

"Sorry for the cold shoulder," he said. "Most of these FBI folks come from the Army. You know, yes sir, no sir."

"That's no excuse," Steve said. "He should at least show some common courtesy. After all, I'm paying his salary."

"You and me both," Kirk said.

Steve nodded. He liked the guy. Easy to talk to.

"Are you a medical doctor?" Steve asked.

"Nah," Kirk answered. "My brain got messed up a few years ago in an accident. I got a large metal plate to prove it. I should've died. Instead, experimental surgery using a donor's neural cells left me smarter and with a strange amount of medical knowledge. Long story."

Kirk gave his head a tap with his knuckles. But the doctor had lost interest in the conversation. He was looking at his phone.

"Sure," Leeds said. "You wanted to ask me something in private?"

"I don't want to take any more of your time," Kirk said. "Just want to run something by you without the FBI laughing at me."

"Shoot," Steve said.

"Don't say that word to him." Kirk pointed at the door. "He might."

"I noticed," Steve said. "Is it really necessary, wearing a gun when talking with doctors and patients?"

Kirk raised his brow, glancing at the ceiling. As he leaned forward, his elbows went onto the desk and he looked Steve in the eye.

"When the arteries dissect," he said, "do they break down, shatter?"

"Well." Steve considered the question. "Not really. Blood doesn't come out. It goes between the layers of the wall, spreads them apart. And the vessel closes because of the bulge compressing the flow."

"Yes," Kirk said. "But there is a break in the layers, at least in one of them."

Usually, a little bit of medical knowledge was worse than nothing. People would come up with all sorts of theories and suggestions and it'd be impossible to convince them they might be wrong. But Kirk didn't look like the arrogant type. The guy was interested in understanding something.

"What's your point?" Steve asked. "What are you thinking?"

"A friend of mine had kidney stones," Kirk said. "They shattered them with ultrasounds. Is it possible the cards' sound box emitted ultrasounds, which shattered the arteries? Just a crazy idea."

Steve remained silent as he allowed Kirk's words to penetrate, then to integrate with his knowledge. In his experience, that was the best way to assess some new outside-the-box theory.

"You may have something," Steve said. "I'm not aware of any sound waves used to affect arteries. But I know one person who could tell us if it's possible."

"Who?"

"My girlfriend," Steve said. "Dr. Silvana Moretti. A biophysicist."

My girlfriend? What was he saying? More like my ex-girlfriend. A weight expanded in Steve's chest.

"She deals with this stuff?" Kirk asked. "Can we bring her in as an expert?"

"Don't see why not." Some alarm went off in Steve's head. "Although there may be a conflict of interest."

"What conflict?"

Steve suddenly felt as if he was under investigation, that somehow he had been backed into a corner, his feet stuck in quicksand, sucking him more and more deeply into a hole. But Kirk expected an answer now. The doctor took a deep breath.

"She and Dr. Nirula had a disagreement," he whispered, "over her brother's death."

Kirk stared at Steve as if he had just had an epiphany. What had Steve done? Way to fix his relationship by throwing suspicion on Silvana. Idiot. He had to defuse the entire matter as soon as possible.

"Sometimes," Steve leaned forward, "I wonder if the government is capable of something so terrible, just to scare people enough to get them to legislate what we can and cannot eat, since they have to pay for the treatment of all these self-inflicted diseases. But seriously, Dr. Moretti is very professional. I'm sure she'll do anything to help."

Kirk's brow went up at the far-fetched conspiracy theory. Steve hoped he hadn't done more harm than good. He wished he could erase the entire conversation with Kirk.

"Can you arrange for me to talk to her?" Kirk asked. "Alone."

Alone, without the FBI bulldog? Or alone without Steve? What was Kirk thinking? Was Silvana on his suspects list now?

"I'll let her know you want to talk to her."

"Great. Thanks," Kirk said. "I want to test my theory before discussing it with the FBI."

Kirk didn't act like a person out to hang people for no reason. Steve felt lighter

He picked up his phone from the desk. No messages. But now he had an excuse to call Silvana again and leave a different message. He dialed the familiar number again.

"Hello," a girl's voice answered.

"Patrizia." Steve sighed in relief. Perhaps talking to the daughter would give him a better chance of getting through to her mother. "It's Steve. How are you?"

"Fine," she said. "Mom went to her car to get something. Forgot her phone. She'll be back in a few moments."

"Okay," he said, wondering about the best way to proceed. "Have her call me back as soon as possible. Tell her the police need her help."

Short and sweet. Did Patrizia have instructions not to talk to him? She sounded a little curt, not like the happy and care-free thirteen-year-old Steve had gotten to like so much he could almost say he loved her. He ended the call and stared blankly, mourning something that had ended even before blooming.

"Thanks so much, Doctor," Kirk said. He stood with his hand stretched across the desk. "Text me her number. I'll call her and arrange for a meeting, perhaps tomorrow. I'll be in touch."

A meeting to explore the can of worms Steve had opened today. Steve got up, shook the PI's hand, and said good-bye. After Kirk left, the doctor sat in his darkened office wondering what effect the meeting between Kirk and Silvana would have on his chances of future happiness.

CHAPTER 6

THE PATIENTS

Kirk rushed out of the elevator and followed the signs for the "ICU." As he approached an area labelled "ICU Waiting Room," he found Mulville perched on a couch. Mullville's red face reminded Kirk of a volcano ready to erupt. Kirk's feet felt as if he was walking on sticky ground. He stopped.

The opportunity to work with the FBI was a new and prestigious experience, and a much higher motivation than the modest compensation he would receive. Kirk had hoped Mulville would make the experience worthwhile, but doubts to the contrary had nagged him since first meeting the FBI agent. He took a deep breath and walked closer.

"Miner." Mulville patted the area next to him on the couch. "Have a seat."

Kirk sat on a chair facing the couch across a coffee table covered with outdated magazines. Mulville must be waiting to interview the ICU patient. Kirk looked to see if anyone was coming to his rescue by inviting them into the patient's room. No one in sight.

"Miner." Kirk hoped not to be the direct cause of Mulville's red face. "Did you read your contract?"

Kirk nodded.

"Does it say anything about blabbering about an ongoing investigation with possible suspects?"

"The doctor?"

"Everyone is a suspect." Mulville slammed his stubby hand onto the table. "We're investigating murders, not petty lovers' squabbles. If you can't keep your trap shut, you'd better go back to your puny fuck cases. The rules are you watch, listen, and learn. If I need your input, I'll ask. Clear?"

"I understand."

"Good."

"Any prints on the card?" Kirk said.

"Nothing useful."

"Do we know where was it purchased?"

"We found only one company selling blank cards in that particular shade of tan. They're in New York City and sell online to people in most states. Impossible to trace who bought what when. But enough of this. We've got shit to do. You talk to Nirula. I'll take the CEO." Mulville pushed back from the couch and scurried to the ICU.

Steve didn't have much time to worry about his girlfriend's future meeting with Kirk Miner. The doctor's phone lit up with a text. Not from Silvana.

"Can't get in to see your patient," Jack Mulville's message read. "In the ICU now."

Anger seemed to emanate from Mulville's text. Steve imagined the FBI agent shouting those words. He got up from his chair, saluted the lighted Capitol in the darkened window, and dragged himself to the intensive care unit.

Jack Mulville stood face-to-face with a middle-aged nurse in front of the Chief Executive Officer's room. The FBI guy's hand clenched his official badge no more than two inches away from the woman's prominent breasts. His face had acquired a new reddish color. He turned as Steve approached and his eyes unloaded annoyance and frustration. The nurse gave the doctor a look of relief, and stepped away from the badge, making room for the doctor.

"A couple of days post-bypass," she said through a tight mouth, "and this man is undoing your work. Goes and tells the hospital CEO his daughter is collateral damage. Heart rate and BP went through the roof. I had to put a stop to the interview."

Steve nodded. He should've guessed that Jack Mulville possessed the bedside manner of an elephant. The man was a real thug. Steve should've come with him in the first place. Where was Miner? Steve had counted on the detective's professionalism and civility to save the day.

"Give me a minute." He signaled Mulville to stay put.

Steve squeezed past the bulky agent and entered his patient's room. The CEO lay still, catheters and lines protruding from his neck and arms, chest tubes gurgling at his side. The CEO stared at the ceiling, mouth drawn in what looked like a combination of submission and contempt. A perfect candidate for an FBI interrogation.

"How are you doing?" Steve whispered.

The patient's eyes turned to Steve. His brow lifted in a sign of helplessness. Steve smiled with sympathy.

"I'm so sorry about the intrusion." Steve pulled a chair closer to the bed. "The FBI got involved because of the card you received. I told you, Dr. Nirula had received the exact same card. So, we're afraid this wasn't just a heart problem."

"Do you mean," a raspy voice asked, "it was done on purpose?"

"I'm afraid so." Steve nodded. "Somebody might have tried to hurt you and Dr. Nirula. Your daughter, unfortunately, was caught in the middle."

The CEO nodded. A small amount of wetness collected inside his lower lids. Steve glanced back at Mulville, immobile as a rock, standing outside the glass door.

"Do you think you can answer a few questions?" Steve asked, turning back to the CEO. "If you're not up to it, I'll tell the FBI agent to come back tomorrow."

"Let's get it over with," the CEO answered. "Let's get the bastards."

Steve signaled Mulville to come in. The agent walked into the room, grabbed a chair, placed his arms on the back, and sat holding his phone.

"This won't take long," he said. "Going back to the card, did any music or sounds come from the music box?"

"No." The CEO shook his head, tugging at his neck catheter. "It wasn't a musical card. That little disc was burning hot. Was it supposed to play something?"

"Not sure," Mulville said. "We're trying to figure out what it was. Did you receive any threats beforehand? Anybody mad at you and Dr. Nirula, for any reason?"

The CEO gave a soft chuckle. The grin froze on his face and his hand went to one of his chest tubes. He grimaced.

"Take it easy," Steve said. "You still have drains in your chest."

"No threats against me," the CEO said, "But I often piss people off. It's part of my job."

"What's one of the major complaints you received lately?" Mulville asked.

The CEO looked at the ceiling for a moment, then his eyes went to Steve, as if asking for advice. After several more silent moments, he shrugged as if he might as well let people know the truth. Steve feared what was coming. His stomach sank.

"About a month ago," the CEO said, "got a major complaint about Dr. Nirula. From Silvana Moretti."

Steve stiffened. He looked at the floor. Bad enough he had told Kirk Miner, but now Mulville knew. That's all Silvana needed.

"Who's she?" Mulville asked.

"Sorry, Steve." The CEO looked up. "I know you like her. She's a scientist. Her brother died recently. She thinks Nirula and the hospital are responsible."

Mulville's thumbs pounded away at his phone. What would happen to Silvana now? Would the CEO's statement make her a suspect? Mulville wasn't Kirk Miner. Steve couldn't put anything past Mulville. Steve wished he could disappear into the shiny tiles of the ICU floor.

"Is it true?" Mulville kept his eyes down. "Are you responsible?"

"Heck no," the CEO said with renewed energy. "We followed the rules. The hospital did a clinical trial for some device she had invented, a thing to detect early heart problems in patients. After a while, there was a concern about its over-diagnosing."

"What do you mean?" Mulville looked up from his tablet.

"Sometimes," Steve cut in, "the device found disease where there wasn't any."

"Yes," the CEO continued. "We ended up with unnecessary tests and treatments, and thus excessive expenses with no chance of insurance reimbursement. We requested a preliminary data review from the FDA to see if the margin of error was excessive. The FDA review team voted to stop the trial until the device could be improved."

"What about the brother?" Mulville asked, his harshness betraying impatience. "What does this have to do with the brother?"

"Moretti's brother came to the ER twice," the CEO explained. "On and off chest pains, but all normal test results. She wanted us to use her device on him. Nirula refused, because it wasn't FDA approved. The brother went home and died. What were we supposed to do? It's not my fault the FDA places a price on human life. I guess Moretti's brother was some form of— what do you call it?—collateral damage. Like my daughter."

Mulville nodded. Steve thanked his patient. Kirk beckoned from the corridor. Mulville joined the PI outside.

"I interviewed Dr. Nirula," Kirk reported.

He pointed at Mulville as if the statement was mostly for his information. Mulville nodded, but his brow went up. Nirula likely had told the detective about Silvana Moretti's grievance against the hospital. How much worse could it get for Silvana?

"Interesting." Kirk added. "Nirula said that, for a moment, he thought this was a government scare tactic. Just like you theorized, Steve."

Mulville shook his head. Steve only wished. Then he remembered. Silvana had mentioned something about doing a project for the government during Christmas. Was it possible the government was running a business that deliberately killed people? The FDA had practically caused the death of Silvana's brother, hadn't it?

CHAPTER 7

BIOPHYSICS

Kirk Miner parked the car in front of Silvana's home, which was located in a residential part of Arlington, Virginia. The structure, a two-story, light-blue house with slanted roof and large windows, reminded him of his home in Brooklyn and made him miss his family even more than he had so far. He couldn't wait to finish the job and get out of Mulville's hair. Luckily, a new last-minute problem was keeping Mulville occupied. Kirk had no doubt he would achieve much better results dealing with Dr. Moretti on his own. At least he could conduct an interview without having to walk on eggshells.

Kirk zipped up his jacket, walked past the iron fence and the dry lawn, stepped up to the door, and rang the bell. He checked his watch. Almost 5:00. The scientist had told him she'd be home after 4:30. He blew on his hands to warm up and listened for approaching noises. His feet couldn't stay still in the chilly late afternoon air. He heard shuffling steps inside.

Kirk had checked out Dr. Moretti online to be familiar with her background and appearance. He expected bright brown eyes, dark hair, and a vibrant personality. The door opened to a pale woman with glazed eyes. Kirk made eye contact and searched his mind for any resemblance to the beautiful image he had seen online. Silvana Moretti in person didn't do justice to her picture.

"Kirk Miner." He offered a business card while showing his FBI plastic card in the palm of his hand. "Private investigator, working with the FBI."

"Silvana Moretti." She gave him an uncertain smile. "Come in."

A black sweater and tailored gray pants, together with a limp handshake, gave her a general appearance of mourning. Kirk followed her inside to the living room. She pointed to one of two armchairs with light-blue upholstery in front of a window. Kirk sat down. Was the woman ill?

"Is this a good time?" he asked. "Sorry about the short notice."

She nodded and sat on the other chair. Her dark eyes made contact with him and held his gaze, as if trying to glean some information about him. A new intensity sprung from her glazed, glassy eyes. Kirk felt scrutinized, as if the woman was judging his character, his worth. Or was she reaching out to him?

He unzipped and removed his jacket, which she didn't offer to take. His eyes rested on an oriental looking carpet under his feet. He placed the coat on the coffee table between the chairs and a matching couch. Through a door, at the other end of the room, a girl walked by, munching on something. A slimmer, younger version of Silvana. Her black hair swung in a ponytail.

"Your daughter?" Kirk pointed at the door.

Silvana's smile lit up her beauty. For a moment, she looked like her on-line pictures. She turned to the door, now empty.

"Patrizia," she said. "She's thirteen."

"You seem very proud of her."

"It's been a rough five years," Silvana said, her face serious again. "Since her father's death. I'm very proud how she's turned out."

"Sorry," he said, trying to assimilate the new information. "Must be difficult working and raising a family alone. Tell me a little bit about yourself. How long have you been in the States? You came from Italy, right?"

The PI felt sad for the woman and wished he didn't have to go through what he had to discuss. Moretti had an air of dignity and strength that made Kirk loathe himself for what he was about to do. But the investigation had to go on. He hoped Moretti would be able to stand it.

"My husband and I," she looked at the window, "came ten years ago. Washington University offered us both positions in our fields. My husband was a mathematics professor. He died in a car accident while he was away, in England, at a convention."

"How terrible," Kirk said.

She nodded. Her hands rested on her knees, as if waiting for the small talk to finish and business to begin. She had long fingers with trim nails and no polish; the hands of a scientist. Her eyes scrutinized him again. She looked resigned.

"What can I do for you?" she asked.

"Dr. Leeds," Kirk said, "mentioned that you are an expert on ultrasound. You may be able to advise us on the hospital situation."

He paused. She kept eye contact, but it was like a shutter had closed on her emotions. Kirk could read nothing.

"Since the matter concerns Dr. Nirula," he went on, "I need to ask if you'd be willing to help us, even after what happened with your brother."

Her fingers tightened on her knees. A frown appeared on her wide forehead. Her brown eyes watched him through narrowed lids.

"Who told you about my brother?" A spark of anger flashed in her eyes.

Tough question. How was Kirk going to answer without getting Steve in trouble? Kirk wanted Steve on his side.

"Routine background check," he said. "Hospital records show Dr. Nirula was involved in your brother's care before he died. The hospital CEO told us about your grievance."

"Yes." Her mouth tightened. "My brother went to the ER twice because of chest pains. The first time, he was admitted overnight and then was discharged after negative tests. The second time, I went with him. I begged Dr. Nirula to use my new device to check his heart."

"What does your device do?"

"It detects arterial injuries." Pride flickered in her eyes. "By measuring the frequency of vibrations."

"You are going to have to put that in plain English for me." Kirk reached for his jacket and retrieved his phone. "I have no biophysics background."

"Healthy arteries," she explained, "vibrate at certain frequencies. With inflammation, the vibrations change. My device detects early inflammation of arteries and predicts imminent heart attack or stroke."

"And it's available?" Kirk looked up from typing notes. "Now?"

"Yes and no." Her shoulders sagged. "I'm ready to start a large clinical trial at the hospital, but the stupid FDA hasn't given us the okay, despite a promising pilot study. How many more rats do I have to kill before we can begin saving people's lives? Like my brother's."

"Why didn't Dr. Nirula use the device on your brother?"

"Hospital's can't use devices that aren't FDA-approved." She shook her head.

She said it as if she was hearing it again from the ER doctor, reliving the agony of her brother's tragic death. She looked on the verge of tears. No anger, only hopelessness in the shiny brown eyes.

"And Dr. Nirula wouldn't admit my brother for observation," she added. "The hospital wouldn't get paid by insurance, because all tests at that point were negative."

"But your device could've detected early damage?" Kirk asked.

"Yes." She nodded. Her hand went to rub her eyes.

"They refused to use it?" Kirk said. "Despite the fact that they'd already worked with you?"

Her enlarged eyes told Kirk how naïve his question was. Kirk couldn't blame her for holding the doctor responsible.

"Dr. Nirula said they couldn't risk being accused of discrimination," she said with a note of sarcasm. "On top of using a non-approved device."

"That's awful," Kirk said. "I can't imagine what you must have gone through. What about the hospital CEO? Could he have helped you…made an exception?"

Silvana gave him a you've-got-to-be-kidding stare. A small burst of air exited her pursed lips. She shrugged.

"That bastard?" she said. "I bet he requested the FDA early review that canned my trial. He's so worried about the bottom line that he would let his mother die to meet it."

Silvana sighed as if to imply the futility of dwelling on the matter, then seemed to recompose herself and return to business. Was the woman innocent, or too naïve to be worried about incriminating herself?

"Going back to your question," she said. "I'm willing to help. But my main research deals mostly with cancer, not arteries."

"Can you tell me a little about it?" Kirk asked.

"I invented a new method." Pride made her face beautiful again. "A way to disintegrate cancer tissues with soundwaves without damaging healthy organs."

"Wow," Kirk said. "Is this available today?"

"Still in an experimental phase," she said. "Very promising. In any case, I'm not sure how this relates to Dr. Nirula's heart attack."

"It isn't just Dr. Nirula anymore," Kirk said.

She leaned against the back of her chair. Her eyes widened and her face looked paler, like translucent china. The woman didn't know.

"Who else?" she asked.

"The hospital CEO." The image of a fuming Mulville flashed into Kirk's mind. But Moretti was going to find out the news sooner or later. And her reaction would be revealing. "And his seven-year-old daughter."

"God." Her hand covered her mouth. "A young girl too? Did they make it?"

She turned toward the door, as if still seeing her daughter walk by. Was she thinking how it would be to have her daughter in the same dreadful predicament?

"They're both stable," Kirk said. "The father's recovering from surgery, and the girl from a coronary stent. The strange thing is their heart attack was also caused by this rare condition called dissection, just like Nirula's. A very unlikely coincidence."

"Is that why you're here?" she asked looking at him again. "The FBI thinks there is a crime involved?"

"What would it take to cause an artery to disintegrate?" Kirk nodded.

"Can it be done with ultrasounds?"

She blinked several times. Her hands came together, her fingers intertwined. Kirk watched her thinking, staring past his chair.

"I guess," she said. "Given the right frequency and the right energy, hypothetically one could damage arteries."

"I see." Kirk nodded. "So it's possible. We found this small device inside a card somebody sent to the hospital CEO. It resembles a sound box. Would it be possible for you to look at it, see if it could produce ultrasounds?"

She looked him straight in the eye. What was she thinking?

"I'll be glad to," she said. "But don't you have FBI forensic experts working on this?"

"Yes," Kirk said. "But the thing is melted and nobody can tell what it's for. Who would know about something like this?"

She shrugged. "I guess I'm the local expert. Is that why you're asking me?"

"You're our last hope," Kirk said, pulling an evidence bag out of his pocket.

He handed her a bag containing the CEO's card, its disk exposed. She reached for the item, held it flat on her palm, and looked at the card through the plastic cover. Her hand started shaking.

"You can open it," Kirk said. "Take your time. Examine it at your lab."

She jumped from her chair and walked to the kitchen. When she came back, her gloved hands retrieved the card from the plastic bag and held up the flap. For a moment, she stared at the words and the dot.

"I don't need to examine it," she said, looking back at Kirk. Her voice was firm, as if she was making an expert's scientific statement. "This is an ultrasound chip from my lab."

She said it simply. Kirk could detect a hint of surprise and a touch of sadness in her eyes. How was he supposed to interpret this? He felt the urge to warn her about saying anything incriminating. He wanted for her to be innocent. There had to be some explanation in which the woman in front of him wasn't a sociopathic monster.

"How can you be so sure?" he asked.

"I've been working with these chips for years." She replaced the card in the bag and handed it back to him. "The Department of Electronics assembles them with my specs, then I program them for a certain frequency, after which we implant them in rats to study ultrasounds' ability to damage different cancer tissues."

"Who knows about your work?" Kirk asked.

"The hospital research committee." She counted on her fingertips. "The hospital CEO. The FDA people who scrutinized the clinical trial. And Dr. Leeds."

Dr. Leeds, the boyfriend, who had volunteered the information about all this, the CEO victim, and the FDA. Could the government be responsible? Kirk was ready to embrace the crazy conspiracy theory to avoid considering Moretti a chief suspect.

"Do you keep these chips in your lab?"

"Yes," she said. "In an unlocked drawer."

Great. Anyone and his uncle would have access. But nobody knew how these disks could be used this way until now. Except for Dr. Moretti.

"Who has access to your lab at the university?" Kirk asked, pushing on.

She thought about it. Her distress seemed to have abated and composure taken over. She answered the questions as if the conversation didn't concern her at all.

"Cleaning people," she said. "A post-doc assigned to me to help with the rats—"

"I'll need a list," Kirk said. "To interview them. Who could program these chips to damage arteries instead of cancer tissues?"

She looked at him in a strange way. Her head shook as if in denial. She released a sad chuckle.

"Me," she said. "Only me."

The woman seemed to be telling the truth. And the truth stacked up pretty badly against her. But she came across as innocent.

"Why do you think it melted this way?" he asked. "A mistake?"

"Not necessarily." She nodded as if she understood something. "If programmed to emit the highest intensity of ultrasounds all at once, these small chips would melt after a one-time use."

Her face changed. Now he could see her eyes shine again. What was going on? Was she guilty or innocent? Kirk couldn't tell. She was being too … too truthful.

"Are you all right?" he asked.

"No," she said. "You see, last week some of my chips went missing."

"Missing?" Kirk's heart pounded in his throat. "How many?"

"Six of them," she said, again looking straight at him.

CHAPTER 8

THE LAB

The university's science center was a six-story gray building with large windows and a brass-rimmed door. Kirk yawned, took a sip from his latte, and handed his card to the uniformed man at the entrance. The guard gave Kirk a questioning stare.

"I'm here on behalf of Jack Mulville, FBI," Kirk said, "to meet Dr. Moretti's post-doc, Donald Emerson, at her lab, at 7:30."

"Elevator number two." The man checked the wall directory. "Fifth floor. Room 503."

"Is he in?" Kirk asked.

"Not sure," the man said. "Haven't seen him yet. But many scientists use the back entrance. They can get in any time with their ID."

Kirk unzipped his jacket and let the warm air in. He followed the directions. "Six stolen chips. Three heart attacks. Three more to go." Those words had been in his mind since yesterday's conversation with Silvana Moretti, like one of those songs one can't help humming. In agreeing to the interview, Emerson had been very cooperative. He must've sensed Kirk's urgency when the PI demanded a crack-of-dawn meeting in the lab.

Kirk didn't have to knock. The door was already open. He stepped inside. The chrome of hoods, shelves, and tabletops shone under halogen light. Screens hung from the ceiling connected to microscopes, computers, and all sorts of electronic equipment. Kirk thought of his high school chemistry lab and smiled. Where were the beakers? Lots of the stuff he was looking at didn't exist then. Even today's microscopes looked like space instruments.

He found Emerson, dark hair wet from a recent shower, bent over a microscope, earbuds in, whistling to some music only he could hear. Kirk had time to walk up to his side before the young man noticed him. Emerson unplugged his ears and greeted the PI with a smile.

"Kirk Miner." Kirk handed him a card. "Thanks for meeting so early."

Emerson placed the card in his pocket and put his hand out. The handshake felt strong. Bright dark eyes held Kirk's gaze.

"Better this way." Emerson, wearing jeans, slid onto a metal stool and pointed at one for Kirk. "Before the day really starts."

"I don't want to take too long." Kirk pulled his phone from his pocket before dropping the jacket on a stool. "Did Dr. Moretti tell you what this is about?"

"The missing chips." Emerson nodded, as if to underscore the gravity of the situation. "And all those dissections and heart attacks."

He grabbed an ID card dangling from his neck and held it in front of a metal drawer to his left. Kirk heard a click. The drawer popped open.

"As soon as we noticed the chips gone," said Emerson, pulling on the drawer, "we placed all ultrasound equipment under lock."

Kirk stepped up. The drawer was full of small plastic sheets covered by chips like the one seen inside the CEO's card. The chips here were enclosed in single bubble wraps joined in groups of six.

"How could you tell chips were missing?" Kirk asked. "Do you keep track?"

Emerson again nodded. His hand reached for a paper log from the bottom of the drawer. He handed it to Kirk. There were dates next to names and number of chips used, followed by the users' signatures.

"The last time you used any chips was two months ago?" Kirk pointed at the log. "And the only persons who use these chips are you and Dr. Moretti?"

"Yes to both questions," the young man said. "I implant them in rats for the cancer tissue experiments. For now, we're done with those. The FDA has allowed human trials. Now we program the chips and the surgeons implant them in patients with various cancers."

"How do you program a chip?" Kirk asked.

Emerson walked toward the wall behind him, where, through the room's only window, one could see a gray sky and the pale pink of dawn. Kirk finished typing, then followed him. Against the wall stood a metal desk supporting a slick black cube with sides of about two feet and dials of various colors. Wires connected the cube to a large screen and a keyboard. A touch of Emerson's finger brought the screen to life with multi-colored lines. Another touch opened the side of the cube to reveal a white empty interior.

"We place the chip inside here." He pointed at the opening. "And we program it using this keyboard. When we're happy with the simulations, we give the chip to the surgeons to implant."

"Do you know how to program these chips?"

"Sure," Emerson said without hesitation. "My post doctorate is on the biophysics of soundwaves. Dr. Moretti taught me how to program the rat chips."

"Why is Moretti's name next to all the chips used during the past two months?" Kirk said. "She's the only one to use them now?"

"She's the only one who programs the human chips," Emerson said. "Programming for humans is complicated. We're still tweaking the number of chips needed for each patient, as well as the direction and intensity of the soundwaves."

Kirk ran his finger along the cube. Was this where the heart attacks had originated?

"Do you use the same machine to program the chips for humans?"

"Yes."

"Do you keep a log on who uses this machine?"

"Yes," Emerson said. "Recently, Dr. Moretti alone. I run simulations."

"In your opinion," Kirk said, pointing his finger at Emerson, "would it be possible to program these chips to cause coronary dissections?"

The post doc's chin lifted at the request for a scientific opinion. But then a deep frown appeared on his forehead. The question troubled him. What was he afraid of? To admit his knowledge and thereby risk becoming a suspect? Or fear of exposing his boss?

"I think so," he said. "After all, the principle isn't much different from what we're doing now."

This was news. Kirk hadn't gotten the same impression from Dr. Moretti.

"Cancer," Kirk asked, "isn't different from a heart attack?"

"Yes, of course it is," Emerson said. "Dr. Moretti's ground-breaking discovery is that every tissue vibrates at a specific frequency which can be detected using her probe. If you interfere with that frequency, you can cause damage or destruction. To destroy cancer, we obtain a fresh specimen and measure the frequency at which it vibrates. Then we calculate the frequency we need to damage or destroy that tissue. The exact same thing could be done for an artery."

"To do it," Kirk said, following a clear line of questioning developing in his mind, "would you need to first do rat experiments?"

Emerson shook his head. He smiled as if he was the only one who could understand a private joke. Then his face became grave.

"You would need rats," he said, "if you wanted the FDA to approve the research trials on humans. Otherwise, you would just need to figure out the normal frequency of human arteries."

"Could you do it?" Kirk asked. "And how would you do it?"

Emerson stared down at the counter, probably wondering if he was considered a suspect. Kirk felt sorry for the guy, forced to cooperate with an FBI helper. Kirk wished he could reassure him, but everyone was still a potential suspect.

"I—" Emerson cleared his voice. "You just need to measure the vibratory frequency of an artery and then use our algorithms to program the chip."

"So," Kirk asked again, "could you do it?"

Emerson looked at him in silence. Kirk read a desperate question in the young man's eyes. Was he digging his own grave? Undermining his brilliant future? Too bad. Kirk needed to know.

"I guess," Emerson said with a shrug, seemingly deep in thought, "but with some help from Dr. Moretti. I wouldn't know how to deliver a strong enough burst all at once. These chips would melt down."

Damn right. The chips did melt down. Were the chips set to deliver a strong all-at-once burst to shatter the poor victims' arteries?

"Who else do you know could do this?" Kirk guessed the answer.

"No one." Emerson looked relieved to steer the conversation away from himself. "Only Dr. Moretti. That's why I'm here, doing my post-doc training with her. She's unique."

More nails driven into Moretti's coffin. But no surprise. She'd admitted as much.

"Who has access to your algorithms?"

"Only Dr. Moretti and I." Emerson smiled. "Everything is locked with multiple passwords. We're both paranoid … because of publications, patents, the Nobel prize."

There was something about Moretti that gave Kirk pangs of regret. He liked the woman. But the investigation had to go on.

"Was Dr. Moretti ever alone in the lab?" Kirk asked. "I mean, working?"

"All the time." Emerson's hand made a swiping gesture. "One time I found her here very early in the morning and didn't know whether or not she had gone home the night before. She was working doubly hard to come up with the best program for a young girl with a tumor in her eye."

"Did it work? Did she save the eye?"

"Yes," Emerson said with a tone of vindication. Kirk couldn't help but cheer for Moretti and her patient.

"Can anyone else use the machine?"

"No." Reluctance was now gone from Emerson's voice. "It's password-locked as well."

"When and how did you know the six chips were missing?"

"Dr. Moretti discovered it," he said. "But it would have come up soon enough. At the end of the week, we take inventory together."

Kirk finished typing his notes. Humming elevators and conversational noises came from outside the room.

Emerson looked relieved. "I'm afraid," he said, "I've got to start working. Lots of reprogramming to do."

Kirk picked up his jacket but didn't move. He couldn't let the opportunity slip.

"As for the reprogramming," Kirk asked, "are you talking about the device the FDA shut down the clinical trial for?"

Emerson's eyes widened. He was probably kicking himself for talking too much. He shook his head.

"How'd you know about that?" he said.

"I work with the FBI. Remember?" Kirk grinned. "By the way, how mad at the hospital and the doctors involved was Silvana when her brother died because they wouldn't use her device?"

"She was incensed," Emerson said. "Angry at the entire hospital."

Bingo. Emerson looked at him and turned pale. Probably wanted to take back those words.

"Wouldn't you be?" he added, as if to mitigate his statement.

"Thank you." Kirk nodded and turned to leave, feeling like a lawyer who had just tricked a witness into self-incrimination.

He took the elevator down to the lobby. Instead of turning right toward the front entrance, he headed for the back of the building. In one of the corners, Kirk found an unmarked door. He exited the building into the alley and turned to look at the access from the outside. At the side of the plain metal door was a keycard lock on a gray wall. Kirk stared at the lock for some time, then slowly headed back to his car.

CHAPTER 9

FDA

The old man shuffled out of the elevator toward the lobby. At least once a day, he had to leave the L-shaped living-room of his Massachusetts Ave. condominium for a change in scenery. The freezing weather lately had relegated his outings to retrieving the mail. That he could do wearing his Harvard sweats and fur-lined slippers.

Gnarled fingers labored to open the metal box, one on an entire wall of similar receptacles. He clenched the short stack of papers—mostly junk—that would keep him occupied for the next thirty minutes or so. He could tell just thumbing through the stuff on his way back up to his two-bedroom apartment. But a tan card caught his eye.

"Honey," he said after closing the door. "I'll be here at my desk going through the mail."

His wife could see what he was doing from the kitchen, but sometimes his need to talk to someone was too strong. He sat down on an office chair and dropped the mail on his desk. The window in front of him looked onto a grime-stained brick wall. After a long career as an ultrasound technician, the view felt like a reproach, as if it represented the little he had to look forward to in life. He stretched his arm and pulled down the blinds.

After turning his attention to the pile of magazines and envelopes in front of him, he freed the tan card from the rest of the stack. He stared at the envelope. No address, only his name and the words "Personal and Confidential FDA Material."

He weighed the thin card in his hand. This was not FDA material. The man had been a team member of several FDA panels. Sitting at meetings and making important decisions about the life's work of scientists and inventors never failed to give him a thrill. He couldn't invent any of the devices the panels analyzed and judged. His job was much more important. The safety of the public was his goal. The team's veto power was the only authority it had. And it was used more often than not.

He placed the tip of his right index finger inside one of the ends of the envelope's flap and smiled. FDA material came in large Fed-Ex packages, not in thin tan envelopes. Pretty obvious what was inside. A begging-for-mercy message, with or without a bribe. That's all it could be. The old man got ready for the feeling of pathetic loathing and outraged irritation that kind of message usually gave him. He had never given into a bribe. Sometimes he wondered if one of the large companies the FDA dealt with could offer him a big enough incentive. Perhaps this was his opportunity. He tore open the envelope and extracted a tan card folded in two.

He pulled up the front flap and brought the card closer to his eyes. How could they expect him to read such microscopically small characters? The man opened the drawer and felt around for his glasses.

"Honey," he called, "did you see my reading glasses?"

"On the coffee table," she answered from the kitchen. "Last time I saw them."

He shuffled to the table in front of the large brown couch. The aroma of his next dinner reached his nostrils from the kitchen. He glanced at his wife's back.

"Smells good, honey," he said, reaching for the glasses.

Muffled steps took the old man to the kitchen. His hand joints protested as he broke off a piece of crusty bread from a loaf sitting on the counter, turned to the range, and dipped it in a simmering pot of beef stew. The woman smiled and went on shaking the salad over the nearby sink.

He returned to his chair tasting the mixture of flavors. Back at his desk, spectacles forked on his nose, the man read the card, which he now held with both hands: "Your stroke will arrive within one hour."

What was this? The FDA team member had received disgruntled letters before, but none that wished him illness or death. He noticed a small gray disk under the words. His finger went to it. Hot as hell. A dull pain started on the right side of his forehead and spread down to his eyeball. Was it true? He would have a stroke? But he had read somewhere strokes weren't painful. The pain escalated, as in a mocking answer. It was like a knife, cutting the side of his neck. Perhaps the stress from the card gave him a migraine. But he had never felt such pain before. Something was wrong. At his age, better be safe than sorry.

"Honey," he moaned, "I'm not feeling so hot. I'm afraid I better go to the hospital."

The woman rushed from the kitchen wiping her hands on a stained apron. She stared at her husband for a long moment as if deciding how to best handle the possible emergency. The man flapped his hand, hurrying her to get ready.

A few minutes later, man and wife sat buckled up in their car on their way to Capitol Hospital. The man's headache and neck pain escalated with the car's bouncing and swerving. To him, the city street lights appeared blurred. Panic sat in.

The squat ER doctor in charge, and the blue-eyed female intern, rushed to meet the old man as he rolled into the ER stroke area on a wheelchair. The wife followed in short unsteady steps, her face crumpled by worry.

"He may be having a stroke," she announced gravely to the doctors. "He got a weird card that scared him to death."

"What kind of card?" the male doctor asked.

"I don't know." The wife shrugged. "What difference does it make? Just help him, will you?"

Medical personnel gathered around and moved him to a gurney. The old man lay still, while his headache spread to the other side of his forehead. The hospital's page system announced "Code Stroke." Hair stood on his naked arms as he shivered under the flimsy hospital gown.

"Get a stat CT scan," the female intern ordered a nearby nurse. "Is the other patient back yet?"

She leaned over him. The scent of her perfume made the old man gag. At the doctor's request, he squeezed her hand, lifted his legs, and showed her his teeth. Everything moved. But the pain throbbed with every heartbeat.

"We had another stroke a few minutes ago," the intern said as if apologizing. "She's in the CT scan now."

They rolled his gurney to a different area. A sign on the white wall read "Computerized Tomography Imaging." Someone parked him next to another gurney with a middle-aged woman facing in the opposite direction. Her pale features and sandy-colored hair looked familiar. The man lifted his head from the gurney.

"Martha!" he called. "Is that you?"

"Please lie down," a male technician said. "Do you know that woman?"

"Yes," the old man answered. "We're on the same FDA team. What's wrong with her? Is she having a stroke too? The ER doc said you just got another patient with a stroke."

"We're not at liberty to discuss other patients with you," the tech explained. "But you are free to ask her while you wait."

The pale woman gazed at him with a disinterested stare. Then a glimpse of recognition lit up her face. She smiled. Was the left side of her mouth lifting less than the right?

"What are you doing here?" she mumbled.

"I'm afraid they're checking me out for a stroke." The old man touched his forehead. "Got this excruciating headache."

"Me too." She pointed behind her. "They told me the CT scan is normal. But I know something is wrong. My neck is on fire. My right eye feels like it's exploding. Also, the weirdest thing happened to me today."

"Can't beat my story." He shook his head. "I got a stroke threat. And here I am. Freaked out like an idiot."

The woman got paler. Her eyes widened. She opened her mouth to speak, when an orderly grabbed the end of her gurney.

"Wait!" the old man yelled. "I need to talk to her for one more moment."

The young orderly gave him a look of impatience. He sighed and let go of the gurney. Martha just stared from her horizontal position.

"Did you get a card too?" the old man asked, bending toward Martha. "A tan card saying your stroke would arrive in one hour?"

She nodded. Her hand went to cover her mouth. The man heard a gasp.

"Perhaps," she whispered, "we should ask the E.R. doctor to check our arteries with the Moretti device. It's supposed to pick up very early damage, even before the CT scan."

The woman's brain had to be fried. Only a demented person could come up with such a suggestion. And she was an engineer. Wasn't she supposed to be smart? Smarter than an ultrasound guy like him?

"I hope you're kidding," the old man said. "How do you think that would go over? We told everyone to stop using the damned device. And now we're going to have the E.R. doctor use it on us? We'll never hear the end of it. As it is, doctors can't wait to discredit us."

The woman looked at him with desperate eyes. The orderly started rolling her gurney. Good. This conversation was insane. Better end it while the old man is ahead.

"Wait." Her hand signaled the transporter to stop, then she turned to the old man. "We could reverse the FDA decision, right now. You and me. If the two of us vote in favor of the device, it would give us four out of six votes—a majority. That would do it, wouldn't it?"

Pathetic. How did someone so spineless get to serve on an FDA team?

"Absolving not," he said. "It outside answer."

"What are you saying?" the woman said, a deep frown carving her forehead. "Doesn't make any sense."

What was happening? The words out of his mouth weren't the ones he was thinking of. Was this what a stroke did? The orderly took his hands off the woman's gurney and came closer. The man tried to reach out for him. His hand didn't follow the commands of his brain.

"He's getting paralyzed!" the young man yelled to the technician at the end of the corridor. "Let's get him into the CT scan, now!"

The gurney rushed forward. The old man slid past Martha. The woman's eyes widened with terror and followed him as he rolled away.

Dr. Leeds slumped in his office chair. Silvana Moretti, from a polished frame on his mahogany desk, smiled at him. He looked at his watch. Five past six. Tonight, for a change, he could make it to dinner with his girlfriend. Wait. The girlfriend is no more.

He reached down for a briefcase packed with all kinds of procrastination items. Steve unzipped the section filled with papers needing more immediate attention.

May as well use the time. Among several standard letter-sized papers, his hand closed around an envelope the size and consistency of a greeting card. A chill ran across his spine. The CEO had received a card just before his heart attack. Same for Dr. Nirula. They both had received notice of the event with a tan card. Dr. Leeds pulled his hand up. The envelope came into vision. Black print winked at him from the tan envelope: his name, along with the words "Personal and Confidential, FDA Material."

At least he knew what not to do with it.

CHAPTER 10

CODE STROKE

S teve froze. He stared at the envelope. His name was on it, but no
address. What kind of FDA material would come in such a format? A
tan card. No coincidence. Could this be another one of those deadly
cards? His hand warned him about the shape and texture. Perhaps feeling
the damn card had saved his life. Steve placed the envelope on his desk with
the care he would have used for an armed grenade. His hand shook, fumbling for a business card from his desk drawer. He reached for his phone on
the desk and dialed.

"Miner," a familiar male voice answered. "What's up?"

"Dr. Leeds here," Steve said. "I received a strange tan card. On the
envelope, it says FDA Material, but it looks like anything but FDA material.
Maybe I'm paranoid, but it reminded me of the cards Nirula and the hospital
CEO got."

"No," Kirk said, "you're not paranoid. Did you open it?"

"No. I didn't."

"Good." Kirk sounded relieved. "Put it down somewhere and move at
least several yards away. Even better, go into another room. We'll come up
to check it out."

Steve pushed off from his desk and walked out to the corridor. The
building was silent, except for distant noise from the elevator shafts. He
leaned against the wall and slid down to the cold floor.

After what to him was too long a wait, a double ping reached him, followed by the whooshing of doors. Kirk and Mulville appeared at the end of
the corridor and rushed to join him. Steve stood as their eyes examined him,
as if looking for bleeding wounds or signs of plague.

"Anything?" Mulville said. "Do you have any pains?"

"Not yet." Steve took a calming breath.

"Where is the card?" Kirk said.

"On my desk." Steve pointed his chin at his office. "Still closed."

"Can I have a word in private?" Kirk asked Mulville. They stepped away and seemed to argue for a long couple of minutes.

"We need to contact Dr. Moretti," the detective said after walking back. "Right now. We need to ask her how to avoid getting exposed."

Silvana had something to do with the tan cards? A tight squeeze took hold of Steve's stomach. Why would he get a card? Something had nagged Steve from the moment he had read "FDA" on the damned envelope. God. Was that it? He was part of the FDA team that had voted on Silvana's device. He had accepted the job to speed life-saving devices through the maze of the Federal bureaucracy. He would never have voted against Silvana's device. Steve believed in its usefulness. His stupid colleagues brought up his relationship with Silvana and insisted that his conflict of interest wouldn't allow him to vote. Was the card punishment for abstaining from that vote? But he had no choice. And Silvana had acted as if she understood and didn't hold it against him. Until now. What was he thinking? Was Silvana—his Silvana—trying to kill him?

No. Silvana Moretti wasn't a criminal. Of this Steve was certain, even if Silvana wouldn't answer a call from him if his life depended on it. But now Steve's life truly did depend on it, if his tan card was as deadly as the other ones.

"Can you call her?" Steve asked Kirk. "I'm afraid she won't answer if I call."

"Why not?" Kirk said. "Is she mad about something?"

"I—" Steve was on a slippery slope. The card added a dreadful twist to the equation, making one reason surface into his mind. "I haven't been able to contact her since the night of Dr. Nirula's surgery."

"Any idea why?" Kirk probed.

"I was part of the team that rejected the Moretti device." He blurted out his answer. "But Dr. Moretti, at the time, seemed okay with my abstaining."

Silence followed. Were the detective and the FBI agent processing his statement? No time to dwell on that right now. For all Steve knew, he was on his way to the Cath Lab, not as a doctor but as a patient. The thought sent his heart thumping.

"Wait here," Mulville ordered.

Steve watched Kirk and Mulville walk away and talk into their phones for several minutes. Then they came closer again. Mulville had seemed to be talking with the crime lab people. From his conversation, Moretti must've given him detailed instructions on how to handle the ultrasound device. Did Silvana know who the new potential victim was?

"Dr. Moretti," Kirk said, "mentioned that opening the card's top flap probably triggers the device. Good thing you didn't."

"Doctor," Mulville said, "tell me more about what you have to do with the FDA."

The slippery slope had led him straight to Mulville. Steve felt again as if he was being deposed in a malpractice case brought against him. No way to predict what his explanation would stir.

"I wanted to vote in favor of the Moretti device," he said. "But I had to abstain due to our relationship."

"If you had voted in favor," Kirk asked, "what then?"

The question felt like a stabbing. What was Kirk implying?

"The clinical trial," Steve admitted, "would have gone on. You need a majority vote against to stop a trial. But I had no choice. People knew Silvana and I were dating. The team forced me to step aside due to conflict of interest."

Had the team forced him to abstain? Or was it more like a suggestion? Could he have put up a better fight?

"If you had voted," Mulville said, "Silvana's brother would still be alive."

Steve gasped. He hadn't quite considered the two events together before, or the potential conclusion.

"Could Dr. Moretti do something like—?" Kirk asked.

"Absolutely not." Steve cringed. "I've known her for some time. She's a scientist, for God's sake. And why would she help me, by telling you how to avoid getting hurt, if killing me is what she's really trying to do?"

"We're going to find out," Mulville said. "Rest assured."

"We have to warn the other three members of the FDA team," Kirk said.

"Again, she's helping you." Steve pointed a finger at Kirk. "How can she be responsible?"

Steve's hand went to his phone. The E.R! Shit! "It's Green," the caller said. "Something is happening. We should let the FBI in on it."

Steve listened. Adrenaline kicked in. He swallowed to alleviate the worsening squeeze around his stomach.

"What's his name?" His heart protested in his chest. "And what's the woman's name? I'm with the FBI right now. I'll let them know."

Kirk and Mulville stared at him. Leeds pocketed his phone. He clenched his teeth and moved his hands and legs. Everything worked. He was still a doctor, not a patient, and had work to do.

"About the other members of the FDA team," Leeds said, "I'm afraid we're a little late. You can go down to the E.R. and see two of them right now, even talk to one, a woman. As far as the other one, a man, you may have to wait until after Dr. Green fixes his carotids. He can't talk because he's having a stroke. Both his carotid arteries have dissected."

Kirk and Mulville remained silent as if processing what they had just heard. Leeds rushed toward the elevator. He heard the two men behind him.

"The woman is freaking out," Steve added, waiting for the ride. "She got a tan card warning her she would suffer a stroke within an hour."

Steve's stomach rose as the elevator descended. Silence filled the space. Nothing but mechanical noises and the pings of passing floors. And his own heartbeat. A stroke? His card was probably predicting his stroke, too. If only Kirk and Mulville stopped staring at him as if expecting something to happen at any time.

Steve walked into the E.R. Kirk and Mulville followed. A familiar voice cursed in the distance. Steve recognized the woman from the FDA team. Two security guards restrained her flapping arms and legs. At least she wasn't paralyzed yet.

"She's one of the FDA team members," Leeds told Kirk and Mulville, pointing at the woman. "The patient with the guards."

Steve surveyed the ER looking for the doctor in charge. Something was odd. Not many people around. Then he noticed doctors and nurses gathered in the Code Room. Through the open door, Steve saw an anesthesia tech standing by an empty gurney with a portable respirator hooked up and ready to go. The crash cart was in place. The different components of the body cooling apparatus draped the gurney, ready to embrace a patient. But there was no patient. All that meant one thing.

"Code DOA," the page system announced.

"What's code DOA?" Mulville elbowed Leeds.

"Dead on arrival." A fleeting twinge of satisfaction arose from Steve's ability to shock Mulville into silence. "The ambulance is bringing in a patient found dead."

The sound of the sirens seemed to grow out of the silence. Intensity increased to the maximum, then the loud whine stopped and the ER door burst open. Two men and one woman in emergency medical technician uniforms raced in with a gurney, like a giant animal, and rushed to the Code Room without interrupting their resuscitation efforts.

"No pulse!" the woman tech yelled, pushing the gurney, one hand on the patient's neck. "Continue CPR."

Inside the room, the medics stood back and the ER personnel took over. The patient was moved onto the cooling unit and CPR was resumed. Orders for adrenaline, defibrillation, and more CPR echoed in the room. Kirk and Mulville stood as if paralyzed by the life-or-death battle.

"You may have to wait for the dust to settle," said Leeds, pointing to the

Code Room. "I have an early start tomorrow and need to rest. I'll catch up with you tomorrow, if I'm able."

He marched away. As he passed the Code Room door, something caught his eye. The dead man's arm stretched down toward the floor, his lifeless hand bluish and open. Relinquished during death's takeover, something had fallen off. On the white tiles below, a crumpled tan card seemed to mock Steve personally.

CHAPTER 11

THE PERP

Steve had never been as afraid of dying as he was at this moment. His head throbbed in a band right behind both eyes. Soon the light might go off for him permanently. Was that his destiny? He had to know for sure. Only one way to find out. Quick steps brought him to the vascular laboratory. His ID card got him inside a largely deserted room with a treadmill and cardiac ultrasound equipment. He walked past several empty examining tables and stopped in front of a closet. At the touch of his ID card, a bar of green lighted, and a click broke the silence. His hand shook as he pulled the door open. Was what he needed still here, despite the interruption of the clinical trial?

Yes. On the top shelf was the Moretti device. He retrieved the instrument, touched the "on" key, and watched a rectangular screen on the side of the probe come to life. A succession of letters and formulae appeared on a clear background. After a wait longer than he preferred, the word "ready" popped up.

Steve placed the flat tip of the probe against the right side of his neck. The carotid pulse pushed against his fingertips. Still open. How much pressure would it be safe to apply to get a good reading without making any possible dissection worse? Steve had examined several patients with the device and had never wondered about that before. Being a patient, on the other side of the fence, was a different situation, full of paranoid uncertainties and unanswerable questions. Steve didn't like that one bit. He couldn't wait to diagnose himself as healthy and jump back onto the doctor's side.

His eyes looked around for a mirror. On the side wall, he found one on top of the sink, and took the probe there. The soft tip was on his neck again.

He held his breath and moved the device up over the arterial pulsation. A beep announced the reading. Steve looked at the screen. The line indicating inflammation was thankfully right in the middle of normal values. The right carotid was normal. His chest felt lighter. Breathing became easier.

He repeated the steps with the left side and got the same reassuring result. He wasn't going to die. Not tonight. Even his exhaustion was gone. What about his coronaries? Should he test them? After all, he hadn't read his tan card and wasn't sure it had anything to do with carotids.

He lifted his scrub shirt and placed the probe on his chest, choosing the space between two ribs on the left side of his breast bone. At the sound of the beep, the line came to rest within the normal range.

He sighed in relief, then replaced the probe and locked everything up. Thanks, Dr. Moretti. Dr. Leeds will never again vote against or abstain from any vote for this device. Though against regulation, he rushed out of the hospital in scrubs, reached his car, and sat at the wheel. Then he stiffened. What was the chance the probe could be wrong? After all, wasn't that the reason why they had voted against it—that it was wrong too often? The team had been worried about too many positive results, resulting in unnecessary medical expenses. But how many of the negative results were wrong? Steve couldn't remember exactly, but it was a small percentage. Only Moretti knew all the statistics. And his life as it had been couldn't go on without knowing for sure. He had to call her. Now.

How was she going to deal with the fact he had used her device for his own benefit? He hoped her anger would have faded somewhat, after almost two months. And what about the FBI's ongoing investigation about her possible involvement in all the dissection cases? He could end up in trouble if caught speaking with her. The story of the tan cards would have to come up. What would Silvana Moretti do if she were guilty? Run? No. Impossible. He shrugged. His thumbs typed out a text message.

"Please call me about your device. Very urgent."

He touched "send." Driving didn't seem advisable in his current state of agitation. He waited in the garage.

The flurry of activities inside the ER Code Room had come to an end. The words "I'm calling the code" by the E.R. doctor, followed by "Time of death 6:34 PM" still hung in the air like a verdict, together with the smell of clammy sweat, bodily waste, blood, and antiseptic. Kirk looked at Mulville. The agent's cheeks had lost some of their usual color. The burly FBI guy must've witnessed many violent deaths in his career. Why would this one affect him so? Did the odor peculiar to hospital-related death bother him? Not Kirk's favorite smell either.

"Are you okay?" Kirk asked. "You look like you're ready to pass out."

"Hell, no." Mulville shrugged and pointed to the floor near the gurney. "Look at that damn card. The stiff must be the last of the three FDA members who voted against the famous device. And the first homicide on our hands. After we work the crime area, we've got to talk to that Moretti woman in person."

Silvana Moretti, a murderer? Everything pointed to Moretti as the guilty party, except for Moretti herself. Something didn't fit. The smile lighting up the woman's face at the sight of her daughter popped into Kirk's mind. Kirk had seen his share of guilty people. Murderers didn't smile that way.

Mulville called the crime lab investigators, then marched into the Code Room and ordered "hands-off" the evidence, dead body included. After grabbing gloves and a plastic bag from a shelf, the agent bent down to retrieve the tan card.

"Perhaps," Kirk said, joining him, "we should involve Leeds. Let him go see Dr. Moretti, test the ground so to speak. He knows her well, even dated her, until recently."

Mulville looked up at him, eyes bewildered, as if Kirk had come from out of space. Kirk could see Mulville's point of view. Still, Steve could be helpful to plan a strategy. They just needed a strategy.

"Listen." Kirk took Mulville by the shoulder and guided him away from the Code Room. "We've got nothing but circumstantial evidence connecting Dr. Moretti to this."

Mulville stared at him with an equal mixture of irony and contempt.

"We can ask Steve to help us," Kirk continued, "if he's up to it. If somebody is framing her, the woman might be more likely to open up to the doctor."

"Framing?" Mulville waved his hand for emphasis. "What framing? She got pissed because the trial for her stupid device got ditched. And more pissed from the screwing-up of her brother's case. What makes you think she'll talk to her ex-boyfriend after also trying to do him in?"

"I understand what you're saying," Kirk said. "You never met her. I did, and something doesn't fit. She isn't the murdering type."

"Oh, yeah?" Mulville face twisted into a smirk. "And what type is that, Detective? I can tell you about serial killers who look and act like Mother Teresa. You never know what's going on inside someone's fucked-up head."

"Don't know much about saints," Kirk said, "but I'd be surprised if there isn't something more going on with Moretti. She's too smart to do this business with the cards. And she looked worried and concerned about the victims, even the people she's supposed to be pissed at. And she started crying when she heard about the girl needing the stent to her left main artery. All too difficult to fake. You weren't there."

"Well," Mulville said, "I'll be there soon enough—to interrogate her."

"It's a mistake," Kirk said. "At least let's run it by Steve first."

"Don't you dare talk to him," Mulville said. "I'm going to question the only FDA member available to talk to—the crazy woman down there."

Mulville turned and walked to the other side of the ER. Kirk followed him. The woman lay still on the gurney. Kirk hadn't heard anything from her since the code. The doctor must've sedated her.

Mulville and Kirk approached the FDA woman and Mulville showed his badge to a nurse at her side. The nurse nodded and pivoted, making room for the men. The woman on the gurney looked asleep, her face flushed, her eyes closed. She wore a fluffy pale pink robe protruding from under a hospital blanket. Kirk imagined her coming back from work, slipping into something more comfortable, grabbing a glass of chardonnay, and relaxing, until the card moment. The card had scared her so much she hadn't bothered to get dressed. Kirk stared at the triangle of pale skin framed by the robe's collar, looking for the slightest movement of a vessel.

"We sedated her," the nurse confirmed, shrugging as if to indicate there had been no other way to contain the outburst.

How could doctors and nurses tell if the patient developed stroke symptoms, if she was asleep? Kirk felt relief as the woman's chest lifted with rhythmic slow breathing.

"Ma'am." Mulville grabbed her forearm. "Wake up. FBI. We need to talk to you."

The woman's head moved from side to side, as if resuming a struggle against restraining hands. One arm went up, the other one struggled against Mulville's vise-like hand. She opened her eyes. Then her head stopped shaking, her arms relaxed, and her fight ended.

"My God!" she shouted. Her free palm covered her left eye. "I can't see from my right eye. I told you something was wrong. Do something. Call a doctor! Don't you all just stand there!"

The nurse stepped up and peeled Mulville's hand from the woman's arm. Mulville stared at the nurse for a moment, then stepped back in silence. The nurse held her fingers in front of the patient's blind eye, but the woman pushed her away. The nurse, ending her examination, dialed her phone instead. Soon the code stroke announcement blasted again from the communication system.

The E.R. doctor arrived. He lifted limp brown hair from the woman's neck and his fingers went to palpate the neck arteries one side at a time. She seemed to relax on the gurney.

"No pulse on the right." He turned to the nurse behind him. "Get her ready for an angiogram. STAT."

The nurse scuttled to arrange for the test. The ER physician looked around as if searching for the right doctor. The patient, with just one functioning eye, stared ahead in terror.

"Dr. Green is still busy with the first stroke. Get the cardiologist on call," the doctor told the nurse. Then he turned to the patient. "We'll take care of this. Don't worry."

"Not much for you or me to do here," Mulville said, waving at Kirk to follow him. "Let's talk."

He led the way to a door labelled "Family Conference Room." The light came on to illuminate an unoccupied room furnished like a living-room. Mulville sank into a sofa where many a family medical tragedy had been discussed.

"Coffee?" The PI pointed at an automatic machine. "I need it."

Mulville refused with a gesture indicating he had no time to waste. Kirk got up, touched the appropriate buttons, and brought his coffee back, opting for a facing chair instead of the sofa. He blew on the hot liquid and took several cautious sips. Mulville gave him an impatient look.

"One dead," Mulville said with an accusatory tone, "and two more having procedures for strokes. The first one Dr. Green said had bilateral, whatchamacallit split of the arteries, same as the heart attacks but in the neck."

"Carotid dissections." Kirk's breath sounded like a soft whistle. He took another sip of coffee. "Pretty rare as well."

"The second one," Mulville went on, "the woman, is half-blind. And they all got cards telling them they were going to have a stroke. The dead one got the same tan card. We're waiting for the autopsy to see if he died of the same thing."

"Tan cards." Kirk nodded wide-eyed. "Just like Leeds."

"These people," Mulville said, pointing at the room at large, "are all part of the FDA team that shut down Moretti's gizmo. It's got to be Moretti. She has motive and capability. She's the only one with both."

Mulville's head turned from side to side as if in search of agreement. Kirk took a few more sips of his coffee. His hand massaged his chin.

"And Leeds almost died," Mulville added. "Luckily, he didn't open his card. Otherwise, he'd be on the table now, instead of his patients."

"I know. But I doubt Silvana would do anything like this to anyone," Kirk said. "The evidence against her is pretty bad, I admit, but it's all circumstantial. Could Silvana have been framed?"

Mulville's hand dismissively swept Kirk's theory away. Kirk placed his empty cup on the floor and stared at the wall behind the couch. His mouth tightened.

"It's a possible explanation." Kirk stressed the word "possible." Then his face sagged with terror. "Unless someone is forcing her to cooperate. What about Patrizia? If she's the one at risk, Silvana will never talk."

"What a coincidence," Mulville said, sitting back and crossing his legs. "The perp forces Moretti to hurt or kill all the people who pissed her off. Why? What would be the motive for someone else to do that?"

"Someone who hates her," Kirk said. "Someone who knows her story. Lots of people know her story. It was in the news."

"Give me a break."

"Mulville," Kirk said, "we've got to convince her to let us help her. Whatever her involvement, she can't handle this alone. These people are ruthless."

"That's all fine and dandy," Mulville said. "But talking to her isn't enough. We need to check her shit—you know, her computer, desk, papers."

Silence followed.

"Get a warrant," Kirk said.

"Yeah." Mulville uncrossed his legs and leaned forward. "We're never going to get the evidence we need if we don't shake some trees first."

"Steve can just ask her," Kirk said. "Then, if necessary, we'll worry about getting evidence."

"Are you listening to yourself? Do you want me to totally screw up this investigation by involving the murderess' boyfriend?"

Kirk's mouth tightened into a line. When dealing with Mulville, it was easy to forget one was in the presence of an FBI professional. But this time the guy was right.

"Fair enough." Kirk said. "If I hadn't met her, and if she hadn't cooperated with us, she'd be at the top of my list of suspects."

"How many people do you have on your list, Kirk?"

"One," Kirk said.

CHAPTER 12

SILVANA

Steve looked up at Silvana's house. He had often paused in that very spot before ringing the doorbell at night, then watching the street light bring the residential walls' blue color back to life. Fantasies about sky and sea would flow through his mind, setting his mood for the romantic evening ahead. Now his chest tightened as he recalled the happiness and pleasure he had once enjoyed there.

Did he still have the right to barge in at nine? Did the past still give him special privileges, or had he been relegated to the role of a regular person in Silvana's eyes? Often, when two intimate people split up, things get so bad, the other person becomes persona non-grata.

Again Steve reviewed the words Silvana had used when dumping him. "It's me," she had said. "I'm not ready. Too many deaths in my family. Have to focus on my daughter."

Their relationship didn't sound irreparable. Yet, afterward, Silvana had never returned any of his heartfelt phone calls, texts, or emails—not even the frantic one he had sent her tonight from the garage after receiving the tan card and using her device. Steve had called her and texted her again, waiting for more than two hours in front of a dinner destined to remain uneaten. A resolution had congealed in his mind like the grease of his steak. He was going to see her at her house. He needed to know what the future held for him, physically and emotionally.

Silvana bedroom's window was the only one lit up. She was probably sitting at her make-up table, the ornate Italian silver mirror in front of her, brushing her hair with a matching silver-covered brush. That's when he would come up behind her, place his hands on her neck, and slide his finger down the lacy gown she'd be wearing for his benefit.

He shrugged the memory away before excitement could turn into disappointment. He walked across the concrete path and climbed the three steps to the front door. His feet felt heavy. He rang the bell.

Shuffling steps could be heard from the other side of the door. Steve found it difficult to breathe. She'd be outraged to see him. And what was he doing there? Getting answers about his chances of survival? Or was he trying to reassure himself she wasn't capable of murder?

Ever since his arrival at the emergency room, along with the rest of the FDA team responsible for shutting down Silvana's trial, he had refused to acknowledge any possible connection between the FDA events and the woman he loved. He refused to even consider such an abomination. An irresistible instinct to turn around and run away seized him. He stepped back. His foot slipped on the edge of the step, his arms and hands went akimbo, and he landed on the frozen concrete below. A sharp pain ran from his buttock up his spine.

"Who is it?" Silvana's husky voice asked from behind a metal door screen. "What's going on out there?"

"It's me," he moaned. "Steve."

The door opened. Silvana's dark silhouette became visible. The entry light went on. She was wearing an aqua-colored robe, which was a favorite of his. He pushed himself up from the icy ground and stood erect despite a burning pain travelling down the back of his right leg all the way to his heel. That one of his lumbar disks might have ruptured seemed unimportant.

She leaned forward. Her face remained in the darkness. He waited for the wrath to hit, grateful for the physical pain to distract him from the emotional one to come. Instead, her hand reached out, wrapped around his wrist, and pulled him inside.

When the light shone on Silvana's face, he noticed swollen eyes, a quivering mouth, and droopy cheeks.

"I'm sorry I didn't return your calls," she said. "What did you want to know about my device?"

Her presence had made him forget he still feared for his life. Now panic returned like a claw clenching his stomach. Steve sighed.

"There were other cards." He concentrated on the tan card he had received to avoid feeling sorry for her. "This time, three people got strokes from carotid dissections."

Her eyes widened and her body stiffened, as if an electric current had gone through her.

"What happened to them?" she said.

"Two went to surgery. One was dead on arrival."

She looked worse now, sagging, broken. The worse she looked, the happier Steve felt, regarding her reaction as a sign of innocence. What kind of nightmare were they all in?

"What about my device?" she said.

The real question burning inside Steve, on which his future and his happiness depended, was: "Did you do it? Did you send the cards?" He wanted to take Silvana by the shoulders and get a definitive answer right now.

"You see," he said instead, "today I got a card too."

The horror he witnessed on her face comforted and vindicated him. Silvana still had feelings for him. Or, at the very least, she didn't want him to die.

"I didn't open it," he said. "Still, I was worried because, at the same time, those other people arrived at the ER with carotid dissections after also getting cards. So, I checked my arteries with your device."

"And?" she whispered.

"Negative," he said. "But I wanted to know if I was really safe."

"You are." Her voice carried relief. Then came her professional explanation. "The device is close to perfect in ruling out disease."

Her cheeks shone in the dim light. They were wet with tears. The next instant, his arms wrapped around Silvana's shaking shoulders, her tears spilling onto his coat, and her sobs and gasps vibrating under his hands and in his ears.

"It's okay," he said. He ran his fingers through her silky hair. "I'm here for you."

She looked up. The pain, visible in her eyes, was unbearable. She pulled the coat off his shoulders. For a moment, his arms were trapped behind him. Silvana's subtle head movement released her hair's fresh scent to his nostrils. Her mouth looked soft and inviting. He bent down and kissed her lips with caution, uncertain what was happening in that moment. Her response caught him by surprise. She dropped his coat to the floor and attacked him with passion he had never witnessed, and with strength he hadn't suspected. Her mouth seemed to seek life force from his. Her embrace spoke of tragic finality, as if this moment was her only and last chance of possessing him.

"I'll always be here for you," he said, more to reassure himself, for he was suppressing the dread fueled by her behavior. "Always."

She answered by reconquering his mouth and squeezing him with greater force.

He freed himself from her hug, lifted her in his arms without breaking their kiss, and walked to the living room couch. His arms lowered her on the pillows with the care he would have used for a baby. He lay beside her, his mouth still on hers, his hands finding her skin inside her robe, under the smooth gown.

He wanted her so much, as if having her was the final goal, the only goal, the only reality. But her body stiffened under his hands, then relaxed, turning limp. Right when his mind had signaled that it was safe to forsake all thoughts and reservations and just feel, right when his body was abandoning all restraints, she released him, turned around on the couch, and stared at the ceiling.

"I need you desperately to love me, now," she said. "But I can't."

He pushed himself up on his elbows and ran a finger on the familiar smooth temple, then the cheek, and down to her chin. He loved when, at work, her chin stiffened with strength, courage, and intelligence. Now it only showed despair.

"Silvana," he said, lifting her chin with his hand and forcing her to look at him in the eye. "What's going on?"

She seemed to wake up from a trance. Her head shook in frantic denial. She sat up, tears streaming down her face again. It was as if the two of them had reached out for each other over a crack of the earth, had touched, locked on for an instant of hope and a glimpse of safety, then the earth had split for good, separating them with ominous finality.

"Two strokes." She choked down a sob. "And a dead patient. On top of the three previous heart attacks. And you—you almost died. All from my chips."

"Your chips?" Steve felt as if the ground under him had opened and he was falling into an abyss. "What are you talking about?"

"Six of my chips went missing." She shook her head. "I recognized one on the card Kirk Miner showed me."

"My God," he gasped, as his mind struggled to integrate the information, and to assess whether it improved or worsened Silvana's odds. "But how are you responsible? Whoever stole them from your lab is. The FBI needs your help to find that person."

She remained silent, nodding without apparent conviction. She looked distraught. Did she know who the stroke patients were?

"Silvana." He took her hand. It was lifeless, as if drained of all hope. "The stroke patients and the one who died were all part of the FDA team that closed down your trial. They're the ones who voted against you. And I was part of that team also, but I abstained. All the people affected did something bad to you. The FBI agent thinks you're responsible."

He waited for her to react to his last statement. His eyes scrutinized her face for any hint of surprise, protest, or resentment. There was none. She let go of a deep sigh and began staring at the ceiling again. What was she thinking? Was she hiding something? Making up an answer?

"You can tell me anything," he said. "I want to know everything."

She turned to him and reached out again, pulling him down to her, squeezing him against her breasts. She kissed his hair. Her body felt relaxed in a normal way, as if she had gained strength from him and now she had some control. "I need you to stay tonight," she said, as if she needed to plead to make him stay. "Hold me, without talking. I need you to trust me. Until tomorrow."

"What will happen tomorrow?" Steve feared she would hear his frantic heartbeat. "Why tomorrow?"

She got up, took him by the hand, and brought him to the bedroom. A whiff of her perfume reached him as she shed her robe. He joined her under the covers and embraced her again. The sheets were cool and fragrant, just as he remembered. The silk of her gown glided under his fingertips.

"I missed you." His mouth found the warmth of her neck. "I want to be here with you, always."

He traced her neck with his lips, pausing to kiss her soft skin, driven by craving and urgency, as if he wanted to commit texture, shape, and scent to memory, in case destiny deprived him of her again in the future. His hands moved inside her gown to the softness of her breasts. She shuddered under his touch and kisses. He took her face between his hands, moving on top of her, ready to forgo and forget any purpose except gaining the highest pleasure from making love to the woman he held.

But hers weren't shudders of pleasure. She was crying again, as if tortured by the pleasure he was giving her and torn by an impossible decision. What was going on inside that beautiful mind? He stared at her shut eyes, clinging to the trembling body. His excitement dissipated and left behind an emptiness impossible to fill.

"Please," he moaned, "tell me what's going on."

"Tomorrow," she begged, her eyes closed not in pleasure but in pain. "I need to rest now."

He rolled off her and held her against his chest, caressing her lustrous hair while fighting his resurgent desire. Moments later, her breathing slowed and the residual soft shudders from the previous crying abated. She was asleep.

Sleep didn't come that easy to Steve. Images of tan cards, hearts with pale areas of death, patients turning blind and dying—all swirled in his mind during different periods of sleep and troubled consciousness. After waking up from yet another nightmare, he reached for his phone and checked the time—eight past two. He ducked into the soft mattress, freed himself from Silvana's arm, and rolled over and out from under the covers. She moaned and turned to the other side. Steve waited until she sounded deep in sleep again. Barefoot, he walked next door to her office and sat down on the chair in front of her computer.

What was he doing there? His stomach clamped down. He loved Silvana. He had never told her yet, and perhaps he never would, but he did love her. Steve had always considered himself a fair judge of character. Silvana wasn't capable of murder. Somebody must be using her, stealing her chips. But why? He needed to find out. She needed his help and he wanted to protect her, help her, and restore their relationship so he could tell her and show her how much he loved her.

So, what was he doing there, in front of her computer? The word "snooping" came to mind. But what choice did he have? Someone had to check this out, either himself or Mulville. Put that way, the choice was clear. Steve needed to know if Silvana was in trouble, so he could help her, defend her against the bad guys, and the so-called good FBI guy as well.

The blue glow of electronics gave the room an eerie feeling. On the desk, the picture of him and her from better times was still there. How much did she still care for him? He touched the keyboard. A request for the password appeared. Steve dug into his memory but found nothing. The room was cold and silent. Air blowing from the heater startled him. Then his eyes landed on Patrizia's soccer picture. The girl looked so proud holding the ball.

He typed "Patrizia." Access was denied. Shit. He shivered. Not from cold. Not from the missed password. From a question again flashing in his mind with exponential dread: Where was Patrizia? Not home. Had something happened to her? His hands wrapped around the chair's arms to prevent him from running back to the bedroom, waking up Silvana, and asking her the question. He had to remain calm. Things always looked frightful at night, in dark rooms glowing with electronic light. The morning sun would bring clarity. Silvana had mentioned there would be an explanation in the morning. A mother would look frantic if her daughter were truly in danger.

He stopped, his sweating hands resting on his lap. But Silvana did look frantic and unable to respond to his love, a different person from the passionate, insatiable woman he knew so well. Steve had work to do. Several deep breaths quieted the pounding of his heart. He had to break into Silvana's computer to find out the truth.

He used various combinations of dates, names, and phone numbers, but they all were wrong. Steve sat back on the chair, hypnotized by the glow of the screen. Thirty minutes of trying hadn't gotten him anywhere. Then Steve remembered. His hand slid under the cold metal desk. He peeled a rectangular piece of paper off the bottom and brought it into the light. How many times had he told Silvana it wasn't a good idea to store her password list under her computer desk? Luckily for him, she hadn't listened. And there it was. A dozen passwords. His eyes scrolled to the one named "main computer." His shoulders drooped as he read "LoveStevetodayx3." The password gave him a jolt of pleasure and hope.

The password set the screen in motion. She hadn't changed the password yet. Did that mean anything for their future together? The answer was hidden right in front of him.

He clicked on several files and found graphics and documents related to Silvana's cancer research. Another file was dedicated to her device. The letter announcing the trial suspension came into view. If only the team had voted in favor, perhaps he wouldn't be here, in the middle of the night, spying on the love of his life.

But he had to go on, to show that FBI jerk that he was wrong about her.

Wait a minute. Mulville had never said anything to Steve about suspecting Silvana. Yet Steve was sure he had. Or perhaps it was Steve himself who suspected her. But how could anyone suspect a woman like Silvana? Steve stared at the computer screen. The sad part was that the absence of evidence couldn't be considered proof of Silvana's innocence. Yet he had to do his best while hoping for the best. He shifted his weight on the chair to ease the pain building up in his back.

An unnamed file carrying a date of about three weeks earlier took his breath away. He clicked on it. Another password request appeared. Sweat poured from his pores as he consulted the password list. He found only one unassigned password—"roadtoHell." He entered it, thinking it could have something to do with him.

A spread of graphics and formulas filled the screen. Steve didn't know where to focus first. After a while, it didn't matter. Wherever he looked, he found stuff he had hoped never to see—all about the effect of different wavelengths and the varying strength of ultrasounds on different-size arteries. He was looking at the biophysics of the cardiovascular disasters he had witnessed during the past week.

A chill ran down his spine. His body sagged. He forced himself to open the next file. Three items came into view. The first was labelled "coronary" and the second "carotid." After each one, wavelength specifications followed. His life as he had imagined shattered in his mind, but he ordered his hand to go on and click on the third item. He stared at the label and the calculations, then slumped down on the desk, head on his folded arms, and grieved.

CHAPTER 13

THE MORNING AFTER

A burning in the small of his back woke Steve up. He lifted his head and saw the computer screen, now dark, which had recently disclosed the explosive information responsible for his demolished future.

The time on his phone showed a few minutes before five AM. Steve tiptoed toward the bedroom. He could see Silvana's back and the pale blue nightgown reaching midway to her spine. The contrast of her curly black hair against her shoulder made her skin look like porcelain. He watched the slow motion of her deep breathing—his Silvana.

Then the artery-shattering formulas flashed into his mind. From now on, contemplation of the woman he loved would trigger images of those dreadful calculations—the love of his life intimately connected with instruments of death and destruction. His mind refused to hold the two items together at the same time. There had to be some plausible explanation. He had to find the truth. She was the key, and he would unlock the truth, forcing her to cooperate in the fight for their future together. The threat of losing her had given him a new awareness of how valuable she was to him. His life didn't seem worth living without her, so he was ready and willing to fight until he had exhausted all resources, and even to gamble his own life to protect and preserve hers.

His hand reached for his crumpled clothes on the floor. Back pain struck him anew and produced a muffled moan. He looked up and assessed the effect of the noise on Silvana's sleep. She remained still. He walked back to her office, dressed, and sat again at her computer, ignoring painful protests from his back. He searched the drawers for a thumb drive. In a few minutes, done copying the critical files, Steve pocketed the memory stick, got up from the chair, and dropped flat on the floor seeking physical and psychological relief from the pain. Neither came. He stared at the ceiling as the daylight seeped through the open blinds, until the soft sound of steps called his attention to the door, where Silvana appeared clad in the aqua colored robe. Sleep seemed to have relaxed her features and healed some of her pain.

"What are you doing on the floor?" she asked, her voice warm with concern.

She squatted next to him. The top of her breasts bulged from the loosened robe. The urge to reach out for her, and to make love right on that hard floor, washed over him. But her puffy eyes reminded him of their present reality.

"I must've hurt my back," he said—anything to delay the moment of truth if only by a few minutes. He felt he had only one chance to say the right words. "When I fell outside."

He rolled on his side and propped his body up with caution. She lent a hand and pulled him up.

"We need to talk." He slid her chair from under the desk and swung his hand around, guiding her to sit down, as he had done only a few weeks ago after swing-dancing at their favorite pub. She nodded and obeyed. Her eyes stared at the cherry-wood floor. He propped himself against the desk to face her. "I have a confession to make."

"You?" She looked up at him with bewilderment. "You have a confession?"

"I came here to see you," he said, groping in his tired mind for the right words to describe something so wrong. "But also to ask you about the heart attacks, the strokes, and the cards."

She remained silent. Steve wouldn't get any help from her. He was on his own to fight for the future. She was part of the problem, and he didn't know whose side she was on.

"I'm worried sick about you. The FBI may be looking at you because all these hurt people were involved in hurting you in the past, one way or another."

"Do you mean," she said, a strange lack of emotion in her eyes, "they're considering me a suspect?"

"Probably," he said, as the path in his mind became a slippery slope too dangerous to travel. "I really want to help you. But I need the truth. And you're unwilling to share it with me."

He waited, hoping her explanation would clarify everything before he had to confess to invading her privacy. What was he going to do if she were to confess?

He refused to consider the possibility. No answer came. He had to jump off his cliff, let her know what he had done, hoping to land on his two feet.

"To be able to help you," he said, monitoring her face for any reaction that would guide his explanation, "I had to look for the truth. In your computer."

Good way to make her angry. But he might need her to be mad. If he had to separate from her, Steve needed all the help he could get. It would be like cutting a limb off his body—hard to do on his own, even if the limb was blackened with life-threatening gangrene. There had to be another way. He saw no anger on her face. No emotions, in fact—not even the despair of the previous night.

"You still keep your passwords under the desk." He lifted her chin up with two fingers to lock his eyes on hers. "I was able to look at your computer last night."

"Then you know," she said. No anger. Only the calm of resignation. "I'm glad you know."

Silvana's face transformed in front of his eyes. A mask of firmness and determination took shape. No more tears. He let go of her chin. Her eyes held his glance.

"Did you program the chips?" Steve forced himself to say. His whitened knuckles clenched the edge of the desk. "To give those people heart attacks and strokes?"

Silvana turned to stare at the blank screen. Steve didn't have to wait long for the answer. It came in the form of a slight nod.

"You wanted to kill people? What about me? You wanted to hurt me?"

"No," she protested. "Not you. Never."

"What about the others?" he said. "Why did you want to kill them?"

"No, not to kill." She shook her head limply. "Just punish. You know why."

No. Silvana was a scientist, a professional, a healer abiding by a "first-do-no-harm" moral code. Steve couldn't accept the fact she had purposefully set out to hurt harmless people.

"I don't believe you." He took her by the shoulder. "I mean, I believe you did it. But I don't think you did it for revenge. That's not you. I know you well enough to be sure about that. You were forced. What did they do to turn you into a criminal?"

Seemingly in answer to his question, Patrizia's picture smiled back at Steve from the desktop. He hadn't seen or heard the girl since his phone call a few days ago. Perhaps she was asleep in her room. If the girl was safe here in her bed, Steve couldn't think of any way anyone could force Silvana to do what she had just confessed. His stomach sank.

"Where is Patrizia?" he asked. "Is she home?"

He waited, hoping she'd dismiss his question as irrelevant to the discussion at hand. No objections came. Silvana turned her gaze away, toward the wall, as if she accepted the question as pertinent and appropriate. Something was going on with her daughter that related to Silvana's criminal-like behavior. Her mouth locked in a straight line. He grabbed her cheeks and forced her head to face him again. But her eyes remained on the wall, looking sideways, avoiding his gaze.

"Where is Patrizia?" he repeated with as much firmness as he could muster. "We're still together. When people are together, they share their problems. They face them together. I'm here for you, to help you in any way I can. If something is happening with Patrizia that made you do those things—"

"You're hurting me," she mumbled. "She's in Florida. With my sister."

"You're lying." He let go of her face. "Vacations are over. She should be in school. Besides, your sister lives in Italy."

She didn't flinch. Her eyes met his. He saw resolve and strength—a will to fight.

"You don't know my whole family," she said.

Steve knew that look. He had seen it when she worked day and night to complete an impossible project. An "I'm going to finish this or die trying" look.

"Where is Patrizia?" he asked again. He forced himself to mention the worst case scenarios his frantic mind was feeding him. "Did somebody take her?"

"Don't be ridiculous," she said with a strained chuckle. "I sent her away, so she wouldn't see me go to jail."

Jail? His Silvana was planning on going to jail? She mentioned this as if she had known it all along. Steve was the one who didn't know, and didn't want to know.

"I'm calling Kirk Miner," he said. "You can tell him your story. See what he thinks."

She grabbed his arm. The phone fell from his hand.

"No." Her squeeze had the urgency of despair, but her face remained composed. "Not Kirk Miner. I'll talk only to the FBI."

What had Kirk done to her? Steve thought he'd be helping her by involving Kirk. He froze. Perhaps that was it. She didn't want any help. He would have to turn her over to Mulville, like a Christian sent to the lions' den. But why?

"You better call your lawyer." Steve tuned down the animosity in his voice. "You're gonna need him."

"I don't need anything," she said. "Only to get this over with. Confess everything. Only to the FBI. Call them now. Then go home. Please."

He forced himself to dial Mulville's number. Silvana wanted to talk.

"I'll be damned," Mulville said. "Did Miner put you up to this?"

"No. I came to her house to ask her about her device. She's not herself. Something is really wrong."

"I bet." Mulville's soft chuckle came through loud and clear. "I'll be right there. My lucky day. Now at last I can send that detective packing."

Silence dominated the house during the next half hour. Silvana went to the kitchen to make coffee. Steve understood. She had to escape from his smothering attempts to rescue her. She came back, handed Steve a mug, then disappeared upstairs. The smell and the warmth of coffee comforted him a bit. The doorbell rang. Mulville walked in as if he owned the place, followed by two uniformed men. He plopped himself down on the couch.

"Where is she?" He surveilled the room with narrowed eyes. "By the way, an autopsy on the dead-on-arrival victim showed bilateral carotid dissection."

"Good morning to you too," Steve said. "She's upstairs. Getting dressed."

Mulville gave him a disgusting, lecherous look. Steve clenched his fists. He had to remain calm, for her, in case he could help her in some unknown and unforeseen way. It was as if she was on the precipice of falling, clinging to him as he tried with all his might to pull her up to safety, but her fingers were slipping away with every passing moment.

"You left her alone?" Mulville assumed a righteous air as he lifted himself off the couch. "If she tries anything, I'm holding you responsible."

"For God's sake." Steve opened his palms in exasperation. "She's confessing to the crimes."

"Go get her," Mulville instructed the uniformed men, using his chin to direct them up the stairs. "Will ya?"

"No," Steve said. "You won't take away her privacy. She'll be down."

"Listen, lover boy," Mulville said, "her right to privacy disappeared the moment she zapped the first artery. Better go home before I slap you with obstruction charges."

"I'll get her." Steve's open palm signaled the men to wait.

He got up and walked upstairs to the bedroom. She sat at her makeup table, hands on her lap, dressed in gray slacks and a white tailored shirt. She clenched the two picture frames Steve had seen on her desk. She looked up at him and stood, placing the photos next to her perfume bottles.

"It's time," he said softly. The unexpected tenderness in her eyes brought him back to better moments. The contrast with the present renewed his pain. "Are you sure you want to do this without a lawyer?" he asked.

She nodded, her face grave, her fingers reaching for the watch on her wrist. It was one of those pulse-tracker sport watches. Steve had never noticed it before and wondered why Silvana needed it now, since he had never seen her jogging. She fidgeted with the clasp until she got it open.

"I want you to keep this," she said, handing Steve the watch. "Bring it to the jail when you visit. I need you to visit."

She didn't wait for an answer, picked up the two picture frames, and marched downstairs. Steve stood speechless, holding the watch between two fingers. He hadn't said goodbye to her, and he'd just missed his last chance to kiss her. His throat closed on him. He swallowed to prove to himself he was still able to. After a moment, he placed the watch in his shirt pocket and followed her downstairs.

The recitation of Miranda rights filled the room, but Silvana didn't seem to listen. Instead, she refused a lawyer and said many things that could be used against her. At the end, she brought her wrists together and offered them to Mulville, who, still slumped on the couch, signaled one of the uniformed men. The man stepped closer, dangling a set of handcuffs, took Silvana wrists, swung them to her back, and expertly locked her hands behind her.

The doctor got up, fetched a long coat from the closet, and wrapped it around her, closing the first two buttons. And then she was gone, together with Mulville and his FBI underlings. Steve grabbed his jacket and followed the grim procession outside.

"Where are you taking her?" he asked Mulville, as the two uniformed men pushed on Silvana's head and shoulder to get her onto the back seat of a black sedan.

"To the federal high-security detention center," Mulville said. "We'll book her and continue to question her about the details. No worry. She's in good hands."

When the creep winked at him, Steve could've punched his eye out. The image of an FBI interrogation room, as seen in the movies, came to mind. Three naked walls with a one-way viewing mirror in the fourth wall. A table with a chair on each side. Silvana, handcuffed to the table, on one chair facing Mulville on the other. Steve rushed to his car and drove away without turning back.

He entered his condominium building, took the elevator to his two-bedroom apartment, and walked straight to the bathroom. Taking a hot shower seemed like a reasonable thing to do. His sore back screamed for it. And he needed to wash off the dirty feeling of Mulville handling Silvana like a criminal.

As he removed his clothes, he tried valiantly to avoid any sudden movements. While unbuttoning his shirt, he brushed against a bulge in his pocket—Silvana's watch. Steve pulled out the thin gadget and turned it over. Nothing unusual. Why had she made such a big deal about it? And why did she want to see him at the jail, after telling him to get lost for good? Steve shrugged, got the hot water going, entered the shower, and felt his muscles relax, soothed by the water massage. Best thing that had happened to him all day.

He toweled off, wrapped the towel around his waist, placed his shirt and socks in the hamper, picked up his pants and shoes, and went to the bedroom to get ready for his day at the hospital. His bed was in its usual state of disarray. He pulled out a cleaners-wrapped shirt from the closet and got ready to put it on, when he heard a strange tapping sound from outside the room.

He walked around, following his ear's guidance. The sound got stronger in the direction of the bathroom. He entered the room. The sound got louder. It was a familiar sound. It reminded him of the monitors in the intensive care unit, or in the operating room. A heartbeat. The source was right in front of him now. Silvana's watch had come to life on the marble counter. A tiny red heart pulsated on the screen, releasing the sound he had heard and followed. That was what those sport watches did. Monitored heartbeats, among many other things. Except no one was wearing this watch.

CHAPTER 14

THE HEARTBEAT

S teve picked up Silvana's watch and looked at the tiny heart. The rate varied. It accelerated and decelerated ever so slightly, just as if someone was wearing the device. Now the rate was at seventy-five, a normal resting heart rate for regular persons. Suddenly, the heartbeat sped up, as if the monitored person had started to run. The rate passed one hundred, reached one hundred and fifty, went all the way up to one hundred and seventy-two. This fast a heartbeat wasn't safe for most adults. What was going on? Whose heartbeat was he looking at?

He sat down, butt naked, on a cold toilet seat. Was this Patrizia's heartbeat? That was the only answer he could come up with. Steve had heard of some new kind of watch that could record and transmit a short clip of a person's heartbeat, but he had never heard of a long transmission such as the one in front of him. This heartbeat seemed to unfold in real time. Perhaps Silvana had found a way to modify a watch to transmit in real time and given it to her daughter, connecting the device to a similar watch of her own.

But why had Silvana felt the need to monitor her daughter's heart, if her daughter was on vacation with her aunt? Might she want to feel close to her daughter? Tears came to Steve's eyes. This would confirm the fact that Silvana knew she would be going to jail. Steve shrugged. No, that was pure speculation. A more likely scenario was that mother and daughter had the watches synchronized for fun, but when Silvana ended up in jail, she planned to use the device to remain in touch with Patrizia.

Steve pondered this last hypothesis while he got ready to leave for the hospital, but his attention snapped back to the watch. The heart kept on going at around one hundred and seventy beats per minute. If this was

Patrizia's heartbeat, what was the girl doing? Exercising, he hoped. Then an extra beat from the ventricle appeared—wider, more ominous. The heart, growing tired, protested.

Why wasn't the girl stopping? Wasn't she tired? Perhaps Patrizia couldn't stop running. Was she running from someone trying to hurt her? Or worse, someone had gotten to the girl and was doing something to her, right now. Was someone torturing the girl, to coerce her mother into silence? He had to stop these terrible thoughts. Steve had no evidence for any of this. Only the fact that Silvana had wanted him to have the watch. His chest felt compressed by a lump. Breathing became a chore. Silvana wanted him to visit her in jail and bring the watch to make sure her daughter was still alive.

Steve grabbed his phone from the marble counter. His hand shook as he called Kirk Miner. He hoped the PI was still around.

"Miner," Kirk said.

"It's me, Steve." He took a gulp of air. "Are you still in town?"

Traffic noise came through the phone. Steve hoped it wasn't New York traffic. The heartbeat from the watch slowed down, to the one hundred and ten to one hundred and twenty range. Steve let out a sigh of relief.

"On my way to the airport," Kirk said. "Trying to catch a ten o'clock flight. I guess it's over. Moretti confessed. Until the last minute, I was hoping it wasn't her. Too bad. Sorry."

"I need to see you," Steve said. "Now. Something's happening. Cancel your flight and meet me at Washington's Federal High-Security Detention Center."

"What's going on?" Kirk asked. "I haven't seen my family in a week. Mulville ordered me home. Nothing more for me to do here. You'll need to call Mulville about that."

"I need to talk to you," Steve insisted. "Silvana's daughter's life may be in danger."

"She told you that?"

"Not exactly," Steve said. "I need you to talk to her with me. Then we need to convince Mulville to investigate some more."

Silence followed. Only traffic noises. He had to have Kirk on his side.

"Good luck with both," Kirk said. "I feel sorry for you, but I don't see how I can help."

"Listen, Miner," Steve said, searching his mind for a plausible way to convince the PI to confront Mulville again. "I'm certain about Silvana. Something horrible must have happened to her or her daughter, or both. You're the only one I can turn to for help. What if I hire you, as a PI? You seem like a good person who wouldn't want an innocent individual going to jail when you could do something to help. Please. I beg you—"

"Shit," Kirk said. "All right. On my way. See ya at the detention center. I'm sure I'll be sorry for saying yes."

Steve ended the call. He wiped his hands on his towel and walked back to the bedroom. The heartbeat was now back to the normal seventies. He got dressed in a hurry and ran to his car. On his way to the prison, Steve arranged for coverage of all his cases and rounds. By the time he stopped in the parking lot of the Federal High Security Detention Center, Kirk Miner was waiting there. Steve slid out of his car into the passenger side of Kirk's rental car.

"Listen, Doctor," Kirk said, "before we go any further, I'm here unofficially. Mulville can never know about this or I'll never hear the end of it. I'm off the case. I don't work for anyone. Not for the FBI, and not for you either. Understood?"

"Yes, and thanks for doing this." Steve pulled the watch from his pocket. "Silvana gave me this just before going to jail. I don't know what to do."

Kirk listened in silence. The heart-rate remained in the resting range.

"You think someone has the girl?" Kirk asked at the end. "And Silvana is being coerced?"

Steve nodded. The big lump in his chest was at last loosening up. Kirk had experience. He would know what to do without involving the police or the FBI.

"That doesn't make any sense," Kirk said. "Why would someone else want to kill all the people Silvana is mad at?"

Kirk was right. Like a glove, Silvana fit the definition of a guilty party. That was the problem.

"I know," Steve said. "I've been racking my brain over this for hours. There has to be another explanation. When I saw all those files with wavelengths that would shatter all kind of arteries, I wanted to die."

"Tell me more about that."

As Steve spoke, Kirk's eyes got wider. Steve saw something he had never seen in Kirk's eyes before. Pure fear. That frightened Steve as well. What was Kirk thinking? How could things be any worse than they seemed now?

"Unless," Kirk said, "the heart attacks and strokes were just try-outs for the real thing. And a way to frame Silvana, to make us think everything was all over."

"Try-outs?" Steve asked. "For what?"

"I wish I knew," Kirk said. "I hope we can find out from Silvana."

"Me too." Steve pointed at the massive building outside. "That's why I wanted you here. To find out the truth."

Steve got out first. The cold air penetrated his clothes. Kirk followed. A dark gray sky closely matched the color of the center's gloomy construction. Steve looked at the spread of concrete stones with reinforced windows and wondered how much suffering had gone on in the building over the years.

He walked up the short staircase, then stopped, allowed Kirk to go first, and followed. Kirk gave his PI card to a burly armed man, requesting an urgent audience with the prisoner Silvana Moretti. The armed guard rubbed his chin as he searched for Silvana's name on a computer screen.

"Sorry." He shook his head. "This prisoner can't receive visitors. She hasn't been arraigned yet."

He turned his gaze to the computer again, as if ignoring the two men in front of him constituted an invitation for them to leave. Steve looked at Kirk. He hoped the PI had some trick up his sleeve. Kirk shook his head.

"Shit," he whispered to himself. Then he turned again to the guard.

"We aren't really visitors." Kirk smiled apologetically. "I'm here to interrogate the prisoner as part of an ongoing investigation. The FBI sent me."

With an elegant gesture, Kirk presented a paper. Steve peeked at it and shuddered. It was a copy of the FBI temporary ID Miner had to give back. The PI had stuck his neck out, ready for Mulville to chop it off, all on Steve's account. The paper caught the guard's attention.

"Okay." The uniformed man's eyes went back to the screen. His radio buzzed alive. "Let me check with the agent in charge."

"Umm," Kirk said, "wouldn't do that just yet, if I were you."

"And why in the hell not?" The man lifted his scrolling finger from the screen.

"Last time I talked to him," Kirk said, "an hour ago, when he ordered me to interrogate the prisoner at once, Jack wasn't exactly in the wasting-time mood."

"Jack who?" The man shut off his radio. "Agent Mulville?"

"Exactly." Kirk nodded. "We go way back."

The man took one last look at Kirk's paper, shrugged, and pointed at the metal detector. Steve was impressed—Kirk was indeed a red-tape master. Kirk pointed to Steve and waved him toward the check point. What was Steve supposed to do? Just walk in?

"He's with me," Kirk said, as if anticipating the guard's objections. "The woman has a bad heart. This is her doctor. Can you have the prisoner brought to the interrogation room at once? The doctor is on a tight schedule. You know, dying patients and all."

The guard shrugged again. Steve and Kirk zipped through the metal detector. Another armed guard met them on the other side and took them upstairs in an elevator with no buttons. The guard chatted into a walkie-talkie with someone who must've controlled the car remotely and, after a short ride, dropped them off in front of a locked door, using her ID card to let them in. The clicking-shut of the lock behind them gave Steve the urge to run. He stood still and his muscles tensed.

The interrogation room was everything Steve had imagined and worse. A cube of concrete wall, glaring lights, two opposing doors, and one mirror on the side, probably masking a one-sided viewing window. Steve removed his jacket, placing it on the table over a metal ring likely used for handcuffs. He sat on a metal stool near one of two chairs. Kirk took the chair next to him. They waited.

After almost thirty minutes, Steve worried that the guard had caught up with Kirk's lie. Wouldn't that be considered a serious offense? Wouldn't he and Kirk end up in jail as well? He glanced at Kirk. The detective didn't give any sign of apprehension. He scrolled through what looked like notes on his phone.

"Don't worry," Kirk said as if he had read Steve's mind. "The wait is our price for that idiot to save face. To show us he's in control after all."

At last, the door opened. Kirk was right—no armed guards to arrest them. Silvana shuffled into the room under the control of a female guard.

Not even the vulgar orange jumpsuit and the clanging cuffs could hide her passionate sensuality. Steve wondered if he was the only one able to see it. Kirk's look seemed to hint at the same kind of sorrow and regret.

The guard parked Silvana next to the chair, let go of her arm, pushed on her shoulder to make her sit down, and left. Silvana's eyes lifted from the floor and came alive with surprise and, to Steve's amazement, a hint of resentment. After insisting that he visit, why wasn't she happy to see him? Was she upset about Kirk's presence?

"Hi." Steve handed her the watch, which was now silent.

She didn't answer. Nor she did ask what the men were doing there. Her cuffed hands stretched at once to grasp the dangling object. She stared at the watch face, touching all available dials. Then she looked up, eyes full of pain.

"She's okay," Steve said. "The heartbeat came up this morning. For a while, it beat pretty fast, then it slowed to a resting rate."

Silvana's eyes widened. Her gaze went from Steve, to Kirk, then back to

Steve, showing renewed resentment. Perhaps bringing Kirk was a mistake. But how else could Steve be talking to her?

"Silvana," Steve said, lowering his voice to a whisper, "where is your daughter?"

She didn't answer. Kept on staring. Resentment escalated to anger.

"That," Steve said, pointing at the watch, "is Patrizia's heart. No sense denying it. I know it, just by the way you look at the watch. You're hoping the heartbeat will come up again, so you can be certain she's still alive."

Silvana took a breath as if ready to talk, but she remained silent. A long sigh followed.

"I paired Patrizia's sport watch with mine." Her mouth upturned in a kind of smirk. "A way of keeping her close."

"Dr. Moretti," Kirk interjected, "is someone doing this to you? You've got to let us help you. You're accused of murder. Even if you're acting under duress, you'll be held responsible...of murder."

Kirk let the sounds of his words fade. Steve watched the battle unfolding in her eyes. He hoped her reasonable side would win. No answer came.

"And how do you even know," Kirk went on, "that this is still your daughter's heart and not some other stooge's while they're doing away with Patrizia?"

For a moment, Silvana looked as if she was going to crumple right there on the chair. Kirk had struck a sore point, but had he gone too far? Steve stood up, wanting to comfort her. Then the strangest thing happened, which made him sit down again on the cold uncomfortable stool. Silvana laughed, but not as if she was happy.

"I'm responsible!" she screamed. "Just leave me alone! Got nothing to say I haven't already told the FBI this morning. I can tell you how the dissections happened for all those bastards responsible for my brother's death. The ultrasound waves were programmed according to the size of the different arteries."

She launched into a detailed technical explanation, as if something possessed her. Or was Steve just reading something he wanted to be true—proof that she was still his Silvana, and not a monster? Kirk remained silent.

"Honey," Steve said, "we're not interested in any of this. Where is your daughter? That's all what we need to know to help you."

"In Florida," she said matter-of-factly. "Where else?"

"Her heart sped up in the watch," Steve insisted. "Very fast. That doesn't worry you?"

"Not at all." Silvana's head shook. "What time was it?"

"This morning," Steve said. "Around ten. For about fifteen to twenty minutes, her rate was around one hundred and seventy."

"She runs at that time," Silvana said without hesitation.

Did Steve detect a hint of panic? She spoke too quickly, with too much urgency. No help came from Kirk. Then the PI met Steve's gaze and nodded, as if to telegraph to him that he was doing a good job, and to encourage him to go on.

"If it's true," Steve said, pointing at the watch, "why did the watch make you so upset?"

"What a stupid question." She looked straight at Steve. "I'm in jail. Don't I have the right to be upset? Who knows when I'm ever going to see my daughter again?"

No. She must be lying. There had to be a way to find out for sure.

"Call her now." Steve handed her his phone. "I want to hear from Patrizia herself."

Silvana didn't reach for the phone. Her eyes looked at him from under lifted brows. Then her gaze went farther, past the two men. Relief washed over her, and Steve realized he had missed the noise of the door opening behind him. He turned. Jack Mulville stormed in, looking furious.

"What the heck are you two doing here?" Mulville pointed a shaky finger at Kirk. "And you're officially off the case. Your ass should be on some airline seat as we speak. All this is highly irregular. I'll report you to the New York City Police. Or even better, I'll throw you in jail for obstruction."

Steve felt clammy. He and Kirk had been caught lying about the FBI, sneaking into a federal prison, and handing a phone to an inmate. Was that enough to go to jail?

"Steve had some concerns," Kirk said, remaining seated and calm. "About Patrizia, Silvana's daughter, being used to manipulate her mother."

Mulville's breath came out in long gasps. Was he trying to calm down? No. From his narrow gray eyes darted anger.

"Look, Miner," Mulville said with apparent control, "we have everything we need. We subpoenaed Dr. Moretti's computer, and experts are examining it. So far, it's exactly as she confessed. So, this is the way it'll go. The arraignment is set for tomorrow. We'll assign her a waste-of-time public defender. She'll plead guilty. No bail. The trial will start in a couple of weeks. Just read the newspapers and see how it turns out."

What was Kirk going to say? Steve, his back burning from pain, fidgeted on his stool. Then the watch beeped in Silvana's hand. Her eyes widened. The heartbeat came back at a rate of one hundred and thirty-five.

"Here," Steve said, prying the watch from Silvana's hands and handing it to Mulville. "I think someone is holding Patrizia hostage. This is her heartbeat. Look, one hundred and thirty-five beats per minute, to terrorize her mother."

Mulville looked at Steve as if he had spoken in a foreign language. His eyes narrowed. He didn't move to take the watch.

"What are you talking about?" He turned to Silvana, pointing at the watch. "Is this true? Do you want to report your daughter missing?"

"No." She looked straight at Steve. "She's in Florida, jogging."

Steve had seen that look before, years ago, during an African safari—the eyes of a mother impala unmoving in front of a male lion, her offspring running to safety. He couldn't fight any longer. Not against this kind of opposition. Time to let Silvana go. He pocketed the watch, the beeping muffled against his chest.

"I rest my case." Mulville's hand signaled dismissal. "Put a lid on it,

Doctor, or it'll explode in your face. Go back to cutting up flesh, or whatever it is you're best at."

In a rage, Steve got a silencing glance from Kirk. The doctor nodded.

"Get out," Mulville added. "Both of you. Leave the prisoner to me. If I see you again, you'll have to yell through a cell wall to speak to each other. That goes especially for you, PI."

Kirk got up. Steve followed. At the door, Kirk turned.

"FBI," Kirk said to Mulville, "you better send an announcement to all government officials not to open any suspicious cards."

Kirk didn't wait for an answer, but called the guard to open the door. Steve stood still and glanced from Mulville to Kirk. The detective believed him. He was on Steve and Silvana's side.

"That's all we need!" Mulville roared. "Spread panic, when there's no need for any. Kirk, your FBI collaboration is over. Keep your idiotic suggestions to yourself!"

The closing of the door smothered the last words from Mulville's mouth. Steve followed Kirk out of the room to the button-less elevator.

As he approached the male guard at the entrance, Steve hurried, his head bowed, his eyes fixed ahead. He got a jolt when Kirk saluted the man. No answer came in return.

"Do you believe she did the programming?" Steve zipped up his jacket.

"Not sure," Kirk answered. "But I'm more and more convinced you're right. Someone is using her."

Something lifted from Steve's chest. The discouragement of having to face defeat alone had been weighing him down since Silvana's arrest. Now he had an ally. But Silvana didn't want Kirk around because she knew the PI had figured her out. The battle was going to be fierce. Not only against the real criminal, and not only against the hindering FBI agent, but against the very person who needed rescuing.

"How can you prove that someone didn't do something?" Steve asked.

"You can't." Kirk gave him a sad smile. "We have to prove someone else did it instead."

Steve didn't like the sound of that. How could the two of them prove anything when Mulville had just thrown the detective off the case and threatened Steve and Kirk with jail?

"How can we prove anything?" Steve said. "Nothing for us to investigate."

"We have to wait."

"Wait?" Steve asked. "For what? Another crime?"

"Afraid we have no choice," Kirk said. "I'll take the next flight home. Call me if and when something else happens."

They reached the parking lot. Kirk's rental car and Steve's sedan stood side by side in the wintry wet fog, waiting to go separate ways. But Steve couldn't let Kirk leave just yet. Kirk was his only chance—Silvana's only chance.

"So it's over?" Steve asked.

"No." Kirk unlocked the car. "It isn't."

"I agree with you," Steve said. "But how can you be so sure? All six missing chips are accounted for."

Kirk looked Steve in the eye. The PI's look carried frustration, anger, and sympathy. Steve felt weak.

"It was what you told me," Kirk said. "In her computer, Silvana had different files with sound waves programmed for coronary arteries and carotids. But then there was a third file."

Steve had wondered why she had that third file. Sitting in the dark office, he had clicked the document open, to find soundwaves calculations for the largest artery of the body, and computer graphics as well. He gasped.

"We're waiting," Steve said, completing Kirk's theory, "for an aortic dissection."

CHAPTER 15

THE WAIT

Kirk looked at Steve and withdrew his gloved hand from the car's handle—for him, a step backward, away from the things Kirk wanted to do most, like get inside the car, start the engine, and begin his trip home. The week away from his wife and son was getting to him. And so far, his FBI experience hadn't panned out at all the way he had expected. The only things Kirk had discovered were Mulville's tactlessness, arrogance, and mastery of four-letter words. And now he might have to explain to the NYPD what he was doing using false credentials to talk to a murder suspect in the presence of her ex-boyfriend. He must be insane, except he knew that Steve had no recourse in Mulville. And Kirk was on the side of justice.

"How would an aortic dissection play out?" Kirk's limited medical knowledge anticipated the answer. "Best and worst case scenarios."

Steve stomped his feet. Kirk watched him considering his surgical experience. Then the doctor shook his head and chuckled. Not a good sign.

"The human body's largest vessel splitting apart in the chest," Steve said, as if lecturing, "is a surgeon's worst nightmare."

Kirk nodded.

"As the wall shreds," Steve continued, "the branches close down. So, we're looking at heart attacks and strokes combined. If the patient doesn't get to the hospital in time, or if the wall ruptures altogether, the blood gushes out and the patient dies."

"But there are warning symptoms," Kirk said. "Pain, if I remember correctly."

"Shearing pain." Steve made a fist and placed it on his chest. "In the chest or upper back, shooting up to the neck or down to the lower back. Best case scenario: People will come in on time."

"Meanwhile," Kirk said, putting out his hand, "I could have the watch analyzed. See if we can get a location on Patrizia."

Steve handed over the watch, which Kirk placed in an evidence bag. Then his hand returned to the car's handle.

"I'll give it to a contact at NYPD." Kirk patted his pocket. "Much more friendly than the FBI piece-of-work we have to deal with."

"Thanks." Steve shook Kirk's hand. "Let me know what they find out. I'll call you at the first sign of a problem."

Kirk's thoughts during the drive to the airport, the short flight to La Guardia, and his wait for the luggage there revolved around Silvana Moretti, her daughter Patrizia, and aortic dissection.

As he waited in line for a taxi, a blizzard-like wind blew through his clothes and chilled him to the core. At last, a cab stopped in front of him. He slid into the back seat and gave his Brooklyn home address to a muscular man with beard, moustache, and a turban.

"Going home?" the driver asked.

"Yeah." Kirk had no desire to converse.

"Who's home?" the driver pushed on.

It was difficult to resist that question. Kirk could always talk about his family. Or was it more like boasting?

"My wife," he started. "She's the best. She's a nurse at Brooklyn Medical Center. Can't wait to see her. Then there is my boy, Peter. He's 11, and very smart."

The man nodded. Kirk spent the rest of the drive listening to New York traffic, still thinking of Silvana, Patrizia, and Steve. When the signs of Brooklyn began to flash outside the window, his hand went to his shirt pocket and pulled out the evidence bag with Silvana's watch.

"Sir." Kirk leaned forward. "I need to make a quick stop at the Prospect Park police station. Got to drop off something."

The taxi driver nodded without looking back. Kirk relaxed in his seat. He phoned his detective friend. The detective was still at work. He always sounded happy to hear from Kirk. Their friendship had been cemented by life and death adventures and mutual respect over the years.

The cab came to a stop in front of the police station. John came out through the glass doors, stood under the entrance's glaring lights, and waved at Kirk.

"Can I scan your credit card?" The driver turned and waved his phone. "In case I got to leave?"

The dim overhead light shone on the man's neck. Kirk noticed a strange shape just behind the beard under the right earlobe. The jagged appearance reminded him of a swastika. Kirk hoped for the man's sake the shape was a scar and not a tattoo. The man pulled up the collar of his leather jacket.

"I won't be long." Kirk pointed at the detective. "I just have to hand something to my friend."

He stepped out of the car. John patted him twice on his arm. His smile told Kirk he could count on him.

"Thanks for doing this," Kirk said. "The life of a young girl is in jeopardy."

"I'll have someone look at it tonight." The detective took the evidence bag. "I'll call you as soon as I get anything."

Back in the cab, Kirk repeated his address. After 30 minutes more of light traffic, he stood in front of his two-story white-paneled house. The barking of his two dogs reached him as the front door swung open. His son Peter was first to welcome him with a tight hug. Wet tongues and wagging tails followed. He was home.

CHAPTER 16

THE CHOICE

The White House Chief of Staff sat in his West Wing office and gazed at the small American flag beside his computer. Looking at the stars and stripes helped him think. He ran his finger through his gray hair and squinted at a screen displaying the names of all the president's cabinet members. Whose turn was it going to be? His eyes skipped down to the last handful of names. Last year, he had chosen the Secretary of Labor. The year before, the Secretary of Agriculture.

The Chief of Staff could've just closed his eyes and pointed at any name, so long as he chose from the last ten names on the list. But political implications were attached to the selection. His choice was held in high regard by other cabinet members. Being selected inferred a certain prestige. It meant the White House Chief of Staff had judged that person good enough to potentially occupy the most powerful position on earth—the presidency of the United States. But some of the people on the list he wouldn't trust as far as he could throw them. He'd better keep his eyes open.

The thumping of small feet and a knock at the door disrupted his concentration and made him look at the time—almost six PM.

"Daddy," a boy's voice bellowed, "we're ready for the President!"

The boy burst in. Long tan pants, white shirt, red sweater, and black jacket. The Chief of Staff hugged his eight-year-old son, who was dressed for dinner at the White House. He smiled at his wife over the boy's shoulder. Blond and slim, the woman looked elegant in high heels and a green woolen dress matching the color of her eyes.

"I need to freshen up," she said, backing out the door again. "I'll be only a moment."

The Chief of Staff touched his lips and sent her a silent kiss. She looked fresh enough to him. She flashed her beautiful smile and left for the ladies' room. If only they could just go home and the hell with the president.

"Daddy." The boy pushed up from his father. "I have something for you."

He rummaged inside his pants pocket. The Chief of Staff turned to shut his computer off. The boy waved a crumpled paper in front of his eyes—a lined yellow sheet from a notebook.

"Wait a moment, Jeff," the man said. "I need to close this or we're going to be late for the President."

"It's very important you read it now." The boy placed the paper on the desk and looked at the door. "Before Mom comes back. It's a secret."

The Chief reached for the paper, his eyes remaining on the computer. He glanced at Jeff standing at attention.

"What do we have here?" Touching one last key, he turned to the yellow paper. "Wow, a letter."

The boy nodded, a proud smile on his face. The Chief of Staff ran his fingers over the paper to smooth out the creases. Words came into focus: "Someone will get hurt unless you choose the Secretary of Energy and destroy this message. No word to anyone. See what happened to the FDA team members."

A typed e-mail address followed. Bcc: FBI@pigs.org

The Chief of Staff's jaw dropped. He took a slow gulp of air and turned to the boy. The proud smile was still there.

"Where did you get this?" He pointed to the yellow paper, trying not to scream. "Who gave it to you?"

"The agent who picked me up." The boy nodded. "He said today you needed help in something important, and I must give you this letter. He said it was like playing a game with secret messages."

"Mommy didn't pick you up today?" Breathing seemed harder. "Who did? Carl?"

The boy shook his head. Who had picked Jeff up? Besides his parents, only Carl from Secret Service and Jeff's nanny had authorization to pick the boy up from school. Steps came from outside the door. How could he inquire about the agent without alarming his wife? And what was he going to do? He looked at his watch. He had to decide—tonight. Or apparently all hell would break lose.

"This," the Chief of Staff said, placing the folded paper in his shirt pocket, "really helped me. But don't tell Mom. It's our secret."

The boy's brows lifted. His head nodded in agreement. His mom walked in rubbing her hands with sweet smelling lotion, no trace of worry or anger on her face. No mention of anything abnormal. She must've known about the pickup somehow.

"Did the Secret Service guy do a good job picking Jeff up from school today?" he asked, looking up and pointing at the boy. "Who let you know you didn't need to get him?"

"Got a text." She looked at her outstretched fingers. "That was really nice of you to arrange. Gave me time to get my nails done before dinner."

What could he say? That their son had been picked up by a criminal? That the boy had spent time in the company of a deranged person, or even a terrorist?

"Sure," he managed. "Do you still have the text?"

Her hand fumbled inside a small black purse. Before she could find her phone, her face assumed an expression of apology. She sighed.

"I erased it," she said. "It looked like a number from the Secret Service. Now that you mention it, it wasn't the usual number we call to contact our agent. Why? Is there a problem?"

"From now on," he said, "I'll let you know personally about something like this. Just in case."

"Is everything okay?" Fear crept into her eyes.

Nothing was okay. A pang of nausea reached his throat from deep inside his stomach. He was going to be sick.

"Fine." He kept his voice from cracking. "I'm also going to use the bathroom before we leave."

The Chief of Staff exited the office. His wife motioned to follow. He pointed to the boy. She seemed to get the message and stopped. The Chief stared at the Secret Service agent standing in attention outside his door. Did Carl know who had handled Jeff? The Chief looked back at his office door. His wife was combing Jeff's hair.

"Carl," he asked the agent, "did you arrange to pick up Jeff from school today?"

The man remained still and stiff. Only his head turned to the side to face the Chief. A frown formed above his questioning eyes.

"No, sir." He looked straight at him, concern in his voice. "Was I supposed to?"

"No. Just checking."

Carl had been a familiar family figure for more than a year, but anyone could be an enemy now. The Chief walked to the men's room, locked the door, turned to the sink, and splashed water on his face. The cold liquid soothed his sweaty forehead. He sat on the toilet seat and speed-dialed the Secretary of Health and Human Services. At least there was a good chance he would get to talk to him. Cabinet members would be especially eager to hear from the Chief of Staff at this time, hoping they had been chosen.

"Hi." A male voice answered after just three rings. "How are you? What's up?"

"Listen," the Chief of Staff said, "it's not what you think. Haven't decided yet. I need to find out if anything happened to anyone serving as an FDA team member—"

"Good God," the man said. "How do you know about that? Who leaked it?"

"No one leaked anything, but I got a strange message, and I need to be informed of any threats to security."

"Well." The Secretary of Health cleared his throat. "Someone died of a stroke, and another man and a woman were treated for the same thing—all team members for a specific case. A local vendetta by some fanatical scientist over an FDA denial. No worries. She's in jail now. It's over. The FBI decided not to make it public in order not to spread panic."

He thanked the Secretary and hung up. 6:19. Dinner with the President was at 6:30. The Chief of Staff swallowed a mouthful of acid. It wasn't over. For all he knew, it had just started. What was he supposed to do now? Call the FBI? The CIA? But then his son would get hurt. How? With a stroke? Could these people initiate strokes at will?

He slumped forward, head on clammy hands. He had signed up to defend the Constitution. But his son hadn't. As White House Chief of Staff, he was ready to die for the president or the country, but he wasn't ready to sacrifice his son's life. He reached for the crumpled yellow paper in his pocket, then pulled at it from both sides. The words straightened out. He read the message again.

They demanded the Secretary of Energy. Not his first choice for sure. According to rumors, the guy was paying allegiance to the bottle more often than to the flag, but tonight the Chief had to do what they wanted. Luckily, he had at least a week before the main event took place. A full week to think about all this, investigate, and decide whom he could trust enough to confide in.

He placed the creased paper on his lap and positioned his phone to take a picture of it. His eyes searched the ceiling for hidden cameras. He detected nothing, but his son's image flashed into his mind. Limp body, bluish lips, lifeless. He placed the phone back in his pocket and stared at the words again to lock them into memory. He tore the yellow paper into as many pieces as he was capable of, got up, lifted the toilet seat, and dropped the contents into the water. The yellow fragments fluttered like flower petals. The flush of water made them disappear. He stood and looked in the mirror. as he smoothed out his damp hair. Releasing a deep sigh, he walked back to his office.

"Are you ready?" His wife's expression changed as soon as she saw his face. "Are you sure you want to go? You look ill."

He had to go. He couldn't change or disrupt anything. Keep the routine going. Also, near the President, he and his family would be as safe as it could get.

"I'm fine," he managed. "But I need to finish something."

The woman looked at her watch and spread her hands. She was used to delays and interruptions for the sake of the country. The Chief of Staff rushed back to his desk and opened the official communication system. The list of cabinet members reappeared. His eye promptly landed on the name of the Secretary of Energy. He emailed his choice to the official address, with a bcc to FBI@pigs.org, as instructed. Then he shut down the computer again and rejoined his family. Outside the office door, Carl was talking with a cleaning woman—more like arguing, though.

"Sir." The agent waved his hand toward the Chief. "Did you call the cleaning crew? This woman insists you called for early service."

The woman was short and wore a scarf around her forehead, seemingly unclear whether to pull her long hair back or use a head cover. A vacuum cleaner hung on the side of a cleaning cart.

"No," the Chief said. "I did not."

"Sorry." The cleaning lady turned to him and checked her phone. She smiled. "You're right. My mistake."

Her accent wasn't Spanish—probably middle Eastern. Hard to tell. She looked at the phone for a while, as if searching for her next stop, then she apologized again and rolled the cart down the corridor.

On his way to the President's dining room, the Chief of Staff wondered what national consequences his action would set in motion tonight. But his mind refused to dwell on the question. One last task awaited him to protect his family. He made his call to the Secretary of Energy, to let him know the White House Chief of Staff had chosen him to be the designated survivor during the President's upcoming State of the Union address.

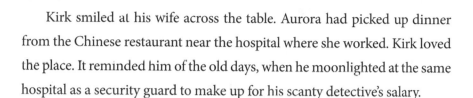

Kirk smiled at his wife across the table. Aurora had picked up dinner from the Chinese restaurant near the hospital where she worked. Kirk loved the place. It reminded him of the old days, when he moonlighted at the same hospital as a security guard to make up for his scanty detective's salary.

"I missed New York's Chinese food." He scooped up some lo mein with chopsticks. "Almost as much as you two."

He reached out to his left to ruffle Peter's hair. The eleven-year-old grinned. Buddy, the Dalmatian, placed his muzzle on Kirk's lap and whined. Kirk gave him a piece of pork.

"Daddy," Peter said, looking sideways, "can you talk about the case?"

"Not yet," Kirk said, chewing. "The FBI is involved. Everything is still top secret."

"Damn," the boy said. "The FBI."

"No cursing," Aurora said, eyeing him.

Kirk wanted to relax and enjoy his family life, but Silvana couldn't do the same with hers. She needed help—he was sure of that. So did Patrizia. The girl wasn't much older than Peter. Kirk checked the time—8:06. Unlikely he would hear about the watch tonight.

"What are you thinking?" Aurora asked. "You better finish eating before it gets cold."

"A young girl's life may be at risk," Kirk said. "Peter made me think of her."

Aurora nodded. That slight motion of her head made her blond curls quiver and his heart flutter. He couldn't wait to be alone with her. He reached for her hand. She responded, wrapping her fingers around his.

"I'm so glad you're home," she whispered.

He squeezed her hand and swallowed a mouthful of sweet and sour chicken. Suddenly, a lump of food stuck in his chest like a fist, pressing and spreading. A shearing pain burst out of the center of his breast bone and travelled up to his ears. Then the ache spread to his back, like a sharp knife cutting the muscles between his shoulder blades. What was happening to him?

"Honey." Aurora let go of his hand and touched his forehead. "Are you okay? You feel clammy."

"I'm not feeling well." He clenched a fist to his chest as if he needed to keep his insides together. "I need to lie down."

He was feeling exactly how Steve had described while explaining aortic dissection. He sagged into his chair. Peter leaped up and placed his arm under his. Kirk needed the support. The pain was so unbearable, he hoped to pass out, so he wouldn't have to feel it any longer. He dragged his feet to the living room couch. Each step echoed inside his chest with renewed agony. He dropped on the cushions, searching for his phone in his shirt pocket and dialed Leeds' number.

"Hi." The familiar voice gave Kirk a small jolt of relief. "What's up, Kirk?"

"I'm sick," he moaned. "Chest pain. And all the other things you said would happen."

"What are you talking about?"

No reassurance from the doctor. A worried-sounding professional meant bad news.

"The aortic dissection we're waiting for," Kirk moaned. "It's me."

A deep breath came through Kirk's phone. Then Steve bombarded him with doctor-to-patient questions to confirm the diagnosis. A soft curse followed.

"Call an ambulance," Steve ordered. "Text me your address."

Kirk mouthed the doctor's order to Aurora. But she was already taking care of that, like the good nurse she was. He gave Steve his address.

"Have the medics take you to Brooklyn Hospital," Steve said. "It's close to you, and I have a colleague there who treats dissections, if possible, with stents—metal tubes put in with catheters, instead of cracking your chest open."

Kirk's chest felt as if a knife had already gone wild inside it. What if he had no time? He reached out for Peter's cheek—wet with tears. Kirk saw helplessness in the boy's smart eyes, but Daddy couldn't come to the rescue. Daddy was dying. The ambulance's sound emerged from a distance and grew louder. Two medics rushed to Kirk's side. After a brief assessment, they got him ready for transport.

Oxygen blowing in his nose, saline flowing in his vein, and morphine dancing in his head, Kirk held Aurora and Peter's hands on his way to the hospital. The comfort he got from his wife's touch helped him transmit a veneer of reassurance to his son, like a transfusion of courage, from mother to son through him. The red glow pulsating on the side window and the whaling of the ambulance soothed him. As soon as the Brooklyn Hospital's E.R. doors popped open in front of Kirk's moving gurney, a team of scrubs-clad doctors and nurses came forward to meet him.

Steve's friend was a sixtyish man with a deep, calm voice. He took charge with contagious confidence. With a calm voice, he gave orders and every-one obeyed. Before he knew, Kirk slid through the round arch of a CAT scanner in the radiology department. The morphine made the pain bearable and fragmented the time into bits of awareness alternated with sleep. What seemed like moments later, Kirk kissed his family and rolled into the operat-ing room.

Anesthesia had cut off a slice of his life, but the following morning, Kirk was back—alive and awake. The events preceding surgery bombarded and overwhelmed his consciousness, yet nothing could suppress the wonder of having beaten death.

"Honey." Aurora's voice soothed him. "The surgery is over. Everything went well. The area of dissection was small and hadn't ruptured to the outside. The doctor was able to use stents to fix it."

Kirk heard her before he could see her. A small dissection? The memory of his agony came back to haunt him. How painful would a large dissection be? He turned to his right side. And there she was, at his side, his wife, radiant, even after crying, worrying, and losing sleep. He moved his feet. His toes wiggled as he wished. His hands curled into fists without problems. No stroke.

"Your friend, the detective, is here too," she added. "Needs to talk to you. And Peter is asleep in the waiting area."

Peter shouldn't be alone. Never. Not for a moment.

"Get Peter," Kirk said, forcing his raspy voice out of his chest. "Don't lose sight of him,"

"Why?" she asked. Her face looked as if she had seen something terrifying. "And last night, why did you say on the phone you were waiting for a dissection to happen? Did somebody do this to you?"

Smart investigator's wife. Kirk wished he could take back his words. But Aurora needed to know, to protect herself and Peter. No way to tell how bad or how wide this matter was going to get.

"I'm afraid so." He watched the expression of her face escalate to panic. "It has to do with the Washington case. Can't say much more. I'll have the local police watch after you. Go get Peter now, then the detective."

She left. Peter rushed in. Joy lit up his sleepy eyes at the sight of his father. His arms reached out, then dropped down again. Kirk understood how intimidating the tubes and wires sticking out of Kirk's chest, neck, and arms could be for an eleven-year-old. Sending a fit of sharp pain down his throat, he smiled, took his boy by the hands and pulled him close. The smell of sweat and sleep reached Kirk from the boy's uncombed hair. But it was the heavy blanket of exhaustion that enveloped Kirk. Better save some energy. He had to talk to his detective friend in private. Kirk kissed Peter and Aurora and ordered them to bed.

John came in next. The eagerness on his face told Kirk he had news about the watch.

"How are you?" the detective said, dropping onto a nearby chair. "What the heck happened?"

"I'm afraid it has to do with the D.C. case I was working on," Kirk said. "Someone didn't like what I was doing. Perhaps it was giving the watch to you. Anything special about it?"

"Everything is special," the detective said. "They started with a regular sport watch and added a GPS and a radio-signals receiver."

"Great," Kirk said. "Can you determine where the signals it receives are coming from? Did you get any transmission of the heartbeat?"

"No, and no." the detective said. "The damn watch has a firewall that defeats anything like that. And no transmissions."

"It figures," Kirk said. "They must use the GPS to locate where the watch is. They stopped transmitting because they know Silvana is in jail and isn't looking at it. By my giving it to you, they knew I was here."

Another possibility was implied: Was Patrizia dead? Had he caused her to die by going to the police? Kirk shivered at the questions. Possible answers were too awful to consider.

"Are you in danger?" the detective asked. "Aurora said someone did this to you on purpose. I don't need to know the top-secret details, but if you need protection, let me know."

"Thanks," Kirk said. "Protection not for me, but for Aurora and Peter, for sure. I'll let you know when it's over."

The detective nodded and bid him goodbye. Kirk didn't need many words to explain. His friend understood. No threat had ever been so insidious. Kirk would take an honest-to-goodness gunshot over these diabolical blows any time. He needed to give Steve Leeds an update, and thank him for saving his life. He reached for his phone. The time was 7:07 AM. Kirk might catch him before his first operation of the day.

"Leeds," the doctor said. "Kirk, is it you? You made it."

"Thanks to you," Kirk said. "Your friend did a great job."

"I know," Steve said. "He called me right after he was done. You were very lucky. A few more minutes and we wouldn't be having this conversation. You should be back on your feet within a week or two."

"I guess we don't have to wait any longer," Kirk said. "The dissection we were waiting for arrived, except it doesn't make any sense. I couldn't have been part of the original plan. I wasn't even in the picture until a week ago."

"You're right," Steve said. "I'm afraid you were an add-on to the original planned list of casualties. My fault for keeping you on the case. The planned dissection also arrived this morning here in D.C. The White House Chief of Staff was brought in around 4 AM. His wife heard him gasp and found him unconscious. Paramedics brought him in and a CT scan showed a dissection of the entire aortic arch across both carotid arteries. Nothing much I could do. He died before we could place him on the cardiopulmonary bypass machine."

"How do you know that's the one we were waiting for?" Kirk asked. "Did he get a card?"

"I don't know for sure," Steve said. "But I have a strong hunch this is what we were waiting for. Haven't had the chance to talk to the FBI about him."

"I'm afraid you're right," Kirk said. "I guess I was just collateral damage. Someone doesn't want me around when the real shit hits the fan."

CHAPTER 17

FEAR

Steve Leeds sat in his office and stared at the report. According to the coroner's preliminary assessment, the aorta of the White House Chief of Staff suffered a two-inch gash. Blood had entered the space between the layers over a foot-long segment spanning the arch from the heart all the way to the other side of the chest. The process had interrupted several major vessels responsible for bringing blood to the heart and the brain. The man never had a chance.

The coroner criticized Steve for refusing to sign the death certificate without an autopsy. Steve could just hear the guy whining about doctors not taking responsibility and dumping unwarranted work on him, with the family having to wait for cremation. In a way, Steve couldn't blame him. There was nothing unnatural about the Chief's death. The man even had a history of high blood pressure and smoking, both known risk factors for aortic dissection. And, as far as Steve knew, he hadn't received any warning. Nor had he received any cards of any kind.

But it was a hell of a coincidence. The day after Steve and Kirk concluded the next event in the Moretti case would be an aortic dissection, not one but two dissections had occurred—Kirk and the Chief of Staff. Steve had learned a long time ago that coincidences often turned out to be connected. Steve had hoped the coroner would connect some cause to these effects. No such luck.

If only Steve could talk to Mulville about the case. Steve had started to dial the FBI agent's number shortly after the Chief of Staff showed up on the verge of death. The doctor was ready to tell the FBI man that the aortic dissection was one of those cases, just like the three heart attacks and the three carotid dissections. But what evidence did he have? Just his hunch. Mulville would've eaten him for breakfast. Steve aborted the call. If only the coroner had supplied some evidence. Now Steve had only one way left to convince Mulville to consider his theory, and that involved speaking to Silvana.

Steve had waited two days for his next chance to visit Silvana. This time, he followed the rules, and Silvana agreed to see him. Or, to be more accurate, she was probably agreeing to his visit because of the watch. He'd be there just as a messenger. Thinking about the demise of his relationship with Silvana brought Steve to a very bad place. In one week, all the happiness and the good times accumulated over months of dating had fizzled out like soapy foam. Now the only things left were anger, fear, and unbearable, helpless sadness.

He pushed back from his desk. A few minutes later, he sat in his car on his way to the Federal High-Security Detention Center. The man at the front desk gave him a hostile look of recognition and took plenty of time studying the appointment paperwork, checking his computer screen, and making confirmatory calls. At last, Steve went through the metal detector and rode the button-less elevator with the guard to the meeting room with gray walls and steel mesh over the windows. Gray partitions separated different cubicles. In each stood a table, half on either side of a glass barrier. Steve sat on one of two blue plastic chairs on his side of the barrier. Muffled conversation reached him from the next cubicle. The two seats across his table remained empty.

After twenty minutes, the room's back door opened and Silvana came in accompanied by a female guard. Steve flinched at her matted hair, swollen eyes, and stooped figure. In less than a week, Silvana seemed to have aged years. Orange, bag-like coveralls mercifully engulfed her shrunken-looking body. She slid onto the chair in front of him and lifted glossy eyes from under heavy brows. Her visible effort hurt him to his core.

"Hi," he said into the handset he found on the table. "How are you doing?"

Stupid question. The answer sat in front of him—slumped shoulders underscoring hopelessness. Steve took the watch from his pocket and placed it next to the dividing glass. Silvana's eyes darted to it with the eagerness of a starving man presented with food.

"How's Patrizia?" Even her voice had changed. Now raspy, it was as if it hadn't been used for days. "Did you check her heart?"

She managed half a chuckle at the reference to his profession as a heart fixer. The impala, fighting for her offspring. Whatever he had told her, John's handling of the watch had to remain secret.

"No more heartbeat," he said, "since the last time I talked to you."

She brushed against her eyes. If she started to cry, Steve would have a hard time not following suit. He had to talk to her while still in control of his emotions.

"Kirk had an aortic dissection three days ago," he said. "So did the White House Chief of Staff."

He waited. Her brows lifted. Judging by her eyes, surprise turned into despair, and tears flooded her cheeks. Was she feeling responsible for what had happened to the two victims? Her response could be that of someone who knew dissections were part of a wider, more wicked plan. Why else would she be crying now? Steve wondered why she didn't ask how the two men were doing. He bet she couldn't bear to know.

"The Chief of Staff is dead," Steve said. "He and Kirk got no cards. No ultrasound chips. How did they do it? How did they make the aorta dissect? What other things were missing from your lab?"

She shook her head as if to clear her face of tears and her mind from hindering emotions. She placed her palms against the glass and looked side to side as if checking for onlookers.

"I did it," she mouthed without using the phone. "All of it."

Steve pointed to the phone. She shook her head, but then she obeyed and brought the phone to her ear. She shut her eyes.

"I don't believe you," Steve said. "I know you. You're protecting Patrizia, but you're wrong. The longer we wait to find her, the greater the chance she'll be dead."

She violently shook her head. The only way to save Silvana was to break down her defenses. An idea lit up in Steve's mind.

"Where did you get the cards?" he asked.

No immediate answer came. She hesitated for a moment. Then she shrugged.

"What's the difference?" she asked. "Anyone can get cards like that from Kinko's."

She was just a puppet, not a monster. Now Steve was certain. A weight lifted from his chest.

"As a matter of fact," he said, looking at her, "today, just before I came here, I asked Kirk about that. I told him I wanted to test you. He said they found only one company selling cards in that particular shade of tan—Arta-merica, in New York City. Kinko's doesn't carry that shade."

She looked pale now. Steve worried that her body would slump to the gray concrete floor and no one would be there to catch her. But then she recovered her color. The impala looked back. She replaced the phone in the cradle.

"I can't talk now," she mouthed. "Come back next week."

Steve fingered the phone again. She didn't move, just stared at the watch. The heartbeat was back, and rapid, at one hundred and thirty-three beats per minute. Kirk was right. The monsters knew from the GPS that the watch was at the jail, with Silvana.

She stood up, her nose touching the glass. Steve pushed back from his chair and placed his palms opposite her face. If only he could help her against those bastards.

The heartbeat continued for several more moments, then disappeared. Silvana stared at the blank dial, terror on her face. A few moments later, the pulse reappeared, faster. One hundred and seventy-three beats per minute. Then it stopped again. A signal. A warning. Silvana's mouth was open now.

Her neck veins welled up. Fog appeared on the glass around her lips. She was screaming.

"Go away,!" she yelled at him. "Please! And stay away!"

The female guard came and removed Silvana. Steve banged a fist on the glass, but Silvana didn't turn back and the door closed behind her. His palms remained against the cold glass for a long time afterward.

CHAPTER 18

INVESTIGATION

As he drove back from the Detention Center to his office, Steve battled the worst of lunch-time traffic. Hypnotized by lights and noises, he soon faded into automatic pilot mode. The bulk of his attention went to review his five-month relationship with Silvana. Memories unfolded in his mind like a movie.

When had Silvana transitioned from a passionate life-embracing human being to a terrorist-directed puppet? The answer to the question suddenly came to mind—Christmas time. Silvana could've been working on the wave lengths' calibration then. Maybe her assignment had come not from the government, as she had told him, but out of sheer terror for her daughter's safety. But why had she accepted him into her house at such a critical time? He stared at snowflakes hitting the windshield and melting into yellowish rivulets. Perhaps she had done it not to raise his suspicions that something was wrong. He started the wipers. Maybe Silvana hadn't found the courage to break up with him during Christmas. Or maybe she hadn't yet realized how terrible the consequences of her work would be.

As Steve rode the elevator to the hospital's seventh floor, he resolved to make the FBI aware of Silvana's innocence. The nightmare wasn't over because the mastermind was still at large. That was an essential piece of information for the government agency to have. He dashed into his office, opened a desk drawer, and retrieved Jack Mulville's business card. His hand shook for a moment as he held it between two fingers and reached for the phone. Recorded messages directed him to select different options until a male voice came on the line and asked him about the purpose of his call. As he explained his reason, Steve wiped some moisture from his upper lip.

"Doctor," Mulville said, after several minutes of silence, "what can I do for you?"

The words sounded appropriate. But the tone came across as if the man resented having to be nice just because Steve was part of the public, and the public paid the FBI's salaries. Steve felt certain the agent would much rather tell him to go fuck himself, but Mulville had to listen this time.

"Kirk Miner had an aortic dissection," Steve said, trying to achieve the most dramatic effect possible. "He almost died. Luckily, with my help, he got to the hospital in time and the docs saved him."

"What are you talking about?" Mulville said.

"A shredding of the wall of the aorta, the body's largest vessel." Steve wondered if Mulville needed the explanation or was just wasting his time. "And the White House Chief of Staff also had an aortic dissection, except he died."

Silence followed. Mulville's breathing came through. Then a heavy sigh.

"They're both part of the same crime pattern," Steve said. "And Silvana is just a puppet in the hands of the master criminal or criminals."

"And you know this how?" Mulville groaned. "Did Kirk get a card? A chip? Cause sure as hell, the Chief got zilch. And the night before his death, he looked like shit, according to his wife. So, you're a doctor. Doesn't it mean something was already happening?"

Perhaps Mulville had a point. Suddenly, the evidence didn't seem all that conclusive, and his gut feeling hardly constituted convincing proof. Steve didn't know where to restart.

"In her notes, Silvana mentioned that the chips could be programmed according to the size of the vessels," Steve explained. "She included the aorta as one of the vessels."

"But there were no chips!" Mulville yelled. "Nada. What part of 'no chips or cards' don't you understand?"

Steve could just imagine the spit coming out of Mulville's screaming mouth. How could he persuade the agent to listen to what he had to say?

Steve pressed his hand on his temple.

"I don't know how the aortic dissections were triggered," Steve admitted. "But it can't be a coincidence that another top government official was targeted, along with the detective investigating the case."

"Kirk Miner was already off the case," Mulville said. "No reason for anyone to worry about him. No motive."

Great. What was Steve going to say now? That he had hired Kirk, and Kirk had investigated Silvana's watch? That the watch had a GPS and a firewall? Without first warning the detective, Steve couldn't get Kirk in trouble with Mulville.

"What do you expect?" Sarcasm colored Mulville's tone. "People to stop getting sick and dying after Silvana went to jail? Didn't you continue to have heart attacks showing up in your ER? We have no evidence that the last two events are in any way related to the previous six. Shit happens, independent of bad guys. Are you a doctor? You ought to know that."

Something vibrated inside Steve shirt's pocket. The heartbeat was on again. The rate was one hundred and nine, one hundred and fifteen, one hundred and thirty-two. What were they doing to that girl? Steve's heart pounded. Did they know he was talking to the FBI? How? Maybe the watch had a bug and they could hear him.

"Hold on," he told Mulville.

Steve rushed out into the corridor, looked around, and walked to the bathroom holding the watch between his two fingers as if it carried the plague. His hands felt sweaty and slippery placing the watch on the floor behind the toilet. He closed the door, ran back to his office, and took a relaxing breath.

"Silvana didn't send the cards," Steve said. "She had no idea where they came from. Someone else is using her, and they're committing the actual crimes. Someone is holding her daughter hostage. Silvana said Patrizia is staying at her sister's in Florida. As far as I know, she has only one sister, and she's in Italy, somewhere in Tuscany. No, in Bologna. Silvana mentioned that she teaches at the oldest university in Bologna. That's what she said. Check it out. I bet she said she was in the States because otherwise the heartbeat watch would be difficult to explain. Or the passport could be traceable. Whatever. Use your resources and find out if her sister is really in Florida."

"Silvana forgot where she got the frigging cards," Mulville said. "So what? Or more likely she's lying."

"I went to see her." Time to throw in everything he had and to hell with Mulville's reaction. "She cried when she heard about Kirk's and the Chief of Staff's dissections. She had little to do with it. She almost told me about it, but then her watch showed Patrizia's heartbeat going on and off. It drove her nuts. She said she couldn't talk until next week. I'm telling you she's innocent. Someone is threatening her daughter."

"Are you done blabbering?" Mulville said. "Next week is her trial. That's what Silvana meant when she said she couldn't talk till next week. Nothing to do with the stupid watch and her daughter's jogging. Silvana didn't want to report her daughter missing because she ain't. We already have the guilty party in jail. Too bad she's your girlfriend. We can't waste government resources on your love affairs. The investigation is over. And stop chatting with my prisoner."

Too bad Steve hadn't kept the watch. This would have been a good conversation for the bad guys to listen to. The terrorists would relax on hearing all this from an FBI agent like Mulville.

"Listen," Steve said, "this case isn't over. The real criminals are still at large. You are the FBI. You're supposed to protect our country from terrorism and serial crimes. So do it. Don't do it for me. Never mind that I pay your salary. Do it because it's your job."

He heard Mulville taking a breath to answer. Then Steve hung up.

CHAPTER 19

CAUSE AND EFFECT

Kirk Miner picked up the black bishop and moved it four diagonal spaces across the chessboard. Deep brown eyes looked up with hidden laughter, his entire mouth stretching into a grin. The expression on Peter's face told Kirk how foolish his move had been. Peter's hand, large for a boy his age, then made a single move for checkmate.

"What were you thinking?" Peter said. But then the grin of victory died on his face. "Dad, this is the third checkmate you've handed me today. Are you feeling okay?"

"I'm fine." Kirk smiled. "We both know how smart you are."

But Kirk wasn't fine. The boy was right. Kirk was thinking about his last conversation with Steve Leeds several days ago, about Mulville's stubborn refusal to reopen his investigation of the Moretti case. From the look on Peter's face, Kirk better let him know the truth, or at least part of it.

"Don't worry," Kirk said, tapping his head with a fist. "I'm not suffering from any brain damage. I just have a lot on my mind."

"Like what?" Peter gathered up the chess pieces. "I thought your case was over."

How had Kirk gotten into this jam? Wasn't it enough Aurora knew the truth about his dissection, that it was as natural as a bomb? For the past week, she'd been walking around closing drapes and blinds and peeking out to make sure the patrol car was still here and the cops inside protecting them. Just before Peter left for school, the look on her face was heartbreaking. She kissed the boy as if it could be the last time.

Now Kirk would have to deal with Peter, and possibly upset him with the truth. Or worse, lie to him. No, Kirk couldn't do that. Kirk had promised himself a while ago he wouldn't lie to his family.

"The case isn't over," he said. "I'm still trying to figure things out."

"Is that why the police are watching us?" Peter's hand stopped in mid-air, holding a few pawns. "And a policeman has been taking me back and forth from school all week? Said you asked him to."

"Yes," Kirk said. "Sometimes I don't tell you things because I don't want you to worry, but I'll tell you the truth if you really want to know."

"Are we in danger?" Peter asked. "Did someone hurt you?"

"I'm afraid someone intentionally did this to me." Kirk pointed at his chest. "I'm taking precautions so no one comes close again—to me, or to you, or to Mom."

"How did they do it?" Peter asked, closing the chess pieces' bag. "They didn't shoot or anything."

"I wish I could figure that out," Kirk said. "That's what I've been worrying about for a week, instead of paying closer attention to my chess moves."

He watched his son. Kirk knew that look. Peter had a new problem to solve. Worry was gone. Only the challenge at hand remained.

"Who came close to you the night you came home?"

"All the people on the plane," Kirk said. "Then a taxi driver. Then a friend I met at the police station. Then you and Mom."

Steve thought about his flight again. He had requested, reviewed, and studied the passenger list. All the passengers' faces hopelessly blurred together in his mind. The Chief of Staff came to mind. Same type of injury to the aorta, but he wasn't on the plane or in the taxi. What did he and the Chief have in common? It didn't have to be a card with a chip. A chip or ultrasound device could be hidden anywhere. The image of the taxi driver waving his cell phone flashed in his mind.

"Yes!" Kirk made a fist and touched his son's. "That's what I needed to think about. The two of us make a good team."

The boy acted much older than his eleven years. He was handling the event better than his mother. Kirk got up and walked to the kitchen. The difficult part would be telling Aurora he had to go back to Washington, DC, on the first flight tomorrow.

The aroma of home-made soup made Kirk re-think his plan. The conversation with Aurora about his leaving again so soon hadn't gone well. How could he blame her, after all he had just gone through? His aorta was kept open by a stent, and the wound in his groin, through which the stent had been delivered, was still healing, and Kirk planned to go back on a plane to Washington, DC to pick up where he had left off on a case that had almost gotten him killed? All this after Mulville dismissed him with the strongest possible condemnation. "Was he out of his mind?" she had asked. Perhaps he was.

Kirk moved closer to Aurora, who was standing beside the range. He lifted blond curls off the side of her neck and placed his lips on the soft skin between her jaw and collar bone. Her perfume spread warmth in his chest. This was life. She seemed to hesitate for a moment, then briefly sighed. And then she shrugged Kirk away.

"Don't you dare seduce me to get me to approve a suicidal mission," she said.

Kirk wrapped her in a hug. At first, her muscles tightened against his arms. Then her anger seemed to abate and he felt her relaxing inside his embrace.

"That girl is still in danger," he said. "I have to try saving her. Plus, many other people's lives may be at stake."

"What about the police?" she asked. "What are they doing? What's the FBI doing? After what happened to you, you can't fight alone. Call the FBI."

She turned and kissed him on his lips. Her eyes shone under the kitchen's lights. If only Steve could rely on someone else catching those blood vessel busters, Kirk thought, he could remain here, enjoy his wife's soft full lips, and play chess with Peter, instead of risking his life.

"The FBI is kind of done," he said. "I spoke with the surgeon in Washington. The White House Chief of Staff died of an aortic dissection like mine. Dr. Leeds tried to convince the FBI to investigate his death as a possible crime, but the FBI guy wouldn't budge. You see, they already have a woman in custody—the girl's mother."

"The mother?!" Aurora drew back. Resentment resurfaced on her face. "Her mother is the bad guy?"

"I think she did what she had to do to protect her daughter," he explained, still holding her in his arms. "The bad guys are still out there."

The tight knots in her back relaxed under his hands. The argument had tugged at Aurora's motherly heartstrings.

"I understand," she whispered, her eyes full of sympathy. "But Peter and I need you. And you're still recovering from surgery."

"I must interview the Chief of Staff's wife," Kirk said. "If I can prove someone caused her husband's injury, and likewise my dissection, I'll be able to convince the FBI to continue the investigation. I'll be very careful. And I'll be home in no time."

He watched the effect of his explanation on his wife's face. He had revealed too much. Something meant to assure her of the necessity of his mission had succeeded only in opening a torrent of fear.

***

The Chief of Staff's residence stood in a cul-de-sac of an upscale residential neighborhood in Virginia. The GPS directed Kirk to stop in front of a three-story red brick house with blue shingles, large windows, and a small front yard. Two burly men stood at each side of the entrance.

His Berretta locked in the car's glove compartment, Kirk zipped up his down jacket and stepped into the afternoon's winter chill. A lonely bird croaked in the distance. The slippery frozen ground crunched under his sneakers. The two men huddled together, side by side, to block the entrance.

"Hi," Kirk said in his most pleasant voice. "Kirk Miner, to see the Chief's widow."

From his wallet, he pulled out a copy of his FBI ID and one of his PI cards. His bare fingers tingled from the cold. He hoped the widow hadn't changed her mind since their phone conversation. The agent on the left nodded. The one on the right stepped forward. Kirk spread his arms and legs and submitted to a pat-down. The same man opened the door and announced his name to a slim blond woman in her late thirties sitting on a black leather couch. Her pale, distraught face and bags under her green eyes testified to recent widowhood. Still beautiful, she stood up to greet him. A young boy, slumped on a black leather armchair, lifted his face from some videogame controls. His glazed eyes bounced off Kirk, then refocused on the screen.

"My sincere condolences for your loss." Kirk grasped the woman's limp but manicured hand. "Thanks for seeing me on such short notice."

She nodded. A resigned smile lit up her face. Then she lifted her head and nodded again at the Secret Service man. The door's cold draft vanished at the sound of the lock closing behind Kirk. Kirk turned to confirm their privacy. The woman took his jacket in silence and gestured for him to join her on the black couch.

"Hot tea?" she asked.

Kirk looked around. A teapot and tray were already in place on an antique-looking coffee table. He thanked her. The woman poured the hot beverage into fragile-looking ceramic cups, sat down, and crossed her black-veiled legs under a dark, high-collared dress. Kirk sat some distance from her, placed one of his business cards on the coffee table, and got busy pouring honey from a small container into his tea cup.

"Mr. Miner," she said, as if she was continuing their past phone conversation, "why all this secrecy? You're a private investigator. And you mentioned you were working with the FBI."

The question required a thoughtful and diplomatic answer. Kirk had to use his former FBI-liaison credentials with the woman. But at the same time, he had to avoid any official scrutiny which would result in Mulville barring his way.

"I was," he said. "But now I'm investigating on my own. As I told you, I'm afraid the FBI has the wrong person in custody. The proof is that your husband was killed while the suspect was already in jail. And I nearly was, too. I suffered the same injury to my aorta as your husband got. I was lucky. I got treated in time."

Hopelessness faded from the vacant green eyes and turned to dismay. Her chin trembled. She looked straight at him.

"You think someone did this to my husband?" she asked. "On purpose?"

"That's what I'm investigating," Kirk said. "I need you to go over what happened the night before your husband died. Please."

Her fine ash-blond hair swayed side to side. She sighed. Kirk felt sorry for the wound he had to reopen.

"I already told everything to Agent Mulville," she said. "Don't you two share notes?"

"I'm afraid not," Kirk admitted. "And he probably wouldn't approve of my inquiry. But I'm trying to find out who killed your husband and bring him to justice. With your help, I think I can."

"Mr. Miner," she said studying him, "I can't be in the middle of a squabble between you and the FBI. I'm the widow of a respected, high-level government official."

Kirk took another sip from his cup, his eyes fixed on hers above the rim. She turned to look toward the front door. Was she considering throwing him out? His breathing got shallower.

"Look." He steadied his hand and replaced the cup on the saucer. "This is the only chance we have to catch the killer. He's still out there. Ready to strike. I believe the woman in custody is being blackmailed. The bad guys must have kidnapped her daughter."

Her eyes closed, as if what Kirk had just told her was too awful to hear.

"But, if the FBI knows this," she asked, disbelief in her eyes, "why don't they do something about it?"

Good question. The problem appeared crystal clear to everyone involved, except for the pompous jerk in charge—Mulville.

"They don't have any proof that the two aortic dissections were caused by someone," Kirk said. "They attribute the injuries to natural causes."

She uncrossed her legs, pushed her feet back against an oriental-looking rug, parked herself deeper into the couch, and relaxed against the pillows. She seemed to accept his explanation. He had to get to the point while he had an opening.

"Tell me," Kirk said, "who interacted with your husband the night he died?"

"We were getting ready to go to dinner," she said, looking at the wall behind the armchairs. "With the president."

"Did your husband look tense?" Kirk said. "Any strange behavior?"

"Now that you mention it, he was fine when I arrived. Then I went to the ladies' room. When I came back, he looked different—upset. Or maybe he was getting sick. He went to the bathroom and returned looking pale and clammy. I offered to take him home, but he insisted on going to dinner. He finished up some email and we headed for the residence."

"Did he say anything odd?" Kirk asked. "Anything unusual that you can think of."

Her face lit up. Kirk liked when this happened. Often some clue would pop out.

"He asked me if the Secret Service guy had done a good job picking up our son from school that day," she said, pointing at the boy. "Then he asked when they had let me know I didn't need to pick him up."

"And that was strange?" Kirk asked. "Why?"

"I usually pick my son up at school," she said, looking puzzled.

"Occasionally, if I'm busy, I ask one of our agents. The school has names on the list for people who can pick Jeff up. I thought my husband wanted to give me more time to prepare for the president's dinner. But then he said something weird—something that almost freaked me out."

"What?"

"He said from then on he would let me know personally if the Secret Service was to pick up Jeff." A veil of panic was visible as her pupils dilated, and she bit her lower lip. "Just in case."

Kirk looked at the boy. His thumbs were in a frenzy, his attention totally devoted to the videogame "Neverland." He would have to interview him at some point.

"In case of what?" Kirk pushed on.

"Right." She nodded. "That's what freaked me out. And there was something else that was strange, in view of what happened later."

A repressed sob interrupted her last sentence. Kirk touched her shoulder in sympathy. He had to move forward.

"What?" he asked. "I'm sorry, I know it's difficult for you."

"The number they texted me from," she said, "to let me know about Jeff's pickup. It was from the White House, but it didn't belong to our agents. At first, I didn't pay attention to that. I even erased the text."

Looking at the guilt on her face was unbearable for Kirk, so he briefly set his gaze elsewhere. But her information was very helpful. The least Kirk could do was to reassure her.

"Don't feel bad about that," he said. "That number would be untraceable. I'm sure. What's important is that you noticed it was unusual, different."

The woman noticeably relaxed. At least he could give her that absolution. It was amazing what kind of guilt-trips deep sorrow propels survivors into.

"Did you tell the FBI about all this?" Kirk asked.

"Not really," she said. Her head moved side to side. "They didn't seem too concerned about this being a murder."

It figures. Why spoil things if a good-enough guilty party is already in jail? That son of a bitch Mulville.

"Who had contact with your husband that night?" Kirk asked. "Besides you and your son?"

"The two Secret Service agents." The woman pointed to the door, then stared at the walls some more. "Oh, there was also a cleaning lady outside the door of my husband's office. Right when we were leaving. She told one of the Secret Service someone had called her to clean early. But nobody had. So she left."

"Did she have any electronic devices with her?" Kirk asked. "Sticks? Chips?"

"Just a cell phone." The woman shrugged. "Why?"

A cell phone is a common object indeed. Perfect for hiding an ultrasound device. In fact, both his cab driver and the cleaning woman had pointed a cell phone at their respective targets. *Bingo!*

"I'm going to get pictures of the cleaning crew on that night," he said. "To see if you can recognize her."

She picked up the teapot and tilted it toward her cup. Only a few drops of liquid fell out. She replaced the pot on a plate.

"Why do you ask about electronic devices?" she said.

"Just a theory." Kirk shook his head. "Sorry, but I can't share confidential information."

The woman nodded. She must have heard the same answer over and over from her husband.

"The FBI asked me if my husband had received any cards." Her shoulders slumped. "I told them no. But they searched the entire house and office anyway. They found nothing. No cards or letters."

"But Daddy got a letter," a loud voice said, "the evening when he got sick. I gave him a letter."

Something had shocked Jeff out of his trance. His mind must've been absorbing the conversation. Kirk looked at the mother. She perked up, looking both surprised and bewildered. The situation required delicate handling. Kirk gave her a signal with his hand to prevent a possible outburst of questions which could jeopardize his investigation. She shrugged, giving Kirk permission to talk to the boy about the new assertion. Kirk got up and squatted near the boy's chair.

"What's your name?" Kirk asked.

The boy turned to him. His hand let go of the bulky remote control. He looked attentive now.

"Jeff," he said.

Kirk's groin wound burned from the stretch of squatting. He stood up, pulled the other armchair over, and sat facing the boy. He racked his mind for clues on the best way to talk to a boy this age.

"Jeff," Kirk said, "tell me and your mom about the letter you gave to your dad. Did you write it at school?"

"No." Jeff shook his head. "Some man gave it to me."

"Which man?" His mother's voice sounded shrill. She leapt from the couch.

"The agent who picked me up," Jeff said.

"Who?" Kirk pointed to the front door. Then he got up, walked to the door, and placed his hand on the knob. "Which one of these men was he?"

"Not them," the boy said before Kirk could open the door. "He was a new man. Never saw him before."

Kirk's hand hovered over the door knob. The woman's face turned pasty. He went back to the chair.

"What did the man say to you?" Kirk whispered. "You can tell me."

The boy glanced at his mother. From the color of her skin, she seemed ready to faint, but she managed a reassuring nod to the boy. Good woman.

"He said Daddy needed help," Jeff said. "Something important. And he would be happy to get the letter. Like playing a game together."

"How old are you?" Kirk asked.

"Eight," the boy said, looking proud.

"Third grade?"

"Second," the woman answered.

"Jeff," Kirk said, "did you happen to look at the letter. Did you happen to read it?"

The boy looked at the ceiling and pursed his lips.

"I'm sorry," he said.

"No?" Kirk said. "Don't be sorry. It's great if you read it. We need to know what it said. Do you remember any of the words?"

The boy seemed to relax. He stared at a screen where robots stood frozen, ready to strike with weapons. A spark of recognition flickered into his eyes.

"There was a difficult word," he said. "Like secret or something."

"Think," Kirk said. "This is very important. Do you remember anything else?"

The woman got up. Her dress hugged her body and twisted as she walked out of the living room. She came back waving a pointed pencil and a yellow-lined notepad.

"Here." She placed both objects on the coffee table. She picked up the teapot and cups, placed them on the tray, and lifted the tray from the table. "Jeff, come here with Mr. Miner and try to write down the words you remember."

She left for the kitchen. Was this a way to give him privacy with the boy? Good idea. Jeff sat on the couch and leaned over the blank paper, pencil in hand. Kirk sat next to him. The boy bit the eraser at the end of the pencil.

"Write the secret word," Kirk said. "Just start. See if it comes to you."

The boy picked up the pencil. Thumb and index fingers tightened around the tip. He wrote "Secret." It was a tentative cursive writing with a slight right slant. He looked up at Kirk. Kirk nodded in encouragement.

"I remember another word," the boy said, writing with renewed energy. "Hurt."

"Hurt?" Kirk felt his stomach churning. "As in getting hurt? Who was getting hurt?"

The PI waited. No more words came. Jeff stared at the paper, pencil still in hand. The mother came back.

"Good job," Kirk said. "Anything else you remember?"

The boy shook his head. A slight frown creased his forehead and he relaxed, dropping the pencil onto the table.

"I'll go to your school and ask some questions." Kirk got up. "I'll be back with pictures of Secret Service agents and cleaning women. Meantime, Jeff, see if you remember anything else. If so, write it down, like you did just now."

Kirk tore the yellow sheet from the pad, folded it in fourths, and placed it in his shirt pocket. The woman's color looked better. She moved toward the door.

"Jeff," she said calmly, "I need to talk to Mr. Miner alone for a moment."

The boy went back to his video game. Buzzing and popping noises filled the living room. Kirk followed the woman to the door. She stopped at the entry and grabbed him by the arm. Her hand had a strength Kirk hadn't expected.

"Did the letter hurt Daddy?" the boy asked from the living room.

The woman let go of Kirk's arm. Her eyes full of astonishment and pain, she turned and rushed back to the living room.

"No, Jeff," Kirk heard her saying. "You have nothing to do with this. Some bad person hurt Daddy. Mr. Miner is trying to find out who. We need to help him the best we can."

She hugged the boy. Her hands combed through his hair, wiping tears from under his eyes. Jeff remained still, the remote control loose in his hands as his eyes fixed on the flickering screen. After a while, her face lifted above the boy's shoulders. Tears streamed down her cheeks.

"I'll call you," she mouthed. Her hand waved Kirk goodbye. "Thank you."

The boy's voice reminded Kirk of his dogs when in pain. Kirk added the event to the list of what he would hold the bastards accountable for.

He opened the front door and walked into the afternoon's early darkness. The Secret Service agents remained still and silent, like frozen corpses. The ground crunched again under his feet. How was he going to convince Mulville to investigate?

CHAPTER 20

SISTERS

Steve Leeds put his stethoscope back in his white coat pocket, his eyes lingering on the angry red line in the middle of Nirula's chest. He felt the familiar sense of pride he experienced when reviewing his work, fueled by the memory of the challenges he had faced and conquered to create that scar. Nirula had entered the operating room in full cardiac arrest. Now, thanks to Steve's expertise, he was sitting on the examining table, smiling.

"Good job." Nirula pointed at his bare chest. "Thanks again for taking me."

Much was implied by the sentence. Only a few weeks earlier, Steve wouldn't have said hello if he had bumped into Nirula in the hospital elevator. In a matter of minutes, Steve had gone from resenting and ignoring the ER doctor, to nestling the man's limp heart in his hands to bring it back to life. All that seemed so far in the past now.

Now the one fighting for her life was Silvana. To some extent, Silvana's fate was a consequence of Nirula's actions, whether she had acted in revenge or under duress. Steve took a breath to push back a short wave of resentment. He was frustrated at his inability to help Silvana. There was nothing for him left to do but wait. And for what? For the week to be over. Silvana's last words kept on swirling in his head. "Can't talk until next week."

"How's Silvana?" Nirula asked, replacing the shirt inside his pants.

Funny that he, of all people, should ask. If only Nirula had treated her brother properly, perhaps Silvana would be at work now, thinking about what sexy nightgown to wear when making love to Steve that night. Instead, she sat in a bare cell wearing an orange jump suit.

"How could she possibly be?" Steve said. "Alone in a jail cell."

The unanticipated sadness in Nirula's eyes gave Steve a pang of guilt. The man was concerned. For real.

"I want you to know," he told Steve, "I never for a moment doubted her innocence. I know Silvana could never plan anything so evil. Not even against me."

He chuckled, seemingly out of sadness. Nirula was on Steve's and Silvana's side. But what good did that do them?

"Did anyone notify her sister?" Nirula said, turning back as he walked out of the exam room. "Silvana's very close to her."

Steve lifted his eyes off his computer. The words tugged at his brain. Never mind the other two patients waiting for him.

"Her sister?" he asked. "What do you know about Silvana's family?"

"When Silvana's brother was in the ER," Nirula said, standing in front of the open door, "the two of them must've spent an hour on the phone with someone in Italy. I think they were talking with their sister."

"Do you know for a fact Silvana's sister is in Italy?" Steve got up from his stool and stepped closer to Nirula. "And are you aware of any other sister?"

Nirula thought about it. How could Nirula know more about Silvana's family than Steve? Silvana hated Nirula's guts.

"As far as I know, she's the only one." Nirula shrugged. "Why?"

Was Steve going to confide in Nirula? What evidence did he have that Silvana had acted under duress? Nothing solid. Only a theory so far. And Silvana could've forgotten where she bought the tan cards. Mulville was right about that.

"Silvana insists her daughter is staying with her sister in Florida," Steve said. "I'm afraid she's lying and that something bad might have happened to her daughter."

Nirula's face morphed into an expression of shock. The man seemed ready to do what he could to make amends for past misguided choices. Steve had made the right decision.

"Do you mean she's not with Silvana's sister?" Nirula asked. "Where is she?"

"Worst case scenario," Steve said, "kidnapped. By someone who's forcing Silvana to act against her better judgment."

"Wow." Nirula pursed his lips and let loose a loud whistle. "Actually, there is a way to know for sure how many Moretti sisters there are."

"How?"

"May I?" Nirula pointed to Steve's computer. "I could review the notes from her brother's ER visit."

Steve pointed to the stool, inviting Nirula to sit. Nirula parked himself in front of the computer and entered his password to access his patients' charts. Steve stood behind him. Silvana's brother's file opened. Nirula selected the family history section. Great idea on his part. The question now was how thorough had the resident been in taking the history. The page scrolled down at the touch of Nirula's finger. Steve leaned forward.

"There it is." Steve pointed at the screen. Nirula lifted his finger and the screen froze. "The patient has two sisters."

Two sisters—Silvana, and the one in Italy. That made two. No sister in Florida for Patrizia to be with. Patrizia wasn't in Florida. By instinct, Steve reached inside his shirt pocket for Silvana's watch and looked at it. The dial was dark and silent. What fluttered was his own heart.

As the exam room door closed behind Dr. Nirula, Steve sat back on the stool near the exam table and stared at the screen. His next patient would have to wait a little longer. He dialed Kirk Miner's cell. A faint melody resonated in the distance. The "no cell phone" rule should be enforced without exception in the waiting room. He should talk to the receptionist about the importance of silence in the office.

"Hello," Kirk answered.

"How are you?" Steve said. "Are you able to talk? I need to let you know something very important."

"Sure." Kirk's voice sounded firm, strong. "I'm good."

A short silence followed. Then the exam door cracked opened and Steve's receptionist appeared, red hair first. She looked up, saw her boss on the phone, bowed in apology, and withdrew. A man came up from behind her.

Now what? The woman not only couldn't control cell phones, but she allowed anyone in during patient's visits. Steve had no time to waste on any drug rep. He took a breath to object, but his eyes landed on Kirk Miner.

The PI just stood there, his familiar blue jacket draped on an arm and a phone held to his ear. He smiled.

"I also have urgent and important things to discuss," Kirk said.

CHAPTER 21

JACK MULVILLE

J ack Mulville reclined in his desk chair at FBI headquarters and took a large bite of a donut. The raspberry filling dispersed in his mouth and gave him a jolt of pleasure. His eyes remained on the document on his computer screen. The hum of conversations dotted with a variety of cellphone ringtones filled the office. Mulville wasn't the type for introspection, but he always knew when he was having one of his special moments. Recently, they were occurring more and more often. This fact frightened him.

Bad feelings were all too familiar to him. Ever since he could remember, his normal state of mind was colored by different shades of anger. No wonder, with all the bullying he had to endure growing up in Chicago's slums. He had learned how to fight in the gym of life. What could he expect from people but the worst? Nine out of ten times, he had been right. In the tenth case, by the time he figured out he was wrong, the person would be too pissed to reconcile.

Besides, Mulville hated admitting his mistakes. He didn't need friends. Or girlfriends, for that matter. Love was for the birds, women were to have fun with, and happiness was a naïve, impossible dream. For an FBI agent, anger, mastery of battle, and mistrust of people were great qualities to have. Mulville loved his job and was proud of it. Only now and then did sadness overcome him, during so-called "special moments" like the one right now.

He took another bite of the greasy donut. Most of the time, the sugar quotient would help him snap out of a bad moment. But not today. Today, the sadness had crept in as he began writing his final report on the Moretti case. Something in the report had triggered a domino effect inside him, sending him into a deep hole. What was the matter with him? He took a slurp of stale coffee from a paper cup. All facts of Silvana's guilt were spread out in front of him—motive, opportunity, means. And she had confessed, for Christ's sake! Who gave a shit about what Sherlock detective Miner and Steve the doc thought? Mulville was used to people misunderstanding him, treating him like a prick. That's why he experienced special pleasure acting like one. If someone was going to hell anyway, might as well enjoy the ride.

So, what was so special about Silvana Moretti? Steve Leeds's call from three days ago came to mind. The moron was focusing on all kinds of inconsequential details in order not to accept the fact that the love of his life was in the slammer and would likely remain there for the rest of her sorry life. The stupid call had set sad moments in motion for Mulville. But the doctor was wrong. No sense in Mulville wasting any more time and energy worrying about him. He saved the document, pushed himself back from his battered desk, and took a break.

***

Kirk closed the examining room door and sat on a chair. His groin throbbed from walking. He felt drawn, marked by illness and the threat of death. Despite the surprise, Steve looked happy and relieved to see Kirk. The trip was the right thing to do.

"What are you doing here?" Steve looked up from his phone. "I was afraid my call would wake you up, and here you are, back to work already. Are you insane?"

Kirk nodded. His smile faded. Exhaustion crept in.

"I couldn't stay still," he said. "Murderers are out there planning God-only-knows-what else and the FBI is doing nothing. Yesterday, I went to interview the Chief of Staff's widow."

"You did?" Steve's eyes widened. "Wait until Mulville finds out. He'll be delighted."

"Somebody has to do it," Kirk said. "And now I have a special stake in this case. As you have."

"What did you learn?" Steve nodded.

"My dissection was not some random disease striking." Kirk pointed at his chest. "Same for the Chief."

"I agree with you, but how can you be sure?" Steve asked.

"The Chief got a note. Those creeps had his boy deliver it to him." Kirk thought of Peter in school. A shiver went through his body. "Then they killed the father."

"A letter about what?"

"I don't know," Kirk said. "No one knew about the letter, not even the wife. They must've made the Chief destroy it. Only the boy knew about it. I think he read it, but remembers little about it."

"The boy is old enough to read," Steve said. "Maybe he's blocking it, because the content was too awful. Poor kid. And how were they sure the son would deliver the letter to his father?"

"I've been going over the same question in my mind," Kirk said. "Hopefully, the boy will remember something more."

Leeds seemed pale under the ceiling light. His mouth stretched as if he was experiencing pain—probably worrying about his girlfriend. But this time she had an iron-clad alibi—jail.

"How did they do it?" Steve asked. "You didn't get any card or note, did you? Did the boy mention any hot disk on the note?"

Good questions. Kirk had pondered this during his entire trip. He had a theory.

"No. No hot disk," Kirk said. "I'm no physicist, but I think they used a device connected to a cell phone to transmit ultrasounds and dissect the aorta. The Chief's wife claims a cleaning lady showed up at his office without being called. She carried a cell phone. My taxi driver pointed a cell phone at me to dissect my aorta. We've got to speak to Mulville."

"Good luck." Steve's hand moved up, indicating futility. "When I tried, day before yesterday, I told him Silvana doesn't have the slightest idea where the cards came from, and she didn't buy or send them. Mulville couldn't care less. Today, I got proof that Silvana was lying about the daughter being with her sister in Florida. She has no sister there. I was trying to find the courage to talk to Mulville again. We pay taxes so the government will keep us safe, and the FBI guy is upset that I'm trying to help with an investigation."

"If only we could speak to someone a bit more receptive than that door-knob," Kirk said, running his fingers through his hair. "If Silvana is lying about Patrizia, the clock is ticking for that girl."

Steve nodded in silence. The distress in his eyes indicated how much he cared about the girl and her mother. Kirk had to find a way.

"I'll arrange a meeting with the FBI." Kirk dialed. "Dinner. The three of us."

"I have to finish with my patients." The doctor waved Kirk out to the waiting room. "Let me know."

Kirk walked out to the waiting room as the call went through. He sat on a comfortable chair next to a fake plant, away from the waiting patients. A sign on the wall in front of him showed a cell phone crossed out with red lines.

"Still alive?" Mulville said at the second ring.

The FBI guy knew about his surgery? Steve wouldn't have told him. But then why such a question?

"Yeah," Kirk whispered, covering the noisy phone with his hand. "We need to talk. How about dinner tonight?"

"You're off the case, Sherlock," Mulville said. "And we aren't friends."

"I'm on my own time," Kirk said. "Got special renewed interest in the investigation."

"Since when?" Mulville said.

Mulville didn't know about his adventure. He was just his usual sarcastic self. Well, Kirk had news for hm.

"Since someone tried to kill me," Kirk said, his tone rising an octave. "By shredding my aorta."

"The doctor told me. Glad you're still with us, but I don't have a job for you."

"I interviewed the wife of the Chief of Staff, who died the same way I should've. Just to compare notes."

"How do you know about that?" Mulville groaned. "We kept it from the press."

Nice concern for his colleague, the PI. No "how're you doing now?" for Kirk. But what had Kirk expected from a doorknob?

"Dr. Leeds told me about him," Kirk said. "He didn't think it was a coincidence either."

"So much for professional secrets." Mulville chuckled. "Son of a—"

"Listen, FBI." Kirk took a deep breath to ease the soreness in his chest. "I got interesting info for you. Don't you want to hear what you missed? After all, I did what you should've done. Investigate."

"What is it?" Mulville's voice got coarser. "Tell me about it. Now. Before I slap you with obstruction of justice charges."

"You're the one obstructing dinner," Kirk said. "You can have a paid dinner tonight at your favorite local restaurant and hear all about what you failed to discover. Or you can be your usual stubborn self. Which one will it be?"

That felt good. Easy to give choices and ultimatums when there's nothing to lose and no one to bow to. What would it take to get the FBI moving again? Kirk waited for the answer. The male patient at his right threw him a look of disapproval and pointed at the "No Cell Phones" sign.

"Official government business," Kirk mouthed, pointing at the phone.

"Dinner at seven," Mulville said. "Charlie's Steak House on Constitution Avenue. You're buying."

"Wow," Kirk said. "Expensive taste. And we aren't even friends."

—◊—

Crisp tablecloth, fancy napkins rolled up inside wine glasses, shining silverware, suffused light from hidden sources—Charlie's Steak House was an atypical experience for Jack Mulville. He sat with his back to the dark wood-paneled wall, the entire restaurant in full view, including the front door. Mulville had gotten into the habit of getting to all his meetings early, to choose the most strategic table, in case something unexpected came up.

He reached for the glass in front of him, took a large gulp of Johnnie Walker, and swirled the liquid around in his mouth. The ice cubes tinkled as he replaced the glass on the paper doily. He could get used to this kind of fancy life.

Kirk walked through the front door. He turned his head from side to side as his eyes surveyed the room. Someone followed close behind him. A taller man. Mulville's spine straightened up against the booth's red leather. What the heck? What was Leeds doing here? Was this a trap? Mulville took a calming breath. No need for his life-saving paranoia to fully kick in. This wasn't a drug bust or a terrorist take-down. This was just dinner, compliments of Sherlock. If the doc wanted to chip in, so what? More dessert and after-night liqueurs for him. Mulville waved the men to the table.

Kirk and Steve shook his hand. A waiter in black-tie bowed and took drink orders. Kirk asked for a Scotch on the rocks and Steve ordered red wine. Mulville refilled. The waiter withdrew and the three men got busy with menus.

"What have you got?" Mulville asked, slurping up the last remnants of his first drink. "Shoot."

"I'll have the chicken parmigiana," Kirk said, looking up from the menu. "With extra tomato sauce."

The detective knew how to rub his nerves. Mulville hadn't decided yet if Kirk was the one out of ten people he could trust. So far, he was sure only of Kirk's ability to piss him off.

"What new information do you have?" Mulville said, speaking each word with clarity. "Don't be smart with me. And what's the doctor doing here if this is official business? He's an outside civilian."

The waiter came back with the drinks and to take their orders. Mulville kept his eyes on Kirk and went first, ordering a bloody Porterhouse with hot sauce on the side. Steve and Kirk followed suit. After the waiter left, Kirk took a small sip of his Scotch.

"Calm down," Kirk said. "Leeds is the one who has the important info. Do you want it first or second hand?"

"Silvana's sister lives in Italy." Steve examined the ceiling's lights through the wine's red color. "Not in Florida. Dr. Nirula confirmed it with me. Silvana is lying about her daughter being in Florida."

"Okay," Mulville said. "I get it. I don't need a committee to shove anything down my throat. If you're done, Doc, take your dinner and go. Sherlock and I have work to do."

With the back of his hand, Mulville made a sweeping motion to dismiss Leeds. Kirk squirmed in his seat. But the doctor smiled. He left without protest.

"Was this really necessary?" Kirk pointed at the door.

"Confidential FBI business."

"So, does this mean I'm on again?"

"No time for engraved invitations." Mulville finished his first drink in a single gulp and slammed the glass on the table. "Silvana lied about Patrizia. And this means the girl was kidnapped? By whom? And why?"

Mulville picked up his second drink, looked at it for a moment, then placed it back on the table. A salad and an order of shrimp cocktail arrived. Mulville turned his attention to the shrimp.

"That brings me to the main reason for this meeting," Kirk said. He ate a forkful of his salad. "Why would someone want to kill the White House Chief of Staff?"

The ball buster never stopped. The doctor must've convinced him the aortic dissections weren't natural. Let's see what new evidence the detective will dish out now.

"What did you find out from the widow?" Mulville asked. "Did she tell you something she kept from us? I hope it was worth it. Impersonating a federal agent gives you a minimum of three years in the slammer."

"Tell that to whoever picked up the Chief's son from school the day before the event," Kirk said, staring at Mulville. "Somebody impersonated a Secret Service agent and gave the eight-year-old a note for his dad."

"What are you talking about?" Mulville said, spraying saliva infused with cocktail sauce. "That's the lamest thing I've ever heard. How could they know the boy would comply?"

"I'm sure they used a convincing argument." Kirk reached inside his shirt pocket and took out a folded yellow sheet. "Luckily, the smart boy read it and I asked him to write down what he remembered."

He smoothed the paper out on the table. Mulville leaned forward. Kirk saw condescension and reproach in his eyes.

"Here's what he wrote." Kirk placed his index finger on the paper. "Secret" and then "Hurt." "Sounds to me like some sort of threat. Whoever did this wanted to show the Chief how vulnerable his son was."

What was the PI up to now? Mulville snatched the paper from the table and read the childish hand-written words. A strange tightness started in his chest. Dread grew.

"Indulge me for a moment." Kirk made a calming gesture with his hand. "Let's assume someone wanted to kill the Chief of Staff. Why him? Why now? What's he working on that's so important?"

Information swirled in Mulville's mind. The Chief of Staff. In January. The note about getting hurt. And about a secret. And the doc had mentioned Silvana couldn't speak until next week. What was supposed to happen next week? Her trial? Perhaps this had nothing to do with her trial. This was something else, connected with all the other things swirling in his head and the yellow note in his hand. Something seemed to click, but then swung away and Mulville lost it. Yet there was a possible explanation that united all this mumbo-jumbo. He had to think harder. Mulville took a sip of whiskey, dipped his last shrimp into the hot sauce, and ate it in one bite.

"Shit," he mumbled. "I'm afraid I know why."

CHAPTER 22

FOOTBALL AND BISCUIT

Mulville stared at Kirk. The entrees had arrived, but the PI remained still, waiting for an answer. Food sat on the table untouched, getting cold. These were good people. Not one out of ten, like Mulville was accustomed to, but two out of two competent, decent people, one of them sitting right in front of him, and the other one he had just dismissed. What was he going to do? Could he reverse course without losing face? Just the thought of admitting they were right gave Mulville an unbearable feeling. He would have to tear down the barrier he had worked so hard at building. He would have to become vulnerable.

"Why?" Kirk asked again. "Why did they kill the Chief of Staff?"

"The note," Mulville said making small circles in the air with his right index. "It wasn't about any secret. I bet the word the boy wanted to remember was 'secretary.' As in Secretary of something. As in member of the cabinet."

"What would the Chief be doing now," Kirk asked, "with members of the cabinet?"

Mulville slumped back in his seat, then spoke. "It has to do with the designated survivor."

Puzzlement lit up in Kirk's eyes. It figures. Most regular morons, even educated ones, didn't have the slightest idea what went on in keeping government afloat.

"Tell me about the designated survivor." Kirk picked up his fork and knife and started on the steak in front of him.

"The designated survivor," Mulville said, as if reciting from memory, "is a cabinet member appointed by the Chief of Staff to be at a physically distant, secure, and undisclosed location, away from the Capitol, when the

President and other top leaders like the Vice President, Cabinet members, Supreme Court members, etcetera gather together in a single place, in case shit happens."

Kirk's eyes widened, his chewing slowed. He replaced the silverware on the side of his dish.

"In case what happens?" Kirk asked. He took a sip of his drink. "If they all die? The entire list of successors?"

"Yes." Mulville nodded. The strange satisfaction he got from Kirk's shock made him go on in lecture mode. "To maintain continuity of government, in the event some catastrophic shit, like 9/11, kills all officials in the line of succession, then the designated survivor becomes the acting president."

"When does this happen?" Steve asked. "I mean the survivor thing."

"During presidential inaugurations." Mulville paused for effect. "And State of the Union addresses."

"When is the State of the Union this year?" Kirk wiped his mouth with a napkin. "It's coming up, isn't it?"

"Next week," Mulville said.

"Silvana told the doc she couldn't talk until next week," Kirk said. "I thought she meant until the beginning of her trial. But next week happens to be the time for this year's State of the Union address. I'm afraid she meant she can't talk until after the State of the Union."

"Probably because that's when the real shit will hit the fan." Mulville took a large sip of Scotch and gasped.

"They sent the note," Kirk said, staring at the tablecloth, "to tell the Chief of Staff whom to pick as the designated survivor. Then they took out the Chief, so he couldn't warn anyone."

Kirk pursed his lips into a silent whistle. His fingers tapped an unknown rhythm on the tablecloth.

"Tell me more about what this survivor does."

The genius detective needed him after all. Kirk better eat his meal while he had a chance. After finding out what was at stake here, he'll surely lose his appetite.

"Best case scenario." Mulville wondered when he would have time to eat his steak. "This president-in-waiting goes through hours of briefings, role-playing disaster scenarios, even outlining the speech he'd make if he were to assume office. All that, while wallowing in virtual power as the staff addresses him as 'Mr. President.' On the day of the speech, the designated survivor is whisked out of Washington by helicopter to a secret spot where a countdown begins and the designated survivor is officially on standby."

"A countdown?" Kirk asked.

"Yes." Mulville nodded. He chewed on a large bite of meat. "There's actually a clock that counts down until the president and entourage enter the House chamber for the speech. This is the time when the survivor starts asking the Secret Service and White House personnel all kind of stupid questions, all too late to be answered, should disaster strike. The designated survivor is then served a superior dinner prepared by the White House mess. After the President is done speaking and back in the White House, the carriage becomes a pumpkin again and the survivor goes back to being a regular cabinet member."

"So." Kirk stared at Mulville's steak. He watched the blood spilling on his plate. "What would one want from the acting president?"

Mulville couldn't wait. Revelation time for Sherlock.

"The football and the biscuit," he said.

"Cut the FBI-Secret Service jargon," Kirk said, giving him a scornful look. "This isn't a game. Real shit is happening if we don't stop it."

True enough. Mulville slurped up the remains of his Scotch and chewed on the last ice cube. He sat up straight.

"The football," Mulville said, savoring the effect of his explanation in advance, "is a 45-pound black leather briefcase full of stuff used to authorize a nuclear launch, in case the Situation Room in the White House isn't available. A military aide or a Secret Service agent carries it and follows the survivor. The President has the same thing for himself, at all times."

He paused. Kirk looked deep in thought.

"And the biscuit?" the PI asked.

"That's a plastic card," Mulville said, "with the authorization code for the launch of nuclear missiles. The survivor keeps it. Same as the President."

Kirk took several big mouthfuls of water, as if he needed to swallow a large pill. "What's the Situation Room?" he whispered.

"That's a room in the White House basement," Mulville said, "where serious national security problems are dealt with, and the orders for launching missiles are usually given by the President. If the room isn't available, the football is a portable launcher, so to speak."

The waiter approached the table and inspected the men's plates. Mulville dug his knife into his steak like it was a piece of land he owned. The waiter retreated.

"But," Kirk said, "what can they do, even if they get hold of the football and the numbers? From what I've read, the president's order goes to the generals. Encrypted. It then must be decrypted and verified. And then there are two people each with a different key for the launching codes, and they all must agree. It'll never happen."

Mulville looked at the congealed fat on his plate. A slight feeling of nausea rose up from the pit of his stomach. Miner had a point.

"Miner." Mulville took another bite of meat and some cold mashed potatoes. "You watch too many movies. Terrorists aren't Einstein. They just want to spread havoc. All we know is they may be planning to get their hands on the football. That wouldn't be advisable even with all the security in place. We don't have the slightest idea what else they're planning, so we're wasting our time squabbling about details."

"Who's the designated survivor?" Kirk asked. "This year?"

Another stupid question. As always, wasting time they didn't have. Instead of working on strategy.

"For security purposes," Mulville said, "the identity of the designated survivor is kept secret until the day of the address. Only the Chief of Staff, some Secret Service people, and a few White House staff members know who that person is."

"But now these terrorists know who it is," Kirk said. "They told the Chief whom to appoint."

Genius. Kirk looked a little pale now. "What's the security like?" he asked. "For the designated survivor?"

"For a few hours," Mulville said, "the designated survivor is one of the most well-guarded individuals in the world. Just like the real president."

"If we knew who it was," Kirk said, "we could change the selection. So the terrorists wouldn't know whom to target. Can't you find out from the Secret Service or something?"

Mulville shook his head. That's all he needed. He pictured himself having a conversation with the FBI chief, or worse, with the President, on how Silvana's sister still being in Italy instead of Florida meant a terrorist attack would be launched on the designated survivor. And they needed to pick a different one. How had he gotten so deep in shit-land? Was this his reward for letting his guard down and allowing morons in? He should've kept his mouth shut about the secretary and all. It was probably just a fantasy. A paranoid fantasy.

"Perhaps there is a way to find out," Kirk said, "whom the Chief appointed."

"How in the hell would you do that?" Mulville said. "There's no clear pattern in the picks from the last three decades. Only thing to narrow it a little is that all cabinet members who serve as designated survivors are lower-ranking in the line of succession. The Chief does it so there are several people in line for the throne who must croak before the stick is given to the designated survivor. So, for example, the secretaries of state, treasury, and defense—the top three cabinets—have never been chosen as designated survivors."

Kirk smiled. He took a large bite of his steak, chewed, and swallowed. Long sips of water followed. What was the PI up to now?

"Okay," Kirk said, "that helps. Mulville, get the line of succession to the presidency."

"Do you mean now?" Mulville said. "What for?"

Kirk looked at his watch and shook his head. The waiter approached, got no resistance, removed the plates, and made no suggestions for dessert. The intensity of conversation must've discouraged him.

"Now is too late." Kirk said. "Tomorrow, we'll go back to see the boy."

"What the hell for?" Mulville asked, a strange hot feeling rising from his chest.

"We'll go through the list of possibilities," Kirk said. "See if he remembers which secretary his dad had to choose. Also, we'll show him pictures of various Secret Service agents. See if he recognizes who picked him up from school."

Mulville took a few sips of ice water. The PI's plan might work. Time to go with the flow.

"Great," Mulville said. "Now, let's have some dessert. Got to make the most of this dinner. I may not be able to afford eating for much longer given the crowd I'm running with."

———— ∿∿ ————

The winter morning looked and felt gloomy. Kirk glanced at Mulville in the passenger's seat as he returned to the brick house in Arlington. Mulville constantly seemed to be annoyed, as testified to by his downturned mouth. Not even the piping hot coffee Kirk had handed him had gotten the line of his mouth to turn up. Luckily, the ride to suburban Virginia wasn't long.

"Let's go to the boy's school first." Mulville pointed to the next exit.

Wow. Kirk had been trying forever to convince him to investigate the school pick-up, and the FBI man had already gotten directions. Mulville was capitulating. No wonder he looked displeased. Not easy for him to admit being wrong.

"Great idea," Kirk said. "I'll tell the widow we'll be late."

He swerved the car onto the exit. Directions to the school came from Mulville's phone and Kirk followed the pleasant woman's voice. Anything constituted an improvement over Mulville's groaning.

The Capitol Hill Elementary School was a red brick building, low and wide, at the end of a cul-de-sac. Kirk pulled into the parking lot and followed the signs to drop-off parking. At 9:24 AM, the dropping-off for the day was over. Mulville got out first, finished his coffee in several noisy gulps, and skillfully tossed the paper cup into a nearby trash can.

"Let me do the talking," he said. "If someone is messing with the Secret Service, I'll have his ass."

He didn't wait for Kirk's consent. Kirk followed Mulville's determined steps to the school's entrance, which featured an impressive white awning. An American flag flapped in the wind at the center of a small front yard.

A bell rang as the door swung open under Mulville's hand. A middle-aged woman with round black-rimmed glasses and unnatural-looking red hair looked up from a desk. Children's work, from writing to math to art, plastered the light beige walls. A banner hung from the ceiling welcoming visitors to the school. The woman stood up. Her gray-blue eyes conveyed mild puzzlement. Kirk couldn't blame her. Mulville looked more like someone on his way to a karate match than to a parent-teacher conference.

"May I help you?" she said. A wide smile produced a multitude of wrinkles at both sides of her maroon-glossed mouth.

"FBI." Mulville showed his badge. He pointed a finger behind him. "And Agent Miner. We're here on official business."

"I'm Amy Pancost," she said, coming around to the other side of her desk. "Head of school. Please follow me to my office."

A narrow black skirt covered her skinny legs to the calves. A plain pink sweater opened in front over a buttoned-up white blouse with small lavender embroidery on the narrow collar. Memories of his childhood teachers flashed in Kirk's mind. After a few steps, she opened a door and waved the two men in. Amy Pancost sat on a blue upholstered chair behind an old wooden desk occupied by a large computer screen and several metal trays with colored labels. The men sat on two matching armchairs on the opposite side. She seemed relaxed, as if accustomed to dealing with high-ranking government personnel.

"This is about Jeff," Mulville said in his usual cutting-to-the-chase style. "The son of the former White House Chief of Staff. Five days ago, the day his father passed away, the boy was picked up from school by an unauthorized individual."

Amy Pancost turned pale. She took a breath but no words came out. Kirk feared she soon might need emergency CPR.

"But," she mumbled, "this is absolutely impossible. We have the highest security for our children. As you may know, the children of many presidents have attended our school. And we've never, ever—"

"Can you describe the procedure you follow for pick-ups?" Kirk asked.

"Certainly." The woman seemed relieved to turn to Kirk. "The students' parents give us a list containing a maximum of four people allowed to pick up their children. When someone comes in, we check their ID and have the person sign an electronic document."

She turned to the computer's keyboard. The clicking of keys filled the silence. Mulville drummed his fingers on the armchair and stared at a poor reproduction of a Monet painting behind Amy's desk.

"You're talking about last Wednesday," she said. Her eyes didn't look up from her computer.

She didn't wait for an answer. Her hand made a gesture for the men to come around the desk. Mulville and Kirk got up and approached, one on each side of her. Kirk smelled a fresh scent. The screen displayed a scrawl. Next to it was a typed name.

"This," Amy pointed at the squiggle, "is the Secret Service agent's signature—Carl Bounty."

"This," Mulville said, marking the screen with a spray of spit, "is bullshit."

The woman looked shrunken and hurt to the core. She turned to Kirk as if searching for support. Nice job, Mulville.

"We're complying with all regulations," she whispered. "They forced us to go all- electronic. Agent Bounty is one of four people listed to pick Jeff up."

Mulville reached for his phone and took a picture of the signature. Amy waited, then scrolled the page to the right. Another typed named appeared: Amy Pancost.

"I checked his ID." She jerked her finger at her own name. "Matched his picture badge with his face. We use your database."

"Show me." Mulville pointed his finger at the screen.

Amy's manicured fingers went to work again. The picture of a clean-shaven man in his late thirties, with a buzz haircut, appeared on the screen. Kirk stared at him.

"That," Kirk said, "is the Secret Service agent I saw at the widow's house. But the boy told me he wasn't the one who picked him up."

"But," the woman said, looking from Kirk to Mulville and then back at Kirk, "that's impossible. I —"

"Do you know this man personally?" Mulville pointed at the picture.

"Not really." The woman's head jerked back. "He rarely comes. Usually, the mom picks Jeff up. I know her well. Do you know how many Secret Service agents come and go here? How can we remember them all? We trust your database."

"Very well," Mulville said. "Thank you very much, Ms. Pancost."

He took one last picture of the screen with his phone. His other hand waved Kirk out as he stormed through the door. Kirk shook the sweaty hand of a flabbergasted Ms. Pancost. His words of apology didn't seem to be of much comfort. When he got back to the car, Mulville stood, leaning on the passenger door.

"It's a fucking inside job," Mulville said, as if talking to himself. "They must've switched the pictures. Only an insider can manipulate the frigging database."

The drive to Arlington was silent. Mulville walked up, badge in hand, to the two pillar-like Secret Service men at the door. Kirk smiled and wished them good morning. Neither agent showed any desire to frisk them. The men must've known the FBI was coming.

"What's your name?" Mulville asked Carl, the man in the database picture.

"Carl Bounty, sir," he said without moving.

Mulville looked at Carl Bounty from head to toe, brought out his phone, found the ID picture from the computer screen, and held it side by side with the agent's face. The man remained motionless except for blinking several times.

"How long have you been in the service?" Mulville asked.

"Three years."

"How long with the Chief's family?"

"One year."

Mulville seemed satisfied. He withdrew the phone and scrolled to the signature picture. He stretched his arm out, phone turned toward Carl's face.

"Is this your signature?"

The Secret Service man's head moved closer to the phone. His eyes squinted. He cleared his voice.

"Sir," he said, "it's difficult to tell with these electronic signatures. The computer changes them as you sign. But if it's the signature of the man who picked up Jeff from school, it isn't mine. I didn't pick him up, as I told the Chief himself on the night he died."

"The Chief?" Kirk said. "He asked you?"

"Yes, sir."

Nothing like the realization that his son was in danger to subdue the father into blind obedience. Kirk winced. He couldn't blame the Chief.

"Thanks," Mulville said.

He pointed to the door. The agent nodded. Mulville rang the bell.

The blond widow in black greeted them and accepted the FBI's condolences. She showed them into the living room. Kirk took the couch. Mulville and the woman sat on the matching armchairs. Tea came in the same ceramic cups Kirk had drunk from during the first visit. Mulville didn't seem one for tea, but the freezing weather must've taken its toll. He poured himself some hot liquid and held the cup with both hands.

"As I explained on the phone," Kirk said, "we'd like to talk again to Jeff."

The widow nodded and went to summon him. Jeff walked in wearing jeans and a thick white sweater, hair still wet from a shower. He shook hands with Kirk, whom he recognized. He nodded at Mulville as Mom made introductions.

"Son." Mulville leaned forward. "We need your help to find out what happened the day the man made you give the letter to your dad."

The boy fidgeted with his hands. His mother sat back on her chair, looking worried. The poor boy seemed to be on a roller coast of guilt. Kirk had to save the day.

"Jeff." Kirk patted the couch with his hand. "Let's forget the letter for now. I'm going to show you pictures of several Secret Service agents. Tell me if you see the man who picked you up from school."

Mulville's head moved back, his eyes dilated. He seemed to get ready to object, but only a deep breath came from his mouth. The boy complied. His shoulders slumped as he positioned himself next to Kirk. He stared at the china cups, while Kirk placed his tablet on the coffee table and opened up the Secret Service file. Several pictures of men and women appeared on the screen. Kirk moved the screen in front of the boy and Jeff looked at the many faces. Jeff bit his lower lip with his front teeth. Kirk watched him and scrolled to the next batch of images. The boy shook his head at each page. Carl's picture appeared. The boy's head jerked up for a second, apparently in recognition of the familiar agent.

"How are you doing?" Kirk asked. "Anyone remind you of the man who picked you up?"

The boy shook his head. His mouth drew to a tight line, and his eyes looked sad. He had gotten to the end. No results.

"It's okay," Kirk said. "It's difficult to remember things just looking at pictures. Maybe we can try something else."

Jeff seemed to perk up a little. Electronic clicking filled the silence as Kirk found a different file. He turned the tablet toward the mother, and she leaned forward to look. Mulville's eyes rolled up to look at the ceiling.

"Ma'am." Kirk pointed at the screen. "See if you recognize the cleaning woman who came in the night before your husband—"

"We have a statement from Secret Service Agent Bounty," Mulville said, interrupting. "He couldn't find her name anywhere. Too bad the idiot waited until the morning-after to check it out. When are we going to cut to the chase and do what we came here to do?"

Kirk grabbed Mulville's biceps, but his fingers were unable to curl around the large muscles. He leaned toward the FBI agent across the coffee table.

"Soon," Kirk whispered. "I want everyone to relax, get comfortable. We have only one chance."

Mulville nodded and slumped back into his chair, blowing a loud sigh of impatience. Soon, his large body went still, his eyes closed, and his fingers intertwined on his abdomen. For a moment, Kirk was afraid Mulville would start snoring.

"How are you doing?" Kirk asked the widow. "Any luck with the cleaning lady?"

She shook her head, much as her son had. Kirk felt sorry for her.

"It's all right," Kirk said. "It helps either way. Now, I'm going to have Jeff try to remember more of the letter to his dad."

She looked up, a frown appearing on her white forehead.

"I need some familiar paper and pens," he said. "Something Jeff uses regularly for his homework."

The woman nodded, got up, and walked out. She came back with a pad and a couple of pens. Kirk smiled with apprehension.

"Here," she said. "Do you want me to stay with you?"

"No," Kirk answered. "If you don't mind, I'd like to try alone. It worked well the first time."

Jeff's eyes filled with anxiety at the sight of the pad and pens. Kirk's concern grew. Poor Jeff. Fear and sorrow were returning—like a conditioned reflex. Mulville opened his eyes and sat up straight, as if ready for action. Kirk felt like a juggler in a circus ring.

"Jack," Kirk pleaded to Mulville, "can you let me and Jeff work on this alone for a moment or two?"

Mulville's face turned reddish. It was a gamble, but Kirk had to take it. The boy would never open up with Mulville around. Mulville took a folded paper out of his shirt pocket, threw it on the table, and left the room without a word. Kirk picked up Mulville's discarded paper, unfolded it, and found the presidential line of succession. He took in a breath of relief and realized he had stopped breathing for several seconds.

"Jeff," Kirk said, placing the pad and pens in front of the boy, "if you help me, we're going to make sure the bad men don't hurt anyone else like they hurt you and your dad."

"But," the boy said, his eyes shiny, "it was my letter that hurt Daddy."

"No, Jeff," Kirk said, holding the boy's shoulder. "It was not your letter that made Daddy sick. These people are very bad, but we can stop them if you help me."

The boy nodded. He sat up straight on the couch. Great kid.

"I'm going to read you some words," he instructed Jeff. "And you let me know which ones were on the letter. You can try writing them down, if it helps you to remember. Okay? You said you wrote the word secret. Was it secret, or might it have been a longer word, like secretary?"

The boy stared into space, thinking. Kirk's breath got shallower. Then Jeff's face lit up.

"Yes," he said. "Secretary. A difficult word."

Jeff wrote secretary. He looked up at Kirk as if seeking approval. Then his eyes stared at the pad.

"Great," Kirk said. "You're doing great. I'm going to give you a few more words. See if you remember if you read them or not."

Kirk looked at the line of succession. Mulville had said the Chief would usually pick cabinet members way down in the list. Better start at the end. Kirk's finger scrolled down to the last name.

"Do you remember reading Homeland Security?" Kirk asked

"Umm," the boy said, His tongue swiped his upper lip. "No. Not that one."

"Okay," Kirk said. "What about Veterans' Affairs?"

"No." The boy showed no hesitation.

Kirk paused. If only he could get some advice on how to conduct the experiment. Go quickly? Slow down? How did a mind of an eight-year-old second-grader work? No time to consult anyone. He had to go on.

"How about Education?" he said. "Does it ring any bells?"

The boy's face lit up. Kirk sat up straight. Something was happening.

"Try writing it," Kirk said, pushing the paper closer to Jeff.

The boy held the paper steady and started writing. After the first two letters, he looked up.

"Give me more," he told Kirk. "It starts with an E. But this one is too long."

Kirk's finger moved up to the previous name on the list. He felt a jolt.

"How about Energy?" Kirk asked.

The boy's hand tightened around the pen. He drew two horizontal lines over the letters E and D next to the word secretary. Then Jeff traced each letter of the new word without interruptions. Energy. Secretary of Energy. Kirk felt a weight lifting. Jeff put the pen down.

Kirk tore the paper from the pad and held it between two fingers. "Great. So, the letter said Secretary of Energy?"

Jeff nodded, staring at the table. He didn't look as certain as Kirk would have liked. Sorrow still filled the boy's large eyes.

"I guess," the boy said. "I'm really tired now. Can I go?"

"Sure." Kirk patted the boy's shoulder. "You helped our investigation. Just like in the movies."

The boy's mouth stretched into a subtle smile of pride. He got up, waved his palm in farewell, and left the room. Mulville marched closer, as if he had been waiting impatiently for this moment.

"It figures," he said, glancing at the boy's writing.

More sarcasm. There was a limit to the abuse Kirk could stand. He had gotten as far as he could,

"What figures?" Kirk said, keeping his tone down. "You of all people, always criticizing, cursing. Never happy with anything around you."

"I can't possibly be happy about this." Mulville chuckled. "The boy must be right. Unfortunately."

"So?" Kirk threw the paper on the coffee table. "What's the problem then?"

"The reason I'm so sure this is our man," Mulville said, an ominous calm in his voice, "is because the Energy guy is the worst possible man the Chief could pick."

"Why?" Kirk asked. "What's wrong with him?"

"The Secretary of Energy's first allegiance," Mulville said, inching his thumb toward his mouth, "is to the bottle. He's a lush."

"And you know this how?" Kirk asked.

"First hand." Mulville winked like a buddy conspirator. "More than once I drove him home and pulled his pants off to put him to bed. Top secret."

"Great." Kirk slumped back on the couch. "Glad my tax money goes to good use. Why don't you call the FBI Director and tell him everything? Shouldn't be too difficult to reappoint some better candidate and defuse the whole thing."

Mulville froze. His blue-gray eyes shone like ice cubes. He knew something he wasn't sure he wanted to share. Well, this time he would have to talk.

"What's the matter?" Kirk asked.

Mulville moved to the couch. A whiff of Mulville's strong after-shave irritated Kirk's nostrils.

"Energy man and the FBI chief—" Mulville whispered, holding together his index and middle-finger. "Don't make me go into details, please."

"So," Kirk said, "if the director cares about him, he wouldn't want him to be killed. Chances are that's what's going to happen, if we allow this to play out without changing anything."

Mulville waved his hand as if to silence him. No. Kirk couldn't stand by and watch someone die, knowing he could've saved him. He'll do it alone if he has to. He would call the FBI director himself.

"Watch." Mulville grabbed his phone.

A stream of secretaries and receptionists, and several minutes of holding in the company of patriotic music, and finally the FBI director's voice filled the room from the speakerphone. Mulville distanced the phone from his ear and held it midway between himself and Kirk. He placed his index finger on his mouth to silence the detective.

"Yes, Mulville," the male voice boomed. "What's more important than what I'm busy with?"

Mulville gave him a full report—from the heart attacks and the strokes, to Jeff handing the letter to his dad, and the Chief's death by aortic dissection. He went on with the fake Secret Service guy picking up the boy from school, and closed with a plea to assign the designated survivor task to a different cabinet member. The story, told by Mulville, didn't sound as compelling as Kirk would have wanted. Kirk's apprehension grew.

"So, let me summarize," the director said. "You want me to take away the fun and privilege to be a designated survivor for the first time in one's career, and why? Because of a letter you don't have, and the testimony of a distressed eight-year-old son, all while a confessed criminal is already in custody. Is that it or am I missing something?"

"Silvana Moretti," Mulville said, lifting his index finger as if he wanted to get permission to speak, "was already in custody when the Chief of Staff got his letter and died."

"That," the FBI chief said, "is proof that the Chief's demise has nothing to do with your conspiracy theory."

Silence followed. Mulville's eyes spoke a loud "I told you so." Kirk took a breath to speak. Mulville silenced him again, this time by drawing two fingers across his throat.

"Listen." The director's voice was calm. "You know better than I. We get much worse threats than this every single day. If we stopped what we were doing after each one of them, we'd be paralyzed. I'll talk to the Secretary of Energy myself and let you know if he wants to be replaced. Don't count on it, though. He was always wondering why the Chief never picked him."

Mulville's clear eyes went up inside his lids. Kirk got ready to speak up again. The agent threw him an incensed glance.

"What about security?" Mulville asked, his voice loud and clear, probably for Kirk's benefit. "Can we at least forbid all electronics at the State of the Union? Can we warn government officials about the possibility of a threat?"

"Yes to the first," the director said. "No to the second. Don't want unwarranted panic. Got to go now. Give me a full written report about this."

Mulville glanced at his phone with a look of contempt. For the first time, he seemed somewhat deflated. He was human, after all.

"I'm not the only prick at the FBI," he said, an unlikely hint of an apology surfacing in Mulville's eyes. "He'll wipe his ass with the written report."

Then Mulville focused on the background. Kirk turned. The woman in black stood behind them.

"Are you still on official government business?" she asked. "Do you need us anymore?"

Had the woman heard Mulville's last conversation? Mulville's curses wouldn't testify to his professionalism. Kirk's face got hot with shame. At least it had gotten half a smile from the poor widow. People like her and Jeff deserved better, and Kirk would make sure they got it.

"We're done, ma'am," Kirk said. "Jeff was very helpful. We got what we needed to do our job. Now it's up to us."

He pushed back from the couch. Mulville followed. At the door, the widow gave them their coats and shook their hands.

Mulville pulled at the door handle twice before Kirk could release the passenger door latch. Kirk slid onto the cold seat and wrapped his gloved hands around the steering wheel. It felt like a block of ice. The start of the engine disrupted the winter's stillness. Hot air blasted in. Frozen droplets started to melt on the windshield. Not much longer before Kirk could hug Aurora and Peter. Mulville and this entire mess would be behind him.

He drove. Mulville sat, his hands deep in his coat, eyes closed, silent. Kirk had done everything he could. Now it was up to Mulville. What was the FBI going to do? Thoughts swirled in Kirk's head, nagging him. If Kirk just went home now, Jeff's help might be for nothing. How could Kirk look at Peter, knowing that Jeff's dad had died for nothing? What about Patrizia? She would die for nothing too. And Silvana? She would rot in jail for crimes she had no intention of committing. Something had to be done with the information he and Mulville had obtained.

"I'm going to embed with the designated survivor," Kirk said. "Arrange for me to be one of his Secret Service agents."

Kirk heard nothing in return. Good. Better than the curses he had expected from Mulville. All he heard were sounds of the windshield wipers swiping.

"Yeah, right." Mulville sounded as if he was waking up from a nap. "We're in good shape. An inexperienced, handicapped PI going undercover as an agent. If anything, I should go."

"Don't be ridiculous," Kirk said. "I'm sure everyone knows you."

Mulville laughed. That was a first. Kirk wondered if the agent's face would crack.

"The curse of being famous," Mulville said. "You don't think it's enough we make sure nothing happens to the President and all those attending the State of the Union address?"

"How sure are you that you can prevent an attack?" Kirk asked. "What about all those strange devices, and Silvana refusing to cooperate with us because of her daughter?"

Kirk listened to more windshield wiper sounds. Was he crazy to volunteer for a possibly suicidal mission? Aurora would never forgive him. Mulville would block it anyway. Home sweet home. Soon.

"How can I be sure?" Mulville said. "I hope all this is just to spread terror. I can't believe that, with all the security and the ban on electronics, they can take down the entire government."

Kirk remained silent.

"But one thing still bothers me," Mulville said.

"What?" Kirk asked.

Something definitely bothered Mulville. The fact that he was sharing that concern with him sent a chill down Kirk's spine.

"Why did they go through all that shit about the designated survivor?" Mulville said. "Kidnapping a kid, making him carry the letter, killing the poor bastard Chief. What for? Unless they've got a plan to go all in?"

Mulville was right. If the purpose was only terror, the terrorist would've made some threatening announcement about the State of the Union address to spread panic. No need to have all the stuff in place about the designated survivor.

"The designated survivor," Mulville said, "seems to be the focus. The key part of the play."

"You've got to get me in," Kirk said. "One of us has to be there when the plan goes down. It's the only way to have some control."

"You fucking sure about that?" Mulville asked. "Got a way to block the deadly ultrasounds? I don't think our consultant jail-bird will be forthcoming about this."

"Perhaps Steve can get that information from her," Kirk said. "I don't think she wants more people to get hurt."

"Are you crazy?" Mulville bellowed, making Kirk's hands shake around the steering wheel. "What don't you understand about not involving civilians? Now more than ever."

"He may be the only chance we have to convince her to help us."

"You can't talk about any of this to anyone. If you do, I'll kill you myself. Understood?"

"Yes, sir." One thing was sure. Mulville wouldn't cut it with Silvana. Kirk was the next best person after Steve. "I'll try myself. I think I may have a chance if I go alone. She trusts me."

How sure was Kirk about Silvana? Sure enough to risk making his son an orphan and his wife a widow? His very life might depend on her willingness to help. And her expertise.

"If Moretti doesn't hurry up and talk," Mulville said, "her daughter is done for. She may be done for already. The sooner that idiot scientist accepts that fact, the sooner we can do our job. People are stupid by nature."

"You can't judge," Kirk said. "You don't have kids."

"But you do, don't you?" Mulville said. "Why don't you go home to him and your wife?"

"And miss all the fun you're going to have?" Kirk grinned and gazed at Mulville sideways. "Are you going to get me in or not?"

"Do you really want to end my career?" Mulville said. "The director will have my ass on a platter."

"Or you may turn out to be a hero," Kirk said, "if we turn out to be right and we succeed. If we're wrong, nobody is going to know I was in the Secret Service for one evening."

"And if we're right and don't succeed," Mulville said, "it won't make any difference either."

"There you go." Kirk suppressed a laugh. "So? What do you think? Do you have a better plan?"

Why was he insisting? The answer was simple. There were things in his life Kirk knew he couldn't live without. Like his wife Aurora. And then there were things he couldn't live with. Like finding out about some disaster knowing he could've tried to avert it. This was one of the latter. Aurora would understand. That was why he couldn't live without her. Kirk would have to call her tonight.

"Have it your way," Mulville said. "For the record, Miner, I'm going along with this suicidal plan, not because I'm looking forward to being a hero. No, I'm just trying hard not to compete with my superior for the stupidity trophy."

"I understand." Kirk grinned. "That's a valid reason."

"You're all right, Sherlock." Mulville nodded.

"But you," Kirk said, savoring every word, "are a pain in the ass."

CHAPTER 23

THE HYZAARS

Patrizia Moretti's breaths came in short gasps. She didn't mind the exercise. Trampoline was one of her favorite activities at gymnastics classes, and she was good at it. Her back flip had improved with hard work and practice. The motion had become so automatic that now she had to order her thigh muscles not to send her body into a spin that would land her on concrete pavement.

As she bounced on the worn-out mini-trampoline, she looked down at her designer sneakers. This wasn't her gymnastics class. And the room wasn't her gym. She looked up and froze inside. She hated the muscular man sitting in front of her. His biceps stuck out of a white t-shirt, and black curly hair protruded from the V-neck collar. Disgusting.

With each bounce, her budding breasts rubbed against her sweatshirt. And the man remained fixed on her chest. Her cheeks got hotter—much hotter than the light exercise would dictate. If only she could stop. Mom had mentioned she needed a bra. The two of them were supposed to go buy one together after the holidays. Would she ever get that bra? She missed Mom. Hadn't heard from her since—. Why would Mom send her away with these people?

Something was wrong. When Mom told her to go with the short woman with the scarf, she had tears in her eyes. Mom looked so scared that Patrizia got scared too. And then they both started to cry. The woman with the scarf pulled her away from Mom. Tears came back to Patrizia's eyes now. Her ponytail bounced on her back with every jump. What kind of a life had she gotten into?

For the past five days, she had been sitting in a room furnished only with a narrow bed, a chair, and a small desk. At odd hours every couple of days, the woman asked her to jump on the trampoline. And she always made Patrizia wear the special watch Mom had given her. Mom had promised she'd be away only for ten days and then they'd be back together. Patrizia had kept a close count of the passing days. Five more days left. One more shower. The rare showers in the small bathroom were kind of awkward. What would happen there today? A spasm ran through her body.

The woman with the scarf was nowhere in sight. The disgusting muscle man with that jagged scar on his neck had taken her place. His narrow dark eyes were still stuck on her body. Droplets ran down her face. Some fell to the trampoline. Patrizia's hands came up from the sides and crossed in front of her chest. The man's face twisted into a smirk.

"Faster," he said. "And move your arms up and down, will you? We need much harder exercise than this."

Kirk looked at Silvana across the glass in the jail meeting room. The changes he had witnessed reminded him of the novel "The Picture of Dorian Gray." In the book, a portrait painting got worse and worse as the man in the picture committed all sort of sins. Here, Silvana deteriorated while someone else did the sinning. Poor Silvana. Could she survive the next few days until the terrible ordeal ended? But what would the end be like? Kirk couldn't begin to imagine. Dread filled his chest.

The only thing in his control right now was to get information to help him do his job. Good thing Mulville had gotten him an emergency appointment at the jail. The purpose and scope of the criminal undertakings remained uncertain, while the person at their so called fulcrum, sat in front of him. This beautiful, smart woman was slowly crumbling into pieces.

"Silvana," he whispered into his phone handset, "what happened to you?"

She shook her head, eyes fixed on the floor. Her knuckles whitened from the effort of holding her handset.

"Tell me about the watch," she said. "Is the heartbeat still there?"

"Not that I know of," Kirk said. "It seems that these people know when the watch is with you."

She remained silent. Her mouth stretched out a little more. How could she bear more pain?

"Silvana, these are brutal people who have no respect for other human beings. And we know your daughter is in their hands. Agent Mulville and I suspect that these criminals are carrying out a very destructive plan of action. Perhaps some sort of massacre. Or worse. Do you know anything about that?"

She sat slumped, pasty faced. A beautiful existence destroyed in such a short time. How could he reach someone who seemed already gone?

"You can put an end to this," he said, unable to keep his voice steady. "For God's sake, Silvana. Please."

"I can't," she moaned.

"I'm going undercover," he said, looking into her unfocussed eyes, "to try to prevent this disaster. Can you at least give me some advice on how to defend myself? How can we block deadly ultrasounds, and how can I prevent my aorta from shattering again? Because, if that happens, I will die for sure, together with God knows how many other innocent people."

Silence.

"I have a son two years younger than your daughter. His name is Peter. He's waiting for me to come home, together with my wife Aurora."

More silence. Her lids half-shielded her beautiful eyes. Kirk had to find a way to get to her. It was then or never.

"Silvana," he added in a last attempt to shock life back into a seemingly soulless corpse, "if I don't succeed, your daughter will be among the casualties."

Silvana looked like a cornered animal, but this time Kirk was on her side.

Her eyes darted all around. She took a breath. He watched her going through all the options in her beautiful mind. Kirk found it difficult to breathe.

"Foam." She bit her upper lip, then her lower lip. "Talk to Don Emerson, my post-doc. The password is perfluorohexane."

Kirk took out his phone and his thumbs went to work. After he showed his notes to Silvana, she proceeded to make the necessary spelling corrections. After Silvana stopped typing, her hands went to the sides of her face. A moment later, she got up and ran to the back of the room to summon the guard. The thumps of her fists on the door filled the silence.

Aziz Hyzaar took a large bite of his apple. A burst of juicy sweetness permeated his tongue. He wondered if the black-haired girl would taste as sweet. His rubber shoes squeaked as he walked along the corridor from the small apartment's kitchen-dining area toward the bathroom. He looked at the yellow line of light under the old wooden door, swallowed, and grinned. But his smile froze. What would his uncle say about that kind of thought? Sex outside the blessing of marriage was prohibited by the Faith.

Aziz had obeyed the Faith during all his twenty-eight years. He could proudly testify to a strict, monk-like adherence to the ideal of sacrificing the flesh for the spirit. Given all that he had accomplished so far and what he was working on at present, he must deserve some reward. Why wouldn't he be allowed to have one little virgin now, if he was going to get seventy of them by the end of the week? In just a few days, Aziz would be in the Palace of Pearls in Paradise, with seventy courts of ruby and seventy houses of green emerald stone. In every house, a mattress of every color, and on every mattress, a dark-eyed virgin would await him. Nothing wrong with him getting a small advance on his holy reward.

He wiped the apple's wetness on his jeans and curled his fingers around the bathroom's door knob. The rush of water muted the soft sound of the slight door opening. His engineering background made it easy to jam a puny lock. The girl hadn't even noticed. At least he heard no protests from her. He walked into the room. The hot smell of steam hit his nostrils. The girlish silhouette appeared and disappeared behind the shower's foggy glass. Her arms were up in the air, swinging and wiping.

He took a breath. A mixture of pleasure and unfulfilled anticipation rose from his groin to his chest. Soon, the soft white flesh of the unholy infidel would be his. He would teach the little bitch a lesson. This wasn't a sin. The entity in front of him wasn't human. She was less than an animal, less than a thing. Just an unholy infidel who would die. He felt his blood vessels dilate. Sweat poured from his pores. His fingers undid the buttons of his shirt, and he dropped the garment onto the wet floor. The black hair on his chest glistened with moisture

"What do you think you're doing!" The woman's voice behind him startled him.

A vise-like pressure encircled his arm and pulled Aziz away from his reward. He stumbled back through the door and had to keep from tripping on his discarded shirt. The corridor's air chilled his sweat. He heard the door swing shut and turned to face his sister. She stood in her masculine-looking uniform of baggy pants and top. A badge carrying her name and cleaning service credentials dangled from her neck. A white scarf kept thick black hair away from her face. Tashfeen's eyes looked at him, loaded with anger and loathing.

"You." She pointed a finger at his naked chest. "You hypocrite. This is how you follow your Faith?"

Aziz pulled his arm from her grip. What was wrong with his sister? Had America messed with her mind? He would have to remind her how to behave properly

"You're teaching me about Faith?" he muttered under his breath. "If it weren't for me, you'd be lost to our degenerate parents."

"What about our parents?" she said. "You have no right—"

"Americanized." He spat on the floor. "Prostituted to a life of greed and cut-throat tactics, pledging allegiance to the infidels' rules instead of Allah's. I have every right."

Tashfeen took a step back. Her shoulders slumped and she looked down at the floor.

"Who showed you the fundamental conflict between Faith and the West?" he said. "Who got our names back—Aziz and Tashfeen, instead of those grotesque American slurs?"

Rage grew at the thought of his parents. Their shame about their Faith had made them change everything. They had often referred to Aziz as their "American child." Aziz hated his American name. For as long as he could remember, he had felt like a foreigner in his country of birth. Luckily for him, his old uncle had come to the rescue and mentored him, providing his fertile mind with proper religious guidance. Aziz had finally understood why America, which represented everything sinful and unholy, deserved annihilation.

"But—" Tashfeen pointed at the bathroom. "Compromising the most important mission of our life for—"

"Shut up." Heat invaded his neck and chest. "While you enjoyed your childlike existence, I've been preparing for this mission all my life, enduring years of total isolation to retain my purity. All so I could pass the stupid polygraph test to enter the agency. It was hell."

"But you did it." Tashfeen's mouth stretched into a timid smile. "All those months at the training center and at the academy in Washington. At last, you are where you need to be, an officer of the Secret Service of the United States. You have everything you need to fulfill your mission, including your perfectly legal American name to open all doors for you. And now you risk everything for a girl?"

Aziz thought about the months he had spent at the Secret Service's Training Academy. The infidels had instructed him in everything he needed to achieve his goal—self-defense techniques, emergency medicine, survival skills, physical fitness, firearms, psychology. He was ready.

"Listen." Aziz let go of a sigh. "It's not what you think."

"You weren't lusting after the infidel girl?" Tashfeen pointed again at the bathroom door. "You've been forever instructing me not to desire anything but our Faith and the Paradise awaiting us. I gave up everything. I did what you asked. I even killed for you."

What had he done? Tashfeen was right to be angry, and he should feel grateful. She had saved him from the worst mistake of his life, right now, when he needed all his energy and focus.

"No, Tashfeen." His hand touched her cheek. "You did what you did for our cause. Our Faith. I thank you for showing me the right way in a moment of weakness."

He walked to his room, took a clean shirt out of a battered dresser, and covered himself. As if by reflex, he bent his knees onto a worn rug and lowered his face to the floor's bare wooden planks. Prayers for forgiveness filled the room like moans of despair.

Inside the bathroom, Patrizia stepped out of the shower. Her foot landed on something soft and cottony: a man's shirt. The disgusting man's shirt. She withdrew her foot as if she had stepped onto hot coals. Her heart felt as if it was out of sync for a moment. Her hands grabbed a worn discolored towel from the rack and she tightened it around her body. The cloth fell short of covering her pubic hair and budding nipples. As she stared at the male garment on the floor, her eyes widened in terror.

CHAPTER 24

FOAM

Kirk rode the number two elevator to the fifth floor of the university's science building. Donald Emerson had agreed to meet him that evening after work. Kirk's life, and perhaps not just his life, depended on the information that would result from the meeting.

The elevator door slid open and Kirk walked to Room 503. The white walls of the corridor held pictures of prominent faculty members of past years. Kirk winced as he paused in front of the door sign before knocking: "Silvana Moretti, PhD." Her name was still there.

The air inside the lab carried a subtle scent of antiseptic. Donald Emerson greeted Kirk with a nod of recognition and a perfunctory handshake. The post-doc wore the same jeans as he did last time, but a different sweatshirt, and no earbuds this time. Emerson motioned the PI to follow him to the back of the room and invited him to sit on a metal stool near the slick black cubic soundwave programmer. The young scientist, looking more relaxed today, obviously assumed the meeting had to do with the same subject as Kirk's first interview. Silvana's arrest must've assuaged his fear of being a suspect. Instead, the young scientist would be the one in charge of Kirk's safety.

"Don." Kirk opened his coat and dropped it on a table after wiping the top with the palm of his hand. "Thanks for seeing me. As I told you on the phone, we need your help urgently. Dr. Moretti told me to contact you and gave me a password to the file with the information we need."

Don looked up. His hand went to his chin. Kirk took out his phone.

"We need advice on how to block soundwaves," Kirk said. "I'll be going on a mission and I need to protect myself from artery-damaging ultrasounds as much as possible."

"Cool." Emerson grinned and rubbed his hands. "Dr. Moretti and I started to work on this just before she left. I've continued on my own after she—. But all this is very preliminary."

With no time to get to the final version. Kirk hoped Emerson had paid close attention to Silvana's teaching.

"Give us what you've got," Kirk said. "We have only a couple of days to make some sort of shield I could wear during my mission."

Emerson swiveled on his stool and went to work on the keyboard. Files populated the screen. He opened one called "Foam Barrier."

"We discovered this almost by chance." He pointed at a series of formulas. "I was testing the effects of different wavelengths. Using the two-syringes method, Dr. Moretti was making foam by injecting air saturated with the gas perfluorohexane into water mixed with sodium dodecyl sulfate."

"What the heck is that?" Kirk asked. "English, please. I need to understand what I'm getting into. My life depends on it."

"Sodium dodecyl sulfate is a surfactant." Emerson looked at Kirk, then added, "something that stabilizes bubbles. We found out because once foam formed, the bubbles expanded greatly without bursting. Then Dr. Moretti asked me to measure the attenuation of ultrasound pulses passing through a layer of foam sandwiched between two polymer films spaced half a millimeter apart."

"And?" Kirk asked. "Give me the latest one. In simple terms."

"At a thickness of one centimeter, the foam can totally block soundwaves." Emerson held up his palms. "It came as a surprise."

"Great," Kirk said. "So this stuff blocks all the damaging ultrasounds?"

"Well." Emerson's brows rose. "Not sure about all. I only tested certain frequencies. It looks like the frequencies the foam blocks depends on the size of the bubble."

Once her daughter was released, Silvana planned to work more on ways to offset the damage done by ultrasound. That the poor woman was dreaming of her daughter's release surely mitigated her actions. Kirk sighed.

"Don," Kirk said, "it might have come as a surprise to you, but it sounds to me that Dr. Moretti was actively working on this when she—had to leave. Perhaps we should look at her files, using her password. We may find more useful material."

"If you wish." Emerson shifted his weight on the stool and switched the user to Dr. Moretti. Many files appeared. "It's probably this one."

He clicked on a file named "Perfluorohexane." His hand jerked. Was Emerson hurt that Kirk wasn't too impressed by his professorial exposition on foam production? Too bad. If Kirk had to bet his life on this foam, the formula might as well come from the master.

"Password she gave me is the same," Kirk said. "Perfluorohexane."

Emerson entered it. The file contained several chemical formulas and several lengthy reports. Emerson focused first on the chemistry.

"I'll be damned." He pointed at the screen. "Dr. Moretti had already figured out what I've tried to find out all these past days. Here is the size of the bubble to block the different waves."

"Great," Kirk said. "See if you can make head and tail of the chemistry. Then we can go to the reports."

"It turns out that we can pick the bubble size for the most likely injury you are trying to prevent," Emerson said. "The shield will work best for that frequency, but not as well for different frequencies."

Emerson looked at Kirk like a fast-food employee waiting for a dine-in order. Kirk let go of his breath and shook his head.

"Okay," he said. "Wait a moment. Let me e-mail the bad guys. See what they're planning."

Emerson kept on staring. No hint of a smile on his face. Perhaps nerds didn't get jokes.

"Look at the English stuff," Kirk said. "Maybe we can get some clues on what's coming next."

Emerson complied. A lengthy description of the experiments and a summary of the results appeared on the screen. Kirk huddled with Emerson at the screen.

"Strange," the post-doc said after several minutes. "The frequencies she tested the most were the one used to damage the aorta. But why didn't she tell me she had already found out all this?"

The thought of shearing pain flashed in Kirk's mind. His hand touched his chest just as he had during that terrible night. He'd rather die than experience the relentless, agonizing pain that nearly sucked all the life out of him.

"I guess we're expecting more aortic dissections," Kirk said. "The other stuff was just a warm-up."

"What are you saying?" Emerson looked up from the screen, wide eyed. "Dr. Moretti programmed the missing chips to cause those dissections and heart attacks?"

Kirk clenched his lips together. He imagined the woman's months of agony.

"I can't discuss details of an ongoing investigation."

"But she didn't." Emerson pointed at the formulas displayed on the screen.

Kirk was stunned by the post-doc's words.

"What are you talking about?" He fished for something in his shirt pocket. "I got this thumb drive with Dr. Moretti's calculations for sound-waves that shatter coronary and carotid arteries, as well as the aorta. I brought it in case you needed that data to plan the shield."

Emerson reached for the stick and plugged it into the computer. Formulas filled the screen. Kirk watched him in silence as he scrolled, examined, and compared.

"These are the same calculations as in the file I just opened," he said. "These sound intensities are too low to cause anything more than minimal inflammation to any arteries, including the aorta."

"Are you sure?" Kirk's voice sounded shrill.

Had Silvana intentionally given the wrong information to the terrorists?

Kirk felt a lightness inside. But heart attacks, strokes, and aortic dissections had occurred and people had died. How?

"You may have to take my word for it." Emerson nodded. "Or Dr. Moretti's. I'm afraid we're the only experts."

"Perhaps," Kirk said, "the terrorist or terrorists we're looking for had enough expertise to take the programming Dr. Moretti did under duress, and hike up the intensities for good measure. What do you think, Don? Is that possible?"

Emerson perked up. The young scientist was back in the expert's seat. After all, he was the only expert Kirk had available for the task.

"That's certainly much more plausible than Dr. Moretti acting like a criminal," he said. "Now that I see all this, I'm pretty sure that's what happened."

"Why?" Kirk said.

"Because," Emerson said, touching the screen, "when she formulated the bubble size to block the soundwaves, she assumed wavelength intensities much higher than the original ones. It was as if she expected the terrorists to increase the dose, and she planned accordingly."

"She expected that," Kirk said, "because she had already seen it happening with the heart attacks and the carotid dissections. The terrorists increased the intensity and innocent people got hurt and died. That's when she knew that her plan had failed, and focused all her remaining time and effort on perfecting a shield for protection against aortic dissection."

That also meant the terrorists would be mighty mad at her. The only reason Patrizia was still alive was the need for them to keep Silvana silent, to make her the scapegoat. The deadline for her usefulness was approaching. Kirk cringed. The new discovery made him forget for a moment the purpose of his visit. Then the importance of the task ahead came back with renewed urgency. Patrizia would need to be rescued before Kirk and Mulville sabotaged the terrorists' masterplan.

"Don," Kirk said, "what can we use to create a protective shield with this kind of foam?"

Emerson acted as if he understood the importance of the question and thoroughly enjoyed answering it. Good. Kirk needed Emerson to give everything he had. It was interesting to watch him think. Eyes to the wall, face relaxed, the young man was in a world of his own.

"It has to be something flexible," Emerson said after some deliberation. "A material able to be molded around the chest, but solid enough to prevent the foam from slushing away or collapsing. And waterproof."

"A garbage bag?" Kirk said.

Emerson looked at him with an earnest expression. Then, his lips stretched, he shook his head.

"Too flimsy," he said. "The foam would shift with gravity. Your chest would be exposed; it would be highly vulnerable."

"What about that bubble stuff used for packages?" Kirk said. "We could put foam inside the bubbles instead of air."

Emerson smiled, as if a bulb had lit up inside his head. His legs jerked to propel his stool backward. He rolled to the end of the counter, to the window and stretched to grab his tablet.

"Genius," he said in Kirk's direction. "Let me call the engineering department. See how busy they are."

Emerson discussed the problem in detail with a woman who sounded just as young, enthusiastic, and nerdy as him. After a pause, the post–doc gestured to Kirk to approach him. Kirk got off his stool. Emerson fetched a measuring tape from a drawer, looped it around Kirk's chest, then called out the dimensions, in inches, into his phone.

"Be ready tomorrow," he said after thanking his buddy. "Who's going to foot the bill?"

Kirk shrugged. Only one entity came to mind.

"The FBI," he said. "But don't send it 'til next week."

Kirk burst into a sad chuckle. Emerson nodded, though not understanding the insider's joke. Kirk gave the scientist high-fives.

After leaving, Kirk walked quickly, eyes to the floor, lost, seemingly, in deep thought. A lot to digest. When he stopped at the elevator, he smiled. Silvana wasn't a criminal or a terrorist. Up to the last minute, she was trying to stop this insanity despite the risk to her daughter. He couldn't wait to let Steve know. He wondered if Mulville would allow at least that much to be revealed to a civilian.

CHAPTER 25

THE LAST SUPPER

The smell of fried grease and beer permeated the air of the Dublin Irish Pub. Despite the fact it was a weekday evening, the place was swarming with enthusiastic sports fans ready to cheer and boo at every opportunity. Kirk took a large sip of pale ale and replaced the frosted mug on a coaster depicting a shamrock. He gazed around the room and relaxed his head against the green, upholstered leather booth. Golden light diffused from wall lanterns to illuminate the bar to his left. The mirrored wall stood plastered with colored liquor bottles and decorative mugs. Martini and wine glasses hung from the ceiling. Singles action appeared to be in full swing.

He closed his eyes and welcomed the slight buzz from the ale. After tomorrow, would he ever be able to enjoy an evening like tonight, or make love to his wife Aurora, or lose at chess to his son Peter? His life as a PI had put him in more than his share of dangerous, even life threatening, circumstances.

But most had arisen from otherwise run-of the mill cases. He had never before volunteered for a semi-suicidal mission. Aurora had reminded him of that fact in no uncertain terms during their conversation this morning. Fear and concern in her voice had turned into panic due to Kirk's unwillingness to reconsider his plan. The chat morphed into an argument and, at the end, outright fighting.

But he couldn't live with himself, let alone look her or Peter in the eye if he gave up without trying his best to stop a possible mass disaster. Explaining the details without throwing Aurora into a frenzy was difficult—no, correction, impossible. Kirk hadn't lied. He experienced guilt-laden relief as he hid behind the "top secret" classification set by Mulville. The final appeal consisted of the technique Kirk reserved for the if-everything-fails circumstances.

"Trust me," he begged Aurora. "This once, I need you to trust me."

Despite receiving insufficient information, Aurora gave him her reluctant support. But the call had left Kirk drained and dissatisfied—another incentive not to die tomorrow. He didn't want this conversation to be her last memory of him. The exchange didn't reflect the deep relationship the two of them had because of life-altering experiences.

"Are you asleep?" a man's voice asked.

Kirk opened his eyes to see Mulville standing in front of him.

"Can't imagine the shit I had to go through to get you into the Secret Service for one day," Mulville said. "That's why I'm late."

Mulville wore his usual black suit, which bulged at the side, and a tie which he loosened before he slid into place beside Kirk. His eyes roamed around the room. Kirk wondered if he was looking for the waitress, checking for danger, or both.

"Hey," Kirk said, putting his palm out to stop Mulville from getting any closer. "Don't sit on this bag. Please."

Kirk picked up a large plastic bag from the bench. He opened the top to show a sheet of bubble wrap. Mulville's eyebrows went up and down.

"That's it?" Mulville asked. "You're going to protect yourself with that junk?"

Kirk nodded. He had to agree with Mulville. The so-called shield looked just like regular bubble wrap. He had to trust Emerson that life-saving foam filled the spaces.

"Emerson filled the bubbles with special sound-blocking foam," Kirk said for his own benefit as much as for Mulville's. "Per Dr. Moretti's instructions."

"Do me a favor: Wear it under a bullet-proof vest," Mulville said, "in case the terrorists fall back on old-fashioned methods."

Kirk nodded. He had been so worried about the damned soundwaves that the possibility of getting shot hadn't entered into his calculations, despite the danger of his mission.

"About Moretti." Kirk nodded at Mulville. "Emerson said the soundwaves' intensity in her formulas would not have caused any significant damage in anybody. And she worked out specs for a shield against the high-intensity waves, in case those terrorists figured out how to use her work for their own ends."

Kirk looked at Mulville. Again, Mulville's eyebrows went up.

"So what?" Mulville said, his hand all but dismissing Kirk's suggestion. "Even if she tried to mitigate her crime, what good did it do? People were hurt and killed, thanks to her science. And she didn't even bother sharing all this info with our experts, who are still trying to make head or tail of all the crap in her computer."

Kirk shook his head and focused on the menu. Mulville slammed his hand on the table.

"What's good here?" Mulville glanced at the waitress approaching. "I see something I like already."

Mulville ordered a beer. The woman distributed menus and rushed away. The men studied the food possibilities in silence. A few minutes later, they ordered two pastramis-on-rye with sides of pickles, coleslaw, and French fries.

"You don't need any soundwaves to get a heart attack," Mulville said, staring at the waitress in the Irish outfit. "You just have to regularly come here for dinner a couple of times a week."

Kirk smiled and nodded. Was this Mulville's way of getting friendly? Mulville took a folded white paper from his front pocket and moved Kirk's mug to make room for it on the table. He spread the paper on the wood and flattened the creases with both hands. A list of names and a row of pictures appeared.

"Here." He pointed at the first name. "As expected, the asshole Secretary of Energy has refused to step down as the designated survivor. Four agents have been assigned to protect him. This one has been around for at least ten years. Decent. Reliable. I once worked in person with him. The other two I've never met. Younger, both active for five or six years. One was requested by the Secretary himself. Apparently, that agent has been with him a few times. Backgrounds check out fine. All born in the U.S. of A. The two from refugee parents may even have a grudge against their own country."

Kirk stretched his neck and tilted his head. He stared at three passport-size pictures and committed the image of the man named Ray to memory with the label "Mulville's guy."

"No Islamic names," Kirk said.

"Way of racial profiling, Sherlock." Mulville slapped Kirk's shoulder. "Do you think all terrorists ride on camels and wear scarves? Unfortunately, most refugees change their names to some Americanized version of the original. After a generation, there's no way to know who's fucking who. And those people who were born here? They all have legal American names to begin with."

"And then there is me." Kirk pointed at his own picture on the paper. "How did you manage?"

The waitress came back with the food. Both men sat up straight. Mulville folded his paper, handing the compacted square to Kirk.

"Review this," he said. "Look at the pictures. Make sure everyone is who they're supposed to be. Not like the guy who fooled that hysterical head of school. Oh, and there's the pilot. Here's his picture as well."

"Thanks," Kirk said, reaching for the paper instead of his pastrami.

"Miner." Mulville held on to the paper. "I'm risking my career for you. Had to call in a couple of heavy-duty IOUs, besides lying and begging to get you in. Don't go dying on me or something. You're gonna be wired and videoed, and protected by bubbles and a bullet-proof vest. And as soon as you smell bullshit, you call it in. No super hero PI stuff. Okay? I'll be ready for you. Won't be far from where you'll be."

Kirk nodded. He grabbed the white square and placed it in his shirt pocket. The pastrami sandwich tasted great. Sharp mustard did the trick.

"I guess this isn't bad for a last supper," Kirk said. "By the way, where am I going?"

Mulville took a gulp of beer, wiped the foam from his lips with the back of his hand, and belched.

"Don't know yet," he said. "Couldn't push my luck that far. You'll have to tell me as you go. So I can follow you with backup."

Could this hulk of a man actually protect him? Somehow, Kirk felt reassured. Or perhaps the alcohol was kicking in. He hoped Mulville's FBI skills beat his social ones.

"Okay," Kirk said. "So, what's my next step?"

"Tonight you'll receive some encrypted e-mail with everything you need to know." Mulville pointed at Kirk. "You can find instructions about decoding the encryption in the same paper I gave you. I don't have to tell you to keep it in a safe place."

"Does the paper self-destruct?" Kirk asked. Nervousness made him chuckle. "Do I have to read it in a hurry?"

The usual Mulville would have shaken his head scornfully, but not tonight. The guy was going soft. If he didn't know better, Mulville seemed to actually care about him, though his main concern probably was his own ass.

"I'll meet you at your hotel to get you ready," Mulville said. "Sometime in the morning. I'll call you. This is no joke, Miner. If we're right, you may be up against the worst, most dangerous people of your career. You're not used to terrorists. You've no idea what they're capable of. Movies or novels don't constitute adequate training for what you're getting into."

"Thanks," Kirk said. "But I'm no fool."

"And remember that your aorta is kept open by a metal umbrella of some sort." Mulville pointed at Kirk's chest and wiped his mouth with a paper napkin.

"Mulville, I'm aware my stent-graft is still bare, susceptible to clotting, and not ready to be traumatized by waves, punches, or bullets. Thank you very much for spoiling a painfully built, beer-induced mind-fog, and for rendering me scared shitless even before I get started."

Mulville smiled. Kirk drank the last drop from his mug, Mulville ordered new drinks for the two of them, and the waitress returned in a flash.

Mulville lifted his mug to Kirk. "To tomorrow. Let's get the fucking bastards."

Kirk lifted his mug, touched Mulville's, and took a sip. Something in the back of his head bothered him. He had meant to ask Mulville about it. Aurora's ordeal had taken precedence in his mind, pushing the other issue to a lower rank of urgency.

"Mulville," he said, "what about the other agents? Shouldn't we warn them? Give them the same kind of bubble protection?"

Mulville darted him with a "you've-got-to-be-kidding-me" look. He took a few sips of his beer. Was he counting to ten before answering?

"Perhaps you should get packing." Mulville looked grave with worry. "That's what I mean when I say you've got no clue whom you're dealing with. Let me explain."

Mulville took another sip of beer, centered his mug on the coaster, and belched again. Kirk smelled the pastrami on his breath.

"The Chief's son was picked up by a fake Secret Service agent," he said. "Someone fucked with the database to make it look kosher. I bet one of the other three stooges on your team tomorrow is fake and, as we say with political correctness, fucking radicalized. Which one do you want to gift-wrap in bubbles? All of them? So, if one or more of them are undercover terrorists, they'll know you're also wrapped in bubbles and will blow out your brains instead of your fucking aorta?"

Kirk nodded. "I guess we're doing everything we can with what we've got. No sense in becoming a martyr. It would defeat the whole purpose."

"Exactly." Mulville pointed at Kirk. "Your mission is to find out who the scab is. That's where I come in. And remember, whatever happens, we've got to protect the football."

"The football." Kirk managed a grin, thanks to the beer, and pointed his knife at Mulville. "And the biscuit."

CHAPTER 26

PREPARATION

Aziz Hyzaar stood barefoot at the bathroom sink. He pulled up his sweatshirt's sleeves and turned the water on. To allow water to fill the space between his palms. He brought his hands together and spread his thumbs apart. Moments later, the warm water soothed his skin, pouring over his face from above his forehead. Using his fingertips, he swiped his eyes, nose, and lips. To ensure that the complete surface of his face had been washed, he put his index fingers inside his nostrils, just as his uncle had shown him when Aziz was a little boy. He proceeded to wash his hands and arms up to the elbows, then he rolled up his sweatpants and brought his feet to the small sink, stretching his legs one at a time to wash his feet and ankles.

The worn-out towel called out to him from the tubular rack. No, not that towel, his conscience warned him, but he reached out and grabbed it anyway. He buried his face in the rough, stiff cotton and inhaled. The scent of the girl inebriated him. Soap. Youth. Softness. Her body had been where his face now was.

No, he shouldn't. He was preparing for his morning prayer, and perhaps the last morning prayer of his life. This was a test—a test of his worthiness to carry out such an important task. The seventy virgins were waiting. He threw the towel on the floor and walked out of the bathroom into the bare corridor. On the way to his bedroom, Aziz passed the girl's room. Silent. Only darkness was visible under the closed door. He sped up his pace, entered his own bedroom, and locked himself in. The rectangular rug next to his bed awaited him. Multicolored and of Persian design, the carpet was the only luxury item in the apartment.

Aziz turned his body toward the corner of the room—northeast—the direction of Mecca from this unholy land. He opened his hands and raised them to ear-level. He prayed while standing, then knelt and prayed some more. His uncle had knelt on the same carpet to pray. And before him, his grandfather. As he bowed, Aziz kept his hands flat on his thighs. Then, with his back prostrated to the ground, he rested his forehead, nose, and palms on the carpet, and prayed for forgiveness.

Today, while undercover, he'd have to use his depraved Anglo name for the final time. The dust in the carpet entered his nostrils and made him cough. Aziz welcomed the discomfort. He sat on his ankles, his feet folded under him, and prayed for his sister Tashfeen, that she would have the courage and opportunity to successfully complete her task, so he could accomplish his.

Kirk Miner woke up in a sweat. His phone showed 7:03 AM. His nightly sleep had been a series of nightmares populated by piercing bullets, burst bubbles, and torn blood vessels. He threw back the bed covers and shuffled into the bathroom in his t-shirt and briefs. The hot shower massaged his skin and reinvigorated him. As he toweled off, he wondered if this would be his last shower, as in the last day of his life. He looked at his image in the mirror and gave himself a glance of reproach.

His best suit waited inside the closet. Luckily, it happened to be black. The color would fit in with customary Secret Service attire. In the pictures, all those agents looked like undertakers. Great. Another good thought. Kirk fingered the soft wool of the black suit. Sitting in the suitcase had unacceptably wrinkled the garment. He took the suit and a white shirt, carried them to the bathroom, and hung them in the shower to steam. Coffee from the room kept him company as he waited on the bed, wrapped in a bathrobe. After the second cup, he took out his phone and dialed.

"Hi," he said. "I hope I didn't wake you. I needed to hear your voice."

"You didn't," Aurora's groggy voice answered. "With the sleep I'm getting these days, I could make lots of money doing double shifts at the hospital."

"I'm sorry," he said. "Tonight, it'll all be over."

His mind ended the sentence with the words "one way or another." She remained silent. Kirk wondered if Aurora was thinking the same thing. But he couldn't share his fears.

"I know how to protect myself." He infused his voice with as much calm as he was capable of. "I have a special shield to protect my aorta, and a bullet-proof vest, and the FBI will monitor every move, ready to intervene. I'll be fine."

"Make sure of it," she said.

"Is Peter there?" he asked.

"Getting ready for school."

"Let me talk to him please."

Silence followed, then the sound of approaching steps. The boy's voice hiked up Kirk's heart rate.

"Hi, Daddy."

"Peter."

Nothing much came to mind. How does one say goodbye without saying goodbye? A lump grew in Kirk's throat that made it difficult to speak.

"Daddy," Peter said, "are you there?"

"Yes."

"Good luck with your mission," the boy said. "And be careful."

It figures. Leave it up to Peter to understand all and to say just the right thing. Eleven going on fifty. Thanks for rescuing Daddy.

"I'll see you tomorrow," Kirk said. "Love you."

"Bye," the boy said.

The sound of distancing steps faded. Kirk waited. Heaviness grew in his chest.

"I'll make a reservation for dinner," Aurora said. "Amelia's, the Italian place. Tomorrow."

"Yes." Kirk closed his eyes and swallowed. "Good idea. Got to get ready now. I love you."

Life was good. He had to make sure there would be more of it in his future—lots more.

Mulville knocked at Kirk's door half an hour later. He looked at the bare-chested detective in dress pants and burst into laughter.

"Good morning," Mulville said. "You don't need to get naked for wiring."

He handed Kirk a tall coffee from a cardboard holder. Then the agent took a sip from his own paper cup and discarded the cardboard holder to pick up a briefcase.

A cup of coffee from Mulville? The guy must think Kirk's survival odds were dismal. Mulville's laughter was a cover, hence Kirk's anxiety escalated.

"Good morning." Kirk stepped aside to let Mulville in. "Thanks for the coffee, even if my heart feels wired already."

Mulville wore a heavy jacket with a badge and an FBI baseball cap. Clothes for action. He walked in, placed the briefcase on the desk, and threw his jacket on Kirk's unmade bed. A Glock, strapped over an FBI sweatshirt, gleamed. Kirk closed the door. He hoped Mulville had something more than his issued weapon. An assault weapon would be nice. Many of them. He started to sweat.

The briefcase's top snapped open at the touch of Mulville's thumbs. Inside were electronic devices and wires, some straight and some curly, all ending with earpieces. Kirk approached.

"This looks like the equipment used by the other three agents." Mulville picked up an earpiece with the curly wire connected to a microphone and a phone. "You can wear it at your waist, like everybody else. Microphone on your wrist. It connects wirelessly to the phone. Only difference is this switch."

When he touched a green button on the side of the phone, a small screen lit up. Kirk wiped his hands on the now-discarded robe and reached out for the phone and the earpiece.

"When you touch the switch, you'll be talking only to me." Mulville looked up. "In the other mode, you'll be heard by the entire team as well as by the backup. By the way, I volunteered my team for the backup. At least that's in the open, so I'll know where you're going."

Kirk nodded. He clipped the phone to his belt, pushed the earpiece into his ear, and strapped the microphone to his wrist. The curly wire stretched. Kirk replaced the devices on the table. Inside the case, a metal American flag caught his eye. He reached out for the small object.

"That's the video camera," Mulville said. "It feeds into our computers. We'll have a van with equipment and weapons, or a room with some sort of set-up. Depends on the location."

"When will I know where I'm going?" Kirk asked.

"Soon," Mulville said. "I'll know first. We'll go ahead and make sure the location is secure, then you and the others will come in."

"How many people on the backup team?" Kirk asked. "I hope you bring enough for a worst-case scenario."

Mulville smiled. Kirk wished he hadn't. A smile at that moment could mean only one thing: No backup was large enough for a worst-case scenario.

"If we're down to the designated survivor," Mulville said, "we're in a 9/11 ish situation. I got the regular Presidential-style backup, in case some terrorists wanna play football—four people with me, and as many as we need on demand… supposedly. Depends on the emergency's level of chaos. That's all I could get from the director without getting my ass kicked out for being part of it at all. As I said, in the FBI, there are pricks and then there is the prickest."

Kirk nodded. The flag had a black dot centered in the middle of the blue stars—invisible from a foot away. He looked at Mulville. The agent paced the floor sipping his coffee. A few drops leaked out from the plastic top and dripped onto the FBI letters. The yellow turned to tan where the coffee hit.

"Fuck." Mulville wiped the area with his hand.

"Hey," Kirk said. "Cool it. What's going on?"

Mulville pulled a chair from under the desk and sat down. His face seemed grave. He placed the coffee on the desk next to the open briefcase. All inappropriate humor was now dispensed with.

"One thing I'll tell you," he said, "but this has to be between us."

Kirk nodded. He placed the metal flag back in the briefcase. He stared at Mulville.

"My team and I," Mulville said, "officially are going back to Washington after we make sure your place is secure. Again, orders from above. They're more worried about threats against the people in the Capitol than they're worried about the safety of the designated survivor. And since 9/11, the designated survivor can't be too far from town anyway."

No backup? Mulville must be crazy. If nobody gave a shit about the designated survivor, why should Kirk give a damn? Innocent lives were at stake, but without backup, his task would be impossible. He had to convince Mulville to do the right thing, despite orders to the contrary.

"Don't go shitting in your pants now," Mulville added. "In reality, I'm going to be where I think I should be—a few yards from where you are. And you'll use a good phrase to signal us to come in."

"Like what?" Kirk said.

"Like," Mulville grinned, "get the fuck over."

"What about your orders?" Kirk said.

"Screw my orders," Mulville said. "And I'm taking the team with me. I'm sure the designated survivor is central to all this shit. Why would they have risked so much to put that loser in place, if all they wanted to do was blow up the Capitol? I don't want to miss the fun."

"What if they want to do both?" Kirk asked. "Take down the Capitol and take the football from the designated survivor?"

"Exactly." Mulville nodded, lifting his palm in a gesture indicating futility. "If someone attacks the Capitol, my small group of people won't make any difference. Drop in the bucket, spit in the ocean. But the survivor would become essential. God save us from that idiot having to act as president. He'll need all the help he can get. You and I would have to save the country."

The country—the entire country—could be at stake. Up to him and Mulville to save it.

"What about you?" Kirk asked. "Aren't you going to need an ultrasound screen?"

Mulville's smile was full of irony. His glance said "You've got to be kidding." Was Kirk a fool to assume that the plastic stuff would protect him? He shuddered.

"If the FBI must crash your party," Mulville said, "we won't be observing the dress code. We'll be way past waiting around for dissections. Believe me. At that point, machine guns would be doing the job."

Mulville tapped his bullet-proof vest as if wishing himself luck by knocking on Kevlar. Kirk nodded. It was all a bit too much to digest. With nothing better to do, he picked up the communication device and placed his thumb on the green button. The screen lit up as expected.

"Quit dicking around with the toys," Mulville said. "Finish getting dressed. You've got to be ready by nine-thirty to be taken away from the Capitol by helicopter, together with the Dick of Energy and The Three Stooges."

The sound of banging on the bedroom door shocked Aziz out of his trance. He pushed back from the floor and stood up. What could be more important than the Morning Prayer? Sayed and Tashfeen should know better than to interrupt him. He stepped to the door and opened it. It was Tashfeen, wearing her cleaning service uniform. The head scarf allowed only her eyes to be seen. Her deep and dark eyes looked wide. Her pupils appeared dilated, likely by adrenaline. Her thick brows met in a deep furrow right above the bridge of her nose. Enough for Aziz to know that something was wrong.

"What's going on?" Panic filled his chest. "Did you do what you needed to do?"

The white scarf swayed, as if to say "no." Tears filled the woman's lower lids. He shouldn't have trusted her.

"Someone called in sick," she said sobbing. "They assigned me to a different area. Almost got compromised trying to access the place."

"The device isn't in place?" Aziz's sounded more than a little angry.

"No." She looked at the wooden floor. "One of the policemen saw me and started to ask questions. I told him I was lost. But I'm not sure he believed me. He reported me to my supervisor. And today I signed in with my real name, and I wasn't disguised the same way as when I went to the Chief of Staff's office."

Aziz stomped his foot on the ground a few inches from Tashfeen. The woman's head jerked in fear. The damn fool. The area would be even better guarded now. What was he going to do? He checked his watch. 8:32 A.M. Less than an hour before they picked him up with the rest of the designated survivor's team.

"You've got to go back and do your job."

"But," she moaned, "what happens if I'm already compromised?"

"The fact that you have to ask," Aziz said with unnatural calm, "shows how your faith crumbles when it comes to the ultimate sacrifice. You have what you need if you get caught. Use it. But first, do what you were destined to do. Tashfeen, today is the day you show how deep your faith really is."

She nodded. Aziz closed his fingers around her arm. His fingertip could have crushed her flesh and bone. She moaned but didn't resist. How could he have trusted a weakling like his sister? He pulled her along the corridor and parked her by the door.

"Wait here," he ordered.

She stood shaking. Aziz rushed to his bedroom. He tossed his sweats to the ground and donned a white shirt and black pants. The gun was next. It almost slipped from his sweaty hands. He pulled the black jacket off the hanger, threw a red-and-blue tie around his neck, and rushed toward the bedroom door. His gaze skimmed past the night table. He stopped, opened the drawer, retrieved a capsule, and placed it inside his shirt pocket. Moments later, he knocked on Sayed's bedroom door, then pushed on the handle without waiting for permission to enter. His sister was a waste. But at least he could count on his brother.

Sayed looked up, black hair damp from a recent shower, his muscular body in black sweats. He completed the prayer and stood up at attention. A sense of pride warmed Aziz as he observed his best recruit.

"What's going on?" Sayed asked. "I heard you yelling at Tashfeen."

"We've got a problem." Aziz dropped onto the only chair in the bedroom. "She failed. I've got to go and get it done myself."

"But," Sayed said, eyeing his watch, "you'll run out of time. I should go."

"No." Aziz extended his palm as if to say "no discussion allowed." "Too dangerous. You exhausted your official duties the day you picked up the boy. We can get away only once with swapping in your face in the Secret Service roster and giving you a fake badge. By now, they must've figured it out. Besides, fooling a head of school isn't the same as fooling agents guarding the Capitol the night of a presidential address. All we need is for you to get caught. That'll sink the entire mission. Let me worry about this problem. I need you ready and available for backup later." Sayed remained silent.

Being in charge was good and bad. All responsibilities fell on Aziz's shoulders. All problems became his problems. The buck always stopped with him. It was lonely at the top.

"I'm the only one who's safe," Aziz said. "And I have to report to the Capitol to get picked up."

"So this is it?" Sayed spread his arms. "Here. I've got everything you need."

Sayed pointed to his night table. On the wooden surface, Aziz saw two devices connected by wire to earpieces. Sayed, the family geek, was at home with anything high tech that needed programming. Division of labor. One of the few American innovations Aziz agreed with. He smiled.

"Yes." Aziz picked up one of the devices. "Did you sync them?"

"If you want to talk to me, touch the green button." Sayed nodded. "The yellow one is for the infidels. If backup is coming and you need me to take care of it, push the green button twice. My device will buzz twice."

Aziz nodded. His brother had never disappointed him.

"Three buzzes," Sayed continued, "if I need to rush in."

"What about the ultrasound device?" Aziz asked.

"I checked your cell," Sayed said, handing Aziz a cellphone. "Still working perfectly. Good wavelength. You're good to go."

Aziz reached for the phone and placed it in his shirt pocket. Then his fingers probed the listening devices. Everything worked. He sighed.

"I'll let you know the location as soon as I find out." Aziz got up. "And I'll make sure we have what we need. Nothing like booze to enhance the resonance, according to the woman scientist's notes. Let the liquid sin do the job. I can't believe how these infidels guzzle down that poison."

Sayed stood still as if anticipating what needed to happen. His little brother had grown up to be a few inches taller than Aziz, and several pounds heavier. But the look in his bright eyes hadn't changed over the years. Still showed the same respect a pupil has for his mentor. Same as Sayed had showed him during childhood. Aziz opened his arms and brought him toward his chest. As they hugged, Aziz's eyes rested on a rectangular black case on the dresser. His heart accelerated.

⌘

Patrizia opened her eyes to the darkness of her prison. Some noise had whisked her away, temporarily providing her relief from the nightmarish reality her life had turned into two weeks earlier. Her hand reached for the wall switch at the side of her bed. A bare bulb in the ceiling came to life. How she missed her pale pink bedroom at home. And her mom, who would welcome her in the morning with raisin-sprinkled oatmeal and sizzling bacon. Instead, the short woman with the scarf would give her stale bread and, on a good day, a slice of cheese. Or worse, the woman would be gone and the muscular man with the hairy chest and the ugly jagged scar would make her jump on the trampoline.

The way he looked at her gave her the creeps. Ever since the bathroom incident, when she had found his sweaty shirt abandoned on the floor during her shower, she feared for her life every time he laid eyes on her. Her mom had said the ordeal would last only ten days. Today was the tenth day.

Was her mom coming to get her? She pulled the thin blanket to her chin, hoping it wouldn't shock her skin with static electricity. Shivers ran through her body, despite wearing her jeans and a sweatshirt—the only clothes she had with her. The smell of her own sweat made her recoil. This morning, Patrizia didn't want to move.

The disgusting man and the woman were arguing. And since yesterday, another man—wider, taller, heavier—who had been coming in late at night and leaving early in the morning, was still there.

Now Patrizia dragged herself out of bed and placed her ear next to the thin wall. The two men were talking. Perhaps they were going to bring her back to her mom. She listened.

"If Tashfeen goes with you, and then I leave, what about the girl?" Patrizia recognized the larger man's voice.

"Doesn't matter," the disgusting man said. "We can leave the girl alone. Nothing matters now. Only a few hours to Paradise."

Patrizia shuddered. *Paradise?* What were they talking about? Paradise as in Heaven? To go to Heaven, one must die first. Were they planning on dying? What about her? Were they planning to kill her? She pressed her ear back on the cold wall.

"Tie and gag her," the disgusting man said. "We can't take any chances."

Patrizia's eyes shut in fear. What she heard had nothing to do with her mom. Mom couldn't have known about this and allowed these people to do such awful things to her. Her heart hurt in her chest. She couldn't stop shaking. Her legs gave out and she sagged to the floor, arms bracing her body, tears streaming down her cheeks.

Aziz found Tashfeen ready and waiting by the door, and just as he had left her—coat and gloves on, with the scarf off her mouth, the way she had to wear her uniform at work according to the rules. Aziz grabbed his coat and pushed her out the door. He hated driving Tashfeen's beaten-up sedan.

"How are you going to explain my going back to work?" She glanced at him from the passenger's side. "My shift was over almost two hours ago. And I already got reported."

"Leave it to me," he said, eyes fixed on the icy road.

How many times had Aziz uttered those words to his big sister? If he dug into his past childhood memories, he couldn't pinpoint the moment of transition, when the two-year difference between them became irrelevant and the little brother-big sister relationship morphed into the strange interaction which defined their lives at present. Of one thing Aziz was sure: Faith superseded all—worldly possessions, love, and blood relatives.

They parked in the employees' lot. Aziz fixed his tie as they walked side by side to the Capitol's north entrance. A plan took final form in his mind.

"Easier on this side." He pointed at a single man in uniform at the top of the steps. "Only one guard. Let me have the device."

The request sounded like an order. Tashfeen looked sideways at him, giving him a quizzical look.

Tashfeen seemed shorter than Aziz remembered. She came up only to his shoulder. She rummaged inside a large cloth pocketbook and handed him a small brown-paper bag. She tried to trot next to him, taking two steps for each one of his. He grabbed the paper bag and shoved it into his pants pocket.

"Let me do the talking," he said. "No matter what happens, go with it."

He bit down on his lower lip until a sharp pain spread to both sides of his jaw. The sting generated the right amount of adrenaline—enough to stir his emotional state to useful anger. He stopped at the bottom of the steps. Tashfeen stopped next to him. Her chest moved rhythmically from the exertion.

"Hey." Aziz waved at the uniformed police officer. "I need assistance. Down here."

The man's gaze roamed around and stopped on Aziz. Aziz grabbed his sister's arm with renewed force. Tashfeen winced but didn't pull away. She knew better than to disobey one of his orders. A guard approached—a clean-shaven man in his thirties, with a crew-cut under a visor hat, wearing a crisp black uniform. His gloved hand went to the gun at his side.

"Secret Service," Aziz said, holding up his badge with his free hand. "This woman tried to grab my badge. She's carrying a suspicious bag. Call the bomb squad. Now."

Did the policeman believe him? Difficult to tell without seeing his eyes. Damn visor. The cop descended the steps. Tashfeen stared at Aziz, bewilderment escalating in her eyes, her body limp under his grip.

"Don't come any closer," Aziz said, putting his palm out, his badge between his thumb and index finger. "Call the bomb squad and stay away. I can handle her."

With his left hand, Aziz twisted Tashfeen's arm behind her back. Terror flashed in her dilated eyes. He invoked Allah to show him the way and to give him strength. Sacrifice was the necessary step to victory and salvation. Locking his right hand into a fist, he shoved it against her chest with vigor. Crunching sounds reached him from ribs underlying soft breasts. A wail came from Tashfeen. Her legs flew up, and her head thumped to the ground. The cleaning company uniform slipped upward, revealing pale thighs. Aziz got a glimpse of unadorned white underwear deep under his sister's skirt.

Aziz glanced back at the guard. The man was busy talking into his wrist from several yards' distance. Aziz's right hand snaked inside his coat and suit jacket to reach the shirt pocket. Steady fingers closed around the capsule.

Tashfeen lay still, overwhelmed by physical and emotional shock. Aziz's fingers remained wrapped around her motionless arm. The guard was still talking into his wrist. Soon, police and FBI agents would storm down the steps. Time was getting close for Aziz to meet the other Secret Service agents for his helicopter ride with the designated survivor. It was now or never. Faith demanded sacrifices.

He let go of his sister's arm and wrapped his fingers around her jaw. The pressure caused her mouth to crack open. He brought the capsule out into the open.

"I'll see you in Paradise," he said, pushing the capsule between Tashfeen's teeth.

A transformation took place in Tashfeen's look. In seconds, glazed-over apathy turned into questioning disbelief and then terror. Tashfeen's head flapped side to side. A spitting sound came from her mouth. Then a loud imploring moan filled the air. The memory of his sister's laughter and last hug filled Aziz's mind.

The capsule flew in the air and rolled on the ground. Aziz stretched out his arm. The small cylinder was outside his reach. The guard stared. Uniformed men gathered at the top of the stairs from all directions. Tashfeen's body shuddered and bounced under his grip. Aziz's right hand went up and struck his sister's soft cheek with unexpected rage. The blow displaced the scarf, exposing dark curly hair. She let go a tired scream. A trickle of blood appeared on the side of her mouth and ran down her lower lip. For an instant, Aziz let go of her face and recovered the capsule. He locked the soft cheeks again in the vice of his hand, crushed the small cylinder between his thumb and index fingers, and poured the liquid content into the small opening between Tashfeen's lips. Then he shoved the entire capsule into his sister's mouth.

Tashfeen coughed and spat out bloody saliva. Then her chest sucked in a few hungry gasps. Her skin and lips turned a bright red color and her body shook violently. Then she lay still.

The bomb squad approached. Four individuals dressed in green astronaut-like outfits hidden behind thick shields squatted next to him. Aziz pulled down the skirt on her sister's legs and repositioned the scarf to hide her face.

"Cyanide," he said to the closest man. "I was able to get some info from her. She wanted to plant something in the House Chamber. She told me where. Can you take over for me here, so I can go check it out? In case she did it already?"

The agents nodded and Aziz left. By the time someone figured out his relationship to Tashfeen, the mission would be over. The very secrecy surrounding the location and the guarding of the designated survivor was Aziz's protection. And soon everyone would be busy with much bigger fish to fry than a flipped-out, suicide-minded cleaning lady.

He ran up the stairs without turning back. At the sight of his badge, the police officers crowding the top of the stairs parted like the Red Sea for Moses. As he walked through the entrance, Aziz nodded his thanks to the police.

The image of Tashfeen gasping for air haunted him. An irresistible impulse to run seized him. Aziz took a few calming breaths and forced his legs to slow down. A wall clock showed 9:01. Tashfeen should be grateful. Her brother had come to her rescue one last time. Thanks to him, she would make it to Paradise after all.

Steady and controlled steps brought Aziz to the south wing of the House Chamber. Only once did he stop along the way, in front of a large ornate mirror in one of the corridors. Here he pulled up his white collar and tightened the knot of his red and blue tie to cover the swastika-like scar on the right side of his neck.

CHAPTER 27

DESIGNATED SURVIVOR

As the helicopter idled on the Capitol lawn, Kirk stuffed the necktie inside his shirt to stop it from flapping in the wind. The icy cold bit his face. A subtle scent of distant fireplaces entered his nostrils and stirred his sad longing for home. Where will he be tomorrow?

Kirk ducked under the rotor. The combined layers of bubble wrap and bullet-proof vest pressed on his throat and induced a light sense of panic, reminding him of the threats the equipment was designed to protect him from. He climbed in through the wide-open door and sat next to a bald man. Kirk recognized him from the pictures as Mulville's guy—the agent who had been around for ten years.

Between his feet sat a black leather case, and a small antenna protruded from it near the handle. It was the nuclear football, filled with classified nuclear war plans. Hard to believe everything needed to start WW III was right there in that bag, the size of an ordinary backpack. Luckily, the critical object was being guarded by Mulville's guy. Kirk wondered where the biscuit could be.

"Ray McGregor." The bald guy squeezed Kirk's hand to the limit of pain. "Nice to work with you. Jack Mulville spoke highly of you."

Kirk didn't know if that fact pleased him or scared him. In front of Kirk was the Secretary of Energy, the designated survivor for the evening, who fidgeted with the x-shaped straps of his seatbelt. The buckle bounced on the man's protruding abdomen with every attempt of his stubby little fingers to secure the harness. Long gray hair fell over his ears and reminded Kirk of barristers wearing powdered wigs in English courtrooms.

Kirk had met the Secretary earlier, when catching the last part of his last briefing before departure. The man was all that Mulville had called him and more. The part the Secretary liked the most about the whole designated survivor deal was to be addressed as "Mr. President." His face lit up like a Christmas tree every time a staff member uttered those two words in his presence. But the man wasn't fit enough to strap the buckle of his harness by himself. How, if called upon, could he possibly run the country?

A second agent climbed aboard and sat in front of Ray. He looked at Kirk as if trying to remember or place him. Kirk took a slow breath to suppress a pang of panic. Time to determine if the bullshit Mulville had dished out would pass muster with the Secret Service

"Marc Bruss," the agent said, putting out his hand.

"Kirk Miner." He shook Marc's hand. "We've never met." Marc seemed satisfied.

To Kirk, all Secret Service agents might very well be clones. Same build from heavy-duty fitness training. Same haircut, either crew or altogether bald, like the guy next to him. No beard or mustache. Same clothes—black suits and white shirts. Only the ties were of different colors, but limited to either black or the colors of the American flag. Dark sunglasses completed the outfit, like the ones agents wore in a movie Kirk fondly remembered— "Men in Black," a flick about Secret Service agents looking for aliens from outer space. In that moment, Kirk felt akin to those men in black. He was looking for the alien from a terrorist country.

One of the requirements to become a Secret Service officer was to be born in the United States, but the man Kirk was looking for was alien in spirit as well as in ideology.

The air smelled of kerosene. The pilot sat still, waiting. The Secretary's buckle at last clicked into place. His shoulders momentarily sagged in relaxation, then his head turned side to side toward the Capitol's exits and surroundings. A deep breath escaped through tight lips. With piercing dark eyes, he examined his wristwatch, then the empty seat next to him. His agent, the one he had personally chosen, was missing.

"There was some emergency," Marc said, "at the north entrance. A woman, possibly a terrorist of sorts, committed suicide."

The Secretary leaned forward. As his brows came together, he took a breath as if ready to answer.

"Finally." The secretary pointed at a man in black running toward the helicopter. "It's about time."

The helicopter shook as the muscular man hopped aboard. He looked around at the three men already seated behind the pilot and squeezed into the free seat on the other side of the Secretary. His hands wrapped around the harness, quickly closed the buckle, then repositioned his tie.

"Greg Hof," he said, shaking hands with the other two agents.

Hands crossed in front of Kirk and the Secretary, then Greg turned to Kirk. The man's dark eyes narrowed. His handshake was firm and strong. Kirk stared at his eyes. A vague familiarity jumped out at him. But all these agents looked the same. The man turned to the Secretary. "Sorry, Mr. Secretary," he said. "You've probably heard about the emergency."

The Secretary's hand went up in a gesture of futility. He again exhaled through pursed lips.

"The problem is taken care of," Greg explained. "The woman committed suicide, but we got information about her intention to place a device in the House chamber. I'm late because I personally supervised a full search of the House Chamber. Nothing there."

"So, that was it?" the Secretary asked. "It figures. Much ado about nothing, despite what Mulville, that FBI fanatic, predicted. And by the way, it's 'Mr. President,' just to stay with today's role-playing."

He laughed out loud. His hand fell flat and heavy on his agent's shoulder. Greg didn't smile.

The Secretary seemed to resent Mulville for asking him to forego his big opportunity. Looking ahead to a long night, Kirk sat back and checked his harness.

"Sir," Kirk said, "we can't assume this little incident was what we were afraid might happen."

"Oh, B.S," the Secretary said, turning to the pilot. "Let's get this show on the road. Don't want to miss any part of my mini-vacation."

Mini-vacation—that's how the Secretary regarded the upcoming ordeal? How stupid and irresponsible could someone be? One more reason to hope that nothing would happen to the real President and potential successors. Then again, Kirk would have to spend the next ten or twelve hours with this jerk.

Ray talked into his wrist, announcing departure. Kirk talked into his wrist also and checked in with Mulville. No green button this time. Official business.

"Place is secure," Mulville said. "Go ahead."

The door slid closed and thumped against the frame. Greg turned the handle to secure the lock. A snapping sound of finality hit Kirk's eardrums. He was alone with five individuals he didn't know, one of whom could be a murderous terrorist. Or perhaps more than one. Who? One senior agent had an impeccable record, as attested to by Mulville.

Kirk looked at Greg. For a moment, their eyes met. A slight sense of familiarity hit Kirk again. The agent diverted his gaze to the snowy fields outside. Hof—the name alone made Kirk think of radicalization. But this was pure profiling, because of the German-sounding name. And the guy with a dark-buzz and dark eyes looked anything but German. Besides, he had just helped defuse a possible terrorist attack, or so he said.

Kirk relaxed his back muscles against the cushioned seat. He reached out for his headset. The agents wore theirs over the earbud wires. Kirk did the same.

The whining of the engine increased and the lazy beat of the blades escalated to a frantic high-pitch whipping. The large mechanical bird with its six-person cargo lifted straight off the ground, drifted to the left to stay clear of the Capitol Rotunda, and headed north.

Thick urban housing and historical landmarks streamed below them for several minutes, then shrunk with increasing altitude. Patches of green and snow-covered ground appeared to mark the D.C. suburbs.

The helicopter's nose tilted toward the ground. The empty areas got wider and became back and front yards separated by curvy surface streets lined with snow. The roaring of the rotors turned into a chirping sound. The thumping of the blades slowed. The aircraft leveled off and steadily descended toward a large area surrounded by hills and trees, landing in a flurry of fine snowflakes. Then everything went silent. Only the whistle of wind could be heard.

A farm-like red wood building with large windows and a slanted shingle roof stood in the background. Snow-covered spruce and pine trees gave the place a peaceful winter wonderland appearance. In different circumstances, this could be a nice place for a family vacation. Peter would have fun sledding down the hills. Kirk pictured himself throwing snowballs at him.

"That's it?" the Secretary said. He looked at his watch, then pointed to the outside. "Less than a twenty-minute flight. All this to be sleeping in a stupid barn?"

The clicking of seat buckles opening filled the craft. The reality of the crazy mission Kirk had volunteered for wiped out the dream-like fantasy the view had prompted. Kirk and the three agents exited the helicopter first, followed by the Secretary. They walked in formation per protocol, with the agents surrounding the designated survivor. Kirk right-sided the survivor, Greg took the left side, and Marc the front. The bald agent walked behind and carried the football. The pilot followed at a short distance. Kirk inhaled the pine trees' wonderful scent.

A wooden sign supported by a low brick wall carried the name of the place—"Silver Spring Ventana Farmhouse and Spa." Steam exited from the side of a flat wooden building next to the main one. The door chimed as the men entered a wood-paneled room with a large fireplace on the left and a reception desk on the right. A comfortable-looking leather couch and chairs surrounded a brown bearskin in front of the fire.

A long narrow table along the back of the room held an assortment of fruit and nuts. Next to the snack display was a bar with blue lights displaying liquor bottles and glasses of different shapes. Several pictures of the surroundings taken in different seasons hung on the walls. No people were around except a man in a red jacket and black pants, and a young woman with straight blond hair and a long-sleeved black dress with a multicolored scarf. The two stood at attention behind the reception desk with large smiles plastered on their faces.

"Welcome to the Ventana Farmhouse," they said. The man patted his side hair, brushing over an obvious bald spot. "Thanks for doing us the honor of using our facility. I'm Paul Ventana, the owner, and this is my daughter Jill."

The owner shook hands with the agents and the Secretary. Jill nodded, still at attention. The owners had cleared the house of all guests for a couple of days and they would personally make themselves scarce after showing the facility to the special guests. But where would Mulville stay? Kirk hadn't noticed any construction nearby—only trees and snow-covered hills. So much for the few yards away where Mulville said he would be with backup. Unless the FBI was hiding in the nearby trees, with a van or such, Kirk would be on his own, it seemed.

"We have reserved the entire bottom floor for you," the owner said, dragging his hand through the air. "Four bedrooms, each with bath and fireplace. You may use this room to relax. And the White House chef is already in the kitchen working on your lunch and dinner."

"Great," the Secretary said. "What about the spa?"

"The spa." Paul Ventana smiled as if the subject gave him pleasure. "Great steam room and an indoor Jacuzzi. Feel free."

"What about the bar?" the Secretary asked.

"Right here." Paul Ventana pointed to his right. He gazed with questioning eyes, starting with the Secretary and moving to the agents. "Dining room on the other side. But nobody said anything about alcohol."

"What's a little booze?" The Secretary waved his hand in dismissal. "It'll help us relax and pass the time. For your country."

Paul Ventana bent down and disappeared behind the desk. Ray and Marc instantly stepped in front of the Secretary, forming a human barrier. Each man placed a hand on the protectee's shoulder and forced the designated survivor to kneel on the ground. The hands of the other agents went to the guns at their side. Greg jumped from the back of the Secretary to the reception desk.

Jill's eyes widened. Her smile turned into a gaping mouth, after which she took her hand to cover the opening. Paul Ventana stood up and turned pale. His hair had fallen down and his bald spot shone under the ceiling lights. Both his hands went up in the air. In his clenched right were some papers that were metal-clipped together.

"What's going on?" Ventana asked. His arms shook in the air, waving the papers. "It's only the contract—the contract for the facility. I guess you can have a few drinks. On me."

"Take it easy, guys." The Secretary got up, shaking his head side to side. "The only one who's going to have a heart attack is the poor guy right here. You stiffs need to relax."

The agents stood down and holstered their guns. The Secretary swept invisible dust from his suit. Paul Ventana dropped the contract on the bar.

"I'll get your luggage," Paul said, still shaking, "and then we'll be going."

He headed to the door with the pilot at his heels. The daughter, still frozen, regained her composure and slipped into a let-me-show-you-your-rooms mode. The three agents followed her to a corridor in the back of the room. Kirk joined them.

On the same side of the corridor were four bedrooms, all in cottage-like décor. Slanted beams on the ceiling, fireplace, queen-sized bed, rug on the floor, sitting area, and marble bath with tub. The agents entered all the rooms first and pulled down shades, despite the pretty view. Ray acted as senior agent and allocated the rooms. Greg and Marc got the room on one side, and the pilot joined Ray in the room on the other side of the Secretary's room.

Kirk took the room after that of the two younger agents. Good for Mulville. He must've somehow arranged for that. Paul arrived carrying a small suitcase. The Secretary pointed to his bedroom.

"I don't know about you," the Secretary said, "but I'm getting into my bathing suit and going for a steam."

The senior agent nodded. Greg looked puzzled. Paul Ventana dropped the suitcase in the Secretary's bedroom, collected his daughter, and rushed away without waiting for a tip. A moment later, the front door chimes rang in the distance.

"I'll take a walk outside for a minute," Greg said, "to secure the living room windows and check the surroundings."

Ray nodded. Kirk felt a pang of concern. Under normal circumstances, Greg's plan would have been considered routine. But a traitor or a terrorist could be among these men. What was Greg going to do outside? Kirk hid his unease.

"Who's our chef?" Kirk asked.

"One of the White House cooks," Ray said. "It's the tradition for the designated survivor. Usually great meals."

The Secretary came out of his bedroom wearing a plush robe labelled with the farmhouse's logo. Kirk and the senior agents dropped their coats and followed him to the end of the corridor, and then to the spa. Kirk heard the door chime again as Greg headed outside.

———— ∽∽ ————

Less than one hundred yards away, beyond the hill at the back of the farm, was an unmarked surveillance van parked in the thickest of trees. Inside, Mulville blew on his gloved fingers and touched a keyboard. The screen in front of him came to life with several black lines. He swiveled on his chair and reached out for the heater's controls.

"I'm freezing," he said, hiking up the temperature.

The van had only two windows, both up front. Different-sized computer screens and electronic equipment, with all kind of knobs and dials, covered the van's inside space. A narrow ledge ran all around to support keyboards, listening devices, infrared binoculars, automatic weapons, a dripping coffee machine, and a large bag full of food bought at a nearby hamburger place. Four swivel seats were bolted to the floor. On them sat Mulville and three other agents wearing FBI jackets and caps.

"Take it easy, Jack," said a younger man with thin blond hair. "We just got started. It'll warm up soon enough."

"Outside back monitor working," a woman agent in her thirties said. "All quiet."

"Outside front monitor picking up fine," the third agent, a man in his forties, said without turning. "I see the entrance crystal clear. The Secretary's personal Secret Service agent, Greg Hof, is outside, talking or texting on the phone."

"Who's he talking to?" Mulville jerked around to the third agent's screen. "Not to us. Zoom in. Increase the audio."

"Too late," the man said. "He's done."

"Go back on the recording from the front camera. Zoom in to see what number he dialed."

The agent did as suggested. Frames rolled and he zoomed in. The rustling of wind mixed with static was audible on the recorder.

"There," Mulville said, pointing at the monitor. "Stop. Go slow. Enhance."

Hof seemed like the son of dark and husky refugees. Fuck profiling. If it were up to Mulville, these Bedouins would all be shipped back to the desert.

"Not sure if he's talking or texting," the agent said. "Wrong angle. Can't make out much. Two minutes and eight seconds."

"Shit." Mulville turned to his screen. "Got to warn Miner. Why he didn't follow and listen in, I'll never know. I'm already regretting this freaking arrangement."

He swiveled back to his screen and tapped into Kirk's video feed. The image of the two senior agents appeared. They stood in front of the spa entrance, their hair damp, cheeks flushed, shirts darkened by sweat. Mulville wouldn't want their job if they paid him his weight in gold. He buzzed a private message to Kirk. The image shook for a moment. Kirk must've been excited to hear from him.

The vibes from the communicator device spread through Kirk's side and gave him a jolt of adrenaline. He wiped sweat from his brow. He couldn't wait to see what Mulville had to say.

"Got to use the john," Kirk said, pointing to a door nearby.

The bald agent with the football nodded. Kirk retreated to privacy. The phone slipped from his sweaty fingers and he had to catch it before dropping the device into the toilet. He checked his messages. Only one. From Mulville.

In the trees beyond the back hill. Large unmarked van. Secretary's agent outside fooling around with windows and texting or calling on phone. Investigate.

Great. Thanks for joining. How in the hell was Kirk going to check Greg's phone? He walked back to the group.

"FBI backup," he said to no one in particular, touching the phone's holster. "Need to check outside. Nothing alarming."

Both guys nodded. Kirk went back to the lobby-living area, grabbed his coat, and headed for the door. The chimes jingled, the door swung toward Kirk, and then caught his forearm. A rush of cold air invaded the room. Greg appeared one foot from Kirk's nose.

"Sorry," Greg mumbled. He stepped back.

"I was coming out to check on you." Kirk stepped back in the opposite direction. "Everything okay?"

Greg dropped his coat and gloves and sat in front of the fireplace. Kirk took off his coat and sat on the couch right behind him.

"Jeez," Greg said. "Edgy, aren't you? I was gone less than half a hour. Wired all around. Six windows. Programmed into my phone."

"How does it work?" Kirk asked. "Can I see?"

Greg smiled, pulled the phone from his holster, touched a few keys, and turned the phone toward Kirk. The memory of the taxi driver doing the same thing flashed into Kirk's mind. Greg's phone could be an ultrasound probe. Was Greg trying to shatter his aorta? Kirk bolted up from the couch as if by instinct and placed his chest at the phone's height, instead of his unprotected neck. Hoping the bubble would work if needed, steadied his hand and reached for the phone.

"Brand new app," Greg said, pointing to a set of six horizontal green bars on the screen. "Each bar is a window. If anyone opens the latch or breaks the glass, a loud alarm will sound and the bar from the corresponding window will turn red."

Sounded innocent enough. But Kirk wanted more. Time to play dumb and electronically challenged. He touched the bottom of Greg's phone. The icons of all apps appeared. Kirk's thumb found the text's icon.

"What are you doing?" Greg asked, grabbing his phone back from Kirk. "Don't touch anything or I'll have to reprogram the whole damn thing."

Kirk had just enough time to see the image on the screen—ready to be analyzed. The screen showed no texts. Either Greg had told him the truth about programming the windows, or he was the undercover terrorist who, wiping the screen clean from the text, revealed the location of the designated survivor to his people. In that case, someone else was coming.

"Lunch time," a male voice announced from the left side of the room.

A portly man with a white outfit and gray hair sticking out of a chef's hat pushed a large cart to the narrow table and started to unload salads and sandwiches next to fruit and nuts.

"Dinner will be in the dining room later." He pointed to the open door opposite the bedroom corridor. "So you can eat, and watch the State of the

Union Address on the large screen."

Kirk nodded. His hand went to his chest, pressing where the pain had been on that dreadful evening only about ten days ago. Nothing. So far so good. Either there was no ultrasound probe in Greg's phone, or if there was, the bubble wrap was working. Or it could be too early to tell. Last time it had taken almost an hour for the symptoms to start. Kirk looked at the time. Only 1:15. The day was still young. More than seven hours to go until the State of the Union. Greg went to the table and served himself a salad and a sandwich. Kirk was starving. Nothing since Mulville's coffee in the morning had hit his stomach.

"I'm going to get the others," Kirk said.

His steps accelerated the closer he got to the bedrooms, as if escalating fear was driving him. Was the Secretary safe alone with the other two agents? Kirk cursed. Worrying about Greg had clouded his judgment. For all he knew, the Secretary could be dead and the football gone.

Starting in the deserted corridor, he ran the rest of the way to the spa entrance. The air felt damp and hot. He pushed on the spa door and a subtle smell of mildew and chlorine hit his nose. The room was full of lounge and massage chairs. A side lamp cast a warm pinkish light and long shadows. The Jacuzzi pool bubbled in a corner next to a coffee table with paper cups, napkins, and a large pitcher full of ice cubes, water, and lemon wedges. The steam room looked dark and opaque behind a glass door on the back wall. Kirk pulled on the handle of the wood-framed glass door. The seal opened with a whoosh and steam rushed out. Kirk waved it away with his hand and surveilled the small room. Empty. Sweat poured out of his pores.

He pivoted on his heels and stepped out. The door hissed closed behind him. He ran to the corridor, stopped at the Secretary's door, and stood still. His eyes went to the American flag on his sweatshirt. He had to slow down. Mulville was probably watching every move he made with the damn little flag. If Kirk wasn't careful, Mulville would soon fly through the door to extract him, and Kirk would be responsible for blowing the plan to save the country. He tried to wipe the flag's eye to clear the steam away. He took a breath and knocked at the Secretary's door. No answer.

Kirk placed his ear to the wood. Nothing. He looked around. Should he get another agent for backup? If so, which one? He couldn't trust anyone. He pushed on the handle. Locked. Now what? He knew from his martial art training that knocking down a locked door with a heel kick happens only in the movies. The rebound from a thick door like this would probably dislocate his hip. Should he shoot at the lock? He had never protected a designated survivor from terrorists before. From his holster, he extracted the gun and removed the safety. The first bullet was already chambered.

"Don't even think of it," a male voice said into his ear.

The sound had come from his phone. The screen lit up but remained blank—Mulville. Kirk touched the green private button.

"What?" Kirk said into his wrist's microphone. "The guy's not answering."

"Probably getting smashed in the shower," Mulville said. "I'm sure he brought his own booze. Not worth me having to pay for a new door. Put that gun away."

"But—" Kirk said.

"But nothing." Mulville sounded firm. "Trust me. Nothing will happen to the designated survivor until the State of the Union. The football is useless unless the President and everybody on the succession list after him are whacked. You have seven hours to relax. Go sit in that steam room you showed me a while ago. Have a Scotch. Now, not later. You've got time to burn a drink. But for God's sake, relax. Otherwise, you'll be a totally nervous wreck when we need you to perform."

This was a different league. Kirk felt like a little league ball player trying to hit in the World Series. But Kirk was the only one who could do it, and he would die trying, if he had to, learning the ropes as he went along.

"Listen," Mulville added, "you're doing great. But call me when you're in doubt, if you have time. If not, I trust your judgment. For now, keep on knocking. No need for firearms at this time."

Kirk replaced the gun. He felt no anger. Mulville had his back, in more ways than one.

He knocked again. This time the lock turned and the door opened a few inches. The Secretary's face appeared. Large frown, wide eyes, tight mouth. Kirk looked down. A towel around his waist was the man's only garment.

"Christ," he said, "can't you all just take a long hike? What instructions did they give you? That I can't take a piss or a shower without someone looking at my dick? You goons are going to kill me before the night is over."

The Secretary's head withdrew. The coffee table in the background showed through the small crack. On it stood a fifth of Johnny Walker next to a tall glass full of ice.

"Lunch is ready, Mr. President," Kirk said.

Kirk didn't wait for an answer. He spun around and returned to the living room. Mulville must be having a ball.

Patrizia opened her eyes. She lay on her side, arms around knees drawn to her face. The fetal position gave her comfort and made it easier to imagine her mom hugging her. But her mom wasn't there, and Patrizia was still in hell. The gray windowless cube surrounded her, her clothes stunk of sweat from her forced trampoline workouts, she was starving, and she was fearful of the future.

She checked her watch. Mom had told her never to take it off. Her finger slid over the smooth dial. Mom had a similar watch and, as long as they both wore it, they were together. She sniffled. The time was 6:37. Already evening. Where had the day gone? She must've fallen asleep. No wonder she was starving. She had had no breakfast or lunch. Had they forgotten about her? Last thing she remembered before falling asleep was the disgusting man yelling at the woman, and talking to the other man about Heaven. Now the house was totally silent. Were they all dead? Her body started to shake.

She threw the thin blanket to the floor and stood up. Slow and silent steps took her to the wall. She held her breath and listened hard. Only muffled traffic noises from the street reached her. If everyone was gone, perhaps she could escape. Her heart jumped at the thought of freedom. How she wanted her mom. Besides, she needed to eat. Kind of silly waiting around for days, only to find out she was alone all this time. She walked to the door.

Her hand went to the handle. She pressed down, pulled. The door opened.

The door had always been locked in the past. Maybe they wanted her to escape. Her heart pounded. She walked into the corridor. The wooden floor squeaked under her sneakers. She turned a corner and the front door appeared at the end of the corridor. Only the bathroom and a bedroom door to get past before reaching the exit. The bedroom door was open. She froze. But her feet kept on moving despite the paralyzing fear.

By the time she got to the jamb, she heard the clicking of computer keys. Her head moved forward to acquire a view of the inside of the room. The larger man sat at a table in front of a portable computer, typing with speed and precision. Numbers and letters rolled onto the screen. What was the man doing? Programming. That's what they called it in the computer class Patrizia had taken. Was he hacking into some system, like in the movies? The good news was he had his back to her. And the man was so busy and focused on the screen she might make it to the front door without being seen.

A long step took Patrizia close to the second door jamb. The next step placed her on the other side of the door. She took a few more quick steps and closed her hand around the front door knob, squeezed the round metal shape, and turned the knob. The door didn't budge. Her breathing now came in rapid gasps. Her eyes went all around the frame and rested on a small latch at the bottom. A padlock secured the door to the wall. She was trapped.

"Time to go back to your room," a deep male voice said behind her. "For good."

She turned. The man towered over her. Patrizia flattened her back against the door. The close-up smell of unclean flesh nauseated her. She was all alone with a monster.

———∽∽∽———

Kirk walked into the dining room, showered and relaxed. He had even fallen asleep for a moment in his bedroom, with all the doors open at the request of the bald agent with the football. Kirk might as well scratch Ray off the list of suspects.

The dining room was larger than he had expected. Kirk counted ten tables. Paul Ventana must be running a restaurant and on top of that had a few rooms for bed and breakfast. Two tables were joined together between a bench and three cushioned chairs. It was set for six with white dishes, glasses, and shiny utensils. Light came from lamps hanging from the overhead wooden beams. The high ceiling and high windows imparted a feeling of rustic elegance. Kirk wished he could one day come back and have a romantic dinner here with Aurora—one day when all this was in the past. Now it was time to fight for that future. He was ready.

"Hey, Kirk." The Secretary's voice reached him from behind. "You finally look relaxed."

A heavy hand patted his back. Kirk detected a whiff of liquor. He turned. The Secretary wore a blue suit, white shirt, and red tie. The other three agents came in with him. Ray McGregor still carried the football. Judging by his wet hair, it looked as if Greg had also showered. He walked to the bar.

The Secretary sat on a chair between Ray and Marc. Kirk took a place in front of him. The pilot joined them and sat next to Kirk. Greg came back with two bottles of wine and a bottle opener. The chef brought in salads on the same cart he had used to bring lunch earlier. He stopped next to Greg, who was fumbling with the foil on the first bottle.

"May I?" the chef asked.

Greg smiled and handed him the bottle, then reached down with one hand. Kirk jumped up from his seat and straightened his spine in attention. But Greg wasn't reaching for a gun. Only for the phone. What about the phone? Was his phone a lethal weapon?

"Hold on," Kirk said, extending out his hand. "Phones should be used only for official purposes."

Greg's smile froze on his face. He stood still, the phone lifted into the picture-taking position. He seemed puzzled.

"Come on, Kirk. Smile," the Secretary said. "Picture time. I'd like to remember this evening. Go ahead, Greg."

The Secretary placed his arms, one on each Secret Service agent at his side, and flashed his teeth with the charm of an experienced actor. Ray and Marc remained expressionless. Greg clicked away, then turned toward Kirk and the pilot and kept on clicking. Was this the moment of no return? Kirk pulled up his vest to cover the base of his neck.

The chef poured some wine. Greg replaced the phone, sniffed his glass, tasted, and approved. Was this a good sign? As far as Kirk knew, very religious people wouldn't drink alcohol. Perhaps this meant that Greg wasn't radicalized after all. Greg took a place next to Kirk. Everyone started on the salad.

"One hundred and twenty-two minutes to POTUS," Ray announced. He placed a device with the time and the ongoing countdown in the middle of the table.

The timer showed 7:02. At nine o'clock, the President of the United States, also referred to with the acronym POTUS, would walk into the House chamber for an address to a joint session of the House and the Senate. The secretary lifted his glass. Only Greg toasted with him. None of the other agents or the pilot touched the wine.

"You and me should play a game," the Secretary told Greg with a conspiratorial wink. "It's called the State of the Union drinking game. Of course, all can join in. I heard this is the best night of the year in the Secret Service.

No responsibilities, no threats, no nothing. After all, we're safe. We've got a designated driver right here."

He pointed to the pilot. The middle-aged military man nodded as if to indicate he had been in similar situations before. The chef came in with an assortment of meats and side dishes and started serving.

"Here's how it works," the Secretary went on to explain. "Every time the President mentions the words 'jobs,' or 'healthcare,' we need to take a sip from our drink. And every time he blames the Congress for something, we finish the drink. Other words like that are worth a different number of sips."

"I read about this game somewhere," Greg said. "In one of his past speeches, the President mentioned "health-care" more than twenty times, and "jobs" more than thirty times. I thought it was a joke."

"Gonna be real tonight," the Secretary said. "We better have quite a bit of booze ready. And don't you all worry about me. Someone once said that anybody with a pulse could do the job of designated survivor."

Was Mulville recording all this? Kirk hoped so. Such irresponsible behavior shouldn't go unpunished. And Kirk's job was to make sure the designated survivor still had a pulse by the end of the night.

CHAPTER 28

STATE OF THE UNION ADDRESS

T he large man's thick fingers closed around Patrizia's arm. Her body stiffened, as if unable to move. He dragged her from the front door, across the corridor, and back into her cubic prison. Her body swayed to the point of losing balance, then her legs moved, coerced by a powerful pull. The man slammed her face against the hard mattress and yanked her wrists back. Pain shot between her shoulder blades as her shoulders protruded from their sockets. She turned her head, moaning in despair. The man held a thick rope in his hand. He had come prepared. She felt the rough rope going around her wrist. Her ankles were next.

Terror made her unable to speak. Panic paralyzed her, as if it knew that submission gave her the best chance of survival.

He was looking at her. What she saw in his eyes made her body revolt in disgust. The rough touch of his thick fingertips on her lips made her scream. The man jammed the rope between her teeth. A thick and sticky tape followed, making it difficult to breathe. She closed her eyes. But in the dark, she could still see the man's blackened teeth and could smell his breath. Was she going to die? She hoped so. Because the man's fingers didn't stop. He was touching her sweatshirt, trying to find her breasts. No, not there! Not the most private parts, the parts that no one except she had been allowed to touch. Not even her mom. Her face burned. She shuddered and bit on the rope as hard as she could. Tears streamed down her eyes. She held her breath and wished she could die.

In that moment, a strange beep came from behind her back. She opened her eyes. The man seemed startled. He stopped touching her, looked around, and turned her over. Her watch was beeping.

His rough hand pulled on the strap and snatched the watch from her wrist. She turned her head. The man looked at the watch, fascinated, as if he had forgotten all about her. Then something seemed to go off in his head, as if a conclusion of some kind had occurred to him. Next thing she knew, the watch had clattered to the floor and a crunching sound filled the room. With his heel, the man had stomped on her mom's gift. The one her mom had told her never to take off.

The man stormed out of the room as if in a hurry to get somewhere soon. Patrizia watched him go, her cheek on the mattress, the smell of dust and mildew penetrating her nostrils. She bit on the rope between her teeth and pulled on her restraints. Acute pain burst from her shoulders. The rope cut into her wrists and ankles.

Would the large man come back? If so, what would he do to her? But if no one came, she would die of thirst and starvation. And without the watch, her mom wouldn't have any way to find her.

Sayed killed the engine and got out of the car. The Jeep had gone as far as possible into the thicket of trees. The GPS on his sleeve showed the vehicle's location overlapping with the pre-selected spot. Aziz won't have any problem finding the car if he were the one left behind.

The Ventana farm was less than one mile away. All nearby hills and icy rocks were covered by frozen snow and trees. Sayed sat back in the driver's seat, reached for a pair of crampons with steel spikes sitting on the passenger front seat, and strapped them to his boots.

As if by instinct, he grabbed a bottle of water from the seat holder, unscrewed the cap, and drank the entire contents on the spot. No sense in carrying more weight than necessary. He popped the trunk open, got out, slammed the car door shut, zipped his jacket over his gun, and walked to the back of the car. From the trunk, he removed the rectangular black case, then locked the trunk. One last look reassured him the car was secure. He lowered the night goggles onto his face and started to hike up the hill.

Silence soothed him. The crunching of his feet and the rhythm of his breathing kept him company. After seventeen minutes, the faint glow of thermal radiation appeared in his visual field. It was in the shape of a large mass—a van. It was the infidels' backup. He stopped walking and stood in position. After surveilling his surroundings, he took a few more steps and saw the Farm's glow appearing through the trees. No other thermal image. He pictured a large triangle, the base a straight line from the farmhouse to the van. Sayed took position at the apex, on a hill. His vantage point gave him full vision of the van and the farmhouse at the same time. He unlocked the black case.

For a better view of the large screen, the Secretary and the four agents moved to the bar area, a few round tables surrounded by upholstered armchairs. The men turned the chairs to face the screen. The Secretary called for a variety of hard liquor. Greg placed a blue bottle of Bombay Sapphire on the round table next to the clear bottle of Kettle One Vodka. Golden Cuervo tequila and the familiar Johnny Walker followed. A tinkling noise came from the kitchen. The chef was loading different-shaped glasses and a bucket of ice. Kirk shook his head and looked at the senior agents.

Ray sat so straight he might as well have swallowed a rod. His eyes stared at the screen as if trying to avoid the Secretary. His hands wrapped the armchair with whitish knuckles. The football was locked between his calves.

Agent Marc sat between his colleague and the Secretary himself. A deep frown crossed his forehead. Kirk wished he could speak freely and in private to these men, but it was impossible to distinguish friends from enemies with any degree of certainty. He pulled a chair and sat next to Ray.

"How're you doing?" Kirk hinted at a smile.

"Okay." Ray turned to him, his face stern.

"Any family at home?" Kirk asked.

Would the existence of a family decrease the chance of terrorism? The bald man hesitated. Kirk worried. Was family a forbidden subject among Secret Service agents sworn to die to protect the President? Had Kirk's question given away his cover?

"Wife and a boy." Ray's mouth stretched into a sad smile. "Missing a birthday tonight. My son is turning ten. Today."

"Can't beat the role model," Kirk said. "I'm sure he'll understand."

Kirk wished he could count on the senior agent being on his side. The contempt he read in his eyes for the Secretary's behavior spoke in Ray's favor. Judging from his behavior, the Secretary himself could've been on the terrorist side. Ray went back staring at the screen.

On the screen, the press killed time, alternating interviews of officials passing by with lengthy explanations of the entry protocols for the expected 600-plus attendees. The Secretary loosened his tie, removed his jacket, and draped it on his armchair. The pilot turned from his chair and pointed at the timer on the nearby table. The countdown to POTUS was at 60 minutes, 32 seconds. "They're starting to come in," he said.

Nobody paid much attention. Only Kirk nodded, out of courtesy. The pilot smiled. Members of the House were filling up the chamber.

The tracking-point precision-guided semi-automatic rifle stood assembled and in position on the hill's frozen ground. Sayed sat on a rock and ran his fingers over the rifle's cold and hard surface as if caressing a woman. He mentally thanked his big brother Aziz for arranging the purchase of the killing machine from a clandestine company located somewhere in Texas.

Officially, the weapon was sold for sport. But what kind of sport was it when you can't miss? His mind named the different features associated with each component sliding under his fingers: compass, inertia measurement device, ballistic calculator, tracking engine, integral laser rangefinder, objective lenses, environmental sensor for pressure and temperature, low light, and infrared filter. His hand lingered on the Tag-Track technology. The innocent-looking plastic tube linked the Networked Tracking Scope with the guided trigger.

Sayed would use the tag button to paint a red dot on each of the targets. Regardless of the targets' movements, the tracker would go to work. The device would lock onto the dot—the moving target—and communicate with the trigger. The trigger would fire automatically, hitting targets as much as 500 yards away. Its two-inch accuracy applied regardless of the shooter's position: keeling, standing, or prone. In his hands was the most accurate shooting system in the world—a fighter-jet, lock and launch technology reduced to a rifle system. He waited.

The Deputy Sergeant at Arms addressed the House Speaker and announced the Vice President and members of the Senate, who entered and took their assigned seats. Kirk glanced at the timer: 8:31 PM. Twenty-nine minutes and twenty-one seconds to POTUS. Then the Deputy Sergeant at Arms addressed the Speaker again and announced, in order, the dean of the diplomatic corps, the Chief Justice of the United States, the Associate Justices, and Cabinet members, each of whom entered and took their seats after being called.

The Secretary placed five shot glasses in a straight line. He considered the different options, then chose the clear bottle and poured vodka into all five. He upturned his palm, pointing to the full glasses as an invitation to the agents. Ray and Marc waved their hands in refusal. The Secretary shrugged. The two agents hadn't touched any alcohol—not even wine at dinner. Good agents or radicalized terrorist? Kirk wondered.

Greg arrived from the bar with a tall glass full of ice and an amber liquid of some kind.

"I'm sticking with this stuff." He lifted his glass as if toasting, took a long gulp of his drink, and dropped into a chair opposite the Secretary. "Great Bourbon."

Kirk pushed back from his chair and walked to his room. He double-locked the door and entered the bathroom. Perhaps the last chance to talk to Mulville and relieve himself at the same time, before something happened, if something did happen. He locked the bathroom door and started to speed dial Aurora, but stopped before he could finish. No time to stir emotions, only time for full focus. He pocketed his phone and took out the official communicator. Time for the green button.

"Mulville," the familiar brusque voice said. "I saw everything. It's worse than I thought. The guy should be at some fucking AA meeting, not acting as President."

"What can I do about it?" Kirk asked. "Should I intervene?"

"If you do, everyone will know who sent you," Mulville said, "and I'll kiss goodbye to my fucking pension. Keep cool and put the bastard to bed if he passes out. I trust Ray to hold the football tight between his legs like a favorite broad. At least you can count on him. That Greg is a wild card. The Secretary must've chosen him because he'd enable him. It's freaking disgusting how they guzzle our tax dollars. Go watch the show. I'll keep an eye out. Good luck."

Kirk poured a glass of water from the faucet and took several long gulps. He sat on the toilet, aware of his breathing and of his heartbeat. He got up, unfastened and removed the bullet-proof vest, lifted his arms, and turned in front of the mirror. The bubble wrap looked intact and covered his entire chest, front, sides, and back. Had the wrap already protected him during Greg's pictures? Kirk would soon find out. He put the bullet-proof vest back on, washed his hands, splashed cool water on his hot face, patted his skin with a paper towel, and went back to rejoin the circus.

As he entered the bar area, Kirk watched the screen. The Sergeant at Arms stood at the doorway inside the House chamber. The time on the screen showed 9:02. The timer had reached and passed 0'0' and had been turned off. The President came into view behind the Sergeant of Arms. The angle changed and the camera showed the Sergeant at Arms facing the Speaker, then turning to the President. The President nodded behind him. The Sergeant at Arms announced: "Mister Speaker, the President of the United States!"

Applause and cheering followed. The Secretary raised the first shot glass and poured it into his open mouth. His lips tightened. He looked at the empty glass and let go quite a whistle. Kirk ran his damp fingers through his hair.

The President smiled and walked toward the Speaker's rostrum, followed by members of his Congressional escort committee. Pausing for handshakes, hugs, kisses, and the autographing of memorabilia for members of Congress slowed his approach. He took his place at the House clerk's desk and handed a manila envelope to both the Speaker and Vice President.

"Copies of his speech," the pilot said, turning to Kirk and pointing at the screen.

The pilot had addressed Kirk directly as if he knew Kirk needed the explanation. Was he questioning and testing his Secret Service legitimacy? Maybe the pilot was talking to him because Kirk was the only one listening. Kirk sat down on the same armchair next to Marc and behind the Secretary and Ray.

On the screen, the attendees' applause and cheers continued uninterrupted for several minutes. The Speaker waited until the noise abated, then he introduced the President to the Representatives and Senators. This led to a new round of applause. Then there was silence. The President looked out over the audience, holding his smile intact, then fixed his eyes on the teleprompter at his right and began to speak.

Thirty minutes later, Kirk took a sip of black coffee and stretched out in his chair. He wished he could change channels and watch a more interesting show. It seemed that every sentence the President uttered had some words that justified drinking in the Secretary's game. After the first ten or fifteen minutes, Marc pulled his seat over and agreed to join in, using only soda or water. Kirk guessed the Secretary's ego required validation. Probably in his mind, he wasn't drinking alone. Greg had stuck with the amber-colored drink. He filled all his shot glasses from the same Jim Beam bottle. Kirk counted at least four shots with ice. But Greg's hand seemed steady. The man must have complete resistance to alcohol. If only Greg went to take a leak, Kirk could check things out. Greg was young—too young for prostate trouble—but his bladder must be exploding by now, no matter what he was drinking.

At the risk of appearing anti-social, Kirk had refused all invitations to join the game. His job required him only to protect people's asses, not to kiss any. Screams filled the room again, glasses clinked, and liquor flowed down throats. What was that about? Kirk refocused on the speech. The President was talking about healthcare.

Above the tilted glass, Greg's eyes looked alert and focused. Kirk noticed a few beads of sweat appearing on the agent's wide forehead. He still wore his full suit. All the agents did, Kirk included. The football still rested between Ray's legs. Kirk could see it from where he sat. The Secretary wobbled in his seat and seemed ready to keel over, but still managed to comply with the rule of the drinking game with each mention of "health care."

At last, Greg excused himself and walked away carrying the Jim Beam bottle. Not stupid. But not smart either. Kirk got up, walked to the table, put down his coffee, and picked up the agent's drained glass instead. He rested his nose on the rim. No pungent whiff. Only the placid scent of tea. The others didn't seem to pay attention or care. The President had just blamed the Congress, and the game players drained their drinks.

"God!" Ray shouted. "Who spiked my Coke?"

He was still in his chair, away from the table, as if in a world of his own.

His face showed an annoyed, puzzled expression. He got up and walked to the sink carrying the football. The Coke gurgled down the sink. Ray centered the waste basket with the empty can.

"Afraid our colleague did," Kirk said. He held up Greg's glass. "And there is no booze in his glass."

Marc looked at his own drink, sniffed it, shook his head in reproach, and went to the sink to empty and wash his glass. He rubbed his mouth with the back of his hand a few times, as if the gesture could neutralize any possible liquor. Had Greg planned to incapacitate the other agents? Might he be planning something soon? Time to confront him. What about Marc? He could be in on it too, trying to keep his own cover with some improvised act.

Kirk took his coffee and went back to his chair. He needed to think. The speech had gone on for about thirty-five minutes. Not much longer now and Kirk could put the Secretary to bed and forget all about this wasted evening. Perhaps the spiked drink had been a gag. Kirk could almost understand Greg. Ray for sure looked as if he needed to relax a little. And Kirk needed to relax also. Tension fostered paranoia. Kirk chuckled, and his smile froze on his face.

Something the President had just said seemed odd. And now the President looked silent and puzzled. Kirk looked around. Ray had noticed it also. He had jumped up from his seat and now was fumbling with the remote control to go back and review the President's words. Kirk watched the President's mouth speak the words backward and fast. Then Ray froze the image.

"Silence!" Kirk shouted to the Secretary and Marc. "Listen up."

The Secretary lifted his tired lids and took another sip of his drink, as if in defiance of Kirk's order. Marc stood and approached the screen. Greg was nowhere to be seen. The recording played. "— Congress to approve a law against fast foods containing excessive animal fats," the President said. "And watch out. Your aortic dissection will come within one hour."

The hair on the back of Kirk's neck stood up. He felt paralyzed. The President paused. The puzzled look on his face came back as it had during the live transmission. A blanket of silence, then whispers turned into chatting. A burst of laughter exploded among the attendees. Applause followed. Kirk looked around. Marc was laughing. Greg was back, laughing as well. The Secretary clapped his hands and filled another glass with tequila, just for the heck of it. Only Ray remained pensive in front of the screen.

Kirk thought of the old TV series, "The Twilight Zone," that he used to watch with Aurora. The main character often was trapped in nightmarish situations, where he'd be the only one who knew the truth, and nobody would believe him or help him. But Kirk had Mulville.

Was Mulville watching? What was he thinking? Kirk rose and rushed out of the room. Before turning into the corridor, he looked back one last time. Greg was the only one aware of his movements. Greg had stopped laughing. His face looked tense, eyes locked on Kirk. Kirk's stomach contracted in a knot.

"Holy shit," Mulville said, pointing at the TV screen. "Did you hear what he just said? The bastards must've hacked the President's speech. They're threatening the entire audience. I was fucking right."

His thumb pressed on the volume button. The President had started to speak again. He was thanking his staff for substituting strong words in his speech to convince people of the necessity of federal controls. Frigging diplomacy. His speech gets hacked and he doesn't bat an eye. The sucker could make excuses if someone exploded a bomb up his presidential ass. Mulville's waist buzzed.

"Yes, Kirk," Mulville answered. "I heard it. They're all laughing their heads off. What do you expect? They told us not to spread panic. Nobody knows how serious this is. The few idiots who know what really happened to the Chief of Staff don't believe it was man-made anyway."

"Should we," Kirk said, "extract? I mean leave? Is this for real?"

Mulville locked eyes with the woman agent and the young blond man next to him. He pointed to their surveillance screens. They both shook their heads in reassurance.

"Stay put," Mulville said. "Go back to the room and keep our visual. Maybe it's just terror they want. Panic."

"But they aren't getting it," Kirk said. "Because very few people know what these bastards did already. What if the terrorists were counting on the State of the Union's live audience to know how dangerous they are from previous crimes? Maybe heart attacks and carotid dissections were done to show that their threats were for real, so that the entire government would be thrown into a state of panic by a statement from the President like the one we just heard."

Mulville remained silent. Maybe keeping a lid on the killings had been the right thing to do. For once, the FBI director might have done the right thing. No knowledge, therefore no panic.

"But what if it's true?" Kirk went on. "What if they want to kill the entire crowd? Then why would they broadcast a warning?"

"Perhaps they want both," Mulville said. "Panic and deaths. Complete disruption. Only one way to find out for sure."

"Silvana," Kirk said. "Silvana would know if this is a real or an empty threat. Call Steve. This time we really need him. He's the only one who can get through to her."

"Okay," Mulville said. "Go back. We need to keep a constant visual. Any problem, give us the signal and we'll come in."

"Yes," Kirk said, his heart beating in his neck. "Tell Steve to hurry."

Mulville looked at the time—9:41. He had twenty to thirty minutes until the end of the speech and perhaps another half hour before all the assembled would leave the House chamber. When would they start dying? If the President was correct, the symptoms would start between then and 10:30.

But why was he thinking this way? Deep inside, Mulville believed it was true. One hour max to figure out if he was right or wrong. It was not often

DISSECTION

Mulville hoped to be wrong. This was one of those times.

CHAPTER 29

PRISONER

Mulville's breaths became deeper and closer together with every unanswered ring of the doctor's phone. What if Steve didn't pick up? What was Mulville going to do? Get a helicopter ride to the jail and abandon Kirk Miner? Mulville's eyes went to his three companions inside the van. The two men and one woman sat in deep focus, glued to their assigned monitors. Mulville saw tension in their hands and in the way their feet stood flat on the ground, ready to spring should an emergency arise. All three were capable, and chosen for loyalty, discretion, and reliability. But Mulville would never forgive himself if anything went sour in his absence. He couldn't go anywhere. Steve Leeds had to answer.

"Hello." The doctor's voice had the muffled, echoing quality of a car speaker. "What's happening?"

Steve wasn't listening to the speech? The thought immediately popped into Mulville's mind as a reproach, but the doctor's question sounded loaded with fear. The doctor must know.

"I'm on my way to the hospital," Steve said. "The casualties will start arriving any time. I hope not all 600 or so at the same time. I'll alert all surrounding medical facilities."

"Doctor," Mulville said, "please listen carefully. I need you to go to the jail. Now. To speak to Silvana. We need to know for sure this is for real, that people have been exposed to killer waves."

"With all due respect, Agent Mulville," Steve said, "are you insane? We don't need Silvana now. We know what these people are capable of. We've already seen the results of their work."

Mulville bit his lip. No cursing. Not now. Steve Leeds was the only chance he had. He had to convince him. Only fifty-four minutes to go.

"Steve, Doctor," Mulville said with all the calm he could gather. "We need to know who's the man in charge. We can show Silvana pictures of the Secret Service agents protecting the designated survivor now. If she IDs any of them as the one she dealt with, we can get him now, and stop the entire thing before it starts. Then, if the crisis is real, you can go and do your surgeries."

Static and traffic noises came through the line. What was Steve thinking? Was he changing direction? Mulville needed something more convincing. Something that would persuade the doctor. What? He slammed his hand on the counter.

"Steve," he said, "Silvana probably never intended to hurt anyone. Emerson told us the intensity of the waves in her calculations wasn't enough to cause any dissections."

"How long have you known this?" Steve said. "And you never told me?"

"Listen, Doc, there's been no time for explanations. All this is confidential FBI business. I'm telling it to you now, because you're the only one who can do what needs to be done. Kirk and I are tied up. Now we need you to convince Silvana to cooperate, so we know what we're up against."

Distant traffic noise filled the silence. Damn. What else could Mulville throw at the doc to alter his thinking?

"She may even have a way to help you decide who's in most urgent need of surgery," Mulville said, "like that gizmo they didn't want to use for her brother—or maybe she can concoct some shit to stop the waves. What do I know?"

Static and the sound of screeching brakes followed. Then Steve's voice came through crystal clear.

"For once, you make some sense, Mulville," Steve said. "Maybe my waiting time can be spent more efficiently. If I have to crack open six hundred chests, I may as well go hide and pray."

"Go," Mulville said. "I'll get you emergency access. And I need a visual with her—Skype or something. I might have to crash Kirk's party any time. If you don't get me, go ahead and call my boss, the FBI director, with what you've found. I'll text you his number. Good luck."

The car sounded like it was accelerating again. The call ended. Thirty-five minutes to mayhem.

Kirk walked back to the bar. His feet felt heavy, as if his sneaker soles were sticking to the floor and he had to peel them off with each step. He stopped at the end of the corridor. The last thing Kirk wanted was to join the party again. What would he find? One more step brought the room into full vision.

Nobody seemed to have missed him. The Secretary had his head on the back of his chair and looked still, his eyes closed. His chest moved with breaths. Still alive. The three agents sat in silence in front of the TV screen. The table stood cluttered with empty bottles and dirty glasses. The speech was still on. Almost one hour long so far. The audience in the House chamber seemed to have recovered from the glitch and continued to act normally. No one clutched his chest or screamed for help. Not yet. Only applause, some scattered boos, and an occasional standing ovation. How much longer? Nothing like all these interruptions to stretch a one-hour speech by an extra twenty minutes.

While waiting for Steve's arrival, Mulville looked at his screen and fought the impulse to talk to Silvana by himself on Skype. He couldn't risk blowing the only chance of finding out the truth about the entire mess.

"Get the prisoner into the interrogation room," he told the prison director. "I want the doctor to have full contact. I don't think you'll have any problem. As I told you, this is a national emergency. And give me a full visual of the room."

The white-haired man nodded. He gazed around as if looking for help, asked for ten minutes to get ready, and kept his word. Within a few minutes, the gray interrogation room came into vision with still thirty-one minutes to go in Mulville's projected scenario. The last message from Steve was that he was getting into the detention center elevator. Mulville took a needed deep breath and a sip of coffee. The warm liquid eased the tightness in his chest.

Silvana appeared. The soft clanking of her leg restraints accompanied her shuffling to a metal chair in front of a rectangular table. Only apathy showed on her face.

Steve entered. He stopped for a moment and his mouth twitched. He reached for the metal chair on the opposite side of the table. Mulville was no shrink, but he knew anger, surprise, and even a hint of excitement when he saw it. He picked all that up from a flicker of Silvana's eye. The woman still felt something for the doctor. Mulville had chosen the right person to do the talking.

"What are you doing here?" she asked Steve, her eyes now alive with reproach.

"Silvana." Steve's voice sounded austere. "We need to talk. Mulville is on the monitor, at the FBI. We know what they're after."

"There is no 'they,'" she said. "I'm alone. I told you. I'm after revenge."

The resistance was back. Up to Steve to find a way to reach her. Mulville sat up straighter and took another sip of coffee.

"I don't believe you," Steve said. "You wouldn't want to paralyze the entire United States government to avenge your brother."

Her brown eyes dilated. She seemed in full panic mode.

"The government?" she asked. "What are you talking about?"

"They are after the State of the Union assembly," Steve said, eyes fixed on hers. "They hacked into the President's speech. The president read: "Your aortic dissections will arrive within an hour.""

She remained silent, biting her lower lip. Steve looked at his watch.

"And that was almost an hour ago," he added. "Is this for real? How can they affect more than 600 people with ultrasound probes that self-destruct after a single pulse?"

Silvana remained still. Mulville nervously shifted in his seat.

"Silvana," Steve said, "I'm afraid we're dealing with terrorists. The Presidential Chief of Staff died three days ago of an aortic dissection. Three FDA committee members had massive strokes. One was DOA, and doctors pulled the plug yesterday on another one, a woman. But that was warm-up time. We think the State of the Union is show time."

Steve paused. Mulville took a breath, ready to yell at the bitch. Silvana looked at his image and flinched. Good. She must've detected some of the homicidal anger on his face.

"Silvana," Steve went on, "we know you didn't mean to hurt anyone. The intensity of the waves in your calculations isn't enough to cause any dissections. But these people obviously knew how to take your work and modify it to advance their deadly ends. And now they know you tried to trick them. Do you think they're going to spare your daughter?"

"What are you saying?" Her eyes widened with resentment, but her tone betrayed defeat. "What do you know about that?"

"Emerson, your post-doc, told us." Steve's tone sounded firm and unyielding, as if delivering the final blow to a cornered adversary. "I'm asking you again. How would they cause dissections to so many people at once? Is it for real, or just to cause panic? At least tell me that much."

She closed her eyes. Mulville watched her calculating the odds in her mind. Her daughter's life hung in the balance. A strange new feeling wrestled with rage in Mulville's mind. Was he going soft on the scientist? Mulville couldn't remember the last time he had experienced compassion for anyone, let alone a criminal. Perhaps the new information had shone new light on the struggling woman.

"It's real." Her eyes opened, revealing a new shade of despair.

Mulville looked at the TV screen carrying the speech. At seventeen past ten, nothing seemed unusual yet. But people would start dropping any time now. The time for diplomacy was up. Time for Mulville to barge into the conversation.

"We know they're after the nuclear football and the designated survivor."

"What?" Both of Silvana's eyes dilated as she connected the old, the new, and her own secret information about the ordeal. Good sign. If only he could scare her into believing the bastards won't return her daughter.

"Dr. Moretti." Mulville's voice boomed and echoed back from the gray room. "I want you to understand the situation fully, so you can make the right choice for you and your daughter. If the government is incapacitated and the terrorists get the nuclear football, we're all finished. Dead. They can launch nuclear weapons. Do you read me?"

Silvana looked paler. Her skin had acquired an unhealthy yellowish tone exaggerated by the glaring halogen light. Shiny beads dotted her forehead.

"They can launch nuclear weapons?" she said. Her metal restraints clattered as she spread her open palms. "Even with the football, it can't be that easy. I read that generals have to be involved—"

Same shit Kirk had said. The conversation was running in circles. He should've been in the room. Then he could've made her talk. He sighed.

"Their purpose," Mulville explained with as much calmness he could summon, "is to paralyze our government and create chaos. As we scrounge around for someone to become president and to take charge, anyone with the football and the nuclear code can make some Army robot push the nuclear switch. The Army is made to obey orders, not to debate them. Are you willing to take a chance with the lives of millions of Americans, including your daughter's?"

Silvana's jaw dropped. Her mouth opened, but no words came out. Steve's eyes locked onto Mulville's image.

"The heart attacks and strokes," Mulville went on, happy he'd finally gotten her attention, "were experiments to cause panic and to set you up, Dr.

Moretti, as a scapegoat. I believe this is the real thing. Keep it up and you'll have on your conscience nuclear blasts in major United States cities. That's what could happen before our government recovers from a mass slaughter. I know these things."

Tears started to stream down Silvana's face. Finally, he had her. Steve jolted in his chair.

"To whom did you give the information about the soundwaves?" Mulville asked. "We suspect at least one of the Secret Service agents protecting the designated survivor may be a terrorist. Dr. Moretti, did you ever see anyone? Could you recognize the man if I showed you the agents' pictures?"

"No." She shook her head. "All communications were by email. A woman picked up Patrizia. Wore a head cover, like a burka."

The Chief of Staff's cleaning lady. Their team must include at least two people, maybe more. Mulville sighed.

"Keep talking. Soon we'll all burn to a crisp."

"They threatened Patrizia," Silvana said. "She would get a heart attack if I didn't go along, or if I said anything. They forced me to give them access to my calculations and to adapt the wavelengths such that they would damage arteries, instead of cure tumors. They took my ID card and got to my instruments at night to program the devices. They researched my brother's case to make it look as if I was sending those tan cards. They said they just wanted to spread panic. No one would die. Not that I ever believed them. That's why I gave them incorrect calculations."

Mulville's eyes darted back to the TV screen. Eighteen past ten and the president was still talking. Behind him, on the right, the Speaker of the House had slouched down in his chair and seemed asleep. But something didn't compute.

Something was wrong with his face. Pale, bluish. The Vice-President sat right next to him. Didn't he realize something was happening?

Mulville saw the Vice-President reach out for the Speaker and shake the Speaker's shoulder. The Speaker collapsed face first. The President turned. A concert of screams and moans filled the room.

"They assured you wrong!" Mulville yelled. "They're dying right now. The Speaker of the House looks dead already. From the screams of the audience, more may be in trouble."

"But the Speaker usually is one of the last to enter," Steve said. "If anything, he should be one of the last to dissect. The President should be the safest one. He entered last."

Silvana looked up through her tears, sat up straight, and began to wipe her face. Mulville and Steve stared at her.

"The man who did the programming," she whispered, "is very knowledgeable—an engineer, or a computer programmer, or both. He obviously knew how to apply my theory to his devices. The transmitter they're using can probably emit different intensities without self-destructing."

The bitch knew more that she was telling. Time to take the gloves off. Screw Steve and his feelings.

"How do you know all this?" Mulville shouted. "Where did they get the transmitter? Did you give it to them?"

Silvana looked shocked. Good. No time for diplomacy.

"No." She stared at Mulville. "They hacked into my computer using my ID. I was working on a larger, more powerful device to be used for cancer therapy. They must've gotten the specifications."

"How many pulses can this device send?" Steve asked.

"It depends on how he programmed it." Her voice had a self-accusatory tone, as if she was confessing to the crime. "He did the programming."

"Worst case scenario?" Mulville said. "What's the maximum number of pulses it can send? Can you guess?"

Silvana seemed to hesitate. Her eyes went to the floor, her face acquiring a reddish color. She looked up again.

"I'm afraid," she whispered, "close to one thousand pulses. And the intensity can be programmed to increase at each pulse. So, the President could be the worst off."

"Wait a minute," Steve said, "you said this device can emit up to one thousand pulses. How? Does it discharge at random, or can it sense when someone goes by?"

"It senses when someone is nearby." Silvana's eyes widened. She nodded. "You have to find it and remove it. Now. Or you'll have more casualties on your hands."

"Thanks for sharing," Mulville said. "I'm afraid it's a little late for that. Over six hundred are attending the speech, and now rescue personnel are coming and going, getting blasted as we speak. Four hundred pulses to go. Great. I'll let my boss know. So where in the fuck did they put it?"

Steve rephrased the question. "Where would they place the device to get everyone?"

"I don't know." Silvana sobbed. "I swear."

"Someplace where one person could do it easily," Mulville said. "Getting in as a janitor."

"Ceiling lights?" Steve asked.

"No," Silvana said. "Too many bulbs to replace. They probably have only one powerful transmitter."

"Somewhere in the bathrooms?" Steve asked. "Mirrors? Faucets?

"No," Mulville said. "The speech lasts around one hour. The President would go into a private bathroom, not into public facilities. It has to be something where everyone passes...without exceptions. Most of all the President."

"The entrance," Silvana said. "On the door jam. A perfect level for aortic dissection. I don't know this for sure, but I think I know how they reason."

"Shit," Steve said. "If that's true, all the people inside have already been exposed. And they can't safely leave until and unless we remove the damn device."

The government was already paralyzed. Trapped like a rat in a cage. Mulville dialed the FBI director.

"Lock the House chamber down," Mulville said after quickly explaining the situation. "Check the door for an ultrasound device and remove it. It's still functional, and deadly, as we already saw. If you can find and remove it, we can prevent further casualties. If not, I guess we have to take our chances and rescue people the best we can."

The silence that followed had an ominous tinge. Only the distressed rhythm of the director's breathing came through. Mulville waited. Was the director going to argue?

"Okay, Mulville," the man said. "I'll go look for it myself."

The line went dead. Mulville stared at the TV monitor. After a short time, the Chamber's front door started to close. Panic rippled through the room in the form of screams, chaotic movements, and faces contorted by fear.

"I got to run to the hospital," Steve said, "and get ready for the casualties. But how can we do all those surgeries? So many, all at once? Many people will die waiting."

"My device could help," Silvana said, her head lifted. "The exposure can be different depending on the angle of the probe. People turned as they passed by the door. Perhaps someone was in front of the transmitter and blocked another person. The terrorists count on the panic, of everybody thinking everyone is at immediate risk. My invention to detect arterial injury can help to tell who is at immediate risk of rupture and needs emergency surgery and who can wait."

"Good," Mulville said. "I'll give orders for the police to escort you to the hospital to work with Dr. Leeds."

"First, I need to get things from my lab," Silvana said. "And I need Emerson. Together, we may be able to do more than just assess the patients. In the meantime, someone must get my daughter. I can reverse the watch's signal, triangulate her location from the previous transmissions, if it hasn't changed. I'll also need equipment from my lab to do that."

"Sure thing," Mulville said. "And what about Kirk? Kirk is with the designated survivor. We've got to let him know he may now be guarding the

President of the United States. What lethal device might they have?"

"But the designated survivor is the most protected man tonight," Steve said. "How could one man take down so many agents?"

Was it pity Mulville saw in Silvana's eyes? The bitch was responsible for creating all these deadly devices and now she was sorry? If she hoped for clemency, she'd better speak up.

"They only need one man in position," Silvana said. "I think they have a portable ultrasound transmitter with them. That's what they must have used earlier against Kirk and the Chief of Staff."

"Do you mean," Mulville said, "like a phone? We think someone used a phone to cause the two aortic dissections."

"A transmitter within a phone," Moretti said, "could be capable of acting at a short distance and with multiple discharges. And the effect could be worsened by the target's fat level, or sugar level, or blood alcohol level. It would easily kill someone with a high alcohol level in his blood."

Alcohol. The terrorists knew, having hacked Moretti's computer. No wonder they had picked the Secretary of Energy as the designated survivor.

CHAPTER 30

AORTIC DISSECTION

Seventeen past ten and the speech was still going. Kirk searched the screen for any sign of distress, while wondering how the Leeds and Moretti meeting had gone. A dreadful sound jerked him away and made him turn to his side.

A moan came from the agent seated at his left. Marc's mouth was twisted, his eyes bulging with terror, and his fist clenching his chest. Kirk knew the signal well.

"What do you feel?" His hand grasped the man's shoulder. "Are you in pain?"

Marc nodded. His mouth opened as if to scream, but no sound exited his bluish lips.

A second moan came from behind Kirk. He turned back toward the dining room. Greg lay on the floor, his mouth also twisted, a palm pushing on his breast bone. Ray glanced at Kirk, rushed to Greg, and squatted down at his side. The football, unsupported, fell onto the wooden floor with a loud thump.

How could this be happening? Both Marc and Greg were down. But Greg was the one taking the pictures early in the evening, and Ray was supposed to be the good guy, Mulville's man. What about the pilot? Could the pilot be the terrorist?

Then Marc's full weight fell on Kirk's forearm, as he crashed from his chair to the floor. Kirk squatted, freed his hand from under the agent, and put his index and middle fingers on the agent's neck. No pulsations. Marc's body jerked and shook for several seconds, then went totally still. Kirk knew CPR wasn't a viable option. The aorta must've dissected across the arch, blocking both carotid arteries—Leeds had described the same thing hap-pening to the Chief of Staff. Or perhaps the vessel had ruptured, causing massive internal bleeding. Either way, the man was dead, as evidenced by his limp body, gaping mouth, and unmoving eyes. Kirk reached for the com-municator and moved toward the couch in front of the TV screen to check on the Secretary.

Last time Kirk had looked at the designated survivor, he had been sleep-ing off his booze. With dread, Kirk approached the front of the couch, where the Secretary's face came into view. His skin color was still normal, but his breathing seemed more labored. His ribcage moved up and down at irregu-lar intervals, separated by pauses and loud snoring. Kirk took a deep breath and switched the phone's green light on.

"Two agents down!" he shouted into his wrist. "One dead, likely of dis-section! Secretary still alive, but may be in trouble as well. I'll go see the pilot now. Call medics to airlift. And come the fuck over."

***

Mulville watched Dr. Moretti on his screen. The woman had at last comprehended the gravity of the situation and seemed willing to help. But was it too late?

"Please go get Patrizia," Silvana begged. "She's all I have."

Steve got up, took the watch from his pocket, and held it at arm's length. "No, you have me, too."

Silvana got up and shuffled to Steve, her hand going to the watch. Steve took her into his arms.

"Are you two crazy?" Mulville said. "Does it look like we have time for this shit? I'll arrange for Dr. Moretti to be escorted by the police to go get—"

Mulville couldn't finish his sentence. The woman agent in the van shook his shoulder. He refocused on his team. The two men and the woman were gearing up, fastening bullet-proof vests, grabbing goggles. Had he missed

Kirk's distress call? He glanced at the time: twenty past ten. He muted his conversation with Drs. Leeds and Moretti.

"What's going on?" he asked.

"Miner gave us the signal," the woman said. "One agent is dead. Another agent and the Survivor appeared in trouble. We sent medics. Permission to move in."

"Go!" Mulville waved his hand. "I'll be right behind you."

Something caught Kirk's eyes. Due to the Secretary's recumbent position and the movement of his chest, some sort of a card was about to fall out from his shirt pocket. Kirk reached out and grabbed the thin orange object. The hard plastic rectangle bore an indentation line in the middle. Puzzlement turned into certainty. Kirk remembered seeing pictures of the object on the briefing papers. His hand trembled. Between his fingers, Kirk now held the precious biscuit—the key to unleashing America's nuclear missiles.

Kirk gazed back at the living room. Nobody was paying attention to him. Ray was busy tending to Greg, who seemed conscious and with fair color. Kirk placed the biscuit in his pants pocket and ran to the pilot's bedroom. No doubt it would be safer with Kirk than with the intoxicated survivor.

Kirk decided not to knock on the closed door of the pilot's bedroom. Greg's and Marc's predicament had hiked the pilot up on the list of suspects. Instead, his ear rested on the wood. Silence. He took his gun from the holster, cocked it, and pushed down on the door handle. The door was unlocked and swung open without noise. Kirk entered, aiming the muzzle at the bed. The older man's jacket and tie stood folded with care on a chair. He was in bed, turned toward the door. His eyes stared out from a bluish, lifeless face. He looked like a corpse. Kirk confirmed the absence of a pulse and raised his wrist again.

"Pilot is dead," he said. "I still need airlift for one of the agents. Now."

He rushed back and approached Ray, still squatting next to Greg. The senior agent had his hand on his colleague's neck. Greg lay still and quiet but was still breathing. Drops of sweat dotted his forehead. His hand had left his chest and rested on the communicator.

"The pilot is dead," Kirk said. "I called for backup. How's—?"

The sentence died on his lips. Ray's hand came off Greg's neck, exposing something under Greg's right earlobe. Something familiar. A jagged shape. A swastika. The same scar or tattoo Kirk had seen on the New York taxi driver's neck. Greg was the taxi driver who had tried to kill him. Greg was the undercover terrorist. But why was Greg down? Nothing made sense. A thump broke the silence and interrupted Kirk's thinking. Then things seemed to happen in slow motion.

A warm slimy wetness sprayed onto Kirk's face and upper torso. He looked down. Red droplets soaked his white shirt. The little flag looked buried under a lumpy, wet material. The pungent and fresh smell of blood permeated his nose. Kirk, eyes refocused, wiped the stuff off his face. The back of Ray's head had been replaced by a wide hole oozing bloody gray matter.

Kirk fought a wave of nausea. The stuff on his shirt and on his face was part of Ray's brain—the brain that had loved his wife and his kid, ten years old today.

Kirk swallowed stomach acid as he watched Greg, still on the floor. But no distress showed on the agent's face. And now, Greg had no problem pushing himself up off the floor. The chest pain had been a well-played act. Now Kirk stared at the barrel of a gun—Greg's gun pointed straight at Kirk's eyes.

Mulville heard his agents open the van's door and walk out into the night. The urgent need to rush after them burned inside him. He turned to his screen and unmuted while gearing up with infrared goggles, heavy Kevlar vest, and an automatic weapon.

"Steve," he shouted, "gotta go now! Emergency with Kirk!"

Mulville hung up on Steve's scared and puzzled face. He dialed the FBI reinforcement team requesting immediate backup. The overwhelmed voice of the woman on the line made the futility of his request clear. The Capitol had already depleted all resources. Mulville and Miner were on their own, alone to protect the only man who could act as POTUS.

He glanced at Kirk's flag feed. Blank. Mulville touched the communicator. No answer. Was the detective dead?

Sayed's phone buzzed twice. Ten-twenty, and the backup was coming. He sprang from the rock and molded himself into position. His knee found a pre-selected flat spot on the ground. Eye on the scope, right index finger on the trigger, he switched on the tag-tracking technology. The small plastic tube lit up with a green glow. The tracking scope communicated with the guided trigger. He focused the scope in the direction of the van. The infrared filter showed the mass of three bodies, maybe four, still inside the vehicle. A strange thumping resonated through the weapon's hard metal. His heartbeat.

Sayed tightened his grip. He inhaled. The fresh scent of pines relaxed him. Silence surrounded him, broken only by his slow breathing and the whistle of the wind. A muffled click and a whoosh announced the opening of the van's door. Three people rushed out in the direction of the building's back entry. Sayed stiffened into position. The warm masses came closer. He touched the tag button and, in turn, aimed the scope at each one of the bodies.

After a few attempts, the three images were tagged, each with a red dot at head-level. Now the targets could run around all they wanted. They were tagged and ready. As soon as the trigger got the signal that alignment was optimal, their heads would blow up. The targets would drop just like the coyote in the movie demonstration Sayed had watched. He aimed at the first infidel.

Kirk stared at the muzzle's opening. As in a paused TV program now restarted, the speed of time became real again. He pushed Ray's body toward Greg to serve as a shield. A second thwack came from Greg's silenced gun. It felt like a metal bat had hit his ribcage full force. He stumbled back, breathless. Never did he so wish he was in top shape, instead of recovering from his recent procedure.

Aurora and Peter came to mind. Adrenaline rushed to the rescue, mitigating pain. Kirk lunged forward with renewed fury toward Greg, still struggling under Ray's body. With his foot, Kirk stomped the man's hand against the floor.

Greg's gun clanked away, but no sounds of suffering came, as if he was too entrenched in his goal to allow pain to distract him. Greg's left hand fumbled some more with the communicator, and then came up clenching his phone like a weapon aimed at Kirk. Sound waves. Close-up. Full blast. Just as in the pictures Greg had taken earlier. Thank goodness for the bubble wrap.

Kirk tightened his fingers, brought his hand to shoulder level, and used a powerful circular motion to land a perfect knife-hand strike on Greg's wrist. The phone crashed onto the floor several feet away. With his hand, Kirk ripped Greg's transmitter from his waist and flung the device to the floor. Then Kirk reached for his gun.

The euphoria of victory surged inside him, but he felt wetness around the gun's holster. Kirk looked at his hand. Clear. Not red. Not blood. The bubble wrap's content. The bullet's impact on the vest had ruptured Kirk's bubble wrap, and the protective stuff was draining from the burst bubbles.

How much of the foamy content had been available to protect his frail aorta in the moment when Greg had zapped him the second time tonight? Time would tell. His chest felt tight. He hoped it was only fear. But Kirk had no time for fear. If he was going to die, only one thing remained for him to do.

"You're done," Kirk said, placing the muzzle on Greg's forehead. "The FBI is coming. Who sent you?"

Greg smiled. Kirk's finger tightened on the trigger. He forced himself to relax. His hand swung to the right, then came back with acquired force and smashed the gun's hard metal against Greg's face. Kirk felt more than heard the jaw's crunching sound. Greg's howl gave him a pang of satisfaction. But the bastard laughed, even with blood trickling from his lips.

"You can't win." Greg spat out two teeth. "They'll annihilate all you infidel pigs."

"Who?" Kirk yelled. "Who's taking fucking credit?"

"United Coalition of Faith." Greg spat out bloody saliva. "Burn in hell, pig."

Things seemed worse than Kirk had imagined. He'd better let Mulville know, while he still could.

Ominously, a series of rapid shots resounded from outside. An automatic weapon. Kirk hoped Mulville had such a weapon in his arsenal. FBI agents should. Greg smiled some more. The bastard must have backup coming as well. He probably had given his signal and was also waiting. Whose backup had fired the shots?

The muffled sounds of feet made Kirk turn, his weapon still in contact with Greg's head. Someone had entered through the back door. And Kirk hadn't opened the lock.

A man rushed in. Not Mulville. He looked and acted like an army tank—wide, strong, and bigger than Greg and, with gun in hand, deadly. Kirk lifted his weapon to the unknown individual. Too late. A bullet came at him without a sound and struck the middle of his forehead with piercing force. The impact propelled Kirk backward to the floor. After that, everything went fuzzy and dark. Was this what it felt like to be shot in the head? But why could he still think, or still hear things?

"Aziz, backup's down." The man's muffled voice seemed far away.

Aziz. Greg's real name was Aziz. And the shots Kirk had heard were from the larger man, Aziz's backup. Mulville was dead. Dead. The words echoed in Kirk's head as everything faded.

An automatic weapon blasted in the distance. Mulville opened the van's door and listened. The cold air bit his skin. No sounds. No motion. Only the pounding of his heart inside his chest and the menacing echoes of the rifle in his ears. Where was his team? A clear sky with peaceful stars and a bright half-moon. A beautiful night. Was it going to be the last thing he would contemplate on this earth? Faint lights came through cracks in the drapes from the back of the farmhouse. He stepped out, ducked, and rushed to the back door, his head low, his rifle pointing forward.

The infrared goggles detected the shape of a warm body on the ground. Mulville squatted. The smaller size gave away the gender. His female agent. He didn't have to check her pulse. The moonlight was sufficient for him to see that there were no arteries left in her neck. In fact, there was no neck. No head either. Only a body topped by shreds of glistening tissue.

Mulville pushed himself up. A painful cloud of anxiety expanded in his chest. He had seen this devastation before. The kind of weapon that had killed the agent at his feet left him no hope of finding any of his team members alive. Anger filled him, helping him to keep going.

A couple of yards ahead, he found an FBI cap at his foot. Mulville picked it up. His fingers slid over the brim. The back part one uses to change the size was gone. Mulville looked around. The body the hat belonged to wasn't far away. The slender male agent. Same result as the woman. The fact that the fallen agents had pledged to defend and serve didn't make Mulville feel any better. Not knowing the man and woman well didn't buffer his pain. Mulville hadn't been there to defend them.

The older agent had made it closer to the back door, but no cigar. He had dropped face-first into a pile of snow—at least whatever was left of his face. Mulville remembered having a beer with the guy, planning this evening. Turns out they had been planning his death. The fate of the mission now rested with Mulville alone.

He raised his arm and got ready to call Kirk again but stopped. Perhaps the terrorist didn't know he was there and alive. Better not advertise his presence. Mulville approached the back door and listened. Silence. His hand pushed down on the handle. The door was open, most likely left ajar by the fake Secret Service agent for his backup to come in after the mini-massacre of the FBI.

He removed his goggles and put one foot in front of the other. Mulville entered, weapon ready to fire. The corridor was deserted. Wood planks screeched under Mulville's weight as he approached the four bedrooms. Three doors stood firm and closed. One—the first one—was ajar.

Mulville entered and secured each room with the sweep of his gun. The bed in the ajar room had been used, as well as the shower. The second room had two unused beds and a few discarded towels. The next one was the Secretary's, as was evident from the Johnny Walker bottle and the dirty glasses. The next room contained a dead body. Mulville recognized the pilot from his picture.

Mulville reached the bar room. Lights were on. Everything was still, silent. His gaze rolled over the table cluttered with bottles, the timer now silent and dark. He stepped into the living room. An agent was down on the floor next to one of the armchairs. Mulville stopped. Kirk Miner lay on the wooden floor a couple of yards away. He faced up, eyes closed. A trickle of blood ran down his temple from a two-inch gash in the middle of his forehead. Tissue and blood covered his face and torso. Mulville's stomach rebelled with violent cramps.

"No." He squatted at his side. "No. You fuck. You son of a bitch."

He slapped Kirk's face and thumped his chest with his fist. His hand picked up slimy matter and blood. Mulville looked at it. The smell of death made him belch out loud.

"Stop," a feeble voice whispered. "You're killing me."

"Son of a bitch, you got whacked. How can you talk?"

Kirk opened his eyes and pushed himself up to a sitting position. He looked as if he had awakened from a bad dream, and now he was recalling what had almost led to his demise.

"Titanium plate." Kirk's knuckles touched his forehead. "From my past accident. Had no idea it was bullet-proof."

"But all this shit." Mulville lifted his hand, which was smeared with organic material. "On you."

"The stuff is from Ray." His hand pointed behind him. "Greg faked chest pains, Ray went to help him, and Greg shot him in the head."

Mulville looked past Kirk and saw the bald agent's body for the first time. The shock of Kirk had been too much. Mulville hadn't even noticed the other body until now. He felt numb inside, except for his stomach, which tightened more with each painful discovery. This felt personal. Too personal. Mulville wasn't used to the feeling.

"Greg had an accomplice," Kirk said. "Outside. He said the backup was down. I thought you were dead."

"Should've been," Mulville said. "My entire team is gone."

"The terrorists belong to some Middle-Eastern coalition," Kirk added. "I'm afraid I know why the survivor is a target."

"Why?"

"They want the football and the biscuit," Kirk started.

"So," Mulville said. "What's new?"

"They want the football and the biscuit," Kirk repeated, eyes full of terror, "not to launch our missiles, but to do nothing with them."

"Nothing?"

"So nobody can use them," Kirk said. "Their goal is to paralyze our government, make us unable to defend ourselves. Then any Middle-Eastern state our government has allowed to produce nuclear weapons can attack us, while we scrounge around for someone to act as President."

Mulville had to give it to the PI. He made sense. If Miner was right, the most urgent priority should be finding a new POTUS, have the football and biscuit handy to defend the country, and counter-attack if needed. The United States of America stood reduced to the status of a sitting duck, and it was up to him and a wounded PI to come to the rescue.

"Where is the football?" Mulville asked.

The question agitated Kirk. He acted as if he recalled something of the utmost importance. His hand went to search his pants pockets.

"The biscuit," he said slumping down on the floor. "I took it from the Secretary. Now it's gone. They took it from me."

"What about the football?" Mulville asked again.

"Ray held the football," Kirk said. "He left it near the chairs by the couch."

Kirk staggered to the couch with the designated survivor. Mulville looked for the football. The black briefcase was gone. Next to the couch, a GPS device lay discarded on the floor.

"The bastards." Mulville kicked the device under the couch. "They separated the GPS from the football and left it behind. No way to track them."

"Mr. President," Kirk said, bending over the survivor, who was still flat on the couch, "are you all right?"

A moan came from the man. Mulville walked over. The Secretary of Energy looked pale and clammy.

"My chest is on fire." His voice faltered as he spoke.

"Stay with me," Kirk said. "Help is on the way."

"Anybody with a pulse," the Secretary whined in a drunk-like drawl, "can do the job of designated survivor."

Then his body shuddered, his breathing stopped, and his eyes stood still, as if staring out at eternity. Kirk's fingers went to the man's neck, then his palms moved to the unmoving chest and performed compressions. After several minutes of futile attempts at resuscitation, the PI gave up and looked up at Mulville.

"Anybody with a pulse," Mulville said. "Not without."

His hand went to the phone. After several rings, a worn-out voice answered—the FBI director's.

"Yes, Mulville," the male voice said.

"The designated survivor is dead," Mulville said.

"How do you know?"

"I know a corpse when I see one," Mulville said.

"You're there!" the director shouted. "What are you doing there?"

Now the moron was complaining. The director should consider himself lucky Mulville had disobeyed senseless orders. But now was a time for calm communication.

"Mr. Director," Mulville said, "you can thank me later. For now, if the President is incapacitated, you've got to find someone able to act as president as soon as possible and give him the President's football. The survivor's football is gone."

"The President is dead," the director said. "Died during transport. Only good news I have is that I found the ultrasound device. As you said, on the door jamb. Thin and clear. Invisible, unless you knew what to look for."

"Great," Mulville said. "So is everyone being rushed to the hospitals?"

"Yes," the director said. "It's going to be a while before we figure out who's in charge of the country."

"Two terrorists are at large," Mulville said. "They hold the designated survivor's football without GPS. I believe their purpose is to prevent our country from retaliating, and thus open us up to nuclear attack from some Middle-Eastern league. Tonight."

"The United Coalition of Faith," Kirk whispered. "That's what Greg called the entity in charge."

A rattling sound filled the silence. It came from outside, toward the front. Mulville looked at Kirk. The director remained silent on the line.

"Sir," Mulville said to the director, "you've got to find a President. As soon as possible. Or we're all going to die."

"The medics must be here," Kirk said. "Not that we need them now."

The sound got louder. The rattling got faster. Kirk looked up.

"A helicopter," Kirk said. "But it's leaving, not coming in. The terrorists must've gotten the keys from the pilot. They're taking off."

Mulville hung up and ran to the front door, his submachine gun in hand. Kirk followed, his gun drawn and ready. The rattling got louder as the men approached the front door. Kirk grabbed his coat from the coat rack. Chimes announced the opening of the front door by Mulville. The rattling intensified.

Mulville looked up. A powerful bright light blinded him. The light shone from the front underside of the large metal bird, hovering a few yards off the ground, and moving up. A smaller red light flashed on the helicopter's tail and intermittently floodlit the military label—"United States of America."

Mulville stepped out into the cold and aimed his weapon at the bottom of the aircraft. A series of rapid thumps ensued. As the chopper wobbled in the air, a long yellow and red flame shot out of the back. The rattling became irregular, like an agonized heartbeat, then the metal bird fell to the ground with a loud bang.

The two passengers leaped from their seats. Mulville aimed again and fired. Mulville and Kirk stepped back into the house. The helicopter exploded in a mass of heat and fire. A large object hit the closed door, causing the chimes to jiggle. Mulville couldn't hear anything. He watched Kirk talking.

"Let's go," Kirk's mouth said. He pointed at the outside. "We've got to stop 'em."

Mulville swallowed. His ears popped. He put the night goggles back on and opened the door, only to see a hellish scene of flames and smoke. Kirk coughed as he pulled night goggles from his jacket. Mulville stepped over a large piece of metal with glass components. He recognized part of one of the helicopter's doors. Kirk followed.

Mulville ran around the flames, hands on mouth, beyond the smoke barrier. He glimpsed the two men running toward the back and up the hill, disappearing into the trees. He strapped his submachine gun to his chest and took off running. Kirk kept up—Mulville sensed the tapping of his feet behind him. The smell of smoke, gasoline, and burned wood permeated the air. Mulville's infrared goggles brought the images of the two fugitives into vision again. The two men now were separating, running in different ways. Mulville turned.

"Can you hear me!?" Mulville shouted at Kirk.

Kirk hand signaled the equivalent of "So ...."

"They're splitting up." Mulville gestured with his hands to mimic his words. "I can't tell who has the football."

CHAPTER 31

CHOICES

Kirk watched the two infrared images separate and head in opposite directions. Mulville grabbed his weapon, aimed it first at the two fugitives, then sprayed bullets at will as he ran after the terrorist on the left. Kirk took off toward the man on the right.

Concussion pain pulsated inside Kirk's head and worsened with each step he took. No chest pain yet. Only a matter of time before his healing aorta, weakened by renewed injury, would act up. Running after terrorists wasn't what his doctor had recommended. Extreme exertion would make his heart pump a larger volume of blood. His blood pressure would increase, pounding the wall of his arteries with every heartbeat, and stretching the aorta, which could explode like a balloon made of worn-down rubber. Kirk thought about Peter and Aurora. Would his family want him to stop now and try to return to them unharmed?

But Kirk was fighting for his own life and future, as much as for his family's and his country's. Peter and Aurora were part of that fight, and part of his reward. And if his life was the price, Kirk was willing to pay it. New adrenaline rose inside him, animating his body. He sprinted as fast as he could toward the enemy.

The air quality was better away from the smoke. With pleasure, Kirk inhaled the scent of pines as he ran. Sweat poured down his spine. Because he was wearing sneakers, he struggled and slipped on the frozen ground. The reddish image in and out of sight among the trees got closer.

Kirk took his weapon from the holster, aimed, and unloaded three bullets. The hot image in front of him stopped and dropped to the ground. Kirk turned to look at the second man, who changed direction and started moving toward the fallen partner. Mulville followed him at a distance.

Radical terrorists were impervious to mercy, good will, and pity. The motivation for the man's change of direction wasn't his partner's rescue. Kirk must've hit the guy with the football. The other terrorist's only purpose was to get the essential object from his accomplice.

Mulville was too far away to intercept him. Kirk had to get there first. Another sprint and Kirk came into full view of the man on the ground. Not Greg, aka Aziz, but the other man, whose left hand held the precious football while his right hand held his groin. The terrorist's gun fell to the ground. Kirk hoped he had hit an artery. He approached him, picked up the gun, and reached out for the football.

"Screw you," the man moaned. "Praise Allah."

The wounded man's hand swung in a wide arc, tossing the black leather briefcase into space many yards away, into the hands of his oncoming accomplice. A perfect pass. And from a prone position no less. The terrorists must've had football practice.

An empty rush of disappointment ran through Kirk, together with the first wave of shearing chest pain. He suppressed a howl. But Mulville leapt toward him. Kirk regretted failing to conceal his pain when he saw Mulville hesitate, looking at him with inquisitive eyes.

"Mulville," Kirk moaned, "go get the football. Don't worry about me."

"What's going on?" Mulville said. "Don't play dead again, you mother-fucker."

"It's the graft." Kirk's breathing came in gasps. "The bubble vest ruptured. Greg zapped me with the sound probe. Nothing you can do to help me. Do me a favor. Go after the bastard. Best you can do for me right now."

Mulville nodded and took off running. Kirk had a mission left to accomplish while he still could. He pointed his gun to the head of the man on the ground.

"Where is the biscuit?" Kirk said, his voice as strong as his pain allowed.

The man smiled, lifted his hand from the groin area, and fished inside his jacket. Kirk jammed the gun muzzle onto his forehead and watched for weapons in the wan moonlight. But the hand came out seemingly empty and went to the terrorist's mouth.

"No." Kirk knocked the hand to the side using his gun.

The man opened his hand like a magician revealing the disappearance of some object. The hand must have clenched a deadly capsule—a deadly capsule now dissolving in the man's mouth. Arabic words and phrases filled the air, then the prayer stopped, the body seized, and the man lay in the stillness of death. As pressure grew and spread inside Kirk's chest, his own death approached, announced by escalating pain. Still, he must continue his search for the biscuit.

His tingling hands went through each of the man's pockets. He found car keys, cigarettes, a wallet, but no biscuit. Nothing under the Kevlar vest, either. He unzipped the man's pants and searched under sweaty boxers and t-shirt. The man's right leg was immersed in a pool of warm and sticky blood. Lightheadedness began to set in. Kirk hoped the pain would renew his adrenalin supply and keep him going to the end of his mission.

He turned to the man's boots—large, heavy, clamped onto the limbs. The task seemed impossible in his conditions, but Kirk managed to undo straps and laces, clenched point and heel of the left boot in his hands, and pulled with all the strength he had left. Pain burst from his chest and ran down both his legs. He ground his teeth and pulled again, this time for Peter, and Aurora, so they wouldn't die in a nuclear fireball. The boot yielded and Kirk fell backward on the frozen ground, the crampons' steel spikes scraping his chin.

He felt like remaining in his horizontal position and just dying, so that the pain would stop. But he managed to get one hand to his mouth and, with his teeth, removed a thick glove. The freezing wind bit his fingers, which were numb now. He turned to the man's boots. The musty smell of sweaty feet assaulted his nostrils.

His naked hand searched the inside of the boot, finding nothing. Then his finger lifted some padding from the bottom. The feeling of flat hard plastic made Kirk oblivious to his pain. He pulled out the credit-card-like object, zippered the biscuit into his jacket's inside pocket, and lay back on the frozen ground, savoring a strange, all-encompassing sense of satisfaction.

Mulville's lungs burned as Greg disappeared further into the trees. The heavy football didn't seem to slow the young man's stride. Kirk's moan still played in the FBI agent's ears and made his legs feel heavy. Was Kirk dying? He momentarily glanced back at the spot where he had left the PI. Two reddish masses. Both immobile. One paler than the other.

Which of the two men had died? Mulville ignored the dread expanding in his chest, turned straight ahead, and resumed running. Running was the right and only option at this point. Kirk himself had said so.

Then a bright light in the sky caught his attention. Not a star or a planet. An aircraft. Mulville noticed the flashing red light. The medics' chopper. He could use it now for Kirk, but he was far away from the Ventana. And with all the chaos going on, Mulville had no way to communicate Kirk's location to the medics. The medics would land at the farm, check out all the dead people, and leave with the corpses. They wouldn't know Kirk needed rescue in the middle of the trees. Kirk Miner would die, if he wasn't dead already. And Greg was getting farther away.

Mulville stopped running. His head jerked and his attention went from the running man to Kirk's immobile body. The pendulum in his mind swung one last time. He turned around and ran back. Unfamiliar apprehension overwhelmed him as he approached Kirk and the terrorist.

He stopped next to the two motionless men and removed his goggles. At a touch of his wrist, a light shone on Kirk's face. The PI looked pale. Was he too pale to be alive? Had Mulville turned around for nothing? He reached out for the PI's pulse, as if his own life depended on the answer. What was going on? Mulville had never before cared so much about a colleague's fate. Why was Kirk so special?

The PI's neck felt cold and clammy. Mulville searched for the carotid artery. A weak pulse. He closed his eyes and shook his head in relief. But Kirk was dying and Mulville had to hurry. He looked at the chopper landing at the side of the farm. In the front of the building, the flames of the other helicopter still lit up the sky.

"Shut the fuck up, will you?" he yelled at the unconscious PI, as if answering his past objections. "The medics are finally here. I'll bring them over. If you fucking die while I'm gone, I'll kill you."

As he moved toward the medics, Mulville texted Greg's picture to FBI headquarters with the order to set up a perimeter and roadblocks. What were the chances his order would be executed during a night like this one? He didn't dare guess.

No sense in sacrificing Kirk for no good reason. The football game was lost. The words rolled in his mind like something Mulville could say when he would have to account for the choice he was making. Or perhaps he wouldn't have to, because he'd be dead too, together with millions of other people. Was he justified in suspending his pursuit of the enemy to save a friend? Was Kirk Miner a friend? As if Mulville knew anything about friendship. Mulville had never had any friends.

"Hey." He waved at the medics as soon as he was close enough. "Up here. Follow me. No one left to save at the house."

The two medics had stopped short of the Ventana front door. They wore protective masks and carried a stretcher. A considerable amount of smoke still filled the air, but the flames from the crash had decreased. Two light-reflecting yellow uniforms moved toward Mulville. He hoped that inside the square little cases the men carried was what was needed to keep Kirk alive until reaching the hospital.

"This way." He pointed behind him. "Agent down in those trees. His aorta is rupturing, for the second time. Hurry!"

He ran ahead to Kirk's place. Filling the air was the idle rhythm of the waiting chopper. Mulville stopped next to Kirk. The medics placed the stretcher on the ground and squatted next to the detective. Mulville stood aside, his breathing shallow. Time seemed to stop. Mulville checked his watch.

Less than half an hour since his team left the van. It felt like an eternity, during which several lives had ended. He watched the medics check Kirk's vital signs. Then the yellow men started an intravenous line and called the hospital to exchange information. Mulville took deeper breaths. The experts had deemed Kirk's status worthy of their rescue efforts. Not so for the terrorist. Good job, PI. Then Mulville noticed the discarded boot. Had the man reached for a deadly capsule in his boot?

Soon, Kirk was strapped onto the stretcher and on his way to the chopper. As the two medics loaded the cargo. Mulville ducked and entered the craft.

"Are you still with me?" Mulville said. "Talk to me, Kirk."

Mulville pulled the gurney's thin blanket up to Kirk's chin. His hands shook as he locked his seatbelt. The chopper wobbled and the ground moved away. Mulville smiled. For the first time that night, he felt as if he had achieved something.

"Agent down," one of the medics said into the radio. "Possible aortic dissection. Operating room standby requested."

Steve—Mulville needed to talk to Steve. Steve should be the one to fix Kirk. Mulville exhaled. Dr. Steve Leeds was busy with 600 other patients, all waiting for his services. He dialed the doctor's phone without the slightest hope the doctor would answer.

Steve leapt out of the police car and rushed to the emergency room entrance. The waiting room looked like a battlefield hospital. Not that Steve had ever been in battle, but he had some conception of war zone hospital wards from movies or colleagues' descriptions. Distressed people occupied every available seat. But the number of seats had been cut back by at least half to accommodate all the stretchers. On the stretchers, more people waited for evaluation and treatment. A mixture of moans of pain, complaints, and fear-driven wails filled the air. Medical personnel moved from patient to patient like bees hovering near a hive. He maneuvered through the stretchers, keeping his head low.

"Dr. Leeds," called the operating room charge nurse in the distance. "Thank God you're here."

Steve lifted his head. He saw her approaching. The blood-smeared uniform seemed appropriate for a war-zone nurse. He stopped.

"All ORs working at capacity. All six cardiothoracic surgeons at work. Fellows need direction. We aren't sure what the emergency justifies them doing or not doing. So far, we had three DOAs. And four deaths here in the ER, one waiting for a CAT scan, two waiting for surgery. And one died on the table. If we could tell who's going to crash next, it would make things a little easier."

She didn't wait for answers or sympathy, shook her thin shoulders, grabbed a gurney with both hands, and pushed it through the door into the ER.

DOAs—Steve never would have thought he would see the day when he would feel a flash of relief hearing those words. Yet he had. DOAs wouldn't require surgery. Fewer people to operate on. What a horrible thought to cross his mind. He walked behind the gurney, past the ER door. Worse than the waiting room. A cardiac arrest code in progress came into view. A nurse performed CPR, doctors tried to get tubes into blood vessels and tracheas, paddles shocked the fibrillating heart. One more DOA. Or perhaps dead while waiting. Or if the patient survived, one more case for him to operate on. He'd better hurry.

"Steve!" Dr. Nirula shouted and waved from the back of the room.

"Down here. I need you."

Steve bumped into a few gurneys on his way to the back of the room. Nirula looked flustered. Not good for someone still recovering from myocardial infarction.

"This is crazy," Nirula said. "We told everyone we're overwhelmed, but patients keep on arriving. I guess all fifteen hospitals in DC with cardiothoracic surgery programs are in the same boat."

'What about the cardiologists?" Steve asked. "Can't they place stents in some of the patients?"

"Dr. Green is doing what he can," Nirula said. "None of the patients I saw were stent candidates. Whoever did this made sure the damage would be as severe as possible."

In fact, the bastards made sure they caused several days of high governmental disruption, with all officials either dead or incapacitated by major surgery. Nirula grabbed Steve by the arm and pulled him to a gurney. The patient looked familiar. He appeared pale and sweaty.

"Mr. Vice-President," Nirula said, "this is Dr. Leeds. He'll take very good care of you."

Steve had time to say hello. Then the gurney moved away to the OR.

"He's really our President now," Nirula whispered after the patient was moved away. "The President was DOA."

Steve nodded. He started to push his way toward the OR. But then someone touched his shoulder. He stopped. Silvana stood by his side. She wore gray slacks and a white tailored shirt—same clothes she wore the day of her arrest only two weeks ago. She stood at attention, escorted by a policewoman. Despite all that was probably going on in her mind with her daughter, she looked composed and professional. Steve gave her credit. In her hand was the foot-long probe known as the Moretti device.

"I'm here," she said. "I can start scanning."

"Great," Steve said. "Start with the people waiting to be seen. Sort them according to how urgently they need surgery."

Donald Emerson stood behind Silvana Moretti. In his hands, he held the slick black cube from the lab with a portable computer piled atop it.

"Perhaps there's something we can do besides surgery." Silvana pointed at the black cube.

Her large eyes suggested both intelligence and confidence. That was what he had fallen in love with. Steve could lose himself just looking at her.

"What?" he asked.

"After I get the reading from my probe," she said, "I can program a chip with a counter soundwave—to correct the problem and reset the tissues to resonate normally."

"Would that prevent dissection?" Steve asked.

"Only in people at an early stage of damage," she said.

Steve looked at his watch. Everyone would have been exposed at least two hours ago. How many early stages could there be?

"I know what you think," she said. "But I know how the probe works. And I have been thinking of a way to counter the situation ever since I realized what these people might be up to."

"Great," Steve said again. "I gotta run to the OR, but you can work with Dr. Nirula."

He pointed at the doctor down the room. Silvana flinched. Of course she did—the guy killed her brother. But who could worry about past feuds when on the verge of a nuclear war?

"I'm fine," she said, as if she'd read his mind.

She walked to Dr. Nirula, followed by Emerson with the black cube. The OR was waiting, but many lives could depend on the use of Moretti's probe. Steve had to make sure Nirula wouldn't object. He rushed behind her.

"Rajesh," Steve told Nirula, "Dr. Moretti is here. The FBI has temporarily released her to help us."

Nirula lifted weary eyes. At the gurney in front of him, a nurse pulled a sheath over a pale-looking woman with a government ID card dangling from her neck. The plastic target kept oscillating at the rhythm of CPR compressions even after all efforts had ceased. Steve pointed at Silvana.

"Dr. Moretti," he went on, "can use her probe to assess patients. And she thinks she can also program chips to generate counter-waves to stabilize tissues and prevent dissection."

Steve saw surprise and uneasiness in Nirula's eyes. Then a flicker of hope lit his face. He smiled.

"Wow," Nirula said.

"I've never done it before," Silvana said. "No one has. What about the FDA?"

Steve cringed. Not that again. And from Silvana?

"I hope you're joking," Nirula said, making a circular gesture with his hand. "With what we're dealing here, why worry about the FDA?"

Silvana nodded. She looked around, pointed to one of the counters, and asked Emerson to set up the device on the chosen spot.

"Besides," Nirula said, leaning toward her, "the FDA people are still recovering from carotid surgery. And the Secretary of Health is having chest pain. I'm sure he wouldn't mind if you check him out. Down there, third gurney on the left."

Silvana left with her probe in hand and Nirula at her heels. Steve, his job suddenly more manageable, was done here. The Vice President's surgery was next on his schedule. He ran to the OR, burst through the door, and took less than a minute to shed his civilian clothes. His hands were pulling the brown strings of his scrub pants when, on the nearby bench, his phone started buzzing and jumping like a jitterbug.

He bent down to read the message. "On medic-chopper with Kirk Miner. Down with chest pain. He needs you. ETA in five minutes. Mulville." Five minutes. Steve slumped on the bench. His heart slammed against his ribs. What was he going to do?

CHAPTER 32

POTUS

D r. Leeds squeezed his temples. Who will it be? The Vice President, now President, or Kirk Miner? No time for long ethical arguments. Severity of disease and not personal preference should dictate the timing of medical action. Steve knew this from medical school. But other important facts affected Steve's mind like a wrench thrown into a delicate mechanism. More than ever, the country needed a president. And the president needed surgery. But Kirk Miner had volunteered for his mission. And now, in repayment for his courage and love of country, he might receive death by agonizing dissection.

Steve couldn't let that happen, president or no president. And that wasn't giving into emotionalism. That was justice, pure and simple. Besides, this president wouldn't be able to govern any time soon. Someone else down the succession line would have to take over anyway.

He pushed up from the bench, finished tying his scrubs, and walked to the sink, committed to follow the old rule: give priority to the sickest patient. From Mulville's description, Kirk sounded as if he fit that role. The charge nurse went by, pushing a gurney toward one of the ORs.

"I need you to go to the hospital entrance," Steve said, intercepting her as he started scrubbing. "Kirk Miner, a special Secret Service agent, is coming in by chopper. Bring him directly to the OR."

The woman had never questioned him in almost six years of working together. Today, Steve saw the glimpse of doubt in her eyes. It was just a glimpse. She parked her patient next to the OR door, turned, and scuttled back to execute his order. Steve held his wet palms up and pushed his way into the operating room. The familiar cold, antiseptic air welcomed him, as did the rhythmic hiss of the respirator and the hum of the bypass pump. The vice president lay draped and asleep under the hands of the senior cardio-thoracic fellow.

"Just in time," the male fellow said, pride in his voice. "Dissection of the ascending aorta up to right carotid. Body cooled by hypothermic extracorporeal circulation. Brain perfused by antegrade selective cerebral perfusion."

"How many dissections have you done?" Steve asked.

"Three. So far." The young man looked up over his surgical mask. "I can repair this one."

"Are you sure?"

"I would never lie to you, Dr. Leeds." The fellow's dark eyes telegraphed a silent chuckle. "Had a very good teacher."

"Let's start," Steve said. "I'll assist you. This way I can go to the next case if you feel you can finish. These are emergency times."

The fellow nodded and went back to work. Where was Kirk? Had his dissection reached the renal arteries? If so, his kidneys would have shut down. Had it reached the spine or iliac arteries? If so, he could be paralyzed from the waist down. No walking for the rest of his life. And how long could the twice-damaged arterial wall stand up to pressure before completely bursting?

"Kirk Miner is here," the charge nurse said from a crack in the door. "Ready to go. The doctor in the next room can take him soon."

"Who's there?" Steve asked.

"One of the junior attendings," the woman said. "And the second-year fellow."

Steve couldn't imagine a junior attending to whom he could entrust Kirk Miner's twice-dissected aorta. But how could Steve justify leaving the acting president in the hands of a fellow to go save Kirk? Steve didn't have a chance to dwell on the dilemma. A deep voice burst through the speaker.

"Code blue, Operating Room waiting area," the calm male voice said. "Code Blue pre-op."

The charge nurse disappeared. Who was coding? Steve needed to know.

"Ask the attending next door to come over here and take over this one," Steve told the circulating nurse. "Straightforward arch. Kirk Miner, next case, is complicated."

The nurse obeyed. There was no such thing as a straightforward dissection. A cardiothoracic fellow learned that truth during his first year of training. But Steve walked to the door, his hands back in the air. The door yielded to his shoulder and he found himself in the corridor. He peeked into the pre-op room.

The Code Blue team was at work. The heart monitor at the patient's side displayed a flat line interrupted only by the wiggles of chest compression. Steve ducked his head below the anesthesiologist's hands in the process of sliding a tube inside the patient's open mouth. He moved to the right to clear his view from behind the nurse performing the compressions and got a glance of the patient's face. It was Kirk. Steve shuddered. Kirk was dead. The aorta had burst and every compression of his chest sent whatever little blood he had left out of his circulatory system and into the chest cavity.

"Bring him inside!" Steve shouted. "We need to place him on pump! Now!"

"But, sir," the charge nurse said, looking up from the crash cart and clearing her voice. "You're the senior attending here. Who's operating on our president?"

"I asked the next room's attending to take over," Steve said. "And the fellow is doing a good job on his own. I'm doing this case. He obviously needs me more than the president."

Steve walked alongside the CPR team pushing the gurney through the OR door. He had to try, even if this was the last thing he would do on this Earth. There was nothing more Steve wanted to do than to save Kirk's life.

Mulville stepped back from the sealed door. Kirk Miner's gurney had disappeared behind the swinging gates, immediately placed under the care of the OR's charge nurse. Steve must've gotten his message. Mulville's mission with Kirk was done. Now it was up to the doctor to do his magic.

Mulville could move on to the next task. It was eight minutes to eleven. He better hurry. Otherwise, even if the doc did a good job, there wouldn't be too much life ahead for the PI, or for many millions of Americans.

He dialed the FBI director's number. Where was that loser? Why wasn't he running around the hospital checking who was available to act as POTUS? If Greg and his maniac accomplices had managed to send word to their beloved Coalition of Faith, anything could happen. Washington could be burning to a crisp before the night was over.

"Hi, Mulville." The director's answer sounded more like a moan than a greeting. "Good timing. I need to talk to you."

"I'm at Capitol Hospital," Mulville said. "How's the search for a POTUS going? Where are you?"

"Third gurney on the right of the ER front door," the FBI director said. "Same hospital. Waiting for a CAT scan."

"A CAT scan?" Mulville looked at his tablet in disbelief. "What are you talking about? Why do you need a CAT scan?"

"When you called me the first time," the director said, "I was already inside the House chamber."

Mulville pocketed his phone and pushed his way to the ER entrance. He found the third gurney on the right. The director lay there, still, pale, and sweaty, a phone in his hand. His arm fell on the gurney the moment his eyes locked on Mulville.

"Are you in pain?" Mulville already knew the answer.

"Worst pain in my life," the director said. "Thank you, Morphine. Listen carefully, since I'm not sure how long I'll last before passing out, or they take me to surgery, or before—"

He stopped. Probably thinking of his family or whoever would stay behind if he died.

"Mulville," the director said, his voice a shade fainter, "you're in charge while I'm incapacitated."

The words hit Mulville in the pit of the stomach—FBI director. If someone had offered him the job in any other circumstances, he would have jumped with joy. That had been his dream job for all his years of service. Now the news made him feel as if he had just swallowed a brick. No slow "bring me up to date," no mentoring or special easing into difficult assignments. Tonight, Mulville would act as Chief, and his first assignment was to save the whole God-damned country from annihilation.

"Yes, sir," he whispered.

"You need to join forces with the military. As soon as you identify the person acting as POTUS, immediately go to the Situation Room. The military person there can execute the President's order on the spot."

What order was the director talking about? Mulville held his breath. The launch of antiballistic missiles, or worse, the retaliatory launch of ballistic warheads after—.

"Are you with me?" the director asked. "The Chairman of the Joint Chiefs of Staff was ill and couldn't attend the State of the Union speech. He's coming over to help. He reports directly to the President and the Secretary of Defense, both of whom I understand are dead."

"But, sir," Mulville said, the power of his new position giving him the courage to object, "the Chairman has no executive authority to command combatant forces. With all due respect, I need a goddamn soldier to fight a frigging nuclear war, not a stooge."

The director grinned. Then he winced in pain. The grin was the first Mulville had ever witnessed from him.

"You're in charge," the director said. "If you can do better, go for it."

Mulville closed his eyes. Who was the toughest son-of-a-bitch general or admiral he had ever met or heard of? The image of a middle-aged man came to mind—the General Combatant Commander of the Marine Corps.

Mulville remembered his official picture. "Solid" was the word Mulville would use to describe him. Calm and strong face. Hooded eyes full of experience. Gaze carrying the promise that justice would be upheld at all costs. Four stars on each side of his collar and on each shoulder. And mouth stretched into a hint of a grin, leaving no doubt that the man would carry out his promises.

"I need a CCDR," Mulville said.

"A Combatant Commander." The director nodded. "Swell, if you can find one. You got four possibilities—Army, Marines, Navy, and Air Force. Hopefully, one of them is still around."

Mulville took out his phone and searched the military directory. The general's picture came into view. Mulville dialed the number. The general himself answered by announcing his name and rank. Mulville felt a jolt of relief.

"I need to speak with you," he said, "on a matter of national emergency."

Mulville listened to the male voice. Then he looked around, puzzled, searching. Best news of the night so far.

"I'll be damned," Mulville said pointing at his phone. "He's already here. Working with Dr. Moretti at finding the next POTUS."

The director grinned and winced again in that order. His color was now faded and his forehead gleamed under the ceiling's lights.

"I guess you chose right," he managed.

Mulville dialed Steve's number. Several rings followed. Mulville winked at the director, but the man's eyes were closed now. Then a woman's voice answered—rushed, frustrated, overwhelmed. Mulville hoped Steve was busy saving Kirk.

"This is Jack Mulville," he said. "FBI director. The patient on the third gurney on the right of the ER entrance has to go to surgery, now."

He listened to the answer.

"I say so," he said. "This man has saved many lives today, at the risk of his own. He's a soldier and a hero. We owe it to him. And we need him on his feet as soon as possible. It's a matter of the highest national security."

"Thanks, Mulville," the director whispered, eyes still closed. "That'll be all for now. Go and do your job somewhere else. And don't make me sorry."

Mulville left without turning back. He had always considered himself tough and acted accordingly. Where was his toughness when he needed it? He found Moretti and the general near a counter at the center of the ER. A young man held a probe next to a black cube, probably downloading information from one device to the other. No one paid attention to Mulville. He stepped beside the general, who looked just as he did in his picture—uniform, stars, and all.

The general's eyes turned to Mulville, but the rest of his body didn't budge. He wore no hat. A black leather briefcase dangled from his right hand. He seemed larger than Mulville remembered. Despite Mulville's six-feet-two inches, something in the man's appearance and posture made Mulville feel small next to him.

"Jack Mulville." His hand touched his forehead in military salute. "Acting FBI director. At your service. How's it going?"

"Great," the general said, turning. "I rushed here as soon as I heard the broadcast, and here was where the President and most of the line of succession would be. My counterpart's colleagues from the Navy, Air Force, and Army are out of the country, and it would take too long to get here. The President, unfortunately, died during transport. I was able to secure the football."

The general lifted the black case. Mulville nodded. At least they had what was needed to act, even with the survivor's football now in terrorist hands.

"I'm glad the FBI is on board," the general went on. "Couldn't locate the director or anyone else in charge. Got a third-hand explanation from Dr. Moretti here about the ongoing terrorist plot. Since you seem to know Dr. Moretti, perhaps you could assist me."

"Mr. Mulville," Silvana said, panic in her voice, "I need to find my daughter. I can try to get a location from the portable ultrasound probe the terrorists are carrying. But I would have to stop my task here for a moment. And the general here would shoot me if I did. I'm sure of it. Can you do anything?"

"Mulville." The general's eyes rolled up in a sign of impatience and perhaps an accusation of stupidity on the doctor's part. "As I wasted time explaining to the good doctor here, the terrorists sure as hell have already sent a message to their overseas masterminds about the success of their mission. These terrorist-harboring countries, thanks to our past foreign policy, have ballistic missiles in their possession. These long-range intercontinental ballistic missiles can deliver one or more warheads to a pre-determined target following a sub-orbital flight trajectory with terminal speeds of over four miles per second. One of these things could travel the 6,000 plus miles from the Middle East to Washington DC or New York City in about 45 minutes. One hour and a half to Los Angeles."

Moretti looked deflated. Mulville remained silent and looked at his watch—10:56. When had Greg escaped with the football?

"If we're lucky," the general went on, "we've got about an hour to get someone acting as President to sit in the Situation Room and broadcast a brief speech to the nation and the rest of the world to make clear the United States is back in the business of defending itself from these and other aggressors. And I need the new president to give me an order to do my job."

Mulville hoped the general was right. The terrorists may well have sent their message earlier. How long would the Coalition of Faith take to execute any launch? Chances were the missiles were charged, pointed to the West, and ready to go. Or perhaps they were already on their way over. He wiped his forehead with the back of his hand.

"What about those missiles?" Moretti whispered. "Can they be stopped? And what's the Situation Room?"

The general looked proud for a moment, as one would look talking about his children. Mulville was curious about his answer.

"The effectiveness of our newer systems against ballistic missiles," the General said, "is very high. The Patriot Advanced Capability 3 had a 100% success rate in Operation Iraqi Freedom. But we need to get to work within the hour, at the latest. Or we'll all be toast, including your daughter, Dr. Moretti. Am I clear? Your priority, Doctor, should be to get someone into shape to act as POTUS as soon as possible."

Mulville looked at Moretti and nodded, as if to second everything the general just said. She retrieved a plastic wand from the counter, turned to the black cube, and talked to the young man. Mulville nodded at the general.

"I don't particularly want to go down in history as a dictator," the general said in Mulville's direction, "but if someone in the cabinet doesn't make a statement to the effect that we're ready to defend our country, I may have no choice but to take over. Someone must issue an order to launch anti-ballistic missiles and to get ready for possible retaliation if necessary. Then I can execute. That's what usually happens in the Situation Room at the White House."

The last few sentences were for Moretti. The General spoke loud and clear in answering her second question. But Moretti was busy with her helper, fidgeting with the black cube.

"This should do it." She slid open the cover to a small rectangular compartment in the top surface of the black cube, extracted a chip, and placed it on the tip of the plastic wand. "Now we'll see if it works."

Moretti grabbed her probe and turned to go, colliding with Mulville, and giving him a brief smile of apology. The general moved his chin up as a sign to carry on.

"By the way," Dr. Moretti said, pointing at the young scientist, "this is Dr. Emerson from my lab. He has programmed this chip using data from my probe to counteract the damaging sound waves."

"Don't let me stop you." Mulville gave her room. "Do what you need to do."

Dr. Moretti, shadowed by the police woman escort, rushed to one of the gurneys. The general followed. Mulville walked at his side.

"Where are we on the line of succession?" Mulville asked the general.

"Down to the Secretary of Agriculture." The General made a face as if he had a bad taste in his mouth. He read from his phone, scrolling down the list. "The President is dead. Vice is in surgery. Speaker of the House and President of the Senate have been airlifted to Washington General for surgery. We can't locate the Secretary of Treasury. Could be in a different hospital. The Secretary of Defense died on the table a little while ago. The Attorney General and the Secretary of the Interior died in the waiting room. So, we're down to Agriculture. Let's go see if we can save him."

The Secretary of Agriculture was a portly man in his late forties. He lay on a gurney in one of the ER's private rooms, undressed from the waist up, looking comfortable but worried. As Silvana and the general approached him, one on each side, Mulville stood behind.

"Mr. Secretary." Silvana Moretti placed her probe on the gurney and held the plastic wand with the chip in front of his breastbone. "We're ready for the treatment I told you about."

The Secretary's eyes widened, and he pressed his hands tightly against the side of the gurney.

"Is this going to hurt?" he asked.

"If it works," Moretti said, "you shouldn't feel any pain. You see, my probe showed that your damage from soundwaves is minimal, but we can't leave it untreated. It could worsen."

"What if it doesn't work?" The Secretary of Agriculture lifted his head off the bed. His neck thickened and his jugular veins became visible. "Am I a guinea pig here?"

"No," the general thundered from his side. He pushed against the Secretary's head, forcing him back to a flat position. "If this treatment works, you may be the next President of the United States. If not, you'll probably be dead sooner than later. So, please allow the doctor to do her job. And rejoice that you were chosen. You may stay alive because of it. Or we may have to move on to the Secretary of Commerce, next in the line of succession. Time is running out. Not enough for lengthier explanations."

The Agriculture Secretary turned paler, silent, and still. The general had a way of convincing people. Mulville watched him in awe. If only the general himself could become President.

Dr. Moretti repositioned the wand over the Secretary, the chip at the tip one inch away from his skin. She touched a key in the middle of the plastic stick. The chip lit up with an orange glow. The color intensified during the next several minutes, then the glow faded, the chip turned black, and a faint smell of burnt plastic spread in the air. The secretary's breath came out in short bursts.

"How are you feeling?" Moretti asked, withdrawing the wand.

At the touch of a different key, the chip popped out of the wand into a nearby waste disposal. Moretti exchanged the wand for her probe. The patient didn't answer but watched the tip of Moretti's probe scanning his chest. He looked flushed. His breathing accelerated.

"Relax," Silvana said. "Your dissection may have been prevented, but if you keep hyperventilating, you'll pass out."

The general looked around, lifted the Secretary's shirt and jacket from a nearby chair, and threw them all onto the bed. The garments landed on the man's abdomen.

"Mr. President, sir," the general said, saluting the Secretary. "Please get dressed at once. The presidential chopper is standing by on the hospital heli-pad. We need to rush you to the White House Situation Room."

"Please," Moretti said, "at least get him a wheelchair. Better we don't push our luck."

The General nodded. The Secretary threaded his arms into his shirt sleeves. Moretti hurried away with Emerson and the police escort. Mulville followed.

"I've got to let Nirula, the ER doctor, know that the chip worked," she said. "I should be able to save most of the senators and representatives who went through the door at the same time. Their exposure was probably limited."

"About Patrizia," Mulville said, trotting to her side. "She may be safe now. She's probably alone. Her only risk is the same we're having—oncoming warheads."

"I hope so." Moretti stopped, her voice choked up. "Unless she's already—"

Dr. Nirula stood near the ER entrance, triaging the oncoming patients from the Waiting Room. He lifted his eyes from a gurney as he talked to the nurse at his side. His eyes gave Moretti a look of hopelessness.

"It worked," Moretti said. "We can program chips to prevent dissections in limited exposure cases."

"Let Dr. Nirula use your probe to assess patients," Mulville said, "so you can take a moment to get your daughter's location from the watch. And you said you might try to get a location on the terrorists' probe. Can you see if you can, before they ditch it?"

Nirula nodded, took Moretti's probe, and went back to triaging, followed by Emerson. Moretti rushed to her equipment in the middle of the ER. A renewed energy seemed to animate her. Mulville grabbed the police woman's arm and held her back.

"I want you to send out the terrorists' location," he said, "as soon as it's available. Let's get those bastards. And send the police or whoever you can find to rescue the doctor's daughter, as soon as she has her location."

Mulville shuddered. His conversation had shaved one more minute from the time they didn't have. He grabbed a wheelchair left behind by a patient placed on a stretcher and ran back to get the new POTUS.

CHAPTER 33

ROCKET'S RED GLARE

A ziz stopped running, bent over, and gulped several mouthfuls of air. He straightened up and listened for oncoming steps. Silence filled the night. He checked the GPS on his sleeve. Sayed's Jeep should be only a few yards away. His gloved hand unzipped the car fob from his pants pocket. The clicking sound of the opening car door calmed him. He found the car among thick, snow-laden bushes. He dropped into the driver's seat and placed the football briefcase on the passenger side.

His breath still came in rapid gasps, but Aziz couldn't rest. He pulled out his phone. At the touch of a key, the pre-crafted message appeared on the screen—the words that would set in motion the demise of the worst infidel country in history, and the beginning of the Faith's revolution. He wished he could live to see the future. His eyes rested on the black leather case. His mission was almost over. He had to hide and protect the football until America's annihilation. Aziz would have to witness the rest from Paradise. He read the message one more time before sending it: "USA Government Paralyzed. Nuclear Football Neutralized. All Clear for Attack."

He placed the phone on his legs and bent over the steering wheel, filling the car with the evening's prayer.

Renewed energy allowed him to perform his final task. He got a shovel from the trunk and dug a hole about a yard from the side of the car. Frozen ground made his job tougher than expected. After several minutes, he lifted the football into the shallow pit, then shoveled dirt and snow to fully hide the black case. In the end, Aziz looked at the snow-covered site with pride. The hiding place had to remain undetected for only a few more hours. He went back to the driver's seat, found the phone again, pulled off his glove, and placed his index finger on the "send" key. A moment later, the engine roared. It sounded like a hymn to victory.

———— ∾ ————

The presidential helicopter sat on the hospital helipad in front of the emergency entry. Mulville ducked under the blade's wind and wheeled the Secretary of Agriculture onto the lift. He signaled the pilot and the wheelchair, with a rumbling noise, moved up to the level of the back door. The Secretary slid onto the chopper's seat. The general, football in hand, climbed aboard and took a seat next to the window, in front of the Secretary. Mulville boarded next and helped the Secretary to strap in. The door slammed shut. The blades drummed, and the craft moved up. Mulville reached for earphones and watched the hospital building shrink into the distance. He wondered if Kirk Miner was still alive.

"What's going on?" the Secretary asked.

"What happened tonight," the General said, "was a terrorist act. Some group called United Coalition of Faith is responsible. We believe their purpose is to launch a nuclear attack on us with impunity. The president is dead. The Vice-President and everyone else on the succession list above you is either dead or incapacitated. You are it. You are the acting President as of now. We suspect hostile warheads may be headed our way as we speak, and could reach us within the hour. We need to place you in a secure place and launch antiballistic missiles ASAP. And we need to send a message to the world that we have a President in charge, that we're able to defend the country, and that we will initiate a counter strike."

The Secretary turned and stared at Mulville as if looking for answers to unstated questions. The man looked clammy, clear droplets shining on his corrugated forehead. Mulville wondered if the sweat was due to his medical condition or his sudden new position.

"But, General," the Secretary said, repositioning his headset, "I haven't been sworn in yet. Can't take any official actions yet, even under these circumstances."

Mulville shook his head in disbelief. Of all people, they had to be stuck with a prick who was anal about protocol? He stared at the general, looking forward to his answer.

"No need to take any oath." The General made a sweeping gesture with his hand. "Not for an acting President in an emergency."

A light scent of kerosene filled the air. The White House came into view below. The Secretary found a phone in his jacket pocket and fumbled with different keys searching for something.

"That's true." The Secretary pointed at a document on the screen. "But only for the Vice President. According to the Presidential Succession Act of 1947, when there is neither President nor Vice President able to discharge the powers and duties of the office, whoever acts as President must resign from his own office. In the section referring to members of the Cabinet acting as President, it states here that the taking of the oath of office—"

"Very well," the General interrupted. His voice sounded deeper than usual.

"I need a Bible," the Secretary nodded with obvious satisfaction.

The helicopter started its descent. The general grabbed the phone out of the Secretary's hand and touched a few keys. When he seemed happy with the results of his search, he shoved the device under the rightful owner's face.

"Here's your Bible." The General placed his index finger on the screen. "Do what you need to do. Fast."

The Secretary looked from the General to Mulville. His eyes seemed to say, "What the heck?" Mulville peeked at the screen, which displayed the image of a Bible. He choked down a burst of laughter.

"But—" The Secretary opened two buttons of his shirt collar and used his tie, which was hanging out of his breast pocket, to wipe his forehead as he touched the phone. "This is highly illegal. I can't—"

"Mr. President." The General's calm sounded ominous. "With all due respect, we have no time for nonsense. We've got to handle a nuclear threat. Place your right hand on the screen and repeat after me."

The helicopter wobbled and touched ground with a thump. The secretary's hand shook. The General grabbed the man's sweaty palm and placed it onto the screen.

"I do solemnly swear," the General said, holding the device sandwiched between the Secretary's hands one on each side, "that I will faithfully execute—"

The Secretary remained silent. He timidly withdrew his top hand from under the General's. The General looked at Mulville. Mulville stared at the Army man's dilated pupils.

The General was a living tank. Mulville had no doubt he would defend his country, whatever it took, but felt an uncontrollable need to assist him in the task at hand.

"Mr. President, I mean Secretary," Mulville said leaning toward the Secretary. "Allow me to rearticulate the matter for the sake of clarity."

The Secretary looked at him and the General. Then he turned back to Mulville, the fear in his eyes similar to that of a trapped animal. He nodded.

"Mister Secretary, sir," Mulville said. "World War Three is about to descend upon our asses. Do you want to go down in history as allowing this country to become a military dictatorship or, worse, burn to a crisp, Hiroshima style?"

The Secretary looked up and shook his head in silent answer.

"Good. Then, with all due respect, Mr. President," Mulville tapped the Bible's image, "place your hand back on the fucking screen and repeat your precious oath after the General. Now!"

The Secretary flinched, but his free hand came up with unexpected determination and landed on the screen. Mulville, satisfied, looked at the General with pride. The General didn't seem to notice.

"I do solemnly swear that I will faithfully execute the office of President of the United States," the General repeated.

The Secretary whispered along. He stared at the White House through the helicopter's window. Mulville knew how the Secretary regarded his new responsibility. It had dropped on his head like a bomb from the sky. Now bombs might be coming for real.

"And will, to the best of my ability," the General said, his head bobbing up and down as the Secretary echoed his words, "preserve, protect, and defend the Constitution of the United States."

"So help me God," the new President added before the General's prompting.

"You're gonna need it," the General said.

The phone disappeared. Sounds of unlocking buckles filled the chopper. Mulville helped the President up, then into the wheelchair. The helicopter's ramp growled and deposited its precious cargo onto the frozen lawn. Mulville stepped out into the cold night. The General picked up the football, exited the aircraft, and straddled the case on the new President's thighs. Mulville looked up. The White House's ivory walls loomed in front of him, the majestic columns suffused with golden light. He wheeled the President and the football over the icy ground toward the West Wing.

"We're going to the right." The General pointed to the White House East Wing.

Mulville stopped. The Situation Room was in the West Wing's basement. What was wrong with the General? His stomach clenched. Instinct guided his hand inside his jacket, where his fingers tightened around the Glock's butt. He turned to face the General.

"No worry." The General lifted his hand. "I'm still on your side. We're going to the President's Emergency Operations Center, a bunker-like structure beneath the East Wing. Serves as a secure shelter and communications center for the President in case of an emergency. Better than the Situation Room. It's nuclear proof."

Nuclear proof. The General made sense. The statement reassured Mulville and, at the same time, gave him the chills. He let go of the gun and returned to the wheelchair handle. The wheels glided over the icy ground toward the East Wing's handicap ramp.

Two dark figures came into view. Mulville hoped the men were on their side. As they approached, Mulville identified them as uniformed Secret Service agents wearing Kevlar assault suits and with submachine guns hanging by their sides. The General must've arranged for presidential protection. He examined the two men's ID cards and nodded.

Three military policemen saluted as Mulville wheeled the President through the East Wing entrance into a deserted, wood-paneled lobby. A buttonless elevator door unlocked at the request of one of the agents. The two rode down with Mulville, the General, the President, and the football.

The five-person convoy unloaded into a windowless room that gave Mulville the feeling of being on a ship. The round presidential symbol hung like a porthole on one of the walls—its only decoration. Light diffused from large ceiling panels. Computer screens and electronic devices plastered the back wall. At the center, an oblong wood table stood surrounded by numerous office armchairs. The air felt stuffy but cool. The subtle hum of the heating system kicked in.

Mulville parked the President at the head of the table and sat down at his right. The General took the opposite chair. The Secret Service agents remained standing by the side of the elevator.

"Don't we have to convene the National Security Council?" the President asked, a touch of petulance in his tone.

"I'm afraid this is it." The General made a circular gesture with his hand. "The Council members are the Vice President, the Secretary of State, the Secretary of Defense, and the Secretary of Treasury, all of whom are either dead, in surgery, or missing in action. The President—that is you, sir—is chairing the Council. I don't think we have time either to find, let alone argue with, the National Security Advisor. The situation is very simple. One or more ballistic missiles are likely on their way to strike us. You and I can handle this."

The General turned to the table's electronic panel and touched a few keys. All the screens came to life with the words "National Military Command Center, Pentagon." A few seconds later, the image of a man in military camouflage appeared. He identified himself as the Vice-Chairman of the Joint Chiefs of Staff. His face could have been a sculpture on Mount Rushmore if it weren't for a veil of grave and solemn fear not even a person of his rank and experience could conceal. Mulville broke into a sweat despite the room's cool temperature.

"General, good to hear from you." The vocal urgency of the camouflaged man testified to how much he meant it. "We've been trying to contact all combatant commanders for some time. We've also been on high alert and doing nuclear surveillance since the events at the State of the Union."

"Sorry," the General said, "I've been busy trying to figure out who the President would be. The Secretary of Agriculture has just taken the oath. We've reason to believe that a nuclear attack from the Middle East is imminent."

"You suspect correctly," the Vice-Chairman said. "We've identified an oncoming ballistic missile carrying a nuclear warhead."

The General's face remained expressionless except for a deepening furrow. Mulville admired his cool. Perhaps the man had known all along the attack was coming and was past feeling shaken. The President closed his eyes and could've been asleep if it weren't for his lip movement. Mulville understood. The man was silently praying. Mulville wiped wetness from his forehead.

"What's the present location?" The General's voice sounded firm and calm.

"Over the north Atlantic Ocean, three thousand miles from DC. Trajectory points at Washington as the first possible target."

"E.T.A.?" the General asked.

"Twenty-five minutes," the Vice-Chairman said, without batting an eye. "Estimated time for impact and detonation."

"Initiate anti-ballistic interception at once," the General ordered. "What are the options?"

"The National Missile Defense system in Alaska," the man said. His mouth twisted in disapproval. "Not very effective against a Middle East attack. Great missiles. But they'll never make it on time."

The General waited. Mulville looked at his watch. Less than twenty-four minutes left now, and the Vice-Chairman had just wasted several precious seconds in describing a non-fucking-viable option. What was wrong with these military morons?

"We've got a Virginia-class SSN submarine," the Vice-Chairman went on, "in the North Atlantic Ocean, one thousand miles from Washington. Antiballistic potential limited in scope, designed to counter relatively small ballistic missile attacks from less sophisticated adversaries. I mean those less sophisticated than us, of course."

"Beggars aren't choosers," the General said. "Use the submarine missiles to intercept at once. Launch the Alaska ground missiles as well, in case the target turns out to be Los Angeles."

"Copy that," the Vice-Chairman said. He disappeared for a short time, then returned with a satisfied look on his face. "Any counterattack orders, Mr. President?"

The President opened his eyes. He stopped mumbling.

"No sense in starting World War Three," the President said, "if we can shut down the oncoming missile. General, what do you think?"

"Mr. President," the General said, his voice loud and clear, "we got to show we're ready to counter. Otherwise, they'll keep sending warheads at us."

"They already are," the Vice-Chairman said. "Pointed ballistic missiles have been spotted in several areas of the Middle East. Getting ready for launch."

"What else?" The President cleared his voice. His head turned from the General to the man on the screen, then back to the General. "What other defense missiles do we have?"

"Thanks to recent cuts," the General said, "not much. The Aegis Ballistic Missile Defense System plan was scrapped in favor of a limited system located on U.S. Navy warships. We have about thirty GBI, or ground based interceptors, most in locations unfavorable for the present threat. We could literally be dead in the water very quickly. We've got to show we have a commander in chief ready to retaliate in defense of the country."

The President nodded. The General turned to the Vice-Chairman. Mulville registered an empty feeling of helplessness. He was out of his turf.

"Have we got anything in position in the Arabian Sea?" the General asked.

"Yes," the Vice-Chairman said. "The USS Greeneville is in position now. Twenty-four launch tubes with four warheads per missile."

"Have it ready to launch," the General said. "The President will make an announcement."

The Vice-Chairman's mouth twisted in an attempted smile.

"General," he said with an apologetic intonation, "you know the protocol. The order to arm and launch must come from the President. And first we need to verify his authority."

The General took a deep breath conveying impatience. Mulville got ready for protests. None came. The four-star man reached for the football. The leather-covered metal box landed with a thud on the polished table. The General clicked open the latch and unfolded the case. On one side, Mulville noticed a keyboard with strangely colored keys. Inside the other side of the case, the General rummaged among loose papers and uncovered two black books and a manila envelope. A second deep breath telegraphed frustration.

"We received the football watch alert," the Vice-Chairman said as if his statement would redeem him from insisting on the verification. "TACAMO is activated. Standing by for the gold codes."

"TACAMO?" Mulville asked.

The General sent him a don't-bother-me look. His forehead looked shinier. Something was wrong.

"TACAMO," the General whispered. "Take Charge and Move Out. It refers to a communication system to be used during a nuclear war, to maintain 24/7 communications between the decision makers—that's us, and the military entities holding the nukes."

Mulville nodded. He reached for one of the black books and thumbed through the pages. The contents looked like a long laundry list. He guessed he was looking at classified site locations for retaliatory options. But no codes.

"So, where can we find the codes?" Mulville asked, replacing the black book and reaching for the manila envelope. "We need the famous biscuit. Wasn't it supposed to be inside the football?"

The General remained silent. He lifted the football briefcase and turned it over, holding back the communication panel with his fingers. The two black books and several loose papers spilled onto the desk. He inverted and lowered the open case to the polished surface again.

Inside the manila folder, Mulville found several pages stapled together giving a description of procedures under the title "Emergency Alert System." No biscuit. He dropped the papers into the case and examined the other black book. It listed classified site locations where the president could be taken in an emergency. He felt his breathing and heartbeat accelerate. Reaching out for the loose papers, he wondered why the General had stopped searching.

"You're wasting your time." The General pointed at the papers in Mulville's hand. "That's just a simplified menu of nuclear strike options—allowing the President to decide, for example, whether to destroy all of America's enemies in one swoop, or to limit himself to obliterate, for example, only Moscow, or Pyongyang, or Beijing."

"Great." Mulville let go of the papers. "We got Nuclear Retaliation for Dummies, but no codes."

The President's brow went up at the word "dummies," but no verbal protest came. Only a look of resignation showed in his tired eyes. The heating system's hum filled the ominous silence.

"No biscuit," the General said, "no codes."

"What do these guys need the codes for?" Mulville pointed at the screen and glanced back at the General. Then he turned to the Vice-Chairman. "Aren't you the one who pushes the red button? And you know we got the president here with us. We just fucking swore him in."

"Hold your horses," the Vice-Chairman said. "Before the order can be processed by the military, the president must be positively identified using a special code on the plastic card nicknamed the biscuit. Given the circumstances, I could overlook the two-man rule."

The world was coming to an end and the military was operating like a reluctant bureaucracy. Even the General seemed resigned to abide by the rules. There was nothing in Mulville's FBI training he could tap into. He suppressed his strong sense of frustration.

"What two-man rule?" he asked.

"To really go by the rules," the Vice-Chairman explained, "the Secretary of Defense is supposed to confirm the President's orders. Where is he anyway?"

"The Secretary of Defense," Mulville answered, unable to hide some satisfaction against the insane demands for protocol, "is likely in a frozen drawer somewhere, a tag on his big toe."

"I'll accept the President's orders without confirmation by the Secretary of Defense," the Vice-Chairman said with apparent condescension. "Best I can do. But I need the codes."

Mulville looked at the General. His solid face conveyed no apparent emotion, only the unquestioning acceptance that came from decades of military life. The General touched the mute key.

"You're right, Mulville," he whispered, "this is very frustrating. Truth is, neither the Chairman, the Vice-Chairman, nor the Joint Chiefs of Staff have any command authority over combatant forces. The chain of command goes from the President, to the Secretary of Defense, directly to the combatant commanders, which is me. But, short of me organizing a military coup, this nice gentleman must confirm the president's identity before the President's orders are executed. And for that, we need the biscuit. Without the biscuit, the president is essentially carrying around a bag of useless papers and wires."

"Stupid eunuchs busting our balls." Mulville spread and reshuffled the strewn papers. "Where's the frigging biscuit?"

CHAPTER 34

THE BISCUIT

The Jeep bumped along the icy dirt path. After twenty minutes, it stopped shaking and the ride became smooth and easy again. Aziz had reached a paved street.

At the first intersection, he placed his foot on the brake and sat still on the deserted road. His head turned back and forth from left to right and from right to left a couple of times. He saw only blackness at either side of the car's light cones.

South was Washington, DC—home during his adult life. Nothing much left there. Sayed was gone, waiting for him in Paradise. Tashfeen—Aziz hoped that Tashfeen was there with Sayed. Now the global truth should be evident to her through the omniscient wisdom of faith. She would understand the necessity of his actions. Tashfeen would be grateful to him for having helped her achieve salvation.

No job was waiting for Aziz in DC, so no more taking orders from infidels, and no more hiding. At last, he was free. His life would be short—he had no illusion about that. His hope was to last until the infidels' destruction started. He would die fulfilled, knowing that his mission had come to fruition. He placed his foot on the accelerator and turned left, heading North. He would drive as far away from the city as possible and take cover waiting for the fiery hell to take him.

Two miles into the journey, a luminous dot flanked by flashing red and blue lights appeared in the distance. Aziz's foot eased off the accelerator. The dot expanded into a heavy armored vehicle bearing the label "SWAT." Two black-and-white police cars completed the roadblock. Armed policemen and members of the SWAT team swarmed behind the vehicles.

DISSECTION

The imminent encounter played in Aziz's mind like a series of short movies. He looked at the icicle-laden trees and bushes flanking the street. Running wasn't useful or necessary. Only limited choices were left. All involved death.

He bit his right glove and uncovered his hand. He found the zipper pull for his jacket, and opened a gap wide enough for his hand to slip inside and find his shirt pocket. The cotton felt smooth and empty under his touch. No capsule. Aziz's stomach hardened in a knot. Tashfeen's face came to mind, blood trickling down her lower lip. The last time Aziz had seen his cyanide capsule was when he had shoved it between his sister's teeth.

Now the SWAT team stood a few yards away like a solid wall in front of his still-moving car. The wall enlarged every yard the car slowly advanced toward impact. Red laser lights danced on the Jeep's windshield, but the pigs wouldn't shoot. Aziz knew why. He was more useful alive than dead. His hand left the shirt pocket and reached around to his holster. The handgun felt hard and cold. The barrel tasted bitter and greasy inside his mouth. When he realized he had no time to pray, Aziz slammed on the accelerator and pulled the trigger.

———〜〜〜———

"This is an emergency!" Mulville shouted, facing the Vice-Chairman's image. "In case you haven't heard, we're on the verge of World War Three, or the USA's annihilation, whichever comes first. And you worry about protocols? The biscuit from the president's football is lost and the president can't tell us where he has put it because he happens to be dead. Dead, like we'll all be soon, thanks to you. Fuck the biscuit."

The Vice-Chairman looked at the General. The General rolled his eyes up, as if in apology for Mulville's immature handling of the situation. The President stared into space as if hoping his presidency had never started. Mulville was on his own in the futile battle against government red tape.

"We're wasting precious time," the General said. "We have only a few alternatives to get the nuclear codes. No time to squabble. I'll call the Situation Room. They usually keep a copy of the codes there. Mulville, you check if they have recovered the designated survivor's football."

Mulville stopped shuffling papers and grabbed his phone, which rang in his ear. He had made a mistake not to go after Greg and the survivor's football. But if he had gone, Kirk Miner would have died. What about Kirk? Was he alive or dead? Perhaps his rescue had been one big mistake.

"Shit," Mulville said after listening to the Bethesda police report. "The fucking bastard."

The General, holding his phone to his ear, paced the wooden floor as they waited for the Situation Room personnel to retrieve the codes. His chin rose in Mulville's direction in inquiry. Mulville shook his head.

"The guy committed suicide," Mulville said. "Crashed his car into the roadblock. No longer had the football or the biscuit. The SWAT team is looking, but he must've hidden it somewhere."

"Yes," the General said into his phone. "Any luck?"

The General stopped pacing and listened in silence. After a moment, he slumped in his chair, still holding the phone to his ear. First time he had seen the General sweat. Mulville winced.

"You better listen to this," the General told Mulville, placing the phone on speaker. "So you know where to look."

"We can't find the Situation Room codes," a male voice said. "The president must have had the biscuit. He liked to keep it in his shirt pocket. Your best bet is to go through the President's clothes. Find his shirt, and you'll find the biscuit, if he wore the right shirt tonight."

Mulville shifted in his chair. His energy seemed to drain, as if the cherry-colored mahogany floor was sucking the life out of him. He was the FBI director. The General counted on him. He wondered what had happened to the real FBI director. No. Mulville wouldn't allow hopelessness to take over. He refused to dwell on anything except his current mission. The future of the country was in his hands. He pushed back his chair.

"On it," he told the General. "I'll call you with the code the moment I get my hands on the President's shirt."

"Great," the General said. The shadow of a grin animated his face. "Meantime, the new president and I have to work on a speech."

The captain in charge of piloting Marine-1 was asleep in the pilot's seat. His chin, surrounded by a bulging neck, was resting on his zippered jacket. Mulville hopped aboard next to him and slammed the door shut. The captain shuddered, startled. The x-marked round patch on his sleeve carried the letters HMX-1, symbol of the Quantico squadron. Mulville felt reassured, as if the patch guaranteed the man's legitimacy—a needed certainty, among the many unknowns popping up that night. The pilot looked at Mulville and reached for the headphones.

"Where to?" he asked.

He started the engine. The scent of kerosene and the rapping of blades filled the air. At last someone who grasped the necessity for informality amidst emergencies.

"Back to the hospital," Mulville said. "Only me. As soon as possible."

The pilot nodded. Mulville buckled up. The pilot worked at the display of lights and switches.

"We're looking for the nuclear biscuit," Mulville said. "The President carried it in his shirt. Do we know where the President died?"

The helicopter lifted off. 11:39. How much time did he have before more warheads came?

"The President lost consciousness on the craft," the pilot said, signaling sideways with his chin without losing track of the sky ahead. "Three of the Secret Service agents worked on him. CPR and everything—until the ER people got him out. He still had his clothes on when they took him in."

Mulville nodded. The Secret Service men were Mulville's best bet.

"I need their names," Mulville said. "Everyone on the craft tonight."

The captain reached overhead and grabbed some papers from a pouch. Mulville took three stapled sheets from his hand. He thumbed through the document, folded the pages in fourths, and pocketed the square.

Six minutes later, Mulville pushed his way through the Capitol Hospital's E.R. entrance. The smell of sweat, slept-in clothes, and fear permeated the air. The scene in the waiting room hadn't improved during his absence. If anything, the sense of panic seemed heightened, likely due to the realization that the hospital couldn't provide care to everyone in need. The death toll was climbing rapidly with no end in sight.

Mulville burst into the main ER room. Three rows of patients met him, instead of randomly interlocked gurneys. Moretti was screening people in the middle. Mulville guessed she had placed patients in a specific row depending on the gravity of their condition. Her post-doc was still working with the black cube. Dr. Nirula looked busy with a dying patient. A Code Blue announcement played and replayed overhead.

Mulville's eyes darted to the third gurney on the right. The FBI director's gurney. Empty. Bunched up sheets and a thin blanket marked the place where the man had writhed in pain. Mulville's breathing paused. Where was the director? Two possibilities. The operating room or the morgue. Both were equal probabilities. Had Mulville saved him with his call? No time to find out. And what difference did it make anyway? For every life saved, so many had been lost.

He retrieved the folded paper from his pocket, opened the page with the president's Secret Service names, and walked up to a young female clerk sitting at a computer terminal near the entrance. Her fingers flew across the keyboard, typing as fast as Mulville judged humanly possible. A hands-free listening device sat on her head.

"I need to locate some people." He shoved his FBI badge in front of the girl's face. "Matter of national security."

He pointed at the printed words on the page. The girl looked up from under brown bangs and thick brows. No makeup. She could've been a high school student but for the tailored white shirt and the hospital patch on the sleeve. She kept on typing a few more seconds, as if she required a cooling-off period. After her fingers went still, she inspected the paper in Mulville's hand. She started typing again. Then she stopped and waited for the computer's answer. The screen changed.

"Our records," she said, looking up at Mulville again and pointing at the screen, "show that the first guy is in surgery. The second agent, the woman, is listed as dead on arrival. The computer can't find the other four. That of course means nothing. Only that we haven't had the chance to register them."

"I need to make a general announcement," Mulville said, pointing at the ceiling. "Now."

"The overhead is taken over by the Code Blue announcements." A smirk fleeted across her lips. "I guess it really doesn't matter anymore. They're all gonna code anyway. Sooner or later."

"We could save the rest of the world," Mulville said, "if you help me."

Awe filled her eyes. The girl wanted to believe him. She hung on his every word.

"What do you want me to do?" she asked, her hands now resting on her pleated skirt. "I can open a communication channel with the operator."

The girl was smart, competent, ready. Mulville got all that in her one sentence. Incredible what a difference a capable human being can make, even in a limited job like hers. Perhaps there was a chance for success.

"Make it so," he said, picking up a phone from the counter and handing it to her. "Let me know when I'm on."

She busied herself at once. Her voice sounded louder and firmer than expected from her body's small frame. In less than a minute, she had put forward and used all her available clout. FBI, national emergency, saving the world, and all.

"You're on," she said, pride in her youthful eyes, handing Mulville the phone. "The entire hospital. Overhead."

He nodded with gratitude. The girl was something else. Awesome.

"May I have your attention please?" Mulville said into the phone. "This is an emergency communication."

The words boomed from the ceiling and filled the rooms like an echo of his own voice. The cacophony of sounds around him dipped for one brief moment, then resumed with defiant indifference.

"Silence!" he shouted. "This is the FBI director. I have an important communication."

The noise dimmed. This time, people looked around with questioning eyes, waiting. Uncertainty provided him with some silence.

"I'm looking for the Secret Service agents who protected the President tonight." He wondered if a terrorist was listening, but what other choice did he have to recover the biscuit? "Please come forward if you can locate any one of them. We need to find the President's clothes. As you know, the President died tonight. He carried something in his shirt—a very important object the size of a credit card. This is needed to ensure national security. Anyone with information should immediately contact me or the operator."

He covered the microphone with his hand. He turned to the girl and bent down to spot her name on the hospital ID dangling from her neck   C. Bloom.

"Bloom," he said in a conspiratorial tone, "do you want to work for the FBI?"

The girl's eyes widened. Her face lit up as if she was living in a dreamlike reality she couldn't believe. Mulville didn't wait for a verbal answer.

"Write down your phone extension here." He pointed at his paper.

She nodded, picked up a pen, and jotted her number down. Her hand was steady, the writing meticulous. Beat the illegible numbers Mulville was used to getting at work. He broadcast the extension.

"You're in charge of forwarding all calls to me." He winked. "And tell the operator to put the call for the FBI through to you. After all this is over, we may make your position official."

The girl went back to typing. Her eyes dashed to the phone at regular intervals. She would do the job. Of that, Mulville was certain. He got up to go.

"Sir," she called, still typing, "I think I know where the President's clothes may be. I saw him coming in. They worked on him right there, in the private code room, next to the entrance."

"Show me," Mulville said.

The girl looked at the silent phone. Hesitation showed on her face. She took her responsibilities seriously.

"If I'm in range," she said, touching her headset, "I can still answer."

"If I find what I'm looking for," Mulville said, "we don't need to wait for any phone calls. Take me to where they keep the clothes."

"The dead people's clothes"—Mulville ended the sentence only in his mind. What would they do with dead people's clothes? Bloom stood up and signaled Mulville to follow. Her petite figure reached up to his shoulder. She hopped away in pink sneakers and white stockings. Mulville followed her.

A man and a woman from the housekeeping crew were the only people in the deserted code room. They were cleaning up after the most recent death. On the bed in the middle of the room, the lifeless body of a woman lay sprawled, shielded in part by a blue paper-cover. The woman's glazed eyes were motionless, turned toward the ceiling. An endotracheal tube stuck out of her mouth, agape at the astonishment of death. Several intravenous catheters, disconnected from life-sustaining devices, hung from her neck and arms. Mulville tried to keep the deceased out of his field of vision. Bloom didn't seem affected by the dreadful scene.

She went for a red container with three interlocking circles and the word "Biohazard" printed on the side. The cleaning woman's gloved hands were pulling out a large plastic bag full of hazardous waste from the receptacle. The girl grasped the woman's arm.

"Wait," she said. "FBI. We need to inspect the contents. National security."

The woman's hands froze in the air and let the bag go. The plastic bundle slid back into place in the red container. Bloom donned purple gloves from a box on the wall and started rummaging through the biohazard stuff. Her small hands lifted drapes, empty syringes, a urinary catheter connected to a half-full bag, various empty and ripped plastic containers, and bloody gauze. The smell of urine and antiseptic shifted in the air. Mulville took shallow breaths to avoid inhaling the odor of death.

"Where do you keep the dead patients' clothes?" Bloom asked the cleaning woman standing by her side. "You can have this bag now."

The woman shrugged. She pointed to a bag under this dead patient's bed. Mulville bent down and peeked through the clear plastic. He noticed the white of a shirt, one black pump, and a black jacket with the American flag on a lapel.

"Were you here when the President died?" Bloom asked the housekeeper. "Did you do the cleaning? We're looking for his clothes."

Bloom was a natural. Mulville could step back for a moment, let some other competent human take the needed actions. He cherished the unexpected relief. Occasionally, a thinking and competent person could be counted on. The thought comforted him.

The cleaning woman stared into space as she considered Bloom's question. Then she nodded and pointed to a door on the back wall. A moment later, she returned to handling the hazardous material.

Mulville and the new FBI recruit walked over to the closed door labelled "storage." Bloom yanked the handle down and out, and they entered a windowless dark room. Light came on in response to motion and shone over a pile of plastic bags like the one enclosing the dead woman's clothes. At least a dozen bags for sure. Mulville wondered if those were only clothes for the patients who had died in the private code room.

"We got work to do," he said. Then he turned back to the open door to address the two cleaning crew workers. "Come and help us. Now."

The man and woman across the door looked up from their tasks. A flicker of annoyed resentment surfaced in their indifferent eyes. Not everyone could be like this girl. Mulville lifted his FBI badge out of his pocket and waved it in the air. The two shuffled over.

"We're looking for a plastic object the size of a credit card," he explained. "We think it's inside the President's shirt pocket. But check everything. Are these bags labelled in any way?"

"By name." The woman's tone implied "duh?" She pointed to one of the labels tied to the strings. "We can look for the President by name."

"Go for it." Mulville pulled a bag over. "Check the names. Let me know when you find it."

Everyone went to work. A clock on the wall showed 11:43. Had the antiballistic missiles reached and destroyed the target? At least Washington DC was still around. He pulled another bag over, checked the label, and discarded it.

"Got it," Bloom announced.

She ripped the bag open and emptied the contents onto the floor. Mulville saw a light blue shirt with a front pocket. He stepped closer, bent down, and lifted the garment from under a pair of black trousers. Human body smell and wetness made him recoil. His hand shook as he swept the pocket. Empty.

"Shit," he said. He blushed, remembering the young girl. "Let's go over everything in this bag."

Bloom didn't seem to pay any attention to his curses. She was already onto her task. White stockings to the floor, sneakers flat under her buttocks, gloved hands spreading stuff on the cold gray linoleum.

"Nothing here," she said after a moment.

Mulville nodded. Bloom got up and seemed ready for new orders. Mulville didn't have any. The President had worn the wrong shirt. The United States would pay the price.

What next? Mulville sighed and reached for his phone. The General would be furious. Mulville was used to being the one unleashing the insults. Today, he would experience how it felt to fail and to have someone rub it in. He dialed the General's number. Time for a military takeover.

An image suddenly came to Mulville's mind. His thumb shut off the call after the first ring. Tied to one of the bags' strings was a label carrying a familiar name. Mulville dove into the pile of bags again, to a particular bag Mulville at first thought was not relevant. Now it looked like the last chance he could think of. Bloom and the cleaning people stood still and watched him. Mulville realized they couldn't read his mind.

"All hands," he yelled. "Look for a bag with the name of Kirk Miner."

He spelled the letters out loud. The detective was smart. He had taken possession of the biscuit already and lost it. If Mulville knew him, Kirk would have spent all the time he had left looking for the biscuit again. The discarded terrorist's boot came to mind. Perhaps the boot had nothing to do with a suicide capsule. Maybe Kirk Miner had searched the wounded man and found the biscuit inside his boot. And Kirk's clothes somehow were right here because he had coded and … he had died. Kirk's clothes were here because he hadn't made it to surgery. Mulville's hope to find what he was looking for clashed with the dread of Kirk's demise. But Mulville didn't have time to wallow in his own possible guilt.

"Here it is," Bloom called out. "Kirk Miner's bag."

She ripped open the plastic and spilled Kirk's stuff on the cold linoleum for inspection. Hands rummaged through shirt, pants, briefs, and a family picture, with total disregard for privacy granted by death. Mulville squatted and lifted the bubble wrap. His hand became moist with the leaking foamy liquid. He discarded the useless shield with contempt and went on with his search.

"Sir," Bloom said, "is this what you're looking for? It was in his jacket."

Under the halogen lights, a slick orange rectangle shone in her hand. She handed the card-sized object over to Mulville. He held the plain solid plastic between his thumb and index finger. The flat surface bore an indentation line in the middle. Thank you, Kirk.

Mulville dismissed the cleaning people and Bloom. He locked the door, dropped his jacket to the floor, and sat on the plastic bags. Air escaped with a hiss in reaction to his weight. Mulville's fingers held the back of the biscuit while he pressed down with his thumbs. The solid plastic separated with a snap. He extracted an orange card bearing several lines of letters and numbers printed in black. The nuclear code. He dialed the General's number and placed his tablet on his knees. His phone showed 11:46.

"Yes, Mulville," the General said. "Got the biscuit?"

"Affirmative."

"Connecting with the National Military Command Center at the Pentagon," the General said.

Mulville stared at the code. He figured there were fifty characters or more. Way more than he had expected.

Static came through the phone line. "Mulville," the General said, "you're on with the Vice-Chairman of the Joint Chiefs of Staff again."

"Standing by," the male voice said, "for the gold codes."

Mulville cleared his voice. "I'm going to read the lines of numbers and letters," he said. "Quite a few. Ready?"

"No, sir," the Vice-Chairman said. "The president and only the president can give us the codes. You see, for an extra level of security, the list of codes on the card includes numbers and letters which have no meaning, and therefore the president must memorize where on the list the correct code is located. It's the only way the president can positively identify himself as the commander in chief and authenticate a launch order to the National Military Command Center. That is us. Otherwise, anyone who finds the football and the biscuit could do the trick."

Mulville's hand went limp. Kirk was so right. The terrorists hadn't hesitated killing the designated survivor because they never had any intention of using the code to launch American missiles. He stared at the number and letters filling the plastic rectangle. Where would the gold codes start? Only the president knew. Perhaps the designated survivor might. And both men were dead. He tasted a mouthful of acid.

"Fuck the codes," he said out loud. "Was the intercept successful?"

Silence ensued. Mulville sighed. What was wrong with these military idiots?

"Yes, sir," the Vice-Chairman said. "Intercept occurred at 11:18 over the North Atlantic Ocean. Fallout away from urban areas."

More silence. Only the rumble of ER activity. Mulville savored the partial victory.

"More warheads being armed as we speak," the General said. "In remote areas of Iraq, Iran, and Afghanistan."

"What about the speech to the nation?" Mulville asked.

"We made an announcement that we have a president," the General answered. "And a commander in chief. But nothing short of armed retaliatory warheads on our part will deter new launches. They expect us to be the usual paper tiger. Suffice it to say, we've got a bad reputation in that department. We need to show that we've got the real thing. Now."

"Doesn't anyone brief the line of successors about codes and stuff?" Mulville asked. "In case shit happens?"

"Actually," a different male voice said, "they do."

"Mr. President?" the General said. "What are you saying?"

"Every year," the President said, "before the state of the Union, the Chief of Staff, God rest his soul, has us memorize the first and the last three characters of the gold codes. This year the Secretary of Defense took his place."

"So," Mulville said, "Mr. President, if I send you a picture of the biscuit, you'll know where to start?"

"Well," the President said, "not exactly. You know how it is. Who pays attention to this stuff, year after year, when nothing happens? Perhaps if I see the sequence, I'll remember where to start."

Mulville found his phone, balanced the plastic card on his lap, took a picture of the packed letters and numbers, and sent the image into cyberspace.

Then he slumped onto the bags, head in his hands. Nothing to do but wait.

"We need a Plan B," the General said, his voice barging onto Mulville's phone. "The President is a no-go. I repeat, the President cannot remember the code's head and tail."

Mulville grunted, shut off his phone, picked up his jacket from the floor, and sprang from the bags. Outside the door, he bumped into Bloom, standing in attention as if waiting for new orders.

"We're done." He waved her away with a sweep of his hand. "Go back to work. If only everyone was as good at their job."

"Sir," Bloom said, staying still, "forgive me for overhearing some of your words. Should we make a new announcement? See if anybody from, what you called it, the line of successors is able to give you the codes?"

Mulville stopped. What was wrong with him? Was he giving up? Did he need a young woman to tell him how to do his job?

"Absolutely," he said. "Make it so."

Bloom did her magic. The headset changed heads. Mulville adjusted the small frame so the microphone wouldn't push up under his nose. Soon his voice boomed overhead, again requesting anyone in the presidential succession line to come forward.

The squeaking of Bloom's sneakers on the linoleum floor followed him through the door.

The cleaning crew seemed relieved to see them go. Like a captain in formation with his followers, Mulville walked to the back of the ER, through the short corridor leading to the operating room, through the doors forbidding entrance to anyone without scrubs or head and foot protection.

The area looked like a gurney parking lot. Patients in different states of consciousness were there in disarray. Two nurses moved from patient to patient, carrying bags of fluid, blood, and medications. Mulville stopped a couple of feet from the closed door. Bloom stood right behind him. One of the nurses turned and stared. Mulville recognized the woman. She had helped get Kirk to the OR. The thought of Kirk Miner dying gave Mulville a jolt.

"How can I help you?" The thin and wrinkled charge nurse approached through the gurneys. "You're not dressed to enter this area."

He showed her his badge. The nurse nodded in recognition but remained steadfast, blocking his way. Her uniform carried sweat stains and blood splatters. Despite the exhaustion evident on the rest of her face, she seemed absolutely determined.

"I need to speak with the Vice President," Mulville said. "It's a matter of national security."

"The Vice President," she said with professional calm, "is still in the OR. Last I heard, he was coming off pump."

"Wake him up," Mulville said. "It's an order, from the FBI director. And the President of the United States."

The nurse's eyes flinched with surprise. Then the exhaustion and indifference returned, as if she had realized that nothing and no one could shock her or intimidate her after all she had gone through tonight.

"May be a while," she said. "His chest is still open. Surgery took longer than expected. Dr. Leeds had to go in and finish."

Leeds was supposed to operate on Kirk. But now Leeds was done with the PI. Was Kirk fixed, or was he dead? Mulville still had no time to dwell on that.

"I need to talk to Dr. Leeds," Mulville said. "There must be a way we can talk to the Vice President. He's our only hope of preventing a nuclear holocaust."

"My first and only responsibility," the tired voice said with the tone of a robot, "is to the patient."

"Move out of my way," Mulville said. "I'm taking over from here. Which room is the Vice President in?"

"You're not allowed past here," the woman whispered. "Everything is sterile."

Mulville placed his palm against the woman's arm. Thin muscles tightened up against his grip. The woman's body leaned sideways, resisting, before wary legs stepped aside to avoid losing balance. With little effort, he pushed her out of his way and marched toward the OR's gurney-crowded entry without turning back. Suddenly, the operating room's main door swiveled open and forced Mulville to move aside.

A gurney came forward. Feet first, body covered with a white sheet, with the reassuring beep of a heart monitor. Life, instead of death for a change. An imposing array of bags, bottles, and equipment, tethered to the patient with tubes and wires, towered above the moving convoy. A masked and scrub-clad man was pushing a portable respirator connected to the patient's breathing tube. Black hair, together with a sliver of pale forehead, protruded from a surgical headcover. Mulville stared at the patient as the head passed by him—it was Kirk. Kirk Miner was alive. A feeling of lightness spread inside Mulville.

With his gaze, he followed the moving mass to the parking lot of gurneys. At least the entire night hadn't been for nothing. He had achieved something. Even if the world as he knew it were to end tonight, the satisfaction would stay with him for the time he had left.

He entered the operating area before the door could close behind Kirk's gurney. Five doors, each with a rectangular glass insert, stood in a row in a deserted corridor. Mulville peeked through the glass into each of the rooms. An operation was going on in every room, except for the last one, which was in the process of being cleaned.

A list of patients' names written with a black marker occupied most of the wall space between the first two doors. The Vice President was listed in Room 4, but Mulville didn't rush away yet. His eyes stayed on the list, searching for another name. The FBI director was in Room 7. He had made it to the OR. Another victory.

Mulville scooted along the corridor to Room 4. He looked through the glass window and counted four people working on the patient—two men, probably surgeons, and two women. He figured one was an assistant and the other an anesthesiologist. The bloody red of tissues and vessels gleamed in the middle of green surgical drapes. The circulation machine stood empty and still. Off pump. Chest still open.

He pushed against the door handle and opened it a crack. The hissing of the respirator and the cool temperature startled him. The antiseptic smell of sterility, and burning flesh, hit his nose. The last one reminded him of barbecued meat. Mulville remembered reading about some cautery the surgeons used to stop the bleeding. He took shallow breaths to counteract a dim feeling of nausea and stared at the doctors, who were mastering raw flesh and blood in their fight against death. No one stopped or noticed him. The futility of his task haunted him. Mulville stepped back. The door closed without noise. He stood outside, helpless and hopeless, staring at the small glass window. Then his phone vibrated in his pocket. A strange, unknown number.

"Mulville," he whispered. "Who is this?"

"It's me," a girl's voice said, "Bloom. I got the Secretary of Education on the line. He says he remembers the beginning and end of the code."

He had forgotten all about her, after leaving her behind in the OR anteroom. Mulville ran to the operating area's exit. The door was locked. He punched a metal pad on the wall and the door pivoted outward. Bloom waved her phone from the opposite side, across the sea of gurneys. Mulville zipped through the labyrinth, bumping patients left and right. When he reached Bloom, he went first to cradle her shoulders, then pushed her outside, back into the ER.

"Where is he?" Mulville asked.

"He's sitting next to the exit." She put her phone back into her pocket and pointed across the room. "They told him he's okay to leave. But I told him not to move and to wait for us."

The Secretary of Education was a bald man in his fifties. He sat slumped on a plastic chair against the wall a few feet from the exit. Shirt unbuttoned, tie hanging by his neck, hospital ID bracelet still at his wrist, he was being kicked out to make room for other patients.

"Jack Mulville." Mulville shook the man's limp hand. "FBI director. The Secretary of Agriculture is acting as temporary President, but unfortunately he can't identify the nuclear code from the biscuit. We need to activate retaliatory pathways as soon as possible to discourage an all-out Middle Eastern nuclear attack on us. We already had to intercept a warhead."

The man seemed deflated. He looked at Mulville as if he had spoken in a foreign language. Perhaps he had already experienced the fear of dying to the maximum of his tolerance. Mulville sat on an empty chair next to him, extracted the biscuit from his pocket, and dialed the General's number. Bloom remained next to him. Her attentive presence gave Mulville comfort.

"That was the reason for all this?" the man asked, as if arriving at an understanding of the situation. "All this was planned for that purpose?"

Mulville nodded at the Secretary while he briefed the General on the phone. The time was two minutes past twelve. He waited for the Vice-Chairman of the Joint Chiefs of Staff to come back on the line.

"What are the first and the last three characters of the gold code?" Mulville asked the Secretary of Education, holding the biscuit in front of him.

Bloom got pen and paper from her uniform pocket and handed them to the Secretary. The man seemed to relax at the sight of familiar objects. He concentrated on the biscuit and went to work. Without hesitation, he wrote down twelve characters, letters, and numbers—the entire code spelled out. Mulville took a picture of his writing and sent the new information to the General. Way to go, Education.

"Here we go." The President's voice broke the unnerving silence. "The golden code. Romeo, Oscar, November, Tango, Lima, 22040, Delta, Tango."

More silence followed. Mulville pictured the Vice-Chairman comparing the code on his own biscuit-equivalent with the code uttered by the President. Already five past twelve.

"Code confirmed," the Vice-Chairman announced. "Standing by for orders."

Mulville thanked and dismissed the Secretary of Education. The man seemed happy to leave. Mulville waited. The General waited. The ER noise drowned everything else out. What were they waiting for now? More fucking protocols?

"General?" the President said.

With no uncertainty in his voice, the General said: "I advise mobilizing and arming all America's fixed ballistic missile silos. And all nuclear subs, and nuclear-weapons-equipped airplanes. Have American pilots climb into their nuclear bombers. Now. Have all warheads aimed at Iraq, Iran, and Afghanistan, ready to be launched."

More silence followed. Thirty-four seconds went by. More wasted time.

"Go ahead," said the President, his tone carrying a tinge of resignation.

"Copy that," the Vice-Chairman of the Joint Chiefs of Staff confirmed.

Amen, Mulville thought. He looked at his phone and hoped the interaction he had witnessed was the right step to prevent World War Three, even if the General's orders sounded much more like the beginning of it.

"Have you identified where the first warhead was launched from?" the General asked.

"Yes," the Vice-Chairman said. "Iran. Same place is readying more as we speak."

A click. Silence. A whole minute went by. Mulville rested his forehead on his icy palm. Then he remembered Bloom and looked up at the girl. She stood in attention, jaw tensed, eyes staring into space. Should he send her away? As if that could protect her from what was coming next. A second click.

"Start launching sequence," the President said. "On all military targets."

"Launch order confirmed," the Vice-Chairman said. "Target selection confirmed. Missiles enabled on the USS Greeneville. Twenty-four launch tubes with four warheads per missile."

"It's a go," the General said. "Let's start with the Iranian missile base responsible for the first attack on American soil."

Mulville looked at the girl, unsure how much of the private phone conversation she had heard. She closed her eyes. Her face turned pale. She knew what was happening and she looked the same way he felt—terrified.

CHAPTER 35

PATRIZIA

Mulville sat in the ER and looked at Bloom, slumped on the chair next to his. The order to launch missiles carrying nuclear warheads to Iran still resonated in his ear. What could one do while waiting for war? After the biscuit rush, the true crisis had just begun. Best bet was to act as if there would be a future later today.

The night had given Mulville an entirely new experience. He wondered what it would be like having a daughter like Bloom, or Patrizia. Sadness hit him as he realized he might not have time to find out, but he could still act on behalf of Patrizia in the time he still had.

"Stay put," he told Bloom. "I may need your help for a short time longer."

"Yes, sir." Bloom seemed to snap out of a trance. She seemed relieved, as if she had dreaded going back to her desk.

Mulville stormed to the middle of the room and found Moretti scanning a patient with her device. He looked for the youthful version of the black-haired scientist, but Patrizia wasn't around. Instead, he saw the police woman sitting on a chair. Silvana's tight mouth, hollow cheeks, and deep frown told Mulville that Patrizia was still a prisoner. Damned police woman. What was more urgent than freeing a young girl?

Moretti looked up. Her eyes, which rested on Mulville, showed both surprise and relief. Her hand, still squeezing the probe, momentarily stopped moving. Then she glanced at Bloom with a quizzical look that turned into sadness. Mulville felt sorry for the doctor. Moretti completed the patient's scan, handed the probe to Emerson, and turned to Mulville again.

"I'm so glad you're here." Grief flooded her voice. "It's about Patrizia. I can't get any reading from her watch. It must be disabled, or the batteries must be dead."

She paused at the word "dead," fear flooding her eyes. Mulville hoped that all the terrorists were accounted for, and preferably dead. Even so, people with nothing to lose did unspeakable things. They could've done anything to Patrizia.

"How can we ever find her?" she moaned. "Did they capture the terrorists?"

"Unfortunately," Mulville said, "all the ones we know of are dead. They committed suicide before we could interrogate them."

Her hands came up to her face, and her shoulders shook and shuddered. Bloom's eyes looked shiny. She placed a hand on Moretti's shoulder, as if crying could help. If he were sure it did, Mulville, too, would start crying on the spot. If only he had gotten his hands around Greg's neck, he could've squeezed the living breath out of him until he spat out the girl's location. Perhaps there was a way to get the information out of that bastard now, even if he was dead.

"Go back to the patients," Mulville told Silvana. "Save as many as you can. I'll go get your daughter."

Moretti stopped crying and considered him for a moment, as if questioning his credibility. Then she was back to scanning possible dissection victims. Mulville stepped up to a hospital computer, sat on a nearby chair, and started typing. Bloom stood by him like a soldier ready for orders.

After the Secret Service database appeared, he scrolled down names listed in alphabetical order. Greg's name was on the list, just as it had been on his FBI badge. And near his name stood his address. A long shot, but the only one available.

Pen and paper appeared in front of him from his new assistant. Mulville jotted down the address.

"Are you in school somewhere?" Mulville asked.

"First year of college." She said it with open pride. "GW."

"Stiff tuition," he said. "That why you work at night?"

"Uh-huh."

He looked at her. Confident and competent and ready. A rare find nowadays.

"I meant it," Mulville said. "If you're interested in an FBI career, contact me when this is over."

When would this be over? And how would it end? Bloom didn't seem too worried about the future. Perhaps the entire night played like a movie in her head. No need for him to spoil her excitement with his worries about imminent death and destruction.

"I always wanted a job with the FBI." She smiled. "I can't believe this is happening."

"I'm the director now," he said. "Just give me a call. You've helped me and the nation a great deal tonight."

Bloom's grin got wider. Mulville could use a smile in rescuing the Moretti girl. He hoped that rescue was what the mission was still about.

He got up, walked to the police woman at Moretti's side, and ordered her to call for police backup to meet him at the terrorists' apartment building. Then he borrowed her black-and-white car's keys. A few minutes later, flashing and glaring lights and blasting sirens announced Mulville's journey.

The apartment building loomed above the street light. The fifth-floor windows, where Greg's apartment should have been, stood dark and silent. Mulville parked in an alley next to the backup's SWAT van and shut off the engine and flashing lights. Exiting the car, he met four men and a woman in full SWAT gear.

The front door was locked. A sleepy and frightened superintendent let Mulville and the SWAT team in at the sight of his FBI badge. Mulville ignored the elevator. The convoy walked up the five flights, weapons in hand, ready to fire. The muffled tapping of steps resonated in the staircase.

By the third floor, adrenaline had chased away Mulville's day-long exhaustion. On the fifth floor, Greg's door stood silent in the dim overhead light of the short corridor.

Mulville extracted the key the superintendent had provided him. The SWAT team spread apart at both sides of the door. Mulville inserted and turned the key, then pushed the door in an inch. No noise or light came out of the crack. He slammed the door wide open. Two policemen darted in.

"FBI!" someone yelled.

The team proceeded to secure one room after the next. Mulville followed. The last door was locked. The SWAT agents got out of the way, against the corridor's wall. Mulville used the universal key, but some other impediment prevented the door from opening.

"Shit," he said. "Locked from the inside."

Mulville aimed his gun at the lock, but his finger couldn't pull the trigger. Patrizia could be near the door. He turned to one of the policemen to handle the task with a crowbar. Mulville kicked the door in and stopped. A bound and gagged girl lifted her head from a mattress and looked at the armed policemen with wide, weary eyes. Mulville was certain he saw relief in Patrizia's eyes. As the police woman went to free the young prisoner, Mulville's next call was to her mother.

CHAPTER 36

BOMBS BURSTING IN AIR

Marine 1, the presidential helicopter, came to rest on the White House south lawn. Mulville ducked out and walked to the East Wing. The guard nodded in recognition and let him in.

"Welcome back." The General greeted Mulville from the same armchair he had occupied when Mulville had left. "How are things at the hospital?"

The wall clock showed 1:25. The President lay on a couch, eyes closed, shirt collar open. Remnants of cheese and crackers and the crumpled paper of a protein bar lay on a nearby coffee table. Mulville sat across the table from the General. All his exhaustion returned as soon as his body flopped onto the cushioned seat.

"Dr. Moretti is doing a great job treating the milder cases," Mulville said. "Last I talked with her, she, her post-doc, and the ER doctors had screened more than three hundred people with her device, and treated about two hundred patients, neutralizing the damaging soundwaves. The most urgent cases were sent to surgery."

"Impressive," the General said. "In less than three hours. What about casualties?"

"The patients requiring surgery were taken care of in the local operating rooms or moved to other hospitals," Mulville said, shaking his head. "Unfortunately, all medical facilities were quickly saturated and some people died waiting for surgery. Not sure of the number. About six hundred people went through the House Chamber's front door."

The General nodded. "Luckily, the guests used a different entry. So, you tell me Moretti saved from surgery close to half of the people affected?"

"Yes, sir," Mulville said. "What's the nuclear situation?"

Mulville had dreaded asking the question. The President didn't seem equipped to handle anything. Mulville hoped a new candidate would surface, if there was the need for an American president in the future.

"Waiting for the report on our retaliatory launches," the General said, pulling a tissue out of his breast pocket and wiping his upper lip. "We had to intercept a second ballistic missile over the Atlantic. Also from Iran. So far, we've been unable to communicate with any of the hostile countries, despite many attempts."

The General pushed back from his armchair and crossed the mahogany-paneled room. He stopped at the side-wall counter. Soon the gurgling of coffee and steam could be heard.

"General," a male voice boomed from all the speakers, "the Vice-Chairman of the Joint Chiefs of Staff here."

Screens came to life and Mulville perked up in his seat. The General turned and took a sip from his paper cup. Images of a Middle East map appeared. The sides of the picture skidded out of view to make room for larger and larger details as the zoom zeroed in on a vast area of devastation marked by rubble, fire, smoke, and dust surrounded by what looked like desert.

"Mr. President," the General called out in the direction of the couch, "you may want to see this."

The General came back to the same chair. The President walked over, yawned, and sat down next to the General. He bit his lower lip while staring at the screen.

"The Iranian military base responsible for the two nuclear launches has been annihilated," the Vice-Chairman announced. "This is the video replay of the bomb hitting the target."

The screen went blank for a moment. Then the image of the desert reappeared, but instead of devastation, several rectangles of different shades of blue and gray occupied the center of the screen. Roofs of the Iranian base. Mulville imagined men at work inside the buildings—people who had launched missiles to kill Americans. They had it coming, but Mulville still braced himself.

A moving white trail announced the arrival of the American missile. As soon as the trail reached the buildings, the screen went white with an all-encompassing flash of blinding light. Mulville blinked several times.

"Oh my God," the President moaned.

The light separated into two circles and one half-sphere below. A cloud of brown bubbling dust rose from the ground and stretched into a stem that connected with the half-sphere of light above, creating the notorious appearance of a mushroom. Then the light turned into a dark grayish-brown cloud of cindery dust that merged with the bottom cloud and engulfed everything in sight.

"Horrible." The President wiped his forehead. "It's so different when you see it happening. And when you know you gave the order."

Mulville agreed, but acknowledged a sense of comfort in witnessing the power of the United States military. The General's tight jaw seemed to indicate similar sentiments. The President looked paler now. Mulville hoped he wouldn't pass out at that critical moment.

"The Iranian President," Vice-Chairman announced, "would like a word with the President of the United States."

"The Iranian President," the President repeated, as if coming back to life. He cleared his voice. His hand shook as he reached for a bottle of water on the table. "Ready for conference call."

The screen went back to the image of the presidential symbol—an eagle on a blue background. Clicking sounds from the water bottle's plastic cap filled the room. The President took several gulps and belched softly without taking his eyes off the screen.

After some static, the figure of an elderly man with a gray beard and a white head-cover appeared. He sat on an armchair upholstered in white material surrounded by ornate golden edges. Behind him, the bright red, white, and green of the Iranian flag contrasted with the black of his tunic.

Brown eyes full of anger looked out from the screen. The American President's eyes darted at the General as if the ex-secretary of Agriculture refused to take responsibility for the retaliatory attack and was telegraphing the silent question, "Now what?"

The Iranian President read from a paper he held steady between his fingers. The language was Persian. Indignation permeated the rage-filled voice. The tone of the content would have been clear even in the absence of immediate English translation. The theme was hatred. The bombing of the military base was an uncalled-for act of war that resulted in several civilian casualties. His hand went up several times, his index finger extended in a threatening gesture. After a short pause, the Iranian President went on condemning the launch of the two ballistic missiles against U.S. soil, and declared the Coalition of Faith a rogue entity with no official connection to the Islamic Republic of Iran.

The American President stared at the screen. The General sat back and sipped his coffee. Mulville wondered if the military man had witnessed similar crises before. Mulville didn't want his assumption to be true. Were such crises kept from the public to avoid panic?

The Persian's speech was over. The bearded man sat still, his eyes daring his American counterpart to produce a suitable answer. The President turned to the General, as if indicating that the General was responsible for placing him in this situation, and the General had the responsibility to get him out of it. The General leaned forward, put down his paper cup, and touched a key from the pad in the middle of the table.

"I just muted us." The General clasped the American President's arm. "I got this, if you want me to. I'll speak on your behalf."

The American President nodded. The General pulled his chair closer to the microphone at the center of the table. He sat straight, on the edge of his seat, and stared at the bearded man. Then he touched the mute key again.

"Hello," he said. "I'm the General Combatant Commander of the Marine Corps. The President of the United States of America asked me to make a statement."

Farsi translation rumbled in the background. The Iranian President nodded. The General took one more sip of coffee.

"We regret having no choice but to take action," he said, pronouncing every word in a slow and clear fashion. "Ours was appropriate retaliation to a nuclear attack originating from your country."

He paused. No comments came from Iran. The General took another sip from his cup.

"Your mention of the Coalition of Faith," the General continued, "in absence of any reference to the group by us, shows your awareness of the entity. We submit that Aziz and Sayeed—their last names are still unknown—and a third zealot, a woman, were clearly guided by an overseas team from your country. The fact that the missiles were launched from Iranian soil is proof you've collaborated with this radical coalition."

No objection came. Only more of the hateful stare. The General went on.

"Today you've experienced a W76 warhead, about five times more powerful than the so-called Little Boy nuclear bomb dropped on Hiroshima and the Fat Man bomb dropped on Nagasaki at the end of World War Two. If we detect any other hostile ballistic missiles coming our way from your country, our future retaliatory launches will include B83 nuclear bombs. These warheads can generate 1.2 megatons of blast energy. That destructive power is equal to 1,200,000 tons of TNT, about 60 times the power of the Little Boy or the Fat Man. And this time, we'll pick more populated targets. Of course, if we feel the threat warrants it, we could always escalate to the more modern Mark 39 hydrogen bombs. They're two hundred and sixty times more powerful than the weapon dropped on Hiroshima."

The General paused. Mulville tried to swallow but found no saliva. The U.S. President looked pasty and green under the ceiling lights. He had to be removed before fainting. Fainting would ruin the effect the General had so well orchestrated. Perhaps there was another alternative.

"Mr. President?" Mulville grabbed the man's arm and squeezed. The President turned, pain and rage in his eyes. Color reappeared on his cheeks. Mulville smiled and winked.

The Iranian President was speaking now. Rs rolled again, accompanied by more irate hand gestures. Mulville waited for the translation. The tone alone didn't telegraph anything good. His fate, and that of the USA, depended on the words the hateful, dishonest, irrational man was uttering. Time to see if the General's gamble paid off, otherwise, World War Three was forthcoming. What would it be?

"The blood of innocent civilians," the translator's voice said, "will be on American infidels' hands."

"No," the General said, his voice firmer than cement. "The innocent civilians' blood will be on the hands of the first party pulling the trigger. The President of the Unites States demands the complete, supervised dismantling of all of Iran's nuclear facilities or you'll face annihilation by forty-six American missiles already aimed at Iranian targets."

Mulville stared at the image of the Iranian President. Redness appeared above the gray beard. The man was obviously incensed. What would happen now? Mulville massaged the back of his neck. His muscles felt like a mass of knots. Then the Iranian President lifted both hands in the air, and spoke with purposeful calm. His total, incongruous control imparted an ominous finality to the short sentence. After one last hateful glance, the image disappeared and the screen went blank, back to the peaceful and reassuring eagle-on-blue background.

"What was that?" the American President asked, his voice cracking. "It sounded like a threat."

The translator's voice, coming through the speaker, cracked as well: "We will not only cut off the fingers, but chop off the arms of the corrupt."

CHAPTER 37

AFTERMATH

D
r. Steve Leeds staggered out of the operating room. The not-so-subtle smell of garlic immediately greeted him, easily over-whelming the antiseptic scent and all the other hospital odors that had permeated his environment for the past twenty-four hours or so. He wondered whether his hunger was playing tricks on his mind. The digital clock above the OR schedule showed 9:20 PM. All the names on his surgical schedule were crossed out. The last thing Steve remembered eating was a protein bar a nurse had opened and fed him three hours earlier, during one of the surgeries.

"Have a slice of pepperoni pizza." The charge nurse pointed to a counter. "Compliments of the President of the United States. Food for all of D.C.'s hospitals involved in the surgeries."

Food. Steve glanced at pizza, chicken parmesan, different pastas, and bread. His mouth watered as he took a step toward the display, but he turned to the corridor in front of the five operating rooms. Three loaded gurneys stood aligned against the wall. A male nurse tended to the patients.

"Post-op?" Steve asked.

The nurse nodded. A tired smile lit up his face. Then he turned back to his tasks.

"All of them?" Steve said.

"All done." The charge nurse stood at attention next to him, pride in her eyes. "Only two ORs left to finish the last cases. The cardiologists are done with their endovascular procedures as well. Sit down, eat, and sleep, Dr. Leeds, before you become a casualty yourself."

He nodded, walked back to the counter, and reached for the pizza. The taste of melted cheese and tomato sauce soothed him. It signaled a return to regular life after a surreal nightmare. He dropped onto a metal chair and fought to stay awake while he chewed and swallowed the best Italian food he had ever eaten.

"How many casualties altogether?" he mumbled.

The head nurse frowned. Her eyes appeared glossy, veiled by tiredness, but her posture remained erect, projecting authority and confidence. Steve had never seen her sit down during the entire ordeal.

"Total of fourteen deaths," she said. "Nine patients died waiting and five more on the operating table. It could've been tons worse, if not for Dr. Moretti."

Silvana's name gave Steve a jolt of adrenaline and triggered in his mind a second name. What about Patrizia?

"Dr. Moretti?" he asked.

"Yes." The nurse said. "She used her device. Together with her helper and Dr. Nirula, they scanned more than three hundred patients. Treated close to two hundred with ultrasound chips reversing the damaging sound waves. No way we could've handled so many more surgeries. People would have died by the dozens. Also, she was incredibly helpful in triaging the patients to decide how urgently they needed to undergo surgery, so we could plan the order."

Silvana. He had to find her. Now. Steve bit off as much as he could of a sauce-laden chicken breast, wiped his hands and mouth on a bunch of paper towels, and scooted out through the automatic door into the emergency room.

He scanned the large room looking for the familiar curly, dark hair amidst the people still swarming the area. The crowd had diminished to the usual size for that time of night, but no Silvana.

In the middle of the room, Steve noticed, was the black cube used to process the chips. It sat lonely and abandoned on a counter next to a pile of empty pizza boxes. Emerson was gone as well. Steve looked at his watch.

What did he expect? No longer deemed useful, there was one place where Silvana most likely would be—jail. Silvana will have gone back to wearing the baggy orange jumpsuit she'd be wearing for the rest of her life. The food in Steve's stomach now felt like a brick.

He pivoted around one more time, narrowing his eyes, ready to be disappointed again. Then his eyes opened wide at the sight of a familiar female face. Steve's tired mind tried to place the features in the right context within the turmoil of the preceding hours. The woman's uniform helped—Silvana's escort. The policewoman sat on a metal chair outside a glass-encased private room. She was dozing off, chin touching her chest, then lifting up again. Steve rushed to her and looked inside the room. Silvana stood with her back to him, tending to a patient on a gurney.

Steve stepped closer. The policewoman stirred and yawned at the noise of the sliding door. Steve waved at her, entered the room, and placed his hand on Silvana's back. She turned, looking startled, then smiled. This was her former smile, the one Steve once knew—before her life had been shattered by terrorism, her coerced role, her daughter's abduction, and so much death. He felt his stomach relaxing at the thought that he was responsible for that smile. But then Steve took a better look at the patient on the gurney. A girl, but not just a girl. *The* girl. Patrizia. Pale and exhausted, shaking under a worn hospital blanket, but alive. Silvana's smile was for her daughter. Only Patrizia could've brought such visible change in Silvana.

"They found her." He cradled Silvana in his arm.

"Is she okay?"

"I think so." Silvana lifted her brows. "From what she's telling me, it was a close call."

She closed her eyes for a moment, as if to suggest all the terrible, unthinkable events that could have happened. Steve tightened his grip around her. Silvana's body shuddered.

"You did great tonight," he whispered in her ear. "You saved many lives."

Silvana nodded. Steve touched her cheek with his lips. She remained still. Her eyes turned to the ever-present police escort.

"I love you," he said.

She nodded again, but the smile was gone. Only sadness remained on her face, and Steve felt emptiness inside.

"You shouldn't stay involved in my mess," she said, her voice low, as if to shield her conversation from her daughter. "Sooner or later, I'll need to face what's coming. They have allowed me some time with Patrizia. By morning, I'm sure they'll take me back to jail."

"Mulville," Steve said, "will help you. He'll testify to how you acted under duress, on how you helped us so greatly. And how many people you saved."

She shook her head. Then she looked into his eyes. He saw pride, and determination, and grief.

"I had to choose," she said, "between my daughter and many innocent people. I would make the same choice again. But I will have to pay for what I set in motion. It'll be what it'll be. I only need to make sure Patrizia is okay and taken care of. Social Services will watch over her until I can make some arrangements."

"You can count on me," Steve said. "Always."

She hugged him, pulling him tight against her. He knew the hug wasn't just gratitude for what he had offered to do for Patrizia. The gesture made him happier and more depressed at the same time.

Steve didn't let go of Silvana as he dialed Mulville. The phone rang interminably. Where was Mulville?

"Mulville." The voice sounded muffled, probably by sleep. "It better be good, Doctor. Shit, I thought I could rest a bit after averting World War Three."

"World War Three?" Steve asked.

The gravity of the situation Steve had encountered twenty-four hours earlier became real again. Lots had happened during his operating time. While he was fighting his battles against disease, Kirk Miner had fought to stay alive, and Mulville had battled deadly foreign enemies. The image of the last time the three met together at the steak house came to Steve's mind. On that evening, he and his colleagues had no idea what they would have to face. Had they won? Was losing only fourteen lives a victory? And Kirk Miner was alive. For now.

"Never mind," Mulville said. "Whassup, Doc? After tonight, I feel I can do anything."

"It's Silvana," Steve said. "She's done here. What's going to happen to her now? Back to jail? Is there anything we can do, considering all we now know? The wavelength data she gave the terrorists was harmless. Those criminals stole and programmed the chips and the devices. And Silvana's inventions saved hundreds of lives tonight."

The silence felt ominous. No assurance was forthcoming. Silvana had helped terrorists. The fact that she had done it unwillingly and under duress, and that she had tried to limit and undo the damage, were both major mitigating circumstances. But only judges, an army of lawyers, and time would determine what effect such mitigations might have on her sentence. Only they could determine how much of her remaining life would be wasted in jail, and how much of Steve's life would be wasted in misery.

"Shit. I guess I'll be on my way," Mulville said at last. "By the way, how's Kirk? Saw him coming out of the OR, alive."

"So far, so good."

"And the FBI director?" Mulville asked. "The one I called about?"

"Not sure," Steve said. "I was busy with Kirk. We'll have to look for him when you get here."

Steve ended the call and tightened his arm around Silvana. How much longer would they have? Whatever it was, he couldn't think of any better way to spend the time left than with the two most important persons he had in the entire world.

Steve and Silvana huddled on uncomfortable metal chairs next to Patrizia's gurney. A few hours had gone by since the conversation with Mulville. Steve had answered calls from nurses tending to his patients, and on one occasion left to check on someone in person. For a while, Silvana's head rested on his shoulder. Her breathing slowed down to the rhythm of sleep. Her face seemed relaxed and serene. Steve wished she could remain in that state. He slowed his own breathing so as not to disturb her.

Mulville's last words reverberated in Steve's mind. "On my way." To where? If Mulville meant to the hospital, he should've been here a while ago. But what could Mulville do at the hospital? There was nothing left for him to do except take Silvana back to jail. The scene of Silvana's arrest was one of the most terrible events Steve had to witness in his entire life. He never would want to go through something like that again. So why did Mulville's words stay in Steve's mind like a beacon of hope?

Mulville appeared at last. He wore a blue suit, starched shirt, and tie. Steve wondered why he had bothered dressing up. Was he going to take Silvana into custody all over again? The attire could be part of the ceremony. Mulville looked perky and freshly showered, and almost happy. Was he happy to re-arrest Silvana? Had he reverted to his usual creepy, dick-like state? That his call to Mulville might have shortened Silvana's freedom made Steve cringe. Silvana stirred in his arms. Her eyes, opening to new events, were filled with resignation. She pushed away from Steve and stood up from her chair to face the FBI agent.

"Thanks for coming in person," she said "I'll make your life easier this time."

She placed her hands together, fingers tightened in fists, ready for handcuffs. Steve felt his chest clutch with despair. Mulville stared at Silvana. Then he bowed slightly, as if he was confirming something to himself.

"How's your daughter?" Mulville asked, pointing at a still-sleeping Patrizia.

"She's fine." A weak smile lit up Silvana's face. "Thanks to you. I told her you saved her life. Also, that I would have to go with you for a while, to sort things out. She understands, I think."

Her hands stayed in position, as if she wanted to get the arrest over with as soon as possible. Mulville remained still. Steve saw none of the arrogance, impatience, and contempt he remembered from the first arrest. What was the man waiting for?

"That won't be necessary," Mulville said.

"Go ahead, Mulville," Steve said, unable to take the waiting any longer either. "You don't have to go soft now. Be soft when we need you. With the lawyers and the judge."

"That won't be necessary either," Mulville said with a wink. "It took me a while, but I was able to convince the new President to do at least one useful thing during his pathetic term."

He fished inside his breast pocket, behind a red silk handkerchief matching his bright tie. He extracted a folded paper, extended his arm, and presented it to Silvana with an elaborate circling of his hand. Silvana looked at the folded paper for a moment. Then she grabbed the document from Mulville and pulled the folds apart to spread the paper open. Steve stood up and looked on with her, his arm cradling her shoulders.

The document had an ornate golden border on all four sides. In the middle, a curved line of words announced: "United States of America." Underneath, two words stood in bold letters: Presidential Pardon. A few lines below, a name was hand-written: Silvana Moretti. Silvana burst into tears.

"Pardon. From the President." She sobbed. "Does this mean—what does this mean?"

Steve squeezed her shoulder. He knew what the paper meant. Life was back to what it was meant to be. The SOB FBI agent had come through in an unimaginable way.

"You're forgiven," Mulville said, upturned his palm in an explanatory gesture. "Like when you go to confession, in the country where you came from. And here you don't even have to say Hail Mary or whatever it is you say there."

"So," she said, "I don't have to go away? From Patrizia."

"No, ma'am," Mulville said. "You're free to do as you please with the rest of your life. As of right now, we can dismiss the sleeping stooge outside."

He stepped back as if getting ready to leave. Silvana leaped to grab his arm, to force him to stop. Her thin arms encircled his bulky body. She stood on the tip of her toes and planted a prolonged kiss on his cheek. Mulville looked frozen. His face turned a reddish color only a few shades lighter than his tie. After Silvana was done, he straightened his jacket and cleared his voice.

"Now I got to go."

He bowed, then pivoted on his feet and left the room waving his hand. Silvana clenched the pardon paper to her chest.

Kirk Miner opened his eyes and saw the very person he wanted to see. Aurora sat next to him, holding his hand. He fought against the anesthesia and drug-induced mind fog and smiled. His chest was on fire, but he was alive.

"We've got to stop meeting like this," Aurora said, as if she was thinking about what to say next. "This time was much worse. You died and they had to bring you back. Dr. Leeds did your surgery, instead of the Vice President's. Everyone in the ICU is talking about it."

He had died? Last thing Kirk remembered was telling Mulville to leave him on the frozen ground in the middle of the trees. What had happened next? Mulville must've come back for him. But what about the terrorists, the football, the biscuit? Had Mulville found the biscuit in Kirk's pocket? Kirk couldn't ask Aurora any of these urgent questions. He had to find Mulville. At least no atomic bombs had exploded. Yet.

"Please don't tell Peter about this," he said.

"Of course not." Aurora dialed her phone. "But I will tell him you're awake. He's waiting outside."

She spoke, then looked at Kirk, as if to make sure that what she told the boy—"your daddy is okay"—was still true. Then Peter rushed in. He didn't seem as shocked about the tubes and intravenous equipment as he had following Kirk's first dissection. Poor Peter was getting used to his dad being damaged and hospitalized.

"Daddy." The boy placed his arms around him. "You came back."

Kirk patted Peter's back. The pain in his chest intensified, but Kirk needed the hug too much to care about the pain. He looked up at Aurora.

"Did you reschedule the reservations?" Kirk asked.

"What are you talking about?" Her eyes filled with worry.

"Amelia," he said. "The Italian place. We were supposed to eat there this evening. Remember?"

Aurora nodded. She looked relieved. Good way to show that his brain was still there. She gave his hand a squeeze, and her mouth twisted into a grin. Then the door swooshed open again and Mulville appeared.

"Oh good," he said. "I'm glad you're up."

Kirk peeked over Peter's shoulder at the burly shape. He noticed the suit and tie. Things must've gone well for Mulville to have had time to clean up. Kirk tapped the boy's back. Peter raised his head.

"Peter, Aurora," Kirk said, "this is Jack Mulville with the FBI. He saved my life. Got me to the hospital just in time."

Mulville didn't object. It was true.

"Wow." Peter stood up. He turned to Mulville. "FBI? For real?"

"Pleased to meet you, young man." Mulville shook Peter's hand. "And you, ma'am."

"Thanks for watching over Kirk," Aurora said, looking up at Mulville.

"Did you give up saving the world?" Kirk said. "For me?"

"Nah." Mulville waved his palm in a downward motion. "Everything is taken care of. Terrorists dead. New President sworn in. Got a good general defending the country."

"Did you get the biscuit from my jacket?" Kirk asked.

"I sure did." Mulville pointed his index at Kirk. "Your biscuit saved the day, and the world from World War Three. The President's football didn't have one. We used the one you took from the terrorist. As soon as your tubes come out and you can eat again, I'll tell you the long version at some bar over drinks and a couple of deadly sandwiches. Worry about getting better for now. I may need you yet."

They had done it. Kirk, Mulville, and the doctor. But what was Mulville saying?

"What do you mean, 'you may need me yet'?" Kirk looked at Aurora, now wide eyed. "I thought you said it's all over."

"Yes, it is." Mulville grabbed a chair and sat next to Kirk's bed. "But today I got good news and bad news."

Kirk nodded, waiting. Aurora frowned. Mulville smiled.

"The good news," Mulville said, "is that, thanks to the good surgeons, the FBI director made it and will resume his position. You didn't know I was acting director all the time you were out."

"What's the bad news?" Kirk said.

"The bad news is you can't get rid of me," Mulville said. "I'm getting promoted. I'll be the director of the FBI's New York Field Office."

New York. The news pleased Kirk more than he would have expected. He couldn't believe he had gotten used to having Mulville around.

"Wow," Kirk said. "You mean we may actually be a team again?"

Mulville nodded and stood, his hand saluting Kirk and Aurora. Then his large body whirled with unexpected agility and stomped toward the door.

"I'll call you," Mulville said without looking back, "if I have to solve some weird shit with a medical twist."

The glass door swooshed open but Mulville stopped. He turned back again and stepped closer to Peter. He bent down, now eye to eye with the boy. Peter watched him closely.

"Oops," Mulville said. "Sorry, Peter. I got to learn my manners. I guess I'm not used to having cool kids around. Now that we've met, I hope I can get to know you better."

Mulville put his palm out in front of the boy. After a moment, Peter's puzzlement turned into awe. Then the boy beamed, raised his hand, and gave Mulville a high-five.

ACKNOWLEDGMENTS

I'm very grateful to my husband Peter, my alpha reader, for his great patience and skillful editing.

A heartfelt thanks to Bill Thompson for his gentle but ruthless editing. So sorry you didn't get to see this milestone. I can hear your deep voice shouting, "Author! Author!"

Much gratitude to Charlotte Cook, for the expert teachings and suggestions I will carry with me through my writing career—I can hear you prompting me as I write.

Thanks to my agent Bob Diforio, for believing in me and for all the work and dedication to make my novels successful.

Thanks to my great friend, Dr. Steven Lansman, who provided me with inspiration and education in the area of cardiothoracic surgery.

I couldn't have done it without my family—your unwavering encouragement cheered me on during the difficult journey to publication.

Finally, a very special thanks to Bruce Bortz, Publisher of Bancroft Press, for the great editing, which paved the way to a much-improved book, and for the contagious enthusiasm. You made it happen.

ABOUT THE AUTHOR

Cristina LePort was born in Bologna, Italy. Her mother was an avid reader and a school teacher. Her father, an accountant who studied mathematics and astrophysics as a hobby, worshipped the USA and was instrumental in his daughter's decision to come to this country. Cristina LePort is proud to be listed on the American Immigrant Wall of Honor on Ellis Island in New York.

Cristina graduated summa cum laude from the University of Bologna School of Medicine and did her residency in Internal Medicine at Long Island College Hospital/Downstate in Brooklyn, NY. After practicing Internal Medicine for 17 years, she wanted to become a cardiovascular specialist. She engaged in cardiovascular research at UCLA, publishing several scientific articles, and was accepted into the Cardiology Fellowship at the West Los Angeles VA/UCLA program. She is board-certified in Internal Medicine and Cardiovascular Diseases and has been practicing Internal Medicine and Cardiology in southern California for 30 years as Dr. Cristina Rizza.

Cristina is the Chief Medical Officer and co-founder of Genescient, a biotech company devoted to genetic research on aging and the amelioration of chronic diseases, using genetically engineered, very long-lived Drosophila Melanogaster (fruit flies.)

Cristina splits her time between her two passions, medicine and fiction writing.

For many years, she conceived novels in the genre of medical thrillers infused with realistic clinical details and cutting-edge science.

She lives in Southern California with her husband of 38 years, Peter LePort, a general surgeon. They have three children and three grandchildren.

She can be reached through her website: https://cristinaleport.com